THE CEMETERY
OF SWALLOWS

Mallock

THE CEMETERY
OF SWALLOWS

*Translated from the French
by Steven Rendall*

Europa
editions

Europa Editions
214 West 29th Street
New York, N.Y. 10001
www.europaeditions.com
info@europaeditions.com

Copyright © 2012 by Jean-Denis BRUET-FERREOL
Published by arrangement with Agence litteraire Piere Astier & Associés
ALL RIGHTS RESERVED
First Publication 2014 by Europa Editions

Translation by Steven Rendall
Original title: *Le cimetière des hirondelles*
Translation copyright © 2013 by Europa Editions

Library of Congress Cataloging in Publication Data is available
ISBN 978-1-60945-186-8

Mallock
The Cemetery of Swallows

Book design by Emanuele Ragnisco
www.mekkanografici.com

Prepress by Grafica Punto Print – Rome

Printed in the USA

C O N T E N T S

THE CEMETERY
OF SWALLOWS

PROLOGUE

The Dominican Republic, 1050 F. in the shade

M y name is Manuel Gemoni. That's all I still know for sure. For the past three days I've been lying at the foot of the wall of a church, a few steps from a dead donkey. Like the donkey, I'm dirty and I stink. This morning, an emaciated cow came to join us. It licked the donkey's nose and then lay down on a pile of straw between us. In the violet-colored shade of the church, the three of us looked like a desperate attempt at a crèche. If we can hang on until Christmas, maybe there'll be other animals to complete the scene.

This blazing square will soon be crossed by the ogre, the island's monster, the abject old man. And I'll kill him, with pleasure! One thing bothers me, though it does not weaken my resolution in the least. Of course, I hate him with all my heart. But I don't know why.

My pitiful adventure began five weeks ago. I'd gotten up at exactly 7 A.M. My wife Kiko and our baby were still asleep. We'd gone to bed late. Dinner with old friends. After I rose, I fired up the percolator, covering it with a towel to avoid waking my darlings. Then I switched on the TV and put in a cassette to watch a documentary a neighbor had recorded for me. It was about making cigars; cigars have always been one of my passions. Fate is bizarre sometimes. It was while I was peacefully sipping my coffee that I saw for the first time, on the flat screen, the face of the old man who was going to change the course of my life. As soon as I saw his face, I knew I had to kill him.

Worse yet, I was dying to do it. Without knowing him, without even knowing who he was, I was already dreaming about putting out his eyes and cutting off his tongue. I, who got depressed when I found a mouse in a trap or a hedgehog run over on the road, all I could think of was killing my fellow man. In any case, that particular fucking fellow man, that horror on legs.

I saw him, and everything I was, everything I believed, everything I thought my life was, turned upside down. Just as suddenly, I no longer felt at home among the people and the objects that a few seconds earlier I had still loved. I had to leave. My only "home" would be facing that man, my eyes burning with hatred, my nails lacerating his face, my teeth sinking into his nose, his eyelids, and his tongue, my hands tearing his heart out of his chest. My place was there, standing over the steaming guts of that dead old man, screeching in desperation because I couldn't make him suffer anymore. There and nowhere else, covered with rage and blood, laughing as I devoured his heart.

During the days to come, hate was going to be my new home, my companion, and my child, and it was good that way.

I didn't try to explain anything, either to my wife or to my friends. I had no hope whatever of being understood. And I was also afraid that they would try to keep me from going, argue me out of it. I was in danger of losing too much time laughing at their common sense, at the sound advice they wouldn't fail to give the madman I had become. I preferred to do what I had to do rather than talk about it.

First I found out where the documentary had been made. I spent two days and a night watching that awful cassette over and over, trying to note down all the details, place names, monuments. Thirty-six terrifying hours of ransacking geography books, atlases, and tourist brochures. As soon as I had identified the country I got on a plane without leaving a letter, without any feelings other than impatience and a malign excitement, seething with rage. A one-way tourist-class ticket for the Dominican Republic.

Once I got there, nothing was easy. I had all kinds of problems. "Stranger" comes from "strange." It was only after wandering around the island for two weeks that I began to get my bearings. Then I finally discovered the place where I was going to be able to cross paths with the atrocious face I'd come there to kill. The old man now left his property only to go to a little cigar factory in Carabello. He was often seen crossing the village square.

So it was there that I was going to try my luck and put an end to his.

With the last of my money I bought an old military revolver with five somewhat rusty bullets and went to Carabello. Each day is more liquid and burning than the one before. I have gradually been taken over by exhaustion and despair. Only hatred sustains me. For a week now, I've been waiting for him, leaning against the church wall.

A sweaty wreck next to my donkey, I no longer have any doubt or desire, only the obsessive dream of killing that old man. My personal tragedy, my destiny from now on, bears the name of that absurd old man, that monster: "Darbier," seven letters that have brought me here to Carabello, to this square under the murderous sun. My sister Julie, Kiko, my daughter, all my former loves no longer exist. I'm waiting for the arrival of the sublime moment when my revolver will emerge intoxicated from my pocket and point its mouth toward the ogre so that I, Manuel Gemoni, can finally bellow my hatred at him. If that scum doesn't come here, I'll know what to do with one of these rusty bullets. I won't go home bearing such a burden . . .

Manuel Gemoni looks pensively at the little square. He has come to the end of his journey. His weariness is mauve and green, queasy like the paint on the houses. Today, three peasants came to see about the donkey. Manuel looked at them without really seeing them, then closed his eyes and tried to go back to sleep, to recover a semblance of strength for a semblance of life. At that precise moment, under the sunny stippling of the acacia leaves, two men appear. One of them is old and wears a light, verbena-colored suit, a silk shirt, and a beige Panama hat. His brown leather shoes shine despite the dust. At his side, his bodyguard is sweeping the square with his eyes. The old man walks with slow but regular steps, without the limp that his great age ought to imply.

An orange dog pisses on the corpse of a motorcycle.

Leaving the shade of the trees, the elegant patriarch is now walking in the full sun. His skin is the color of a glazed chestnut, with wrinkles and fissures that are almost black, and pale blotches like dried sugar. His shoulders sway mechanically, as if driving his whole body.

Had he awakened at that moment, Manuel could have seen, glowing under the brim of the Panama hat, the old man's terrifying, yellowish eyes with golden irises. Then he would have been sure that he had chosen the right nightmare, the right man. There is no doubt that this skeleton about to come around the corner of the church is the detested being he came to find. The guy whose photos he has tucked into the hip pocket of his pants.

The dog, lying next to the motorcycle, his tongue hanging out of his mouth, watches the old man go by. But he doesn't bark to warn Manuel. The man will soon leave the square. It will be too late. Three pink and black pigs cross the other side of the square, stopping to explore a mud puddle. Manuel doesn't wake up. A few more steps. The two men are now out of sight behind the church.

Manuel hasn't budged.

It's over! He doesn't know it yet, because he's sleeping, but his journey to the other side of the world has led to nothing. How many days can he hang on before using his own revolver to leave the island?

An hour goes by. The dog has joined Manuel in the land of dreams. The quiet of the square is now disturbed only by the cheerful grunts of the little pigs. The cracked bell is trying to announce that it's noon. Manuel opens one eye, coughs, and goes back to sleep. Before going to lunch, the three peasants return to deal with the donkey. Tomorrow is Sunday, there will be a mass. The animal's stench could spoil the celebration. As for the gringo, they'll ask him to move on. They pick up the beast's carcass and stumble off, the strongest man taking the front legs, the other two the hind legs.

Suddenly they drop the donkey's cadaver and swear. Manu wakes and sits up. The sight is disgusting. A swarming liquid is escaping from the animal's underside. Without worrying about this detail, one of the bearers spits on his hands and seizes the donkey by its ears. The two others grab the tail. The donkey has to die in order to be carried in its turn by man. That's how it is.

Manu sighs and finally looks in the other direction. On his left, a few yards away from him, he sees Darbier!

He is returning from the cigar factory to his lair. Contrary to his habits, today he has decided to go the same way. Has fate finally decided to put an end to the ogre's insolent luck?

Despite his drowsiness, Manuel tries to rise and get hold of his revolver. But the bodyguard is already upon him. He has sensed the danger and is rushing with all his bulk toward the young man. Luckily, the guard has hesitated to drop the precious boxes of cigars that his boss has just lovingly selected. Eleven boxes he's holding. And that's what saves Manuel. Thanks to that extra second, he's able to dodge the attack and get out his revolver. Without quite knowing what he's doing, he points the weapon toward the guard's crimson face. He hears a crack and sees the man fall, holding his right temple. The boxes burst open and the cigars roll across the sand.

Darbier, who hasn't moved during the attack, lurches toward him as well. His lips are open in a grimace of hatred. Manuel lifts the barrel of his revolver and tries to fire. But the old man grabs the end of his weapon and directs it toward the ground. The young man pulls the trigger nonetheless.

The revolver shots ring through the square.

The first bullet pierces the old man's left palm and with a spurt of blood tears off three of his fingers. The second explodes his big toe. Darbier's torn flesh is covered with sand and dirt. He falls backward, screaming with rage.

Manuel is surprised that a man so old still has such red blood; it's almost fluorescent. He'd have imagined it would be black, like his soul, or white, like a kind of pus.

Darbier sits up and shouts at him in French:

"But you're . . . It's impossible!"

Terrified, he adds:

"Don't kill me, I can pay you . . . I can compensate you!"

Then, seeing Manuel's face, he knows that his proposal is useless.

So don't move, keep quiet.

Time stops, seconds rub their black paws together. Above the two adversaries, the sky is a definitive blue. Manuel, his legs spread in his dirty clothes, looks down on his target, his two arms outstretched. His revolver, hammer cocked, is aimed at his victim's forehead. On the ground, Darbier tries to protect himself by putting his wounded hand in front of his face. How can he still be so attached to life?

He breaks the silence, imploring and swearing at the same time:

"Don't kill me, you little piece of shit!"

For some old men, living a hundred years is not enough.

Instead of running away, the people of the village are gathering around. They are gravely watching the scene. Manuel suddenly feels like the executioner at a public execution that a tortured people has long awaited.

What could he have done to them?

It doesn't matter! Manuel has come to avenge himself. He has suddenly understood the reason why, even if it makes no sense. If he wants to kill this man, this revolting old man, it's because one day Darbier killed him, Manuel Gemoni, after having tortured him for hours. Manuel, without realizing the absurdity of what he has just discovered, and simply to put an end to his questions, pulls the trigger.

The third bullet digs into the dust six inches from Darbier's head. His yellowish skull is covered with gray earth. He utters a cry of anger that is cut short by the fourth bullet. Entering above his mouth, it shatters his teeth and the right side of his palate.

Manuel stops firing to look at his enemy writhing and drowning in his own blood. It is grotesque, like his ridiculous groans and gurgling as he desperately tries to breathe and reposition his broken teeth. His legs begin to jerk. His bladder empties, making a large, dark-green stain between his legs. At the corner of his mouth, a mixture of saliva and blood forms a mass of pink bubbles that slowly slips down his chin to join the dusty aridity of the soil.

Manuel fires his last bullet.

The old man's hair explodes and his brain begins to spill out, white and shining in the sun.

Manuel doesn't have time to allow satisfaction to fill his heart; he feels a sudden blow to his back. A projectile fired by the wounded bodyguard has just hit him. As he collapses, Manuel looks at the man who is approaching to finish him off. He says to himself that all things considered, this is the perfect end to an imperfect story. The sun has gone cold. He shivers and looks down at the ground, where everything is going to come to an end.

A second explosion, a second pain.

One doesn't write his own life, neither its contours nor its limits, one doesn't choose what bites him. Manuel and his last thoughts sink into the earth. The coolness of eternity. He has just enough time to think that now he has to die; his life depends on it!

BOOK 1

1.

Mallock is alone, stretched out under a row of coconut trees with manicured leaves. Their curved trunks rise up, as survivors, from a disturbing, almost excessively white sand. They reach for the sky to find the wind. Beyond the beach is the tropical ocean, and his son who is swimming in it. Since he died, he hasn't grown anymore. He's still five years old and has his father's absinthe-colored eyes, his pupils match the waves of the sea. Here is Thomas, his little Tom, his little fellow, in the lukewarm waters of the Atlantic sheltered by the reef, that amniotic mother. Here is Thomas Mallock among the blue crabs that run sideways, the sea horses and microscopic, silvery jellyfish. Look at him! In that sea, that's Thomas you see. He's flying, my little angel, on the glassy, limpid waves of the ocean.

His father, a police superintendent, smiles, astonished to feel so well, here in the full sun, in his heavy suit striped by the shade of the palm trees . . .

"Monsieur, your tray, please?"

Mallock wakes up in a sweat. He says, "Excuse me," and pulls down the gray plastic tray.

"I'm really sorry to wake you, but we're going to bring you something to eat soon."

The flight attendant has a little scar on her forehead and a nice smile.

"It's okay, you did the right thing," Mallock replies, smiling back at her.

In any case, as long as he lives, his son will remain dead.

Superintendent Mallock is flying to the Dominican Republic. He has been assigned by Dublin, the head honcho at 36, Quai des Orfèvres, the criminal investigation department in Paris, to bring back Manuel Gemoni, a French citizen who has murdered an inhabitant of the island.

Any normal person would have jumped for joy at the idea of leaving Paris and its gloomy, cold November weather. To escape from the gates of winter, cross the Atlantic, and return to summer, with beaches and palm trees.

But not Mallock.

Amédée Mallock, the king of homebodies, hates to travel. In his view, neither fauna nor flora nor historical stuff can justify the displeasure of going away, being deprived of all the little possessions with which civilized people surround their bodies and their minds to protect them from the inevitable collisions with the rest of the world.

When he is forced to leave home, Amédée sulks like a frustrated schoolboy, resenting those who have forced him to perform an unnatural act: moving! He has been a hundred yards from Niagara Falls without deigning to look at them; in Egypt, he didn't even glance at the pyramids; in India, he ignored the big white thing, and in Copenhagen, the little mermaid. Even in Paris, where he has lived for a long time, he has only recently gone up the Eiffel Tower, and not to see the view, or to admire the metallic monument, but to investigate a mass murder.

Now, going off to be a stupid tourist on a remote island in the Antilles didn't appeal to him at all. Normally, he would have taken sick leave. If he didn't protest, it's because he knows Manuel Gemoni personally. Especially his sister, who has worked for him ever since Fort Mallock—Mallock's office within the criminal investigation department, known as "36"—was set up.

*

Six days before, Julie Gemoni, a captain in the police, came to see her boss. Outside, the caramel-colored Seine was awaiting winter. The capital was enjoying a classic Indian summer.

Julie had come into his office with her lips tight and her chin jutting out aggressively. She asked for a special leave. Like most of the Fort's staff, she had been on duty all through the case of the "massacre of the innocents." She had a lot of over-time hours, loads of vacation time, and credit for all the weekly days off she hadn't taken during the crisis. Some time ago, she had submitted the request for a combined leave, explaining that she wanted to go away for a month. She needed her super-intendent's permission.

"Really? That long? You're hard on me. But then you must have your reasons," Mallock said to her. "And then it'll spare me having to look at your ugly mug. I mean, the one you've been wearing for the last two weeks. You look like you're going to a funeral and that affects everybody's morale."

Julie hesitated for only a few seconds. She'd probably just been waiting for an opportunity to talk about it.

"It's my brother," she finally managed to say.

"Manu? What's up with him?"

The mention of this name revived all the feelings and concerns the young woman had been bottling up inside her for several days. Her tears were welling up behind her eyelids, ready to overflow them.

She tried to speak: "He's been . . . They've . . . "

But she began to sob, furious with herself, and ashamed to let herself be seen crying, especially in front of her superintendent.

"Excuse me, I'm sorry. Usually I can . . . "

Mallock went up to her. He felt like a dolt for having talked about her "ugly mug." She fell into his arms. Embarrassed and worried, he awkwardly stroked her back. Then he continued with a series of little taps, more masculine and less compromising. But also more ridiculous.

"Only macho jerks and hard-ass bitches don't cry."

Then she opened up and told him about her sadness and her little girl's fear of losing her big brother.

Under Superintendent Mallock's hard and intransigent shell there were herds of tenderness galloping free. Julie had always suspected as much. Today, as he held her in his arms, she had proof of it. She could clearly hear the hoofbeats of those herds.

Once she'd calmed down, Amédée helped her to a seat and went back behind his desk to make a cup of tea for her. That was one of the rare things he knew about women. Those marvelous hominids had very few sorrows that couldn't be assuaged by a cup of tea, a nice bouquet of flowers, or the purchase of a red jacket. He had only Lipton's on hand.

He performed the tea ceremony, like a kind of geisha. Like a man who respected traditions, at least when they were culinary. He manipulated the delicate Chinese porcelain with his big, meaty hands, lifting his pinky and bowing fussily. He scalded the teapot, poured boiling water on the tea leaves, emptied it out immediately, and repeated the procedure. When he finally decided to serve Julie her tea, his associate's reaction seemed to prove him right as soon as she had taken a second sip. At the third sip, she began to contemplate the bottom of her cup, running the pretty tip of her tongue over her upper lip. At the fourth, she straightened up. At the fifth, she began her story.

It was the first time Mallock had heard about the case. It was no longer a matter of a missing person; now it was a murder investigation. And what a murder! Her brother had just been wounded after having, it seemed, killed an old man in cold blood on the other side of the world.

She knew nothing about the crime itself except the memorable sentence he'd uttered when he was arrested. Whether it was a motive that was still incomprehensible or a simple expression of madness, to the policemen who came to arrest him Manu had said: "I killed him because he had killed me."

The plane's air-conditioning system is setting records.

Amédée reaches up to adjust the ventilation control with his big fingers. A refined bear of a man, he has slender wrists onto which a butcher's hands seemed to have been grafted. Glowing eyes like precious stones light up a face that is half Nick Nolte and half Depardieu, with the same hank of blond hair, a shapeless nose, and a delicate mouth. His body, six feet tall and weighing 220 pounds, makes him look more like the American, and it will not be too big for solving this unlikely case. Mallock, who likes to be in control of his environment and the development of his investigations, is preparing himself for some trying days. It will take two or three superintendents to cope with the strange enigma with which Manuel Gemoni is about to present him.

That's fine, Mallock is several.

His thoughts return to Julie and what she told him in Paris.

"Tell me everything, right from the beginning. What happened to Manu?"

Mallock was fond of Julie's brother.

"It's a very common thing, but when it happens to you, it's not the same, it's tragic," the young captain began.

"The facts, please. What happened?"

"Manu disappeared exactly two weeks ago, without the slightest explanation. Jules and I looked for him everywhere. No gambling debts, no enemies, no depression or likelihood of suicide. As you know, he's married to a Japanese woman, Kiko, and they have just had a marvelous little daughter."

She took a deep breath; she was still on the verge of tears.

"Manu is two years younger than I, but I've always considered him my big brother. I don't know if you remember, but he has a degree in archaeology and is a teacher-researcher at the College de France, where he works on everything that concerns ancient Egypt. He is sought after the world over."

Julie was proud of Manu. No doubt he must be proud of her, too. The young woman had had a brilliant career in the police. She was now entering what Amédée called his blood brotherhood, his right arm, a virtual hand whose five fingers corresponded to his five main associates.

At five feet tall, with her wasp-waisted, feather-light body, Julie was its little finger. She stuck her nose into everything and used her pretty ears exactly where they were needed. She had no peer for uncovering the most . . . secret information. Mallock suspected she was making unhesitating use of her Corsican family's various networks. When he said that it was his little finger that had told him, most of the time he was referring to Julie. Her acute intelligence and her ability to synthesize information were a kind of recourse for Mallock, a lifebuoy for use in the event that his own system of reflection failed.

"Frankly, how could anyone have had anything against him? He is . . . was happy, and made everyone around him happy, too."

"That's true, he's a good guy," Mallock agreed.

"Plus," she went on, piling up her arguments as if she were trying to finish convincing him, "they'd just moved into a spectacular apartment with a view of the Madeleine. I've never seen him so radiant. To the point of being annoying," she added, trying to add a touch of humor.

"And all that," Mallock concluded, "didn't prevent him from packing a bag and going out the door to kill an old man on the other side of the world?"

"I know, it's completely absurd!"

"After all, Julie, people don't kill somebody for no reason at all! This guy over there may be responsible for the death of one of his friends, or . . . "

To shut him up, she sniffed, with a charming wrinkling of her nose.

"No, among the people around him, no one died, except for one of our aunts whom he adored, but it was a natural death, apparently."

"You know, Julie, there's always a reason for things, even if it escapes us at the time."

"That's just what Jules has been telling me from the start. But after all, you know Manu, he's a model of balance and moderation. When he was a child, he was already wisdom itself. In a baby, that was pretty astonishing. People said he was the reincarnation of an old soul. Mama called him her 'Little Gandhi.' He didn't even have the usual childhood illnesses, or go through an annoying phase, even when he was an adolescent. He had no weaknesses, none. Except, maybe . . . "

Mallock encouraged her to continue by simply nodding his head.

"His only weak point was his fear of forests and the dark. Ever since we were children, it had been my job to protect him and reassure him when night fell. But even that peculiar panic has never prevented him from being one of the most courageous men I know. Once, when he was seven, I got lost in a little wood east of Ajaccio. In the middle of the night, he came to look for me. He was terrified and dripping with sweat, but he found me and took me home."

Julie repressed a huge sob before saying something that touched Mallock's heart.

"Today, I'm the one who has to take him home."

The Airbus's engines are humming with a reassuring regularity. At the end of the aisle, the food cart has just appeared.

The sound of glasses clinking and liquids being poured. Amédée will soon be able to get some sustenance. And he likes to eat, and drink, too. A double whiskey, that will relax everything, the body and the mind, in a single, saving wave.

As for the rest, as an experienced man used to the trials of life and the wrath of heaven, he has learned to guard against excessive hopes. He has given this meal that is advancing toward him one and only one objective, that of filling part of the void he has in his stomach. Period. But the naïve fellow has once again expected too much of the gods' magnanimity. An unidentifiable chunk of meat swims among the remains of lukewarm vegetables. He waves it away and closes his eyes again.

"I'm the one who has to take him home," Julie had said gravely a few days earlier. Mallock had looked at her with tenderness, that particular tenderness he reserved for the marvelous little girls who had become women, courageous, beautiful women. Yes, her brother was a good guy and he had a wonderful sister. With her very light hazel eyes, her olive skin, her short hair, and her little, slightly hooked nose, she was beautiful enough to eat. But what made her still more beautiful was her lively mind, along with the methodical, stubborn side that is peculiar to feminine intelligence. Mallock was very lucky to have her on his team. And Jules was lucky to have her as his partner.

"You hadn't been able to track him down before these recent events?"

"Yes, I had, just before I learned about this murder business last night, I'd finally found out where he'd gone. Too late."

"Why didn't you ask the whole team for help right from the beginning, instead of trying to find your brother by yourself? In the Fort, within the blood brotherhood, we take care of each other. You ought to know that."

There was a touch of reproach in what Mallock said.

"You were all busy with the most recent developments in the 'massacre' case, and I didn't want to mess up everything with a personal problem that was far less important than the horror we had to confront this summer. I took advantage of Jules's convalescence to put him to work. I really thought we were going to be able to handle it by ourselves."

Jules was still recovering from the bullet wound that had sent him to the hospital during the previous investigation. It had struck him in the forehead but was small-caliber, and it had saved him by passing between the two lobes of his brain. He had only a small, crescent-shaped scar.

Mechanically, Mallock turned on the two tape recorders that he used so that he could listen to depositions again.

"Tell me about the beginning of your investigation."

" Jules and I began with the supposed contents of his bag, as it had been reconstituted by Kiko. She'd noticed the absence of certain clothes and toilet articles. Then we viewed together the videocassette that he'd constantly been watching and that, according to his wife, is supposed to have started it all."

"What kind of video?"

"A documentary on historical and ethnological stuff. Manu not only watched it several times, but also took digital photos of it. He must have taken some of them with him, but the ones that remained allowed me to tell what he was looking at so attentively."

"The parts of the documentary that interested him?"

"Exactly. There were one or two that seem to have fascinated him. In those pictures, we can see a town square, a few trees with trunks painted mauve, the color of a local political party, so far as I could understand, and a church constructed from pink earth. In fact, it is the presence in the photo of black people with green eyes and red hair that allowed us to identify the village: San José de Ocoa."

"Because?"

"It's a specific ethnic group found in only four places in the world. Ocoa was the only one that had the same vegetation. The church provided the final proof. In the film, that was also the most obvious thing."

"Can I see it?"

"No, the crime squad and the guys from Foreign Affairs came to Manu's house and confiscated all his personal effects. The morons even took fingerprints off the cassette and the tape recorder, as if they were weapons. Conservative steps, they said. They were meticulous."

At the time, Mallock felt personally insulted by such a procedure. Then he calmed down. Wouldn't he have done the same thing?

"That's okay. I'll take care of that later. On the other hand, I'd like you to have your brother's blood tested as soon as possible. Have the authorities in Santo Domingo send us the blood. We have to find out everything about his physical condition. He might have been drugged or caught some disease there."

Julie felt a little better. Mallock's use of the pronoun "I" helped her enormously. Not only were she and her close friends and relatives no longer the only ones, but the Mallock machine was in gear. And she was in a position to know how effective that was.

Somewhat reassured, she went on: "After discovering where and when he'd gone, I had no difficulty in confirming his departure. I borrowed Ken's computers and connected to the databases of the airline companies and the customs and immigration authorities. In two hours we found the schedule and the number of his flight. I also discovered that he'd paid for his ticket in cash and, more disturbingly, hadn't bought a return ticket."

A one-way ticket to the ends of the earth, Mallock murmured, closing his eyes. And all those miles to go murder an old man whom he didn't even know. What could he have been thinking?

It seemed to Julie that she heard her superintendent's brain starting up, like a powerful steam engine. She felt the heavy circumvolutions of his imagination shaking the ground under her feet, eating up the steel rails she'd just put in front of him. She knew he wouldn't stop until he'd reached the terminus: the solution of the enigma.

She was infinitely grateful to him.

The food cart comes back to his row:

"Sorry to have awakened you again, superintendent."

Superintendent! Damn, he's been recognized again. Since the last investigation, he's had trouble not being noticed.

"What would you like to drink?"

The flight attendant's smile is so dazzling that Mallock catches himself counting her teeth. It isn't possible that she has only thirty-two. At least twice that many.

"Whiskey, please."

"Ice cubes?"

Mallock looks at the label on the bottle:

"Yes, please. And a little soda." A nectar like that can be drowned ruthlessly.

After the past, the future. Mallock has started thinking about what he has to do when he gets there. Dublin, the big boss of the 36, the occupier of the prestigious Office No. 315 and his direct superior, had been clear. If he was okay with Amédée being responsible for this investigation, even though it involved someone who was close to him in a way, that was because his favorite superintendent had improved with age, like a fine wine whose bottle was embellished with the flattering label: "As seen on television." His presence would satisfy the egos of the local authorities and it would be easier for him to get access to the investigation's files. The procedure of extradition might thereby be simplified. For its part, the chancellery had begun working to arrange the repatriation of its citizen, probably with the help of Interpol, the Dominican Republic having contacted the international police organization.

The old man Manuel had killed was named Tobias Darbier. He had a French passport. The Ministry of Foreign Affairs had emphasized that the victim and the murderer were of the same nationality. A little incentive on the economic level had made it possible to foresee a satisfactory outcome. A "transfer agreement" had been signed, and then everything had moved very quickly. But many promises had been made in order to permit this extradition.

Far too many promises, Amédée was to discover later on.

For once, he thought he would play the starring role, that of the savior. The one who is awaited and who arrives at the right moment, with trumpets, drums, and lightning bolts. Zorro the horseman, the great superintendent, all askew, with his little cape flying behind him. Mallock the centaur and flawless knight. Obsolete and ridiculous, like a medieval hero with his plumes and revealing tights.

As a child in the schoolyard, Amédée was already the boy who gallops straight ahead, slapping his thigh, shooting invisible arrows and defeating a whole army of bad guys all by himself. Mallock had the hero's whole panoply. And while he'd gotten older, he hadn't grown up. So yes, he took pleasure in this mission. He would go find little Gandhi and take him home.

A mixture of Cyrano and Don Quixote, Mallock was poorly adapted to his time and to life on Earth as a whole. He had seen hypocrisy and mendacity win out and the words of the Just become inaudible, but he continued nonetheless to fight to save sand castles from the rising tide. An emperor of paradox and the king of the oxymoron, Mallock combined in a single heart modest pride, tears, and fierceness, tender hardness, empathy, and misanthropy. Thanks to a kind of melancholy-based glue, he managed to construct out of all these contradictions a homogeneous, almost monolithic whole. People talk about the hopes of youth; Mallock was instead the despair of age.

A questionnaire appears, falling from on high. Great, something to do. He starts to check the "tourism" box, but then chooses "business" instead, wondering what diplomatic intrigues and administrative complications—two redundancies in a row—he is going to have to cope with. The Dominican authorities no longer oppose Manuel Gemoni's extradition or having him tried in France, on the condition that they be allowed to send two observers to monitor the trial as a whole. Regarding that aspect of the accord, it only remains to choose the observers' hotel—the George V or the Crillon?—and to agree on the amount of their expense account. Aside from that, the Dominican officials ask that everything be done in due form and in conformity with their national prerogatives. Face has to be saved, and no one must be able to interpret this accord as an indication of weakness on their part. Dispatching someone like Mallock, and not a simple captain, helped calm the last local sensitivities.

When he gets there, he'll still have a few courtesies to perform, two envelopes to deliver in person and a raft of thank-yous, and then he'll be done, he thinks. The only thing that still worries Amédée, who is peacefully falling asleep, is how long it will take him to get through all these formalities. A day, a week, a month? What would a bureaucrat who was an islander be like? A day, a week, a month? Sleep, the humming of the engine . . . A day, a week, a month?

He wakes when the plane, after having touched down with a violent thump, is bouncing up again. Jesus! The guy must be a fucking beginner! Stupefied, Mallock hears the other travelers applauding like mad, congratulating the pilot. He sighs, almost philosophically. "After good judgment, the rarest things in the world are diamonds and pearls."

Flight attendant's announcement that they have arrived in the Dominican Republic. A bunch of jerks already champing at the bit to get out. Bags by the dozens descending from the overhead compartments. Mallock stays in his seat, looking out the window. He wonders, once again, whether he'll be able to live out his life without becoming completely misanthropic, or even psychopathic, a mad killer mowing down passengers in a train, an air-conditioned bus, or—why not?—a plane landing in the Dominican Republic.

2.

Except for the humidity, the noise, the gray, overcast weather, and the strong odors, the arrival in Santo Domingo was not all that bad, even for someone like Mallock.

In the main hall of the airport, there were a dozen passport-control booths, salmon-pink and numbered in yellow. A great idea—the booths, not the color—that would have been enough to control the flow of white tourists and swarthy businessmen had the authorities not decided, in obedience to the international agreement to ignore public convenience, to open only one of these lovely booths.

Arriving passengers found themselves forced to pass through the bottleneck thus produced in order to get the sacrosanct *tarjeta del turista*, full of typographical flourishes, gilt stamps, and royal watermarks.

Once they had this precious document in their hands, they all scattered, every man for himself, to try to take possession of one of the rare places that had a counter on which they could fill out the aforesaid questionnaire. This assumed of course, that everyone was the fortunate owner of a pen. Then all one had to do was keep a paranoid eye on his baggage while pressing hard enough on this carbon copy, which was very tropical in its quality.

Fortunately for Mallock, Commander Juan Luis Jiménez and his assistant, *el capitán* Ramón Cabral, had been assigned to meet *el comandante* superintendent from Paris. These two local police officers had been instructed to spare Mallock any hassles, and they gave him a warm welcome. The term was all the more apt because he was still wearing one of his usual suits, with a tie and matching socks, and heavy leather shoes. He realized how important the two officers thought he was by the simple fact that neither of them dared smile at his clothes, which were inappropriate to say the least.

They had straight white teeth beneath black mustaches. They took his passport and, without asking him to pay the ten-dollar entry fee, left to deal with his paperwork:

"Stay, we'll take care of everything."

They spoke French about as well as Amédée spoke Spanish. They weren't out of the woods yet . . .

Imprisoned in his suit, Mallock feels sweaty and a little stupid. Then, for the first time since he was allowed to get rid of the horrible short pants his mother made him wear, he considers the possibility of buying himself that unimaginable article of clothing: Bermuda shorts. To make the idea acceptable, he has imported it into his brain only in the form of a simple working hypothesis, depending on a whole series of conditions: the shape, the material, the color . . . But the worm is in the apple, the idea is making its way, and the world may soon be able to see Mallock in shorts!

In the middle of the hall, the superintendent's eyes make a slow, discreet panoramic survey to locate a store specializing in things for the tourist who lacks foresight. There is none. He sees nothing but bodies that are moving slowly because of the heat: a two-year-old child wearing camouflage clothing, a giant bent down like a question mark, dyed animals, heavily-laden tourists, and then, here and there, men in uniform sporting revolvers and mustaches. Blue caps, riot guns, colonial kepis, Kalashnikovs . . . there are watchmen, private security men, *tur-*

istos, municipal police, vigilantes, national police in blue shirts, forest guards assigned to protect the island's vegetation, *testas negras*, rather like the French riot police, but more tropical, and finally policemen in gray uniforms, wearing American-style caps, whose exact function is not known to anyone.

The superintendent will have time to realize that democracy always has trouble "taking" in countries that have been too long drained by colonialism, socialism, or a good old family dictatorship.

Often all three of them at once.

In the pink-sided glass passport-control booths, pairs of officials with dark skins were concentrating so as not to think about anything. It's a whole art. With half-closed eyelids and pouting lips, they waited to seize the official scrap of paper and, without even checking to see what was written on it, tore it in half and gave the traveler, who was in the last stage of exhaustion, a completely illegible copy. Then they opened the passport and, with a majestic gesture of authority, slammed a stamp on a blank page in a ritual tattooing that was the final act of the initiatory ceremony of welcome.

Jiménez and Cabral reappeared on the other side of the booths and signaled to Mallock that he should join them. Amédée passed in front of the passport-control men without any of them asking him anything at all, or even deigning to glance at this guy who was crossing the broad yellow stripe symbolizing their sacrosanct border.

Tómalo suave, a translation of the American "keep cool," was the country's official motto, and it was clear that everyone was following it to the letter.

The two policemen with their big mustaches were waiting for him with a big, empty baggage cart. Amédée had a little difficulty in making them understand that he didn't have any baggage. Most of the gringos landed with loads of luggage, not to mention those who were going to the Amber Coast with enormous silvery bags containing one or two sailboards. In the carry-on bag he was rolling behind him, Amédée had managed to stuff his aluminum cell phone, a Nikon Coolpix, an iPod, a bunch of extra underwear, and the strict minimum of lightweight shirts, his toilet and medicine kit, which even included, at Julie's insistence, sunblock, a powerful mosquito repellent, and two little plug converters for American outlets.

Then he looked at his hosts more carefully.

Jiménez was dressed in civilian clothes. Pants and shirt in unbleached linen, his white hair clashing violently with the color of his skin, which was completely black. He was as short and thin as his sidekick was tall and stocky. Cabral, whose skin was much lighter, was wearing a uniform that looked like that of the regional police: white shirt with a captain's epaulets and navy blue pants. Through the shirt Amédée could see a T-shirt bearing the word *Cabarete* inscribed in a circle on a big blue wave from which a windsurfer was taking off. On his feet, Cabral wore heavy black high-top shoes. Finally, held under his left arm, a white, colonial-style cap intended for traffic police added a pleasant exotic touch to the uniform.

Despite what morphopsychology might have suggested, it was the little skinny guy, all dried up and somber, with his snow-white hair, who proved to be the most easygoing. Mallock, in accord with his old habit, nicknamed him Cappuccino. *El capitán* Ramón seemed to either have a stick up his ass or a terrible horror of gringos who thought they could just come into his territory and tell him how to do his job. His beige skin and plumpness won him the sobriquet Double-cream.

Cappuccino and Double-cream would be the two victims of the same loss of income. Every day they spent taking care of the gringo would be so much time lost for the rackets they and their men ran on tourists alongside the island roads, systematically but genially. This pastime, curious but inoffensive, was in fact part of the policemen's compensation. The government hadn't raised their salaries in years, but had unofficially authorized them to exploit the country's new natural resource: the "gogo-bobo-gringo."

"My hotel is in Puerto Plata, right?" Mallock asked, in an attempt to strike up a conversation.

"Puerto Plata is *mierda*, and Sosúa, the closest village, is *mierda de mierda* . . . "

Seeing the dark look given him by Ramón, who didn't like his boss to talk about their country that way, Mallock decided to reply with a simple "Is that right?" whose intonation, simultaneously interrogative and doubtful, even reproachful, was there only to signify his surprise, and, consequently, to imply the high opinion he had of this superb republic.

The result went beyond his hopes. Ramón lowered his guard and went so far as to hold out his arm to offer to carry Mallock's bag. Mallock refused and dealt him the final blow by saying:

"*Muchas gracias*, Señor Ramón," which completely won over *el capitán*. Which just goes to show that in life, sometimes it takes very little to spare yourself problems, the wise Amédée told the hotheaded Mallock.

Once they had left the airport and its air-conditioning, a great draft of the Caribbean filled the Parisian superintendent's lungs. It was hot and humid, almost oily, and he wondered with concern whether this atmosphere had enough oxygen in it to keep him alive. For the moment, he doubted it did.

"Don't worry, you'll quickly get used to it . . . "

Jiménez and his perfect teeth were amused to see the French supercop breathing with the gracious ease of a fish on the deck of a boat.

"It'll be better on the *otro* side of the island. We've reserved *uno* big penthouse in Cabarete, on the Amber Coast. Very good spot for windsurfing, so much more air for you."

Double-cream Cabral, annoyed by Jiménez's gobbledy-gook, finally decided to speak up himself. A marvelous surprise: he spoke perfect French, which was probably why his superiors had selected him for this assignment. However, he had a curious accent that took Mallock a while to identify. At first he thought it was American-influenced, but then realized that it was more like a Canadian accent. The higher-ups must have figured that it would be easier for the superintendent-commander from Paris, and that it would also help them keep a closer eye on him. Mallock decided to be careful when he was using the telephone.

"Your countryman murdered *el comandante* Darbier on my territory, the north coast of the island, between Sosúa and Cabarete," Ramón explained. "More exactly, halfway between Caliche and Punta Goleta."

He belched and went on: "We call that part of the country the Amber Coast. Over there you'll feel much better, there are winds that constantly blow in off the Atlantic. Here you're in the worst of the Caribbean mugginess, the Tropic of Cancer."

"How far is it?"

"About four hours, at least one of which is just getting out of Santo Domingo. Then we take the Duarte *autopista* that runs along the central mountain range. Up there you'll see how beautiful our country is."

That was a criticism of his superior. They'd reached the police car, which was painted sea-green with white, black, and white stripes.

"Did they tell you that I have to stop at the French consulate to finalize Gemoni's repatriation?"

"Yes, *edificio* Heinsen, 353 Washington Avenue. *Allez, en route*," Cappuccino Jiménez said, proud to show that he knew French, too.

As he got into the front seat, Mallock said *Vamonos!* in the same convivial and resolutely cosmopolitan spirit.

3.

First Impressions of the Island

In the Dominican Republic, traffic greatly resembles a gigantic bumper-car game, with only two rules: force your way through, whatever it takes, and full speed ahead between the enormous potholes while trying to avoid, if possible, hitting other vehicles or being hit by them. And also push your luck, there being an impressive number of accidents on the island. *Guaguas*, community taxis, small motorcycles, Japanese cars, and big Mack trucks engage in a kind of joust punctuated by the regular use of the horn. People honk to draw attention to themselves, to intimidate their adversaries, to say hello, to tell off another driver, or for no reason at all. In fact, one can drive without headlights, without brakes, and with tires that have been repeatedly patched up by one of the many *gomeros* who specialize in unauthorized recaps. The only thing that can keep a vehicle off the road is a dead motor, or worse yet, a broken horn.

The enormous fuzzy dice attached to the rearview mirror were swinging violently back and forth. Sitting in the suicide seat, Mallock spent the first half hour automatically braking with his right foot while nervously pointing out the various obstacles to a beaming Jiménez.

"Here, *ça passe ou ça casse*, as you French say," the *comandante* said jovially.

There was no doubt that this little bumper-car game and the effect it produced on the big superintendent from Paris greatly amused Jiménez. Then Mallock resigned himself to his fate, wondering only if he'd thought to update his last will and testament, and if he had, where he'd stashed it.

George Washington Avenue ran quite close to *el mar de las Antillas*, as the Caribbean is called there. When they arrived in front of the imposing Heinsen building, with its tall columns of pink marble, Mallock, his legs shaking, left the two policemen in the cool of their air-conditioned car and plunged again into the tropical steam bath. Once he'd crossed the sidewalk, he was delighted to find that the building's lobby was also air-conditioned. The concierge told him where to go, pointing with a dirty finger to the elevator door. The French embassy occupied the third floor, and the ambassador, Jean-Pierre Delmont, had a huge air-conditioned office that looked out on the sea.

He was a tall, gaunt man with silvery hair. He wore an expensive suit with custom-made Italian shoes, a tasteful silk tie, and a crocodile-leather belt. He came up to Mallock to shake his hand. His smile smelled of shaving soap, tobacco, and cologne. At the end of his arm, like a bouquet, his hand with slender, frequently manicured fingers. Mallock shook it with his big paw. *Another pampered desk jockey*, he thought.

But he was wrong.

Watch out, Commander Mallock, Amédée whispered, *it's not a crime to have an ugly or a handsome face, the great river of acrimony flows over the shallows of "bitterness."*

In fact, Ambassador Delmont knew his trade well and practiced it perfectly. After the usual courtesies—polite inquiries as to how his trip had been, "You must be tired after such a voyage, Superintendent," initial commentaries and advice concerning the climate, flattering remarks on Mallock's fame, etc.—Delmont had the excellent idea of suggesting that they have some Lagavulin: two inches of it in a glass filled with ice cubes. The diplomat hardly had his whiskey in his hand before he got to down to business:

"I think you've understood the situation as well as I have. The immediate repatriation to France is explained and justified chiefly by the state of Manuel's health. He is not in danger of dying, but here, on this marvelous island, the longer your 'stay' in a hospital, the greater the chance that you'll stay there permanently. Sepsis is as common here as flu is at home. That said, the carelessness of their medical system and the obvious incompetence of their doctors are the last arguments to give if you want to get somewhere with the Dominican authorities. They get angry at the smallest perceived slight. Let's just say that their insular sensitivity is as stupid as our European arrogance."

Mallock smiled with approval.

"Here, like everywhere, whites and natives are not prepared to speak openly to each other, Superintendent. And fortunately, because otherwise, what would I be doing here? So you'll have to indulge in a little flattery and smile more than you initially planned, if you don't find that too unbearable?"

Even though he was a professional diplomat, the man went to the heart of the matter with great clarity and without the slightest dissimulation. Fine, Mallock would do the same.

"I get the message regarding repatriation, but I'd also like to be able to gather the maximum amount of information in preparation for the trial."

Delmont set his empty glass down on the table. "It seems there's no doubt about Manu's guilt, and I'm sorry about that. He himself admitted the facts in my presence, and there are seven witnesses, three of which are credible."

The affectionate use of the diminutive "Manu" made Mallock think that the diplomat had taken his job seriously. He must have met with Manuel Gemoni several times. Delmont continued:

"So, for your investigation I hope you will verify the most important points, interrogate the witnesses, but proceed no further once you've covered the essence of the case. The local authorities could dig in their heels and Manuel would be lost. I've seen that happen almost every day, and with two bullets in his body, I can tell you that he won't long survive the not-very-hospitable hospitality of their hospital."

Delmont had his own peculiar sense of humor. Semantic.

"Darbier's bodyguard was restrained by the villagers, otherwise he would certainly have finished him off. I'm sure that in Paris they'll know how to treat him and save his life. Whereas here, with those wounds, he's as good as dead."

"By the way, while we're on that subject, is there any hitch regarding his repatriation?"

Delmont slowly ran his fingers through his hair. "Let's be clear, Superintendent, we have only one plausible political argument in the context of the extradition agreements between the two countries: the offender is French and his victim is 'supposed' to be French as well. That has allowed us to undertake negotiations that should move in the right direction. Two or three days from now, if things go well, we'll have the official papers and you can leave with your prisoner."

After he'd registered in a corner of his brain Delmont's doubt regarding the victim's nationality, which he planned to ruminate on later, Mallock couldn't help asking: "If things go well? Is it possible they won't?"

"We . . . I don't know, but so far as I'm concerned, I'm always in doubt. In a country like this one, you can't be sure until your plane's wheels have left the ground. There will be negotiations right down to the end, and concessions to be made at the last minute: that's how things work. It's a complex process whose details will remain strictly confidential. If the French government follows my advice without either resisting or giving in, we'll move slowly but surely toward a positive outcome for both parties."

Mallock understood that the ambassador wouldn't say anything more on this subject. And he chose not to pursue the matter or allude to the exceptional powers that the government had given him for his investigation. In any case, Delmont must know about that, and it would be more elegant not to brag about it. Nor did he find it necessary to mention his personal connections to Manu. It is incredible how often, over time, you realize that most of the time it's better to keep your trap shut when you feel safe with someone and feel a desire to spill the beans.

He limited himself to a polite formula: "I want to thank you for having done so much to help Manuel Gemoni. His sister and his wife will be very grateful to you."

"To tell the truth, I've only done my job, and I'm far from satisfied. You should thank instead a man called Juan Antonio Servantes, my Dominican counterpart. He was very cooperative. We would both have liked to move Manuel to another hospital so that the leg where the second bullet was lodged could be operated on before he is taken back. We still haven't been able to arrange that. By the way, I've made an appointment for you with Professor André Barride. He offered to pick you up tomorrow morning at your hotel, the Blue Paradise, and take you to see Manuel and negotiate his transfer together. He's an expatriate surgeon who knows the country even better than I do. I called him last night, and he says he has managed to set up Manu's transfer to a private clinic where the operation can be performed. I sincerely hope that everything will go well. Manuel didn't seem to be a bad fellow. On the contrary, he's a good guy. Anyway, I'm preaching to the converted. You know and like him, as I understand it?"

Mallock should have suspected it: "Through his sister, Julie Gemoni, who works with me."

Delmont smiled faintly. "That young man is as likeable as his victim was detestable."

Even if still very far from suspecting what he was going to

discover, what Delmont meant by "detestable" interested Mallock in the highest degree. But he really no longer had time for it. His two guys were waiting for him down below and his bed was beckoning to him from the other side of the island.

"Could I call you from my hotel tomorrow morning to ask you a few questions about Tobias Darbier?"

"Of course, Superintendent, that's what I'm here for."

"Thanks in advance. I've got to go now, I have to hurry if I want to reach the hotel before nightfall. And then there are two pairs of mustaches in uniform parked in front of your building who must be getting tired of waiting."

The ambassador smiled as he accompanied him as far as the door. "For male Latinos, the big tuft of hair under the nostrils is part of their virility, but it's far from being the only one. Burping after drinking beer and carrying a revolver between his *cojones* are still indispensable."

Mallock burst into laughter. He rarely laughed, but when he did, the walls began to shake and his conversation partners looked at him with concern.

There was madness in his laughter.

Down below, the two Dominican stallions were obediently waiting for him, sipping beers. Mallock smiled when he thought of Delmont's remark. They were clearly eager to resume their bumper-car game. Even before Mallock had time to close his door, the car took off with wheels spinning.

The superintendent decided to rely on God, and turning his eyes away from the road, he took up the subject he was dying to discuss.

"Who was this Tobias Darbier, in fact?"

The answer emerged from Ramón's mouth in a sibylline manner.

"*El Comandante* Darbier was not really well-liked around here."

Mallock divined that this was a prudent understatement, a diplomatic euphemism that was begging to be encouraged.

"A real bastard?"

Ramón nodded. "A real piece of shit."

Mallock waited a few minutes before he continued:

"A complete biography of this guy would help me understand why this young Frenchman came here to kill him. We could close the case and move on to something else. Among policemen, we have to tell each other everything, right?"

Double-cream Cabral glanced at Jiménez in the rearview mirror. The latter stopped smiling long enough to imperceptibly nod his head. Then the captain knew he could start talking, move on to telling secrets, or at least the ones that could be shared between Europeans and islanders.

"He was without any doubt the most hated man on the island. A complete asshole. A foreigner to boot, and white! At least half of the Dominicans would have liked to kill him themselves. He thought our little island should be under his boot, or at least he did in his heyday. That 'chalk-face' talked about the Dominican Republic as his 'empire.' He even thought about raising his own army to invade the other side of the island, Haiti. But at the same time, he was trying to remain unnoticed by foreigners and by the puppets who were running the country, so he dropped the idea."

"What did he look like?" Mallock said, encouraging him and disregarding Double-cream's assumed xenophobia.

"A caricature of a monster. He had a beige complexion and an S-shaped nose, with a negroid mouth, light blond eyes, and curly hair. Long scars on his face. He was about 6' 5" tall. As he got older he shrank. He had more murders on his conscience than anyone else on the island. He was hated as much as he was feared."

"How did it happen that he hadn't been killed earlier?

Ramón grimaced. *He'd have liked to have done it himself,* Mallock thought.

"He was too well protected, surrounded by a veritable army of paid bodyguards. He paid them well and they were extremely effective. Most of them had belonged to the former dictator's security team. Darbier's *brutos* allowed him to escape more than thirty assassination attempts during the past seven years. So what happened to him is not really surprising. What's surprising is that it was a young gringo from France who killed him. They must not have known he was on the island."

Mallock remained silent. Pensive. The slightest bit of information could be of the greatest importance. It might help him find a motive for this crazy act and above all it might help him gather extenuating circumstances for the trial. Since there was no doubt about premeditation, they would be crucial.

Amédée was being bounced around in every direction, and his ankle was beginning to hurt from slamming his foot on an imaginary brake pedal. Jiménez Cappuccino was passing on the right, using the crumbling, narrow emergency vehicle lane, weaving in and out and blowing the horn every three seconds, never losing the smile that he seemed to have stuck on his face that same morning, like his mustache, with neoprene glue.

"How did Darbier end up in the Dominican Republic?" Mallock asked again, in the most relaxed tone he could still manage.

"His story is the same as the island's. He arrived in 1946 and spent the first three years working for the dictator, Rafael Leonidas Trujillo."

The way Ramón pronounced this name made it seem that he was spitting three times on the ground.

"Trujillo, the head of the national guard, had overthrown Horacio Vásquez, the first president to win a free election, in 1924. For thirty years, that fascist dominated the island, and believe you me, it was not a nice little banana republic. He ruled by terror, torture, and political assassination. My father was one of the twenty million Haitians massacred by the national guard on Dominican territory. My mother was Canadian, from the Quebec area. That explains my ability to speak your language and the color of my skin. 'A bit of milk in very black coffee,' my mama used to say."

The word "mama" was touching coming from such a hulk of a fellow. *El capitán* Ramón Double-cream Cabral had loved his mother, and he probably still mourned her, Mallock thought. He was also pleased to have chosen such an appropriate nickname for him. Beneath his walrus-like appearance, he was in fact a cream of a man.

"May 30, 1961, is a holiday for the whole island," Ramón continued. "Abandoned by the Americans after he tried to have the Venezuelan president, Betancourt, assassinated, Trujillo himself was assassinated. It happened in Moca. One of my friends has kept as a memento the chromed swan the bastard had had installed on the hood of his car. So far as I'm concerned, he should've thrown it in the sea. That shit Tobias was not only an ally of the dictator, but also a friend of Balaguer, his vice-president. The surviving family and that whole little world divvied up Trujillo's fortune after he was assassinated. At the time, people spoke of a billion dollars, without counting agricultural land and industries. When you get that rich on an island like ours, you also become untouchable."

Mallock found that way of putting things very significant. It was true, and it was terrifying. The last dictatorships, which could be classed as part of the world heritage of inhumanity by Unesco, namely North Korea and Cuba, were overhangs from an earlier period. On the whole continent of Africa and in many countries, the leaders had blood on their hands and didn't have to answer for it to anyone.

What Ramón went on to say confirmed this. "Darbier had five pretty difficult years during the presidency of Juan Bosch, Balaguer's perennial opponent, and then during Godoy's presidency. As incredible as it seems, Balaguer became president again in 1966. Not only had he manipulated the elections, but he was able to take advantage of the Americans' complicity. They didn't want another Cuba so close to their shores."

El capitán Ramón Double-cream Cabral gave a loud beer-belch before continuing: "Though Balaguer's dictatorship was not as violent as Trujillo's, it was still twelve years of undivided power for the dictator's former right arm. And, once again, twelve years of good business deals for *el comandante* Darbier, who was always at his side. Amber, rum, sugar, coffee, cocoa beans, and tobacco, that was their gold."

"Was he finally assassinated?"

"Balaguer? Absolutely not. Starting in 1978, they both worked behind the scenes, for eight years, in fact. Particularly under the presidencies of Guzmán and Blanco. And then, in 1986, guess what?"

"I think I see . . . "

"Yes, indeed: the people called the former dictator to power once again. And Balaguer, with his henchman at his side, was president until 1996. And everything started up all over again. Ten more years of exploitation and exportation of amber, rum, sugar, coffee, cocoa beans, and cigars: *para tabacos hechos a mano.*"

"And now?"

Cappuccino joined the conversation by pointing, with his left hand, to the mauve paint that covered many of the trees and fences:

"We play *los colores* . . . That *es el color* of Bosch's party, but he has . . . retired. Peña Gomez and Jacobo, the two . . . *contradictores*, chose *blanco* and *azul*. They're dead now. The people is a . . . *con*, that's what you say, isn't it?"

"The syntax is good, but as for public opinion, it can hold its own," Mallock told a beaming Jiménez. "What about Balaguer?"

Mallock, more and more curious, was discovering a whole world of corruption and bright colors.

"He's blind and an invalid; he's ninety-three years old," Ramón said. "And you won't believe it, but he's running for president in the May 16 election."

"I suppose he has no chance of winning?"

"Don't count on it, he's the king of alliances. I think he's probably going to win again. Even if Hipolito Mejia, his new opponent, seems to be off to a good start."

"But why?"

In perfectly choreographed synchronism, Mallock saw the two policemen shrug their shoulders:

"You have to think that people are less afraid of an old dictator than change and the settling of political or ethnic accounts," Ramón said. "And then a dictatorship always has two main actors: the dictator and the people that serves as his accomplice. Don't forget that in Europe Hitler and Mussolini were elected democratically, Superintendent. Stalin and Lenin . . . a little less democratically."

The laughter in the car was interrupted by a sudden swerve. A few seconds in the ditch, and then back on the road. With a former choirboy's reflex, Amédée surreptitiously crossed himself.

4.

Crossing the Island, from South to North,
from Santo Domingo to Cabarete

S ix P.M.: the car had left the embassy more than an hour
earlier, and they still hadn't covered even a quarter of the
distance. Here the road was broad and for the last few
miles, miraculously, paved. They were in the northern part of
the San Cristóbal region.

"Villa Altagracia," Jiménez announced, like a good tourist
guide. "*¡Admira!*"

In fact, there was much to admire. The natural scenery was
splendid. A sort of paradise. Mallock thought about Darbier
again. He couldn't believe that a criminal, brutal foreigner
hated by a whole people had been able to walk the streets that
way for so long. In the video that Julie had played, he didn't
look furtive. At this point it seemed clear to Mallock that
Darbier and the old man crossing the square in that documentary were in fact one and the same person.

"Have you really told me everything about this Darbier? I
don't understand how he was able to live to over eighty without
someone taking care of him, settling his account once and for all."

A ponderous silence was the only reply. The air-conditioning had transformed the car into a refrigerator. Mallock realized that his feet and hands were freezing. He opened the window to let a little warm air in from outside.

"Wait a minute, please," Cappuccino said. "I'll adjust the
air-conditioning."

Amédée reluctantly closed his window.

At high speed, they crossed Piedra Blanca and then Bonao. The ugliness of the houses contrasted with the beauty of the vegetation. Two building materials prevailed: corrugated metal and cement blocks. For the poorest people, simple wooden planks, poorly fitted, served as a wall. Steel reinforcing rods projected from the tops of the larger houses.

"They all look like they're under construction," Amédée remarked.

"Once the house is finished, you have to pay the government a tax on it. And then people are often waiting to have the money to build a second or third story. It's easier to leave the reinforcing rods sticking up. Here, time doesn't have the same value it has in Europe."

It was silent in the car again. Mallock, who didn't want to doze off, struggled against invisible weights that were trying to close his eyelids. He thought he had succeeded, but he was wrong. When he woke up, he saw a broken sign indicating that they were entering La Vega, the regional capital.

"How much farther is it?"

He'd almost asked, like an impatient child, "Are we there yet?" He'd caught himself just in time.

"We'll be there in a little less than two hours, Superintendent."

Here people didn't talk in terms of miles, but of time. It was another philosophy of life.

"Could we get something to eat and drink?"

"*No problemo*. Everything has been arranged. In twenty minutes there is an excellent *comedor*. Otherwise, there's a *parada*, not nearly as good but only three minutes away."

"The *comedor* will be fine," Amédée replied. He was starving, but never enough not to care about cuisine.

His patience was rewarded: the grilled chicken with garlic sauce was delicious. The rice with red beans in a béchamel sauce was not. The local beer, Presidente, served ice-cold, proved to be a blessing.

When they got back on the road, night had fallen, spreading its dark, flattering cloak over the world's imperfections. With the help of the beers and the coolness, they were now driving more calmly, with all the windows open, a concession Jiménez made at Mallock's and Ramón's joint request.

It was during the last part of the trip that they began to speak more freely. As they entered Moca, the regional capital of the Espaillat and the sacred historical site of the dictator's assassination, Mallock, who had patiently bided his time, struck up the conversation again:

"Tobias Darbier was lucky he wasn't here on that day," he said.

"*Mucho, mucho, mucho* intelligence," Jiménez mumbled into his mustache. "And he got . . . power, *puissance.*"

Wasn't there a touch of admiration in Cappuccino's remark?

"It's especially that he knew too well what was going to happen," Ramón said, without wanting to say any more.

Amédée decided to be blunt for once:

"Did he have paid spies in the police here?"

Silence.

"They can't be called spies. In any case, you wouldn't understand."

"I wouldn't understand what? Corruption? Treachery? Torture?"

The silence, this time, was shorter. Ramón broke it by turning toward Amédée.

"You're way off base. If I add voodoo, curses, and zombies, are you prepared to . . . envisage such things? No. You French are pragmatic, more Cartesian than Descartes. You think all that is a bunch of superstitions fit for niggers, right?"

Mallock hesitated. The door was open, but this was the wrong time to make a mistake. First of all, he had to ignore that word "nigger" that resounded like a rather childish provocation:

"You know, I've seen some pretty awful stuff in my career.

More than you can imagine. Nothing surprises me and I'm entirely prepared to believe you, but don't try to fool me. If in fact you're scared, I would understand that very well. Don't try to blame that on a colonial superiority complex that I don't have."

El capitán Double-cream Cabral took a few minutes to think before he spoke again:

"From 1945 to 1948, Tobias Darbier spent four years in Haiti, on the other side of the island, learning the cruel meanderings of the Left-Hand Path. But he already knew all about torture."

Bingo! They were off and running again. Mallock sat up on his seat.

"What are the known facts?"

Ramón smiled broadly:

"Here, facts and legends are one and the same thing. Everything is transmitted orally, and words get deformed, imbued by the personality of the storyteller. Stories live their own lives, and Tobias Darbier was an inexhaustible subject of conversation. Today, nobody could claim to be able to separate truth from legend. One thing is sure: he was Trujillo's teacher in matters of torture and black magic. For a long time, he was the unofficial emperor of this island. The rest . . . it is better not to mention."

Ramón might have been able to pursue his revelations a little further had Mallock forced his hand. But the superintendent knew how to conduct interviews and preferred, on the contrary, to talk about something else. For example, about the subject that had led him to haul his heavy body around a paradise far too tropical for him.

"What does Manuel Gemoni have to do with all that? What do you think?"

"Nothing. It was made clear to us that it wasn't our problem. Your presence here is the confirmation of that."

"Touché," Mallock smiled. "But from one cop to another, how do you analyze that?"

"If we want to remain logical and simple, I think he killed him for revenge. Darbier had made hundreds of enemies here. He must have made others before or elsewhere. In any case, your Manuel went all the way. It's up to you to look into your compatriot's life, among his ancestors or those close to him. Maybe you'll find one of Darbier's victims or one of his henchmen, and that will provide an explanation for this murder. Your friend is a Corsican, and I believe the notion of vengeance is no joking matter on his island."

Mallock could find no fault with this analysis. *El capitán* Ramón Double-cream Cabral had just scored a point and given the complicated superintendent a simple lesson in logic.

Whether because he was getting used to Captain Cabral's brand of driving or because he was interested in what he said, Amédée no longer kept his eyes on the road and finally let his legs relax. Outside, the air smelled of cinnamon and the waves. They were arriving in Cabarete. Jiménez slowed down. The village ran along the beach in a continuous line of shops and restaurants. After dark, hundreds of bare light-bulbs had been turned on, tinting with yellow and orange the lower parts of the setting. If one looked up a little, one saw the effervescent green of the palm trees. Then, still higher up, a third color, the cobalt blue of the night sky studded with stars.

The car stopped in front of a garden gate. While Ramón Double-cream Cabral went to get the key to his room, the superintendent in charge walked off toward the sea. His pace slowed when his shoes sank into the lukewarm sand. The ocean's sounds called out to him: "Ah! There you are, Amédée, my waves and I have missed you." The horizon was lost out there somewhere in the night. Mallock took a few steps as far as the line of palm trees to escape the lights of the hotel and the restaurants along the beach.

Closer to the water, the wind was waiting to free him from the Caribbean humidity. He raised his head to loosen up his neck after all the tensions of the day. The sky was spangled with stars, but the Great Bear had disappeared. Their constellation, his and his Thomas's, the one that connected all nights with his little angel.

Suddenly he felt lost.

5

Second Day, Cabarete, Amber Coast
Six P.M. Local Time

H is first awakening in the tropics, on the third and last floor of a five-star hotel, gave him a more positive impression of the Dominican Republic. The sun was beginning to light up the cobalt of the night, and the air, which was already lukewarm, was being stirred by the immense fans attached to the ceilings.

The preceding evening, Ramón had been so kind as to make the rounds of the rooms to turn on the ventilators. He'd also opened the windows, which were fitted with Venetian blinds and screens in order to produce one of the secrets of survival in these latitudes: a draft. Then he had informed Mallock of three other constraints. First of all, wash your hands only with the distilled water from a little spigot to the right of the faucets. Secondly, drink only *agua minerale* in bottles, served sealed. And thirdly, don't throw your used toilet paper in the bowl; instead, put it in the wastebin next to it. Mallock, although he didn't like such an unhygienic practice, pretended it was normal, in order to avoid offending Ramón's *nacional* sensitivities.

That morning, as he went out onto one of the three balconies at his disposal, he had the impression that he'd dived into a postcard or been forced to go on a tourist excursion:

"You will note the incredible luxuriance of the vegetation: creeping vines, bougainvillea, conifers, coconut trees and palms, mango trees, tree ferns, banana trees. Look up at the sky, the fauna is just as rich. Our republic is an amazing aviary of exotic birds, among which can be seen the dazzling nightingale or the Dominican parrot, *Amazona ventralis*, with plumage of *verde cotorra*, which has become the island's emblem. You will also note, behind this splash of colors, the white of the beach and the fluorescent jade of the sea. See how generous Nature has been. So, enjoy it . . . and don't forget to tip the guide."

But Mallock silenced that little internal voice, which was often too caustic. There was nothing to object to. Even an old spoilsport like him couldn't help being amazed. The sun's heat was beginning to bring out the scents: pepper, mango, damp earth. To complete the picture, a flock of tiny hummingbirds, the great masters of stationary flying, were cleaning the parasites off the leaves. Mallock's eyes were dazzled, but his heart ached. He couldn't help thinking that he would never be able to show this spectacle to his Thomas. So many things he could no longer share with him.

He looked up at the sky and asked his son:

"Tom, my dear, is this what your paradise is like?"

He put on a white short-sleeved shirt and unbleached linen slacks, his bare feet in leather sandals, and went down a circular staircase to the garden. A dark-skinned man was watering the plants. His right hand had been cut off and his eyes were bloodshot. Mallock said, "Good morning," and the Haitian replied with a nod and a broad smile.

His teeth were in lamentable condition.

From the other side of the garden, along the coast road, the Blue Paradise was giving off scents of fresh-squeezed orange juice, bacon and eggs, and coffee. An irresistible combination. That was where Mallock was supposed to meet André Barride, the physician who was going to examine Manuel.

The French superintendent was not the first one up. Coming out from behind his bar, the owner of this strange *cantina* approached him, holding out his hand:

"So you're the famous Mallock, France's savior? I'd been told you were here. I'm Jean-Daniel, and I've never saved anything but my own skin."

"That's already something," Mallock retorted, smiling in spite of the "famous" which was no longer in any way flattering since that word was now applied to any boob who'd been on television.

The owner of the *cantina* had blue eyes washed out by the sea, the sand, and different suns. A hooked nose and blond, almost white hair. A slight accent colored by travels, a muscular body, a skin that told stories, and the rich smile of people who have already lived several lives, full of the bitterness and repentance that go along with them, and the humanity as well. Mallock decided to call him Mister Blue. That name fit him perfectly, with his look, his rough elegance, and the all-blue place he'd set up for himself.

His Blue Paradise was an empty space between two houses whose walls he had appropriated by painting them in cyan blue. On the right was a smooth façade decorated with naive images; in the center, a palm tree grew through the corrugated metal roof; high up, three rows of ventilators; and on the left, a window looking out on the store next door.

Mister Blue was one of those barnacle-like men who sometimes rest, between two battles, by attaching themselves to a rock, a ship's hull, the walls of houses, or to a tree trunk, like an epiphyte.

"Your neighbor didn't object?" Mallock asked, intrigued.

"About what?"

"About your appropriating the walls."

"No, he's very nice, an exceptional guy." Then he broke into laughter. "I'm the neighbor. That's my amber shop. If you have time, I'll show you my treasures."

He pointed to a table: "Sit down there, it's the coolest place and there's no fan right above it. What will you have?"

Mallock ordered a big glass of orange juice, tea with milk, and three fried eggs.

Later, when Mallock's plate was empty, Dr. André Barride arrived. He went directly up to Mister Blue to shake his hand and exchange friendly smiles. Then they both came over to Mallock.

Jean-Daniel introduced them. "Dr. Barride, this is the famous Superintendent Mallock."

Like Mister Blue, André Barride was square-jawed and had a fighter's body. But his skin was much less tanned, uniformly orange, in fact, salmon-colored, and he weighed sixty or seventy pounds more. If age had caused his skin to sag a little, the muscles were still there, well hidden and ready for use at the first occasion. The doctor had an imposing build and even a bit of a potbelly, a big, flattened nose, and dark hair. As for his eyes, they were not South Seas blue but black, like two pools.

"There's no time to lose. We have to go first to Puerto Plata to negotiate a bed in the clinic and reserve a surgeon to assist me. Then we'll head for Santiago to get your friend out of the hospital."

At a discreet sign from her boss, one of the waitresses brought them a drink. Without thinking much about it, Mallock downed it all at once. A wave of heat. It was rum, but fortunately, it had been made on the island, so that it was sweeter and not as strong as the industrial alcohol from Martinique. Although they had been able to produce cigars that could sometimes almost compete with the Cuban ones, their rum still had a long way to go.

"I'm also going to Santiago to purchase a few fossils. I'll be leaving around 3 or 4 P.M., so if you need me, don't hesitate to call."

Jean-Daniel scribbled a number on the paper tablecloth, cut it off, and gave it to André.

"If you need help, you can reach me at this number starting at noon. Get going, boys, and good luck."

The somewhat mocking tone in his voice, and Barride's grimace and worried look, attracted Mallock's attention. This wasn't going to be a pleasure trip or a cruise, it was going to be a hassle. He was right, but he was still far off the mark. Light-years off.

The flame trees in bloom were sprinkling with crimson drops the monochrome green of the island's vegetation. Taking his time, the doctor stopped here and there to drop off medicines, improvise free consultations, do his errands, or buy a little hashish.

"It relaxes me and keeps me from drinking too much," he said as he lit a joint before getting back on the road. "Alcoholism is the main problem for Westerners who live in Africa or South America," he went on. "A way of holding on, I suppose, of enduring the cultural gap, or maybe simply the temptation of a way of letting oneself go that will never be criticized or punished. So I prefer a little joint; does that shock you?"

Mallock reflected on his own weaknesses. He hesitated as to how to reply: "not at all," which is what he thought, or "not really," which was more in tune with his status as police superintendent.

"We all need crutches to put up with life," he finally said, philosophically. "Having difficulty handling things in such a crazy world is actually a sign of good mental health, isn't it?"

André smiled as he cast a furtive glance at Mallock. He'd feared being stuck with a stuffy, pretentious bureaucrat. He felt relieved. Pothole: his pickup swerved. He swore and decided to slow down. These potholes were gigantic by European standards and axle-deep.

There were clumps of greenery on both sides of the road, and the low, mossy hills along the coast were studded with palm trees. The sky was a sumptuous blue. The sun bronzed the brown of the tree trunks and brought out the multitude of greens. Around every curve, Nature revealed all its generosity. Water and earth were copulating in the sun, and their children were dazzling. Time passed, punctuated by the peaceful appearance of donkeys alongside the road. They were tied up there to graze and clean up the shoulders. Twenty miles farther on, they entered a series of endless curves.

"We have to watch out," Barride remarked, taking up a subject that miles and silence had put to rest. "The authorities here are serious about drugs."

Taking advantage of this opening, Mallock brought up his favorite topic: "What do you think about this Darbier fellow?"

André smiled. "Finally! I would have worried about a cop who didn't ask me questions when I was at his mercy."

"Don't feel you have to answer."

"I'm joking. But you have to recognize that here history is not written day by day, respecting the facts. Tobias Darbier became a legend on the island, and it's very difficult, today, to separate the true from the fantastic. Personally, I pay attention only to eyewitness testimony."

"Have you heard any about Darbier?"

The doctor's eyes grew harder. He reflected for a few seconds. Mallock knew how to wait.

"There's one thing I've kept to myself for a long time. And now there you are with your question."

Was he hesitating, or was he collecting his memories? No matter, it was for him to decide. And that is what he did, two miles farther on.

"Darbier is dead, and so is my patient, so I suppose I can talk now."

A grimace of disgust.

"One day, I had X-rays made of an old man whom I'd been treating several months, in particular for kidney stones and arthritis. It wasn't easy to do; he could hardly move anymore. With the help of two members of his family, the radiologist and I spent four hours taking as many pictures as possible. It was trying; the poor man had had almost all his limbs fractured and his joints dislocated, it was terrible. When I asked him the cause of his injuries, he simply waved the question away. But to me it looked very much like the effects of *strappado*, a form of torture, favored by Torquemada and his death squad. The victim is hoisted to the ceiling using pulleys and with his wrists tied behind his back. Because of the weight, the joints all end up breaking. Then the torturers let him fall toward the ground, and by suddenly stopping his fall, break his bones, one after the other."

André Barride frowned, as if blown away by the violence of what he was describing.

"Later, when the old man began to trust me, he told me that it was the infamous Darbier who had tortured him. Three days in a row. And he broke his joints, ankles, elbows, shoulders, wrists, and even fingers, not with ropes and pulleys, but with his bare hands. Then he worked him over with a hammer to break his bones. Thinking he was dead, he had his henchmen throw the poor man in a ditch alongside the road. When I asked him what Darbier wanted to know, he laughed in my face: *Nada. ¡Esta por la felicitad, señor!* The bastard practiced torture the way other people pay tennis or bridge, just for the pleasure of it. That gives you a good idea of what the man was like, doesn't it?"

Homo homini lupus, Mallock murmured.

Although they were painful, all the horrors he learned about Darbier would be grist for his mill. He had set himself three tasks. The official one was to bring Julie's brother home in good condition. The two others were unofficial: to take advantage of the opportunity to discern whether there might be the slightest doubt about his guilt; and if not, to find as many extenuating circumstances as possible. On this last point, it seemed that there might be material that would strengthen the defense's case. But he still had to find people to testify, and then prove that Manuel knew about these practices, and that his act was connected with Tobias's barbarism, indeed could even be seen as a duty to take revenge if there was a victim who was associated with him. It wasn't clear that he could do that.

"Could you make a statement for me?"

"Testifying to all this?"

"Yes, with a copy of the old man's X-rays?"

Barride frowned doubtfully.

"I could, but that wouldn't prove that it was Darbier's work. As for the X-rays, they disappeared from my office a few days later, as if by magic. You'll have to get used to that; everything concerning that individual is highly volatile, especially human testimony. Anyway, be careful, his *brutos* didn't die with him, and they probably won't like this kind of investigation."

By the time Mallock had digested this last bit of information, they had arrived in front of the entrance to the Puerto Plata clinic. It took them two hours to negotiate a room, the surgeon's fee, and the rental of an ambulance. The first one wouldn't start, and the second, which got there half an hour later, couldn't leave again. A dozen phone calls later, they ended up reserving a third ambulance that would wait for them at the Santiago hospital.

"For the happiness and the radiant future of the people" might have been the translation of the faded inscription that adorned the pediment of the hospital, a building covered with cracked stucco. Inside, the cast iron grilles and doors, like the armed guards with shotguns, made it look more like a prison than a place of healing. The *C* in *URGENCIAS*, put up backwards, formed with the *I*, which was also in bad shape, a symbol close to the hammer and sickle.

They spent more than half an hour getting through various barriers and making their way through the crowds that were piling up in front of each of them. Calmly, as someone used to such things, André presented the authorization for transfer, and then, armed with a few dollars, he shook the guards' hands. Finally they entered the part of the hospital reserved for emergency care, where they had to step over the ill and injured who were occupying the halls, at the same time being careful not to slip on an old bandage or a puddle of bodily fluids. The odor and the heat combined to make breathing unbearable.

In front of a steel door, two soldiers asked Barride for his papers. Mallock noticed that no one could enter without an official document countersigned by Delmont and the island's authorities. So many precautions to guard a poor, wounded Frenchmen seemed excessive. Unless they were there to protect him? From whom? In the farthest reaches of the hospital, behind a final grille protected by another pair of mustaches with riot guns, Manuel was waiting for them. He was in a room one of whose sides was being invaded by a mountain of old crutches and recycled casts.

Mallock was shocked. Manu no longer resembled the young man he had known. He was an aged and emaciated phantom of himself. A hysterical mummy with red eyes and protuberant bones, the mummy of a pharaoh who had gone mad on the brink of death. Far from all humanity, his expression looked like that of a murderer. As for his smile when he recognized the superintendent, it also resembled a grimace: a monstrous mask stapled on for the occasion.

What had happened to him?

6.

Puerto Plata National Hospital, 1 P.M.

For a week, Julie's brother had been bathed in a mixture of sweat, raw pain, and urine. With a constant desire to throw up. But overcoming this torture, making it almost bearable, he felt a marvelous happiness, a kind of satisfaction, a sweet euphoria that flowed through his veins like a river of morphine.

The old man, the monster who had haunted his nights and all the forests of the earth since he was a child, was dead. He didn't remember the exact moment when he attacked him, but he still felt on his lips the sugar of his blood, the strange humor of iron, and he saw perfectly the shiny dullness of the ogre's brains sprawled shamelessly in the dust of the square.

And, if he was prepared to admit the facts alleged against him and to recognize his full culpability, it was not out of contrition, but pride. To be sure, he still didn't know why he'd been led to kill him, but he felt satisfied by the idea that he'd done it. He had the incredible certainty that in this way he had atoned for multiple offenses against God and the people he cherished in his heart of hearts, without really being able to give them names.

Kiko, Julie, and his little baby had also resurfaced in his consciousness. All their love, and the infinite love he had for them, was coming back to life. He let them approach him, but timidly, with great slowness. And even holding them back.

For he knew that Hell was still within him.

Before opening the door, Amédée hesitated. He knew only too well the horror and the tears that openings could conceal. Behind them were hidden helplessness, bruised faces, agonies, murders, hearts burnt to ashes, incest, fears, odors . . . everything that constitutes man, and the rest as well. Mallock didn't like doors, he'd never liked them. Noble apartment doors for sordid crimes, hospital doors half-open on deathbeds, regrets, and bodies, under the same load of saltpeter and mold, secret doors hiding dirty eyes playing doctor with children's hearts, soft doors wetted by tears, or steel doors with codes and padlocks barring access to the shameful riches of a greedy world. Vocation and damnation. Mallock knew that he was doomed to open these doors, all of them, one after another, without ever being warned of the horrors awaiting him, and that he would have to go on opening them for the rest of his life.

When André entered the room before Mallock, he swore. The hospital's doctors, having removed the bullet Manu had received in his upper back, had put a full-body cast on him down to his stomach. His knee was traversed by a pin, and the bandages around it were saturated with pus.

André was furious, but he was able to restrain himself, at least until the young intern on duty announced that he had decided not to let the patient leave without removing the infamous pin. He must have been short of them. Without worrying about anesthesia, before André's incredulous eyes the intern grabbed an ancient drill, plugged it in, and attached the chuck to one of the extremities of the pin. Then he simply pushed the switch. Miraculously, the electricity wasn't working.

André immediately attacked. With all the diplomacy he had left in his big orange body, and smiling constantly, he explained to the intern that it really wasn't necessary, that they were very grateful for his trouble, but that they had to leave because the ambulance was waiting. Then he asked him for a simple piece of cotton with a "dab" of alcohol. He was planning to give Manuel a shot of analgesics as soon as they were in the ambulance, but didn't have anything to use as a disinfectant. The little drop of alcohol took a quarter of an hour to reach them and cost André the last of his bills.

Twenty-five minutes later, they were finally in the ambulance. The two soldiers, three police technicians, and the two mustaches with riot guns had followed them. A kind of elite commando, they played their part. But oddly enough, they seemed to believe in it, their fear even making them sweat heavily. A local tradition or an excess of zeal?

Mallock, quite wrongly, decided not to pay any attention.

Another miracle: the all-white ambulance was there, where it was supposed to be. Manuel, who had emerged from his lethargy, had begun to moan. André decided to give him an initial shot in the hospital's parking lot, before the ambulance's bouncing around on the Dominican roads made this operation more dangerous.

While he was preparing the anesthesia, he turned toward Mallock.

"Do you really want to go with us? Personally, I don't see what's in it for you. You're going to waste your time in Puerto Plata. When we get there, he'll be taken straight to the operating room. It could be quite a while before . . . "

"No problem, I've seen enough hospitals for one day. Could you try to reach Mister B . . . Jean-Daniel, so he could take me back to Cabarete?"

Just as Mallock was turning around to get out of the ambulance, Manu sat up on his stretcher and screamed: "The ogre's belly! You can't understand. And his teeth . . . my God, his teeth!"

When the ambulance finally left for the private clinic, five motorcyclists and two police cars followed it. Five short minutes went by before Mister Blue arrived at the Santiago hospital's parking lot. Good timing. His mauve minivan, his nice face and smile were a blessing. It's often like that, when one is on foreign territory, the slightest familiar face quickly becomes a friend.

The way back to Islabon and Cabarete ran between the Yásica and Jamao rivers. Surfaces carpeted with red earth, damp and rich. Vegetables, fruit trees, and grapevines grew there effortlessly. Even the logs used to make barriers along the road were rooting and becoming trees again. But here, too, the villages were mere jumbles of corrugated metal, billboards, mud, and rubble.

"They're really poor."

"Probably," Jean-Daniel replied, without much conviction. "But that doesn't excuse everything." And he added, in his colorful language: "You don't shit where you sleep!"

Down deep, Mister Blue loved this country and its people. But like a demanding father, he was not prepared to excuse their weaknesses without a fight. He left that to right-minded tourists.

On the side of the road, a barrier consisting of three policemen in gray uniforms signaled to them to stop. Mister Blue drove on without slowing down. When he was alongside them, he shouted something accompanied by a smile.

"They're just trying to make ends meet," he decided to explain to Mallock. "But you have to understand their position."

Then he began to talk about this people, its strengths, its customs, and its obsessions from the past. All the muddy habits that a man who has experienced communism and dictatorship accumulates under his shoes. Then he fell silent. Probably to let Mallock admire the landscape and thus understand the reason for these things he'd taken too long to explain.

Minutes and miles passed. Curve after curve, the road tipping the car from right to left as a hand turns a glass of wine in order to assess its color. To be sure that Mallock was enraptured, the sun turned orange. On both sides of the road, the magical encounter between this golden tint and the green of the leaves, dazzling in its beauty, suddenly raised once again the question of God's existence.

"It's this same light, this sunset imprisoned in drops of resin, that one finds intact in a piece of amber."

Mister Blue had broken the silence.

"Each of those stones is like a hologram going back to the dawn of our Earth. With this ochre and golden light, and these insects captured in full flight or as they are laying eggs. When I examine one of them for the first time before deciding to buy it, I always feel the same emotion."

"Do you know what each piece of amber contains?"

"No, that's the name of the game. I try to guess by wetting them and looking through them, but I'm allowed to polish them, to "open a window," as they say, only after I've negotiated a price and paid it. I've bought pieces of amber for next to nothing in which I've found treasures. But that's rare, unfortunately. Seven years ago I paid a relatively high price for a stone because I thought it contained at least a fragment of a lizard. That's an amber-hunter's dream. It was in fact there, and by a wonderful surprise, whole and almost intact. A miracle!"

"Will you show me that when we get back?" Mallock asked.

"Alas, I can't. I was forced to resell it in order to be able to continue to negotiate other pieces of amber. I've always regretted it. It was shortly afterward that I decided to construct a *cantina* next to my shop. It allows me to earn enough money not to have to separate myself from my most beautiful pieces.

Ah, we're almost there! Come see me tomorrow, I'll show you."

They covered the last miles that led to Cabarete without Mister Blue ordering his foot to press more lightly on the accelerator. He seemed determined to run over someone. If not a person, then at least a pig or a chicken.

"In St. Petersburg there was a room entirely covered in amber," he went on without slowing down. "I believed that it was a legend until the day when I found, right here on the island, and very oddly, among the belongings of the father of one of my men, a black-and-white photo showing that room. Unfortunately, the poor guy had died in a collapse at one of my mines. For a reason that still escapes me, in his cabin he had a whole file on this treasure."

Mallock would never have imagined that this room was also going to be part of the fabulous enigma that had brought him here. He felt he was nearing the stable and was dying to take a good shower.

"In the summer of 1941," Jean-Daniel continued, "the Third Reich began its offensive on the Russian Front by bombarding Leningrad. Hitler wanted to wipe that city off the face of the Earth. But inside Catherine the Great's palace there was an exceptional room completely paneled in a kind of amber parquetry."

"Made on this island?"

"No, it wasn't. It had been made for the palace of the king of Prussia, Frederick William I, by an architect named Andreas Schulte and a jeweler, Gottfried Tasso. In 1716, Frederick made the incredible decision to trade these fabulous panels to Peter the Great of Russia for two hundred and forty-eight elite soldiers he wanted to enroll in his guard. The exchange was made and this fantastic puzzle in amber was transported from Berlin to St. Petersburg. In 1755 a certain Rastrelli was finally able to reconstruct and install the amber cabinet between the green dining room and the great picture gallery in Catherine the Great's palace at Tsarkoye Selo. But the story doesn't stop there, Superintendent. In fact, at this point it becomes even more exciting."

"Cabarete": the sign announcing the city had a radical effect on the driver's behavior, unless the effect was produced by what he was about to say. Mister Blue turned his tanned face and South Seas blue eyes toward Mallock. He was no longer looking ahead of him, and accordingly the car was now moving very slowly. Behind him, people began to blow their horns, but not excessively. Mister Blue and his pickup were known in these parts.

"Two centuries later, two German officers who knew about Hitler's destructive intentions conceived a plan to save this little marvel. With the help of their men they managed, during the invasion of St. Petersburg, to dismantle the whole room and get it out of the country. The rest of the story is a little vague. The panels are supposed to have moved through Prussian palaces before disappearing again. The legend was born. Since then, historians, treasure-hunters, and members of the amber guild have been trying to find out what happened to the panels without ever being able to learn anything further. The location of the amber room is still completely unknown. Unless you listen to certain rumors."

"What rumors?"

"More about that later!"

With that, Mister Blue's car stopped in front of the hotel.

"Many thanks for the ride . . . and for the story," Mallock said with a smile.

"I'll see you at breakfast tomorrow, and *tómalo suave, 'commisare.'*"

In his penthouse apartment, a crate of mangos and red bananas was waiting for Amédée. After a long, lukewarm shower, he started to fall asleep as he was watching the sun sink into the sea. At the last moment, he asked his mind to give him a clue, a lead, something that would keep Manuel from being given the maximum sentence. But he dreamed only of the clicking of boot heels and rooms covered in amber.

7

Wednesday, Third Day on the Island
Cabarete-Sosúa, Round-trip

Mallock's headache was still with him in the tropics. It also wanted to know the exoticism of the mangroves and bromeliads, the colorful beaches, the aromas of the jungle and the unfamiliar bamboo. It dreamed of the turquoise transparency of the creeks and the tentacular clumps of polyps. So it had gotten him out of bed around 4 A.M.: "Let's go for a walk, you big lazybones, I'll hurt you less," it had promised him.

So the superintendent went out into the night to walk on the sand and try to calm his old companion. The earth was still warm from the preceding day's sun. Amédée looked up at the stars. This time, he recognized the friendly constellation that connected him with his son: the Great Bear. It was there, but upside down, a little sheepish, its neck lying along the horizon. He stretched out on the sand, upside down too, with his head toward the sea. He spoke to Thomas, told him about the beach and the palm trees "that you would have liked so much." Then he thought of Amélie and closed his eyes, suddenly nauseated by his solitude. Imprisoned in a coma from which she had never returned, she'd been buried with Mallock's ring and his heart. They spoke to each other, he about the past, she about the future, her Amédée's future. She told him: "I'm keeping your ring, take back your life." He ended up saying: "Yes."

Mallock returned to his suite around 8 A.M. and called André.

"You were right not to come," André told him. "I got home at midnight. Forty-eight hours from now, if you have the repatriation agreement, you can take him away. He will need a good year of physical therapy before he'll recover full use of his shoulder and especially his knee."

"Can I come by to see him?"

"I don't know. In principle, yes, but call me a little later, I'm going back there. By then I'll have examined him again and I can give you an answer."

Mallock thanked him and hung up. Then he called Julie, as he had promised before leaving. He did his best to reassure her.

"Don't worry, he's out of danger and I'm going to be able to bring him back to France. Where he is now the hygienic conditions are satisfactory. We can talk about the trial later."

Then he added, to calm her: "I haven't had my last word yet."

"Is he guilty?"

"I'm afraid he is."

"Did he tell you why he did it?"

Julie's voice was trembling.

"He wasn't really in a condition to be questioned, but when he woke up he repeated that he has no idea."

"That's inconceivable. People don't go off to the other side of the world to kill somebody without a motive."

"Except for professional killers," Mallock replied, without realizing what he was saying.

"What are you talking about? Manu would never . . . "

"Calm down, Julie. I have to consider everything. If I don't keep a completely open mind in an investigation of this kind, I may as well give up. He killed a man, comma, he will be convicted, period. We have to do our best to see to it that he comes out of it as well as possible. And believe me, I'm going to do everything I can."

Julie thanked him at least three times before she hung up. Mallock left his room, wondering how he was going to be able to keep his promise.

Jean-Daniel was waiting for him at the Blue Paradise. He was so friendly that each of his customers must have believed he was special. Mallock ate a copious breakfast. The fruit he'd eaten the day before had barely held him until the morning, and he was dying of hunger.

At 9 A.M., he had to face the facts: the policeman who was supposed to come pick him up and take him to the police station and prison in Sosúa was not there. He went out on the sidewalk and yielded to the temptation to take a *motoconcho*. Basically, two dollars to get him safe and sound to his destination on a motorbike. He told himself that the wind would do him good, and of course he didn't know the nickname the locals gave these strange taxis: *muertoconchos*.

After having risked his life at every turn, every pothole, every animal or human being they encountered, his ass and his back hurting, his hair in disarray, he arrived in front of a big building painted green and bearing a sign: *Policía Nacional*.

"Sosúa police station," his driver confirmed, smiling amid a big cloud of dust.

Mallock felt a sort of dizziness, a great retrospective fear of the kind in which your whole life passes before your eyes in three seconds. With his thighs and calves traumatized, his legs could hardly hold him up. But he was alive. So he smiled back, grateful to have been spared by the island's merciful gods.

Inside the building, *el comandante* Juan Luis Cappuccino Jiménez and *el capitán* Ramón Cabral fell all over themselves making excuses. Each was convinced that it was the other's turn to pick him up. Mallock didn't go on about it.

The series of witnesses, organized, perhaps a little too well, by the two policemen, left little doubt regarding Manu's guilt. Four Dominicans, a couple of Germans, and an Englishwoman all confirmed the identification they had already made concerning the murderer and the way the killing happened. The same facts, the same chronology, with perfect coherence and using practically the same words to describe the scene. Had they learned their lesson well? But what more could he ask for? And then Gemoni had confessed, as Ramón and Jiménez never ceased to repeat. They also showed him the photographs taken from the television program that had upset Manuel so much. They had been found, dirty and wrinkled, in his hip pocket. Mallock thought of Julie and felt devastated.

The pictures proved premeditation.

Except for a lunch break in the canteen next to the police station, Mallock, Ramón, and Jiménez worked nonstop until 4 P.M., when Amédée called André to find out if he could question Manuel. The answer was negative. The young man had still not come out of the fog of the anesthesia, and he needed, moreover, to catch up on his sleep.

"Sorry," André concluded, "questioning him now would be pointless. He's going to sleep like a log for another twenty-four hours. Afterward, he'll be in better shape and able to answer all your questions."

Mallock hung up, pensive. He felt a sort of uneasiness, without having the slightest idea what was troubling him on this point. Had Dédé-the-Wizard, one of his multiple nicknames, run out of inspiration again? Why had the investigation seemed to drag on this way from the outset? Was it due to the density of the vegetation, the heaviness of the heat, the spongy mud that slowed one's pace after every rain? Or was it something else altogether? A Mallock who couldn't concentrate, who avoided the cruelest hypotheses, for Julie and for himself, and who refused to associate the name "Manu" with the words "killer," "mafia," "assassin," "madman"? But it was in that direction, and no other, that he now had to go, whether he liked it or not. He could no longer close his eyes to certain facts, or to the last image he had of Manu, his last words. The question was not and had never been: "Did he kill him?" The question was: "Why?"

After one of those deep sighs he so often heaved, Mallock asked his police buddies if one of them could take him to Cabarete. Jiménez agreed with enthusiasm, happy to put an end to a workday that had been much too long by local standards. A little nervously, Amédée went back to the suicide seat and the enormous fuzzy dice attached to the rearview mirror.

When they arrived in Cabarete, he went directly to Mister Blue's shop. He felt irascible and demoralized. Fortunately, Jean-Daniel was able to make him forget his nightmare for a few moments.

"Okay, to begin the show, a curiosity: blue amber!"

Without further ado, the adventurer turned on two neon ultraviolet lights attached over the display case. Each piece of blue amber was instantly transformed into so many minuscule aquariums in which age-old insects were suspended over a floor of artificial corals. So many crepuscular worlds frozen by the gods in a cosmogonic order. Within each universe, billions of things—stardust, insects' feet, amphibians' eyes—were hidden, still frightened, in the same electric mist, metaphorical reflections of the multiple questions and thoughts that had been amalgamating in Mallock's brain since the beginning of the investigation.

There was something infinitely poetic about the cerulean, electric shimmerings, the commemoration of a miracle or a genocide. A fatal twilight, a meteor shower, an atomic deflagration. The deinonychuses had stopped devouring the red, the diplodocuses had stopped grazing on the green, and all the dinosaurs had raised their heads toward the sky before dying.

Gorged on light, the tree's resin had been immediately transformed into microscopic oceans.

The miracle of the blue amber was supposed to result from two extraordinary events: insects getting caught in a tree's resin at the very moment when an asteroid struck earth and put an end to the reign of the dinosaurs. By exploding when it struck the earth, it is said to have produced light so intense that it "exposed" the still soft amber, giving it that incredible bluish luminescence.

For more than an hour, Mallock traveled over these interior seas. In each case, Mister Blue sought the best possible angle before putting them on the glass plate of his old microscope. The silence in the room was disturbed only by his informed commentaries. After a dozen blue stones, he turned off the ultraviolet lights and moved to different specimens tinted by a Jurassic moss, green amber.

Finally, in the third and final act of his show, he brought out his most beautiful fossils, drowned in crystalline golden amber, specific to the Americas.

"In Europe," he explained to Mallock, "people sought amber without insects, in order to be able to cut it for jewelry or objects. But it was a much less transparent stone, much milkier than this one. The famous amber room was made with this kind of amber. Moreover, I am going to show it to you. One never knows—if you wake up someday on the inside, you'll have to be able to find your way!"

He broke out laughing at his own joke as he looked for a photo in one of his multiple drawers:

"Damn, where did I put it? Ah, here it is!"

In an old snapshot, Mallock saw a room in Louis XV style with strange panels. The faded black and white probably didn't do justice to the amber cabinet.

Jean-Daniel put the photo back and resumed bringing out his most beautiful pieces of amber, as so many treasures.

"You must have a small fortune in this shop. Aren't you afraid . . . ?"

Mister Blue smiled: "You do what you have to do. I go to the shooting range twice a month with Ramón, the most respected policeman in the area. But of course you know him, I forgot. Naturally, I'm the one who buys all the ammunition, including Ramón's, all his friends', and even his family's."

"Is he married?"

Oddly, Mallock had imagined Double-cream to be a bachelor who still lived with his mother.

"Since he was sixteen years old. He's a good fellow, Ramón. He devotes everything he earns to his little family: seven children, two boys and five girls. And with what remains, he helps out two other families in need. So I'm happy to help finance the target practice sessions. And then they allow the men to relax a bit; they laugh like crazy, and that also has the advantage of letting all the would-be burglars know that they'll meet with strong resistance on my part."

"The art of dissuasion."

"Exactly. And of reputation, as well," Jean-Daniel went on. "They take me for Buffalo Bill, Clint Eastwood, and Bruce Wilson all rolled into one."

Normally, Mallock would probably have laughed, but he hadn't forgotten that the next day he had to call Julie, and that the news wouldn't be good. Mister Blue, a subtle psychologist, understood his friend the superintendent's mood, just as he divined, more or less, the reason for it.

"Are things going badly for the young Frenchman?"

"Not well," Amédée conceded. "I don't really see how I'm going to get him out of this mess. However, I was convinced, deep down, that he couldn't be the killer, and that I'd immediately locate the mistake that had been made. If you knew him, you'd understand. He's a rather exceptional young man. I hope there's a good explanation for his act, because for the moment, at this point in the investigation, he's in danger of receiving the maximum sentence."

The two men fell silent, engaging in the kind of meditation such a pronouncement calls for.

"The worst thing is that I haven't much to go on," Mallock resumed. "Between Manuel, who seems to be in a bad state, and the local police forces, who are very satisfied with what they have, I'm afraid I'm going to go home empty-handed."

Mister Blue observed a second silence, as pregnant as the first, but longer. He was reflecting.

"Listen. I'm going to close the shop. My girls will take care of the bar, and we're going to go eat a good meal in the only restaurant around here that's worth going out of your way for. As far as your problem is concerned, I have only one solution to propose. Tomorrow I'm going to the mines to buy stones. Near the most remote of my deposits, there's an old woman who is—what?—rather unusual."

"A historian of the island?"

"Not exactly," Mister Blue smiled. "She doesn't know this island, *she is this island, and then some*. How can I explain it to you? We undergo things, whereas she knows, she's . . . "

He stammered, almost ashamed of what he was trying to say.

"Listen, I've always been a rational kind of guy, but I've seen things, and then . . . I mean, after all, it doesn't cost anything. You can always try to meet her. It's not easy, but I think she likes me and she'll make an effort if I ask her to."

"But what could she know about Manuel?"

"The wrong question, Your Honor. She knows, period, and without any direct object, without explanation. She doesn't receive her information by, let's say, traditional channels. And even if she doesn't know your particular case, she'll open up your mind. I've resorted to her on two occasions, and I'm still astonished."

"But who is she, this woman?" Mallock asked.

He really didn't feel like going off on a wild goose chase with the local witch or fortune-teller. He didn't care at all for tarot-crooks, Sunday astrologers, blind seers, and illiterate numerologists.

"You have to see her to understand," Jean-Daniel insisted, a little hurt by the superintendent's reticence. "But I won't force you. Be here at nine o'clock Friday morning if you want to meet her. I'm doing this for you. It doesn't amuse me. On the contrary, that old . . . "

"I get it," Mallock cut him off. "It's nice of you, and at the point where I find myself . . . "

"O.K. In the meantime, I'm going to close up and we'll go enjoy ourselves," Mister Blue concluded.

They sailed off in the direction of the harbor in question. And in fact it was extremely good.

8.
Thursday, the Fourth Day,
Trip in a Guagua *to Puerto Plata*

The superintendent is in the sea.

There's no one on the shore. Only dark phantoms with cut-off arms extended by pipes are walking there. Banished gardeners, Haitian thieves exiled from the other side of the island, doomed to tourist paradises in perpetuity.

Dawn. The sky begins to weep, a monsoon, a dense cluster of raindrops that fall while the sun persists, transforming this deluge into a curtain of golden pearls.

The superintendent embraces the waves with his arms, as one embraces a faithful companion. It seems to him that here, more than elsewhere, by slipping into an apnea, he could melt his pains and free his tears, banks of jellyfish children who will leave him and return one last time to bid him farewell before disappearing behind the mother-of-pearl of the coral.

At 9 A.M., Mallock goes back up to his penthouse.

This morning bath does him good. He feels a little better.

Then he summons all his courage and telephones Julie:

"Nothing to report," he lies. "I think I'll be able to see him this afternoon. Don't worry. Everyone here likes him."

"But why?"

"Let's say that the man he killed was not much appreciated around here. I'll tell you all about it."

He hung up and called the ambassador.

"Hello, Monsieur Delmont. I'd like to know where we are with this. No problem?"

"I was about to call you, Superintendent. The authorizations have been negotiated and I'm hopeful, unless there's a last-minute reversal. In the series of things we have to swallow, one is that they want you to go in person to the National Palace to sign the final papers of repatriation at the Santo Domingo branch of Interpol, and take the documents authorizing the expulsion by the Dominican Republic to the courthouse in Puerto Plata. These are signs of allegiance and good will. I hope that doesn't bother you too much?"

"We'll do what we have to. In any case, I intend to go see Manu."

He felt much too relieved to take umbrage. Repatriating Manuel meant saving his life. And that's what he was there for, nothing else.

"How is he?" Delmont asked. "I haven't had time to call André."

"The operation went well, but he was still in a fog yesterday. I hope he'll be able to travel, I have no desire to say here forever, although . . . Anyway! We'll see. No special instructions?"

"Regarding Manuel?"

"No, the fools at the courthouse."

"Oh, yes! Well, no, nothing in particular . . . Or rather yes," the ambassador went on, "I'm clearly not quite awake yet. Ask for Juan Antonio Servantes, he's the one assigned to your case. I spoke to you about him, I think."

"A Spaniard?" Mallock replied, astonished.

"About as much as I'm Tibetan. He's the product of a post-war import, if you see what I mean. We had a few of those around here, people who came here to recover their health. Germanic down to the heels of their boots."

They both laughed and hung up, promising to keep each other up-to-date.

Just as angels pass without being noticed, a first clue had just passed through the room. Mallock didn't hear it, but a corner of his mind put it aside for later. Then he realized that he still hadn't grilled Delmont about Darbier. He might know more than the two policemen. Or at least he would have a different version, official and even, and, with a little luck, unofficial.

But he didn't feel like calling the ambassador back.

He was hungry enough to eat a horse, as the English say. He left to eat at Mister Blue's place. Under the door to his suite, somebody had slipped a two-day-old French newspaper. He opened it and automatically looked through the obituaries. He did not find his name. Good news! He must still be alive!

Mister Blue was there, faithfully at his post.

"I've just received a call from our friends in the police. They are very sorry, but they can't come to pick you up this morning. They left me a telephone number and instructions. Their whole office is at your disposal, but if you want a driver to come pick you up and take you to Puerto Plata, you'll have to call and ask for him. They themselves can't do it."

"That's fine with me, I'm not in a talkative mood today anyway. I'll get along on my own."

Jean-Daniel, who had his fits of misanthropy as well, didn't argue with Mallock.

"There are *guaguas* that go to Puerto, but they're very hot and packed to the gills. If I were you I'd take a taxi."

Mallock noted that everyone, including Mister Blue, took care to address him with the formal *vous*. No matter how much people sometimes felt drawn to him, he was still a French police superintendent, with the rank of commander. In addition, he was a national hero, and potentially a big, nasty cop.

Jean-Daniel picked up the receiver of his telephone and negotiated for two minutes with a taxi driver connected with a company in the village nearest Sosúa, judiciously named S.O.Súa, to get him to take his friend to Puerto Plata. Then he let Mallock eat breakfast in silence.

Ten minutes later, the taxi arrived. The superintendent got up:

"See you," he said, in the mood of a neurasthenic mastiff that came to visit him with a fidelity and regularity that had to be admired.

This morning, it was with a belly full of fried eggs, potatoes, bacon, and melancholy that Mallock traveled by taxi to Puerto Plata and its courthouse.

In the halls and waiting rooms of the courthouse a crowd of humble people was languishing. In rags, their eyes shining with naive hope, they were waiting for a justice in tatters, a whore with blindfolded eyes who would go upstairs only with those who could afford to pay for her charms.

Mallock was in a position to know that his own country had no lessons to teach. From the judges who cost too much and commercial tribunals that could be paid in stardust and a Scorpio luxury cruise to Saint-Martin, to venal Attorneys-General, crooked lawyers, and pompous magistrates. Wavy blue hair, long neck, and evasions for the 1 P.M. news, then a waxed jacket at night, to read the meters. The feckless judicial system no longer fed on anything but warmed-over ideology, virtuous laxity, and categorical mistakes.

Here, on the island, it was similar, but on a smaller scale, and on a larger scale with fingerprints left almost everywhere. The everyday practice of baksheesh and "greasing palms" was much too developed to be able to claim the slightest discretion.

Mallock had himself announced. And, while he waited, he decided to spare the seat of his pants by standing. A good decision. After only three minutes' wait, two men came and escorted him to the office of Mr. Juan Antonio Servantes. Amédée felt a kind of regret. He would have liked to be forgotten in a corner so that he could scream and yell, have a pretext for being disagreeable. He was in the mood for that. He could pour into it his fear for Manuel, his sadness for Julie, and all the negative energy accumulated by his own impotence.

But a "Mistah superintendent from Paris" couldn't be abandoned amid the common people. He was an influential man and this status incontestably put him at the top of the social ladder, alongside the notables who did him the supreme honor of recognizing him as one of their own. Too bad that would have allowed me to avoid waiting, Mallock cynically concluded, following the two henchmen of the official in charge of the Puerto Plata courthouse.

Juan Antonio Servantes resembled the stereotypical image of a white neocolonialist in a banana republic. His shoes, his watch, and his belt were tobacco-colored, made from the same arrogant, duly tanned crocodile skin. He walked toward Mallock, his hand extended to greet him, his shoulders, neck, and chin held excessively high out of his awareness of his office and his importance.

"Superintendent, what a pleasure to meet you!"

His slightly rolled "r" didn't go well with his appearance. He was very much the handsome Aryan—the eyes, the imposing presence, and the blond hair. Stupidly, Mallock imagined him in an SS uniform. He would have been splendid. Maybe his father wore one of those beautiful black coats?

Prejudice, Amédee said to himself reproachfully.

Servantes's office was full of files. Clearly he was a busy man. After an hour spent talking and making phone calls together, Mallock revised his judgment. Juan Antonio Servantes wasn't his cup of tea, but like Delmont, he was doing everything he could, with a great deal of skill and persistence, to pave the way for Manuel's release and repatriation. Without any fuss or the slightest affectation. What would have already been astonishing in a French bureaucrat became admirable in the case of a tropical expatriate. Everybody made snap judgments on the basis of appearance, but Mallock had no excuse.

To redeem himself, he asked the young official:

"Would you like to finish this conversation over dinner this evening?"

He hoped to be able to take advantage of the occasion to question Servantes about Tobias Darbier.

"I'd love to, Mr. Superintendent. I also have things to tell you. Where would you like to meet?"

"At my hotel, there's a kind of bar, the Blue Paradise. Do you know it? It's not very luxurious, but it's quiet. How about meeting there around 8 o'clock?"

"That's fine with me, I'll be there at 8 sharp."

Mallock thought he heard heels clicking. But with crocodile-skin loafers, that was impossible. He reflected that to make this diplomat really acceptable, the rest of the broomstick up his ass would have to be removed.

Late morning.

Amédée returned to the capital and its National Palace by way of the Matías-Ramón-Mella Bridge, the Avenue of Mexico, and Doctor Delgado Avenue. The famous palace, constructed in 1947 on Trujillo's orders, was the seat of the executive power. Mallock smiled slightly. Two big pretentious lions framed the royal staircase leading to the imposing, four-story building. Built in a neoclassical style, with all the options and supplements, it was topped by an impressive dome 35 feet high and 36 feet in diameter. The *Oficina Central Nacional*, Interpol's central office in the Dominican Republic, had been located there since the country joined the other two hundred-odd other members of the international police agency in 1953.

Superintendent Mallock was well received. He was given several papers to sign and two officials carried out the repatriation in his company. An hour later, he was already outside in the sun again.

He decided to eat lunch on the street: white coconut, red

bananas, and green mangos. Enormous clouds were passing overhead in the sky, sweating. But Mallock wasn't. He was already beginning to get used to the climate and even to feel a certain bliss at having the great yellow circle always present above him.

At exactly 2 o'clock, he arrived at the clinic.

The authorities had posted policemen on guard duty in front of the main entrance and in the two hallways that led to Manuel's room. This time the superintendent didn't have to show his papers. The news of his presence, as well as his face, had spread all over the island. A message was waiting for him. Ramón and Jiménez were trying to reach him. A policeman dialed the number for him.

It was Ramón who answered:

"Jiménez says he has new information for you, Commander."

"He didn't tell you what it was?"

"No, he wants to tell you himself. He told me it might help Manuel. He would like all four of us to meet."

Mallock was intrigued. Was this finally a breakthrough in this case?

"I'm just about to question him, could you meet me here?"

"That's what Jiménez wanted, so far as I could tell, but he told me we'd need authorization to get access to Gemoni's room."

"No problem, I'll put you on the list at the desk. I'll wait for you."

Mallock hung up, feeling hopeful. Two halls farther on, he entered Manuel's new room. Julie's brother was lying on a makeshift bed. A brand new splint surrounded his knee and his shoulder was in a cast.

He smiled when he saw Mallock appear.

"I'm very glad to see you. Please excuse me for the day before yesterday, but I didn't even recognize you. I hope this trip around the world didn't tire you too much, at least? I'm going to try as best I can to help you in your investigation."

Amédée smiled. This was the real Manuel he had in front of him. With his big, soft eyes and his slightly old-fashioned politeness.

"No problem," Mallock replied, relieved.

"I must have caused everyone great concern. I'm truly sorry about that."

Mallock had an idea.

"Wait, I'll be right back."

Three minutes later he returned with a cell phone.

"We're going to try to call your sister. She's worried sick. I don't think anything would please her more than to hear your voice."

"And I'd like to hear hers!"

Mallock dialed Julie's direct line at the Fort.

"Hello, Julie? Ah! Hi, Jules. Yeah, I'm fine, is Julie around? Thanks."

He handed the phone to Manu. He realized, with dismay, that his fingers were still all sticky from the mangos he'd eaten for lunch.

"He's going to put her on. But don't talk too long, I borrowed the phone from a doctor here."

Discreetly, he left the room on the pretext of wanting to smoke a cigarette. Something he never did. When he came back five minutes later, Manuel had hung up. His eyes were still wet.

"Thanks with all my heart, Superintendent."

"Listen, Manu, if you can't say *tu* to me, or call me Amédée, at least don't call me 'Superintendent.'"

Mallock had a fatherly feeling for Julie's brother. He'd seen him as a young man, as a young lover, a young husband, and a young papa. Being addressed with the formal *vous* bothered him a little.

In general, he couldn't get used to the idea that as he got older, it would become more and more difficult to get people to use the *tu* with him. Through a kind of pagan superstition, young people said *vous* to their elders as if, by putting them at a distance linguistically, they hoped to also distance themselves from death.

"Well . . . Amédée. I suppose you'd like me to tell you the whole story."

"You think?"

9.
Private Clinic of Puerto Plata, Manuel's Story

Mallock, after hesitating between the indeterminate color of the sheets and the orange spots that stained the only chair in the room, decided on the bed.

"I'm listening. We all need to know what got into you."

"I feel that I'm going to disappoint you. What I have to say makes no sense, not even to me."

Manuel managed to smile. He did not intend to complain or bemoan his fate. He seemed to be more concerned to help this poor superintendent than the other way around, as if his own future were not really important, or in any case much less so than that of the people around him. Mallock remembered his sister's comparing him to a holy man, or his mother calling him her "Gandhi." There was something exceptional about Manu, in addition to his big, ebony eyes: a kind of wisdom and sweetness, something tranquil, outside time. With his broad forehead and his brown hair always brushed back, he almost seemed to have come out of a prewar film.

Manuel began his story:

"I got up that morning, making as little noise as possible in order not to wake Kiko and my little honey. I made myself coffee and went into the living room. I slipped into the video player a cassette that contained the documentary my neighbor had kindly recorded for me. I'd decided to watch it before going to market. I always go early to avoid the crowd. And there's also more choice, isn't there?"

Mallock smiled his approval.

"Go on with your story!"

Manuel's eyes looked through Mallock's body into a dark corner of the room. It was the look of a man trying to extract from the past, from the back of his skull, true images and words, in order to bring them back for his friend.

"Everything is still a little confused, but I remember very well what was on the cassette. Just before the main report, there was a short, horrible piece about Haiti. Two guys in British uniforms were laughing like mad as they devoured the brains of living monkeys. The principal documentary, which was about the manufacture of cigars, took us to Cuba and the Dominican Republic. It was toward the end of the film that my life changed."

He lowered his head under the weight of the memory.

"I saw an old man's face, and my heart stopped beating. When he appeared on the screen the first time, the camera followed him for three or four seconds. The second time he appeared, he was crossing a small square, with two swarthy men wearing white suits and dark glasses walking beside him. He passed in front of the camera, at a distance of less than two yards, without even seeming to notice its presence, and then suddenly he turned his head toward the lens. I have absolutely no idea what happened to me. There was no longer anything but that image in my life. For several days, I did everything I could to identify that man and that place. Believe me, I didn't know who he was, and I didn't even know then what I would do with that information if I succeeded in finding it."

Mallock had said nothing; he hadn't made the slightest gesture. But Manuel couldn't help attributing negative thoughts to him:

"I'm not a liar, Superintendent, I even abhor lying. I know this story is absurd, but it's the truth."

Mallock repeated: "Go on with your story," as his only encouragement.

"The next day," Manu continued, "I bought a professional video player and a Betamax-formatted copy of the documentary: "Tobacco and Cigars in the Dominican Republic: A Mirage or a New El Dorado?" Then I spent hours watching these two scenes, using the slow-motion and stop-frame functions. There was something insane about the fascination and hatred that this old man's face awakened in me. Then I ordered stills of them."

"They found three of them on you, in poor condition, but still recognizable. Just so you know, that's enough to prove premeditation."

"There's no point in denying it, there was in fact premediation," Manuel admitted, "there's no doubt on that score. I had only one idea in my head, and that was to find him and kill him. But I swear to you and repeat that I hadn't the slightest idea of what led me to want to eliminate him."

"Did he resemble anyone else, somebody who could have justified so much animosity?"

"That's impossible. I've never felt such hatred for anyone in my whole life."

Mallock thought the young man was very lucky. As for himself, he'd detested more than one man. Enough to fill the four thousand holes of Blackburn, in Lancashire.

"Why did your neighbor record this cassette for you? Maybe he wanted . . . "

A sad little laugh from Manu.

"My God, leave that poor old man alone. Since I love cigars, he recorded a program broadcast on a cable channel. It was about the breaking of the agreements between Davidoff and Cuba, and the development of the quality of Dominican cigars."

There was no lack of dead ends in this case. Mallock moved on to another subject: "Do you feel remorse for having killed him?"

"No, on the contrary. I'm glad to have done it. Every time I think about it I feel a kind of ferocious joy, a sense of euphoria. And at the same time that's unbearable for me. The idea that I killed a man, his blood . . . "

Manuel fell silent, overcome by emotion.

Mallock was confronted by either a brilliant actor—a possibility that could never be excluded—or one of the annoying enigmas that life sought to put in his way.

A third possibility: Manuel was simply crazy. Schizophrenia could explain the twofold feeling he had with regard to this crime. For a moment he began to hope that the psychiatrist would confirm the young man's insanity. Wasn't that the best solution? They take him home and have him cared for. He's put in a psychiatric hospital and the case is closed. Then he thought of Julie and was angry with himself.

Well then, since he cannot and must not be either mad or guilty, let's go with the enigma, he said to himself.

That was the only choice left, and fortunately it fell within his competence.

It had grown muggy. Outside, a storm was building. The clock in the room showed 3 o'clock.

Manuel resumed his narrative:

"I spent my first week on the island in a kind of fog. The combination of heat, palm trees, rum, hate, and contradictory feelings seemed totally unreal. But I quickly understood that this man was anything but unknown in the Dominican Republic. People gave me strange looks when I showed them the photos."

Mallock, who knew Tobias's history, was not surprised.

"I finally understood that they were afraid of him, terribly afraid. And that's what caused me the most problems. To get people to talk I had to pay them. A bad idea: they led me all over the island, telling me all sorts of nonsense. I was so blinded by my desire to find this guy and do him in that I didn't see anything. A stupid moth caught in the glass chimney of a kerosene lamp. Since I didn't want to use my credit card, for fear it would allow me to be located, I used my remaining cash to buy a weapon. That wasn't easy, either. All I could find was an old, prewar gun, half rust and half oil, with five bullets in it. After that, I was broke, so I left my lovely four-star hotel and slept outside. A bad trade. But things are odd. I should have been afraid, even terrified at the idea of being on the streets on an unknown island. But I wasn't. As I went out the door of the hotel, I felt an extraordinary excitement, a kind of blood-thirsty exaltation. Yes, that's it. The night smelled of blood and I loved it!"

Mallock listened to Manuel's account. Contradictory feelings coursed through him, each trying to draw him into its camp.

"It was at that point that I began to fall lower and lower," Manuel went on. "From village to village, from garbage can to garbage can, I hunted my prey all over the island. I washed myself with water from the ditches or potholes. I ate rotten fruit that had fallen off trucks. I no longer had any pride, any desire, or often any strength, but I never gave up. After a rainstorm that covered me with mud, the sun reappeared and I set out again, coated with dry clay. It was really strange, Amédée, I left a trail of pottery along the road like bread crumbs. Partial molds of my body that detached themselves and fell to the ground, sometimes making a sound like a broken saucer."

Manu's face was looking more and more serious.

"I wouldn't have lasted long if people I met along the way hadn't helped me. I always found, at the very last minute, someone who gave me a hand, made it possible for me to go on, as if they were aware of the mission I'd been given and approved of its goal as much as they shared the reasons for it. That was all the odder because I myself didn't know those reasons, and I still don't."

Manuel clenched his jaw and furrowed his brow. Fear. Pain. His eyes grew larger and his lips disappeared in the chalky white of his face.

"I was hunting a dangerous animal . . . and on its own territory."

Mallock saw the significance of this. Manuel looked like he was hallucinating, thus giving preponderant weight to the most rational hypothesis: a fit of madness.

Although puzzled, Mallock encouraged him:

"Go on, Manu."

"Finally I was given the name of the place that corresponded to the photos I'd brought with me. The people who informed me said it must be San José de Ocoa. I went there and waited. For several days, I don't know exactly. A month or two, maybe. But one day, the bastard walked past me without paying any more attention to the bum I'd become than the donkey that people were burying. I got up and walked toward him. I recall the second when I was finally able to point my revolver at him. I see everything in my mind's eye—his suffering, the blue of the sky, the pink of the church, his yellow eyes, and the red impact of my bullets. His fucking revolting brains. Then nothing. I found myself in a hospital, my body imprisoned by pain and my mind submerged by that feeling of accomplishment I already mentioned."

Manuel paused a moment to think before concluding his story.

"I have to tell you one last thing, Superintendent."

Mallock was tempted to remind him of his request not to call him "Superintendent," but changed his mind. On reflection, it wasn't a good idea to ask a guy who was half-crazy and probably a murderer to call by his first name the cop who was assigned to pick him up. For the moment, "Superintendent" would do just fine.

"In fact, I'm happy that this Darbier, if that's his real name, didn't die immediately," Manuel went on. "He had to see his death approaching. It's terrible, but that makes me happy. Like the certainty that he suffered during his last moments. I can't stop replaying in my head the image of his blood in the dust, of his fingers torn off, of his brains on the ground and the urine that was leaking out between his legs. I can't help thinking with joy about his cries of rage, his gurgling with pain, at the same time that I hate myself for having taken a life. You're going to think I'm sick, Amédée, and you're probably right, but for me his miserable death agony was and remains something euphoric, at the same time exciting and calming, a moment of deliverance, not to say bliss."

Mallock, embarrassed by this admission, asked an entirely different question:

"Weren't you ever afraid?"

"No, never. But there's nothing unusual about that; I was born like that. There's only one thing that scares me, and that's the dark. Put me in a forest at night and you'll transform me into a frightened little boy. I feel there's a presence, something terrible. My mother and Julie will tell you. They constantly explained to me that at night there were exactly the same number of people and objects in a room as in the daytime. They went so far as to count them. But I was convinced that there was at least one thing more, more than during the day, and that . . . thing always terrified me. During this whole business, nothing has frightened me, neither the unknown, nor poverty, nor death. The day on which I killed Darbier will remain the greatest day of my life, as important as the birth of my child. It's a kind of foundational act for me, even though I still don't know why."

And then, as if all this still wasn't complicated enough, he felt obliged to add:

"You know that he seemed to recognize me, too, when I attacked him?"

It was at this point that Ramón and Jiménez knocked on the door to the room. It was 4 P.M. Outside, heavy clouds were darkening the city. An initial grumbling resounded like a warning.

The two policemen seemed delighted to see the now famous Gemoni. Mallock even wondered whether they were going to ask for his autograph. If Ramón asked for one for each of his children, they weren't going to get out of there any time soon. Proving that they wanted to stay a while, they went out again to bring three plastic chairs back to the room. Ramón Double-cream arranged the chairs in a circle in front of Manu's bed. Mallock sat on the chair in the middle, with Ramón on his left and Jiménez on his right.

It was Amédée who opened the discussion by addressing himself to Manu:

"This is Commander Juan Luis Jiménez and his assistant, *el capitán* Ramón Cabral. They have served as my guides on the island ever since I arrived here. If I have asked them to come here, it's because the commander says he has interesting revelations to make regarding . . . "

But Mallock didn't have time to finish his sentence. Manu had suddenly opened his eyes wide on seeing Jiménez. At the same moment, a dull explosion had resounded in Mallock's right ear. When he turned around, he saw Jiménez pointing an automatic at him. Out of the smoke emerged the silence that had been ended by the gunshot.

The storm broke and a lightning bolt illuminated the room. Instinctively, Mallock turned toward Ramón.

Double-cream was still sitting on his chair, his arms on the armrests. The bullet had penetrated his left ear, leaving a circular hole. His brains, which had splattered on the wall, were slowly running down toward the floor, licking the whitish paint on the partition.

For Mallock, it was clear. If he said nothing, if he did nothing, in a few seconds he and Manu would be dead as well. Following the lightning bolt, a first thunderclap, enormous and belligerent, exploded over the city. To gain time, Amédée held his open hands out to Jiménez, asking him:

"Why, *comandante*? Before you shoot, tell me, between policemen, why?"

Jiménez's hands were trembling. His eyes were wet and his jaw clenched. For Mallock, this was clear, too: he was acting on orders. And what he had had to do was far from easy for him.

"Why did you kill Ramón?"

"Ramón is collateral damage."

Mallock doubted that. He'd shot him first because he was the only one in the room who was armed.

"Now I have to kill you two as well, both of you, I'm sorry . . . "

Another lightning bolt. Mallock, who no longer had any hope, lowered his arms and looked sadly at Manu. The grumbling of the thunder, colossal, shook the windowpanes.

"I'm sorry," Jiménez repeated, as he raised his automatic and aimed it at Mallock's head.

A third lightning bolt. Amédée started to say:

"Jiménez, I understand. Sometimes there are things in life that the meaning of the . . . "

Then his arm shot forward as if to slap the air. His hand closed on the silencer, he twisted his wrist, and two seconds later Amédée was holding the gun and pointing it at Jiménez.

As he hoped, the third thunderclap had been even more violent. By counting twenty seconds, twenty syllables, he'd acted at the right time. In his heart of hearts, he thanked his friend Gilles Guédrout, who had made him repeat a hundred times the twisting motion of the wrist after having grabbed the barrel.

Then he called: "Guard!"

When the guards entered, they were stupefied.

Was that because they saw Ramón with a bullet in his head?

Or because they didn't see Mallock and Manu in the same con- dition? Did they know what their *comandante* intended to do? Or did they have nothing to do with this attack?

Still more questions, Mallock thought, the answers to which he would not have for a long time, if ever. Didn't matter. Hardly had the guards come into the room, after three seconds of hesitation, before they pointed their weapons at Jiménez and put him under arrest.

When he thought about it, Mallock realized that he already had his answer.

They would have pointed their guns at him if they hadn't known what was going on. He was the only one who was armed, and he was a foreigner to boot. If they hadn't known otherwise, they would therefore have concluded that it was he, and not Jiménez, who had just shot Ramón. The soldiers in this country, as in many banana republics, knew the smell of putsches and failed assassinations. *Vae victis!* Jiménez, by fail- ing, had instantly found himself alone.

Mallock had just enough time to ask him one question before he was taken away.

"Why, Jiménez? Was it to avenge Darbier?"

"No, *para que no hable!*"

"Who? And so he wouldn't talk about what?"

But Mallock didn't have a chance to hear the reply. So that Jimenez himself didn't talk in his turn, the guards took him away roughly and without waiting.

During the whole attack, Manu had remained immobile in his bed.

"Thanks, Amédée. My God, I really think I owe you my life."

Mallock smiled at him. Julie's brother had been so shaken that for the first time in his life he'd finally been able to say *tu* to him!

10.
Cabarete, Thursday, the Second Part of the Evening

Water was starting to fall out of the sky as Mallock was returning to Cabarete. He had seldom seen such a downpour. It was a compact mass of large, heavy raindrops. Vertical rivers that greedily rushed onto the aridity of the soil. The landscape, which had been dull and matte, became shining, colors became vivid and the greens became fluorescent. The windshield wipers couldn't keep up with such a deluge, and the *guagua* in which he was riding had to slow and almost stop while waiting for the rain to let up. It was almost 8 P.M. when Mallock arrived in front of the Blue Paradise.

Shocked by the attempted killing and Ramón's death, Mallock had forgotten his rendezvous with Juan Antonio Servantes. The latter was waiting with a glass and a bottle of single malt in front of him. He must have come directly from his office, and hadn't changed clothes.

"Good evening, Commander. Would you like to go upstairs and freshen up a bit in your room or should we go right away? I know a very good little restaurant that I'd like to show you."

Mallock decided it was pointless to tell him what had happened in Manuel's hospital room.

"Give me five minutes to take a shower and I'll be right back."

Of course, a quarter of an hour later, they dropped anchor in the same harbor where Jean-Daniel had taken him the day before. But Amédée pretended to be astonished. Sometimes he acted in an almost civilized way, and was capable of the required minimum of hypocrisy.

Juan Antonio Servantes waited until the waiter had taken their order before leaning toward Mallock:

"I still don't know whether what I'm going to say will be of any use to you. And in fact, telling you this could put me in a difficult situation if you were indiscreet . . . "

Servantes was beating around the bush. He was waiting for a response or a sign of encouragement. But Mallock knew only too well the virtues of silence. He endured three minutes of embarrassment and questioning looks without flinching.

The young diplomat finally cracked:

"Can I count on your total discretion?"

"Everything depends on what you've got to tell me," Mallock said, resolved not to force a revelation. "I can't promise anything before knowing what it's about. It's up to you to decide."

The bureaucrat was an intelligent young man: he understood that Mallock's very correctness, his refusal to make an unconditional promise to keep quiet, was the best guarantee of his possible silence. He lit a cigarillo, drank a sip of red wine, and settled back in his chair.

"You're a man of considerable experience, and I'm sure my physical appearance struck you as odd, associated with a name that is so . . . Mediterranean."

No sign of denial on Mallock's part.

Servantes went on:

"You must also know that many former German military men, and especially the Nazis, took refuge in various countries in Latin America, forming small groups who regretted or yearned nostalgically for the Third Reich. You don't have to believe me, but my father belonged to the first category. He'd been mistaken about the notion of the Fatherland and about his *Führer*'s true nature. As a soldier, he'd learned to obey and had taken longer than others to become aware of what he'd been asked to do. That's not an excuse, but it is the beginning of an explanation. Today, it's very easy to judge and condemn a whole nation. Germans are no better or worse than the other peoples that vilify them. However that may be, to come back to my father, he asked for no favors, for no leniency, and he never really tried to conceal himself. Sometimes it even seemed that he wanted to be captured, in order to atone, no doubt . . . "

Juan Antonio Servantes hung his head.

"Not seeing punishment coming, he finally hanged himself shortly after my birth. My mother told me that he refused to be happy, and that my presence was too great a pleasure for him, a blessing he didn't deserve. In fact, I'd become an unbearable happiness for him."

He waited a few seconds for his sorrow to subside and then added:

"To sum up, he hanged himself because of me."

The young man choked up. To give himself time to recover, he filled the superintendent's glass and then his own. Although, or rather because, he was innocent, living was not easy. Juan Antonio Servantes was suffering and his wound was deep. The waiter came with two steaming plates of spiny lobster.

"Begin right away. It's better hot," Juan advised.

Mallock looked at the young man and asked frankly:

"This Darbier whom Manu killed . . . Did you know him?"

The diplomat smiled painfully.

"Not personally, but Tobias Darbier was a legend among the people of the 'exiled,' as my mother called us. In fact, 'legend' isn't the right word, I should rather say 'taboo.' Every time I asked her what the man had done that prevented any of his former companions from trying to take advantage of his success, my mother waved her hand, as if to tell me that there was nothing to know and that I had to stop asking questions about the guy."

Juan waved his wrist in front of him, imitating his late mother's movement of denial.

"I think no one knew the whole truth. The man was surrounded by rumors and inspired fear. For us children, he'd become something frightening, the villain, the devil, the very face of fear and the dark. He was 'the incarnation of the bogeyman in fairy tales.' I think he also bore all our little world's guilt, he was our collective bad conscience. In any case, he was a monster, not a man!"

Mallock thought of Manu again. He, too, had emphasized this point by speaking of an ogre.

"In Sosúa," the young diplomat continued, "there was a group of Ashkenazi Jews who had been living there since the 1930s to escape the Nazi regime. Three or four years ago, I questioned members of one of these families. The little community was convinced that Darbier was a war criminal. There were rumors, confidences, reported declarations—there was hardly any doubt. But they didn't have enough proof to inform the Israeli authorities. And then, they were terrified. If there was a leak, if it was learned that they had accused Darbier, they were risking the worst. Rumors of torture were common on the island. It would be suicidal to attack a man who governed the territory where they lived, and who had made them rich. Because business is business, and they had dealings with him."

"And your mother never told you anything more explicit about Darbier, about what he was supposed to have done?"

"She did. And that's what I've come to tell you."

Juan Servantes sat up straight. Took a deep breath. Mallock recognized the importance these admissions had for the young man.

"My mother was really shocked when Tobias Darbier

regained favor and then power in l996, for the third time, alongside Balaguer. In fact, it made her crazy with rage. According to her, he had gone beyond all limits of barbarity. And even if she refused to tell me more precisely, she finally fed me a few bits of information in the form of anathemas against the ogre. It was so violent and so astonishing, especially coming from her, that I still recall the exact words she used. She screamed at me that the mere existence of that man on Earth was 'an insult to God,' his coming into the world 'a blasphemy,' and his incredible survival 'the devil's doing.' Caught up in her surge of hatred, she also told me something I hadn't heard before: the legend of his birth."

Juan leaned toward Mallock and murmured:

"The scars this accursed Tobias had on his skull are supposed to have been made by his mother's teeth when he was born. It's said that she gave birth to him through her mouth."

Amédée concealed his uneasiness by picking up his glass. He drank its content in little sips, while the young diplomat continued his story:

"The doctors are supposed to have pried apart and disjointed the poor woman's jaws in order to let the baby emerge. It's absurd, but most people around here believe it. And then my poor mother added that the man who succeeded in cleansing the earth of his presence would have 'a place in heaven for all eternity, alongside the Lord.' Now, my mother was very religious, very orthodox in her Catholicism, if I dare say so. I was stupefied to hear her assure me that she would find it acceptable that someone who had committed a murder be admitted to heaven. It was that statement, more than all the rest, that really affected me. And that is perhaps also why, twelve years later, I am so concerned about Manuel."

He fell silent and sat back in his chair to let the waiter fill their glasses again. He waited until the waiter had left to continue:

"I'm not a practicing Catholic, and hardly even a believer, but I did in fact detect a kind of . . . saintliness in Manuel. He has an extraordinary good will toward the people and things around him, and then there is this acceptance of his destiny. Either he is completely mad or . . . Anyway, I'm really no longer sure what to think. Do you believe in God, Commander?"

"No, nor in the devil. God forbid. Come on, let's eat."

They both attacked the lobsters. But they were already completely cold.

Mallock returned to his hotel around midnight. The rain had stopped. He decided to go back to the beach to try to fight off a new fit of sadness. In the distance, at the exit from the bay, he could see white lines in the dark, the last ocean waves still playing with the coral reef, pink barriers for baby waves.

The superintendent stretched out on the sand. He imagined himself digging into the sand with his face and his webbed feet in order to give birth to his pains there. So many little soft eggs whose inhabitants would soon wriggle free from the sand and run off to the sea.

Half asleep on the beach, Mallock smiled. At himself and at his internal lunacies.

This evening, he imagined himself a giant tortoise, a survivor from the Jurassic. Sometimes an aquarium phenomenon for laughing children, sometimes a wheezy deep-sea diver, a tranquil observer of deep ocean trenches. His eyes, too, were full of tears. And his child, too, had been devoured by the crabs. Since then, the superintendent's life had been askew, his heart the wrong way round, waiting to have, like these nice animals, his back recycled in the form of combs and his abdomen cooked up in a soup!

11.
Friday Morning,
Fifth and Next-to-last Day on the Island

M allock's night was traversed by black uniforms, white lightning bolts, and eviscerated regrets suspended from hooks. There was the red of the flags and blood, and then the frightening drums, broken crosses, and things draped in leather. Anyone else would have called it a nightmare, but not Mallock. He had recognized the characteristic blue odor of his visions, as well as the cold imprint they left at the very back of his head in the morning. For the first time in this case, Dédé-the-Wizard had just received a message from heaven, from the beyond or from his own subconscious, which was sometimes faster and much smarter than he was.

He woke up with a question.

If Tobias Darbier was a war criminal and Manuel had executed him for that reason, why hadn't he admitted as much? He wouldn't have escaped a trial, but any attorney could have emphasized the extenuating circumstances. Unless he had been paid to do the job? A contract? Mossad? That Jewish community on the island? Was that plausible? Bad question. Everything was possible and everything had to be considered.

He had only one day left to learn more about the ex-emperor of the island. He got up, grimacing, and dragged himself over to the telephone. A first call to talk with Delmont about the preceding day's events:

"Jiménez has never been suspected of being a *bruto*, or of hanging out with Darbier?"

Mallock had gone straight to the point.

"No, otherwise he wouldn't have been assigned to this case. The investigation will tell us more, but we already know that in absolute terms, few people on the island are beyond Darbier's powers of corruption and his ability to do harm. The fact that Jiménez is both a good policeman and a *molo*—that's what the *brutos* call the non-*brutos*—probably played a role in his recruitment by Darbier's team. That made him a person above any suspicion.

"What about Ramón? His family?"

"I know, superintendent, it's very sad, but it is not, unfortunately, within my jurisdiction."

Silence. Sometimes there's nothing to be done, and Mallock hated that. Out of personal pride. Out of hatred of destiny. And out of empathy as well.

"Could you at least check to see if everything is in order for the burial and the payment of his pension? You must have a Dominican counterpart in that area?"

"I promise, I'll keep an eye on it."

"Why not both?"

"I wouldn't have thought you so sentimental, Superintendent."

"Me?" Mallock interjected. "I'm a real softie, Mr. Ambassador. But don't spread that around, it could do me great harm."

Delmont laughed a long time, like a diplomat, a little dose of pure amusement accompanied by five or six seconds of professional laughter. He interrupted this great musical moment by begging Mallock to excuse him:

"Pardon me, I'll be back in a moment."

Receiver set down . . . sounds of doors opening and closing, footsteps in the distance . . . paper being torn up, crumpled . . . the receiver picked up again.

"A courier, and for once it's good news. I've just received, this very moment, the repatriation agreement. You can take Manu away. As for the final details, I'll take care of them. Since he's suspected of murder, it's not going to be easy to get him on a regular flight, but I'll see what I can do."

"Thanks very much. And what about Darbier? I'm sorry to insist, but I still haven't had your version. What do you know about this Tobias?"

Delmont didn't hesitate for a second. Either he was being sincere, or he'd prepared his reply:

"One thing. When I took up this post, it was explained to me that he'd been powerful and dangerous, and that it was better to avoid getting close to him. And that's exactly what I've done."

"But in your position you must have heard things about him?"

This time Delmont paused. When he spoke again, his voice was lower:

"Listen to me, Superintendent. Tomorrow, or in no more than two days, you are going to leave the island, but I . . . stay here."

And once again, he let a few seconds go by. Mallock had understood.

"I'll wait for your call regarding the details. Goodbye, and thanks again, Mr. Ambassador."

Have to know how to hang up.

Especially when there's no longer anyone on the other end.

The second call of the morning was to Julie, to inform her of the latest developments. He hesitated a little, and then, after telling her the good news concerning the repatriation, ended up telling her about Jiménez's attempt to kill her brother.

"Not a word to Kiko, boss, please," Julie said. "We'll tell her what happened when he's back here."

"That was my intention. But I assure you: I've taken steps to prevent it from happening again."

At that moment, Mallock realized that he felt guilty. His

negligence appeared to him to be so flagrant that he experienced it as a message, a form of revelation. He was on foreign territory, not only in the geographical sense of the term, but also in another sense: he was in a strange, different land. The reality of the facts, like people's motivations, was dangerously out of his control. And then, what did he know about Darbier's past, and Manu's? Nothing tangible.

Then he asked Julie to put Bob on the phone.

Daranne was very happy to hear his superintendent's voice. When he learned that Mallock had chosen him for a delicate task, he was exultant. Ever since his suicide attempt, he no longer felt that he was in Mallock's good graces. A difference in age, in culture, and many other little things he was only vaguely aware of. Mallock's three other captains formed a brotherhood from which he was increasingly excluded. That was how it was. Nobody's fault. Daranne didn't hold it against them. He was just sad about it. His relations with his wife hadn't improved, either, and he was beginning to think about his old P38 again.

"What can I do for you, Boss?"

"It's delicate, Bob."

Mallock was one of the few people who called him "Bob," as Robert asked. The others couldn't even use his first name. For all of them he was Daranne, a use of the family name that expressed the lack of brotherhood or simply the difference in age. All he had to do was to stop wearing that little red and white mustache, farting all the time, and making faces, Mallock's collaborators would have said to justify themselves.

"Discreetly, without talking about it with the others," Mallock explained, "I'd like you to look into the state of Julie's brother's finances. A complete rundown, including any foreign bank accounts. Examine that with the tax men. And also check his car. We didn't find his cell phone, it might still be inside the car. If you find it, go through it with a fine-toothed comb."

"What exactly are you looking for, Boss?"

"I have two paranoid hypotheses I'd like to be able to forget about. One is that of a professional killer. For himself or for a government. Manuel Gemoni doesn't really have the profile, but I've already known some whom you'd never have suspected. The other, and this is a more believable hypothesis, probably even the most likely, is that it may be a matter of vengeance. This old man who, for your information, is a real bastard, may have already crossed paths with the Gemonis. Broaden your investigation. Try to find out if among the victims of revenge or those who disappeared there are any Gemonis, or someone related to them. For that, and for that only, take Ken's assistant into your confidence: you're going to need to have access to the data banks. With the internal security branch, also see if there have been any trips to Israel or contacts with Mossad."

Then Bob understood why Mallock had come to him, and he was hurt by that.

He objected, just on principle:

"Are you sure that's useful? I don't much like doing things that have to be kept secret from the group, Boss. So far as Julie is concerned, I think that . . . "

"I agree, but believe me, it's better for her. I'm almost certain that you won't find anything and that will be that. But I absolutely have to have the confirmation. It's pointless to upset her for nothing, right?"

Daranne reflected for two seconds before yielding. Whether it was a matter of profound conviction or the habit of obeying, no one could have said.

"Fine, you're the boss, and I'll get started this morning."

Just as he was about to hang up, Mallock had a last idea:

"Listen, there's one other thing to look into. This Tobias Darbier seems to have a past that is much more complicated than it first appears to be. Just to see, put in a request for a DNA search."

"How? Your guy's corpse isn't here!"

"Go through Dublin. Get him to request the authorities to take a sample from the old man's body and have him send it directly to Mordome. *Capice?*"

"Okay, Boss," an obliging Daranne said.

"Thanks, Bob, I appreciate it. Ah! By the way, I'm returning on Saturday, but I won't be in the office until Monday."

"Do as you like, Boss," Daranne said, and hung up.

Mallock also hung up, with a feeling of guilt. He'd taken advantage of a slight dissension within his team to manipulate one of its members. The goal being above all to help Manu get out of this mess. But even if the intention was praiseworthy, the way he'd done it left much to be desired. Especially since Daranne was a loyal man.

He resolved to put matters straight at the first opportunity.

12.
There are More Things in Heaven and Earth

Outside, it had been raining steadily since the day before. Tons of lukewarm water were striking the island, its houses, trees, earth, and inhabitants. There was nothing to do that day except wait for Delmont's call. Still forty-eight hours to spend on this island, and there was only one question in Mallock's head. How could he learn more about the ogre of the Dominican Republic?

Mallock thought again about Mister Blue's proposal. What did he have to lose by going to see the old woman he'd talked about? He had no serious lead, no step to be taken, and not even the unlikely temptation of spending a day lying in the shade of the palm trees.

An old witch, even if she had no gift whatever, would at least make for memories.

He looked at his watch: 9 A.M. *Would Jean-Daniel still be there?* Mallock put on a shirt and linen trousers. He went out into the rain, running.

By a stroke of luck, or of destiny, Mister Blue had waited for him. Ten minutes later, they were crossing Ingenios and its cane plantations.

The valley of Cibao.

The air was fragrant with the perfume of brown sugar. Cinnamon-colored streams of mud were running along the road and torrents of rain were falling on their vehicle's windshield. They continued to meet fast-moving cars, despite the fact that most of them were almost blind. Miracle upon miracle, they managed to avoid each other. Mallock began to wonder if, in the end, he had been right to leave the refuge of his hotel to risk his life by setting out in search of an old woman.

"I really need more information about this Tobias Darbier, in order to make connections. Do you think we'll be able to see this famous woman of yours?"

"I really don't know. First we'll have to go by a cigar factory where a man works who can let her know and take us to her. He'll be the one who decides, not me."

It took them a good half hour to reach the cigar factory and to find the mysterious intermediary. When they arrived the old man got up from his sat. His body resembled a Panatela cigar. Dry, slender, and wrinkled. His skin, in perfect harmony, had all the nuances of a tobacco leaf. Zagiõ was his name, and his job was to keep the humidifier going in the holy of holies, the wrappers room. Each time he turned on the ancient machinery, the whole room and its occupants were invaded by an opaque watery fog. Mister Blue went up to the man and began to speak to him in a confidential way. Zagiõ listened to him, interrupting only to slip new questions into the hollow of his ear.

Fascinated by the factory, Mallock had forgotten his mission. The perfume of the damp wrappers, the powerful odor of the harvests compressed into hundreds of cubes made of canvas, their monochrome colors, ranging from green to dark brown, the variety in the form of the cigars . . . Mallock the cigar-lover was in heaven. He caressed, smelled, and then, in the packaging department, lit a few of different calibers. He declined the initial offer of a *domingo turisto* with a sweet, disgusting perfume, and had them open the special reserve for him. He dug around, asked for a stool in order to reach the higher shelves, where the oldest types were stored, came back down, and tested them again, until he had six different cigars slowly burning between his fingers. He finally selected three very large types with noble insides and perfect wrappers:

maduros. He had two hundred of them packed up for him. And the same quantity of *robustos*, but with a still darker wrapper, almost *obscuro*. Finally, he asked that some of them be subjected to a special treatment that involved putting a bit of fabric imbued with cane sugar and rum on the end that goes into the mouth.

During all this time, Zagiõ had followed Mallock as he moved around. They looked at each other one last time. Zagiõ's dark eyes seemed to be trying to penetrate the superintendent's soul by way of his absinthe-colored irises. Apparently satisfied with what he'd seen there, he slipped his papery hand into the pocket of his tattered pants. He took out an object that Mallock would never have expected to be there: a state-of-the-art cell phone. He opened it and dialed a number. A few sentences later, he closed it and put it back in his pocket.

Mister Blue thanked him, patting him several times on the shoulder. Zagiõ finally replied with a big smile, revealing the presence of white teeth in a mouth with black gums.

"Zagiõ has sent the message," Jean-Daniel said. "He has announced our arrival, but there will be no reply. We have to take the risk; she may not be there. In any case, during the time it will take to inform her, we can go eat lunch."

"Is there any decent place to eat around here?"

Otherwise, Mallock preferred to go without.

"There's an exceptional place. I'm going to take you to Camp David, on Trujillo's summer estate. His old supporters have turned it into a museum glorifying their dictator, and above all, there's a superb restaurant. It's not open to everyone, but I know the chef. Jean Jeansac, known as Jeanjean, is French, a native of Ribérac, the land of foie gras, but he was already here when I arrived. I'm sure he knows more about Trujillo and your Darbier than most people do. We can try to question him as well, we'll see. Okay?"

A quarter of an hour later, the mauve pickup drove through an old gate decorated with a series of surveillance cameras. The residence was usually protected by guards armed with riot guns posted all along the drive that led to the main building, but the rain had made them take refuge inside. Mallock and Mister Blue were checked only once, when they got to the top of the hill, in the reception hall of the restaurant. The residence was vast, flat, and white, a sort of gigantic cheese plate with red roofs over it. The first surprise was to find the place empty. Except for the guards and the employees, who were all standing, no visitor was seated at any of the twenty-one large tables, or on the glass-roofed terrace.

The second surprise was that a large part of the main reception room, which had been transformed into a restaurant, was occupied by cars, the tyrant's old Chevrolets, with their personalized license plates: "BENEFACTOR OF THE FATHERLAND," dusty little flags on the sides, and a big revolving red light affixed to the front fender. The chromed radiator grilles looked like the maws of voracious beasts. With their enormous silvery teeth, they expressed their owner's desire to hold power and to devour. Only one of the dictator's favorite automobiles was missing, the one in which Trujillo had been riding when it was pierced by the bullets.

In front of El Generalísimo's bar, a big guy with cheeks streaked by broken veins was waiting for them. Jeanjean's eyes did not contain the bonhomie that his body expressed. The smile was there, but frozen, blurred by an eternal sorrow. They were welcomed effusively. The Frenchman must be dying of boredom, alone on his hill after so many years.

Without having agreed to do so, Mister Blue and Mallock made the same decision: eat lunch first, then question. The man had doubtless been reduced to silence because of the privileged position he occupied. And maybe also by a sense of fraternity and complicity that all the years had finally caused to grow in him, perhaps in spite of himself. So the superintendent, like a good cop, told himself that a little patience and a few well-placed compliments about his cooking might calm Jeanjean's fears and lead to two or three bits of confidential information at the end of the meal. After all, Darbier wasn't Trujillo, and there was every likelihood that Jansac was not involved in the secrecy and veneration surrounding the former dictator.

In fact, Mallock didn't have to force himself to praise the cuisine. The meats served, with their natural taste of grass and milk, were nothing less than exceptional, as was the way they were prepared. Mister Blue devoured a huge piece of lamb, as succulent as it was delicious. For his part, Mallock enjoyed an enormous rib-eye steak, more tender than the filet, but with the flavor and rareness of a back steak. The chef joined them for dessert and was showered with compliments.

Confronted by the enthusiasm of his compatriots, Jeanjean broke out in a smile again. He set his past aside and let his eyes shine. They talked about the different kinds of meat to be found on the island and the ways of preparing them. Mallock, who had quickly won the chef's esteem by his display of culinary competence, thought it was finally possible to bring up the subject of Darbier. He did so by asking a question that was logical and, he thought, neither polemical nor indiscreet.

"What about Tobias Darbier? Which meat did he prefer?"

The response was as surprising as it was sudden. As if he had a flock of parasites under his skin, Jansac's face undulated and turned vague.

He rose and stammered:

"I have to go now."

At the back of the restaurant two hefty men in civilian clothing were watching them from a distance. The "chef" added, pronouncing each syllable very distinctly:

"Be careful, very careful."

Three seconds later, Jeanjean was back in his kitchen. The subject was far more delicate than Mallock had imagined. Without pursuing the matter, the two Frenchmen paid the bill and left to look for the witch.

A rain squall. On both sides of the road, the green jungle was exhaling odors of mossy rot. Mister Blue's minivan was navigating blind on this liquid mirror, drawing its own rails of mercury on it. In the drainage channels, the dead-drunk soil was puking up its excess ocean water in the form of slick, ochre-colored mud. All around them, in the vegetation, thousands of greedy mouths were swallowing the water.

Mallock and his guide met two or three jungle-taxis coming in the opposite direction. The rain was beating down on the minivan, making a tremendous racket. Inside, the two men remained silent, concentrated on the vehicle's trajectory, mute and appalled by their insignificance and nature's omnipotence, its discreet but crushing superiority over man.

In La Cumbre, the car took a red-mud track that led to La Toca. When it was no longer wide enough, at least for a car, the two men got out. Without anything to cover themselves, they courageously plunged into a nowhere of wet grass, passing through the green humps of the hills and the intoxicating odors of humus and licorice.

Mallock and Jean-Daniel were now walking on old mule-paths, following in the footsteps of the *marrons*, the fugitive slaves of the last century who tried to escape the cruelty of their masters. Each of them had seen one of those near him mutilated by the little white tyrants who cut off the noses or ears of their slaves with a machete to prevent them from committing suicide or running away. The masters concealed these bloody appendages somewhere in their sumptuous homes and returned them to the families only at the moment of their death. The poor creatures thought they would never find peace if all the parts of their bodies were not buried in the same place.

A dozen children emerged from the rain. There were smiles on their faces. In their hands they carried plastic bags full of pieces of amber caught in their gangue of coal and sand. Mister Blue greeted them with a nod of his head. They recognized him and understood that they would make no deals with him that day, or with the foreigner accompanying him. In this case, the latter was a Mallock concentrating on not falling on his face.

His blond hair was dripping wet. The next day, if he was still alive, if he had not slipped into the bottom of a ditch, he would leave for Paris with Julie's brother on a stretcher, and without the slightest new lead.

Good Lord! What the hell was he doing there?

They walked for almost an hour. The sky had disappeared. The earth, the world, reality itself, seemed to be liquefying, while swarms of bare-chested children ran around them. The children ran ahead of them on the steep trail, then waited for them farther on. At every step, Mister Blue's and Mallock's feet sank into the mud without ever slipping. Finally, Mister Blue stopped at the edge of a large, strange hole and a little hill of lignite. He grabbed a piece of wood and began to strike a big, concave boulder with all his strength. Then he sat down on a rock and waited in the rain. Mallock did the same without asking any questions. He was simply done in by fatigue and the strange turn his investigation had taken.

Usually it was he, and he alone, who decided to stray into intuition, when he really needed it to resolve a difficult inquiry. Recently, on the contrary, it was events that had constantly led him further toward the strange.

This trip was the culmination of the strange, its metaphor.

The hole in question was one of the last amber mines Jean-Daniel had worked. In it he employed Dominicans whose whole production he had agreed to purchase. From this earthen mouth, barely supported by timbers and braces, one of these men emerged. Jean-Daniel moved forward to help him climb up the last few yards. And there, at the edge of what they called a mine, under the sticky, cold rain, the two men began to laugh and talk.

Mallock decided to take advantage of this pause to roll up his pants as far as the knee. By capillary action, water and mud were rising higher and higher: it was time to stop the inundation, even if he had to go back to Bermuda shorts.

A few minutes later, the group plunged back into the jungle, with the children behind and the miner in front. Seeing the new direction the adults were taking, the youngest children started to show signs of nervousness, which turned into fear when they arrived at the top of the next hill. Below it stretched a vast mangrove swamp.

Jean-Daniel briefly explained to Mallock that beyond this area of mud and brackish water there was another, higher hill studded with giant palm trees. It was there that they were to meet the old woman. When Mallock turned around one last time before beginning the final descent, all the children had disappeared.

Mister Blue, in a toneless voice, said:

"Let's hurry."

No time for politeness. Jean-Daniel was no longer the same man. His face was a solemn mask, and the water outlined on it a sheen of superstitious fear. Mallock would never have thought Mister Blue could be intimidated by anything, whatever it was, and especially not by an old woman on a hill. In Mallock, his guide's concern was transformed into an increased interest in this expedition. Perhaps his day had not been wasted after all, if what was waiting for him way up there was capable of disturbing a guy like his companion.

When they arrived at the bottom of the hill, the two men

were confronted by a new apparition: two splendid Blacks with gray, almost transparent eyes who had risen up out of the rotten vegetation of the mangrove swamp. Identical twins with muscular bodies covered with clay, licorice-colored hair, and ageless faces. Jean-Daniel, with water running down his face, explained to his friend that these two ebony statues were the sons of Niyashiika, the name given to the old woman by the island's inhabitants.

"One of them speaks French, but I don't know which one."

No one was allowed go any further, except Mallock, whom the magician had agreed to meet.

"Good luck. Set your prejudices aside and take advantage of this interview," Mister Blue advised him, addressing him for the first time with the familiar *tu*. "I've been around enough to know how right Shakespeare was."

He turned on his heel and went off down the path to the mine.

Without turning around, he called through the rain: "There are more things in heaven and earth, Horatio, than are dreamt of in your philosophy."

Mallock smiled, caught his breath, turned around, and bravely entered the heart of the jungle in the muddy water of the mangrove swamp.

13.
Friday, November 29

Mangroves drunk on blood, defunct rivers, plants interlaced in a single marshy nightmare, the swamp was cluttered with drowned birds, aerial roots, and giant crustaceans.

Niyashiika's sons walked in front, up to their mid-thighs in water, without even turning around to see if the foreigner was able to follow them. Mallock, who was not reassured, said to himself that he'd never been so wet in all his life. Even completely immersed in the water, he would have felt dryer. He followed the twins step by step, because he saw that the route they were following, full of turns and reverses, was not a matter of chance.

They took an infinitely long time to emerge from the swamp.

Without the slightest pause, they began to scale the hill. Water was running down it in serpentine rivulets. The three men climbed on all fours, taking care to keep their balance. Mallock used his hands as claws, sinking them into the grass and holding on to it. When they arrived at the summit, they finally sat down on the fallen trunk of a coconut tree. The twins put giant palm leaves on their heads to serve as umbrellas, and one of them explained, in perfect French:

"We have confidence in the fossil man, and Zagiõ compared you to a piece of amber still stuck in the sadness of its coal. He also spoke of the generous orangutan that you are. He mentioned uprightness and good will as well. So our mother asked us to come to get you at the mine and to answer you, if you really want to ask questions."

The violence of the rain had caused the palm leaf he'd put on his head to slip off; he replaced it and waited.

Mallock was astonished by what the twins had said. He was dying to know more about this woman. But why was there so much mystery and so much fear surrounding her? He hesitated to speak, as if the expression of his ignorance might be seen as blasphemous, or a crippling sign of weakness . . .

He finally said:

"Please don't hold it against me, but I've never heard of Niyashiika."

The young man gave what he thought was an explanation.

"Our mother is the child of the union of a Yanomami shaman and a fairy. She was brought to this place by the winds and the waters. Here she has moved the axis of the world every day. Fifty years have passed. She has become an *ayahuasquera*. Now she speaks to the spirits of the universe. And she questions the cosmic serpent as an equal."

A shadow passed over the shiny Bakelite of his face.

"If she gave birth to us, my brother and me, it was to become still stronger, to add to the telluric powers of the shamans that of the mothers. That is what I had to say; it is said."

He stopped speaking and stood up, leaving his brother sitting alone on the tree trunk. Then he signaled to Mallock to follow him and started climbing the last few yards to the summit. In front of the door of a crude, dilapidated wooden house, he left the superintendent with his perplexity and the black mud that was running down his white calves.

Amédée wondered how he could have let himself be led so far from his lair just to interview a witch. But that was not the last of his questions. When Niyashiika appeared on her doorstep, his perplexity changed into a mixture of anger and hilarity. What stood in front of him, a little, old black thing, all stunted, clearly had no chance of being able to help him in any way at all. If one of them could help the other, it was he, by giving her a little bit of money and something to eat. The woman's destitution, like the dilapidation of her makeshift home, was absolute.

However, an atmospheric phenomenon aroused doubt in Mallock's Cartesian mind. Without any possible explanation, within a few seconds the rain stopped and the sun came out. Niyashiika's amber-colored eyes lit up like strange embers and then became brown again and concealed themselves behind their lids. She looked down to watch where she was going and went back into her cabin without paying any further attention to her visitor. After a moment's hesitation, Mallock followed her. Behind him, the rain began again, transforming the hut's bare doorframe into a curtain of glass shards.

On the dirt floor, three hens, a cock, and about a hundred chicks were turning in circles. They, too, were amber-colored, some of them streaked with gold, others with coal-black. Between the cabin's planks an ambiguous sunlight penetrated, forming sharp-edged halos with the dust. Kitchen utensils and a few colored plastic bowls hung from the corrugated metal ceiling.

Without asking his preference, the old woman started making what Mallock at first took to be coffee. A wood fire. Socks used as a filter. Multiple metal bowls used to decant several times the liquid thus obtained. Probably to produce a homogenous beverage. At each stage, she added powder, sugar, and murky water in which roots and herbs were steeping.

Mallock would have opted for a good whiskey. But he had nothing to say about it. So he warily drank the liquid. It was hot and peppery and, in fact, had an aftertaste of coffee. The old woman signaled to him to follow her outdoors.

Her white hair combed back into a tight bun was resplendent in the sun.

Her face was surprising.

She did not resemble the people in this area; she looked more like an Indian. And the more Mallock observed her, the more he realized that she had a strange beauty. Without his actually being aware of it, reality was being deformed all around him, disappearing and then reappearing a hundred times more clear, as if he had always been myopic and had finally been given a pair of glasses to correct his sight.

Then the old woman started to talk to him, volubly, without stopping to take a breath. In a monotone and in a language close to Spanish, with a few German, French, and English words, and others more guttural. She said that a "double dragon" lived inside us. That it was from its multiplication that we are born. And that it was this twisted ladder, this spiral staircase, that connected, from all eternity, the earth and the sky. With an index finger covered with bark, she drew on the ground a double serpent, the symbol of twins, a double helix, a sketch of DNA. She said that Manuel's dragon was pure, that his ladder was made of glass. She said Mallock had to save Manuel, and for that reason he had to share his most elevated hallucinations, the ones produced by the *ayahuasca* of Oba, the final drug. She said she had spoken to Darbier's "Quetzalcoatl" and to Manuel's, that she had been forced to use her science to go back up the whole sequence of their rebirths. She said that Tobias Darbier, the creator of black voodoo, was called Don Pedro, himself the reincarnation of a Carib chief, a cannibal, a soul-eater, Solote-Soum-Ba. She also said he had been "Damballah-Flangbo," the one who each night transmitted his orders to Lucifer. Finally, she said that she had given Mallock the drug, and that he was soon going to have to die. "Just time enough to smile at me," she simpered, her eyes blazing.

Amédée was surprised to find himself thinking that he was going to see Thomas again and that he had never taken his old Jaguar in for its technical inspection, before his heart sped up, then stopped. There was no long, luminous corridor, and still less a son standing there waiting for him.

Then he was cast into Hell.

Thousands of Carib savages were devouring Arawaks and sycophants. The earth was mauve and white, composed of guts and bones intertwined, woven with care. In the distance fires made of children's arms were glowing. There was a brief storm of red snow, luminous embers, descending from the sky. Then the cosmic serpent appeared, the one called Ouroboros in Africa, Shesha among the Indians, Typhon in Greek mythology.

Mallock was trembling but he was not afraid. It was the heart and the spirit of the universe that he was looking at, its source and its beginning. A single entity, God and Chaos. Infinitely large, disproportionately small. Simultaneously a universal serpent and a chromosome with bilious eyes.

Accompanying the magisterial arrival of the initial wonder, he heard Satie's first *Gnossienne*, played on a minuscule piano by a little monkey with a bare skin, whose yellow brain gleamed in the moonlight. The young animal was sitting on the edge of a well. Around him, three big, black dogs were keeping guard, while above them thousands of squawking swallows turned in a vortex as far as the firmament.

Mallock walked on, as far as the intersection of seven paths. On each, people were standing, sitting, and lying, strangers whom he recognized despite their differing garb. As he walked among them, there were also powerful feelings with bodies filled with water, incredulous eyes, finally obvious smiles. He felt horizontal rain, deflagrations of melancholy, a barrage of the imperial artillery, the army of leaden bullets, spit out of ancient muskets. Hundreds of sharp rancors fell from the sky. But love as well. Silent tongues. Tsunami joys.

And he saw himself swimming in the earth.

He was making broad breaststrokes to move forward, astonished that the earth offered so little resistance. Only his fingers felt the movement through matter, a little like a child when he scrapes up sand to build a castle at the seaside. Sometimes, the dreamer went around rocks, the biggest and most dense, sometimes he crossed great lakes of oil, slipping faster than the wind.

Mallock was still swimming in the earth when he suddenly felt himself pulled backward and upward. Piercing the surface, his body sprang up into full light. He had time to glimpse, in the center of a gigantic arch, another little monkey wearing a tarboosh and beating on a drum. Higher up, an enormous French flag, blown by the winds, was twisting in vast waves.

He woke up in the middle of a prodigious room.

A chapel of candles and amber, it was without any doubt the most beautiful thing he'd ever contemplated since his mother had taken him to town, when he was three years old, to see the crèche in the cathedral. The flames of thousands of candles seemed to come from inside the walls. Walls that looked as if they had been fabricated in a kind of melting gold, which simultaneously retained its mobility, its luminescence, and the reflective capacity of the purest mirrors. It took Mallock a few minutes to understand what he was looking at. Lit by a hole situated very high up on the ceiling and by hundreds of candles, it was the fabled amber room. Not affixed with precision to straight and vertical walls, as in the photo, but beautifully set into plaques on the walls of an immense cavern.

One of the twins, sitting alongside him, was wiping his forehead with a damp cloth. Mallock didn't have to say anything, the question marks were evident on all of his features.

The twin explained to him:

"You are just under my mother's house. My father discovered this natural grotto years ago. He closed it in and constructed this wooden hut just above it to protect the entrance."

"But these amber plaques . . . How . . . "

"You are going to learn all that. It takes time . . . Stay lying down, your heart has just started up again."

Chameleons, the young man's gray eyes had taken on, in the candlelight, the color of gold. He dipped the cloth in cold water again, and put it on Mallock's forehead.

"The amber panels were stolen by *el Diablo* Darbier and his killers in a European city, just before it was destroyed. They brought this war booty to the island, where he thought it would be safe. My father happened by chance to find out where Tobias *el Diablo* had hidden it. The day Trujillo died, my father and three of his friends stole the crates and brought them all here. Only one of them was missing, the one that was supposed to contain a music box. It is thought that it was forgotten in Germany."

Mallock listened, fascinated.

"Our father had always been very poor and full of love for his wife. He would never have been able to offer her all the gold in the world and the things that provide comfort. That pained him. After he discovered Darbier's treasure, he conceived the mad plan of constructing the most beautiful palace in the world for her, and for her alone, in her honor and in the honor of what she represented for him. He did not leave the panels in the crates, where the amber was languishing; he reconstructed the room as he saw it in his head. My father was will and strength incarnate. For twelve years he worked on the cavity of the grotto in order to be able to reconstruct the room like the dream he had of it."

He paused long enough to dip the cloth in the cold water again and put it on Mallock's forehead.

"He died too soon. My brother and I finished the work in accordance with his plans. When our mother leaves us, we will leave her in it with the candles and fill it in with earth. No one will ever know."

"But I now know the place . . . "

The young man smiled and tapped him on the forehead in a friendly way.

"Now that you are dead, you've become much better, haven't you? It is the awareness of the imminence of his own end that makes man a dangerous animal. And you are not merely a man, you are half bear and you were a cat, and also a precious stone, and an old baobab tree as well, my mother said. And she also said that your own serpent is a kind dragon! And then, without wanting to disrespect you, you have to be able to find your way back, *gringo*. We have seen you walking, you and your arms, in the swamps!"

"With my headache, my bad back, and my pale white calves, you mean?" Mallock added with a big foolish smile.

The twin broke out laughing. A laugh that ricocheted for a long time on the thousands of pieces of amber that formed the most beautiful marquetry in the world.

BOOK 2

14.

Saturday Morning, November 30,
Return to Paris with Manuel

Sitting in the fuselage of the 747, dry and clean, Mallock was wondering what he had actually experienced. A nightmare, a Mallockian vision, an opium dream? No, the object was very real. His left hand touched the strange vial cut from amber, a gift from the old witch. He had placed it in the middle of the tray and a ray of sun, amplified by the cabin window, gave it still more life. A very odd kind of energy. The stone seemed to contain a small electric lamp. All around it, the gray plastic Air France tray on which it was set was like a golden gouache.

He looked up and heard:

"Hello, Superintendent. Did you have a good stay on the island?"

A flight attendant was leaning over him, her body bent at the hip like a loving mother over her baby's cradle. Her breasts were in position.

Mallock put the vial back in his pocket.

"Do we know each other?"

"I know you. I was on your flight over and I even woke you without meaning to when I served your meal."

"You have an amazing memory," Mallock smiled.

"Not really. I've often seen your face in the newspaper. If you need anything at all, please don't hesitate to ask. I'm entirely at your disposition."

Mallock mumbled a thank-you as he looked at her, and promised himself he wouldn't hesitate . . .

"Wait," he added, as she stood up to leave.

He finished his champagne and handed her the glass. She took it and gave him a splendid smile.

"Another one?"

She was really very appetizing with her satiny skin and her lovely hands.

Calm down, Mallock, he reprimanded himself.

"Thanks, that's very kind. I'm going to stop there with the champagne."

She disappeared down the aisle.

As much as Mallock loved wine, he had little liking for this acidic drink, a symbol of the farewell glass, the endless party, and Christmas without Thomas. On the other hand, pretty women . . . Even at Easter or Trinity.

His back told him that he must have been seated for more than four hours already. In fact, they had taken off at 8:07. This time, the plane had flown straight from Puerto Plata to Paris. A direct flight that avoided crossing the island and stopping off in Saint-Martin.

At the airport, where the Interpol officers were waiting for them, he had had time to buy a complete set of colorful shirts before checking in. They were all intended for his friends, including one for Anita, his housekeeper. She wore a size XXXL; she was adorable, but really not slim.

When he got on the plane, he hadn't had time to look for his seat. The company had "spotted" him and insisted on putting him in first class: "Sorry about the flight over, but we're going to try to make it up to you."

Mallock had ambiguous feelings with regard to this fame. The antisocial part of him hated being recognized or approached in the street. Since the 1980s, the media had paid attention almost exclusively to self-declared VIPs and brainless celebrities. Being put in the same category as these mediocrities was in no way flattering. On the other hand, he couldn't deny that his new fame now allowed him to have less paranoid, more open relationships with the people he met. He had to be honest with himself: he'd long been afraid of others.

He'd been like that from the outset, and then for various reasons that had steadily piled up. This recognition, which he thought not utterly undeserved, opened up for him an area of conviviality he would never have been able to construct on his own. With what he knew about people, without that big slap on the back on their part he might never again have held out his hand to anyone . . . Now, things were different, as when you walk down the street with a dog on a leash. People smile at you and come up to you, thanks to this nice mediator.

That was how Mallock used his fame: "with a collar and a leash," and taking care that it didn't shit all over the place.

He looked at his watch and got up. It was time to see if everything was going well in the back of the plane. Given the small amount of traffic between the Dominican Republic and France, he had obtained the authorization to repatriate Manuel on a regularly-scheduled flight.

The last rows, isolated by a curtain, had been requisitioned and set up for the wounded prisoner.

Asleep, his body saturated with drugs, Julie's brother was delirious:

"My God, please! In the fireplace . . . that's not possible . . . "

The two doctors turned to Mallock, their eyes reflecting the same professional concern.

"We've given him everything necessary to calm him. He should be knocked out. In fact, every injection we've given him has just made him even more absorbed in his nightmare."

"Try something else?"

"Sorry, but to keep the toxic effects of the drugs from

becoming a problem, we have to wait a while. I'd give him Haldol, but he's already on the edge of a coma. He remains coherent, but just barely."

At that very moment, Manuel's body tensed like a bow. He grabbed Mallock's arm.

"Don't you understand? It's the ogre."

Then he fell back on his stretcher, inanimate. One of the doctors pinched his arm, then stuck his middle fingers on each side of Manuel's jaw.

"Damn, he's going under! We're going to have intubate him."

"What did you give him?"

Mallock was dying with concern. He didn't see himself bringing a cadaver or a vegetable home to Julie as the epilogue to his expedition.

"Nothing unusual," the emergency doctor replied, "rehydration solutions, valium to calm him, and analgesics to reduce the pain. These reactions can't be explained by the drugs alone. I'm afraid he's still in danger."

Mallock had a terrible foreboding:

"Did all your drugs come from Paris?"

"Of course. Why?"

"Are you sure?" Mallock insisted.

Then the other doctor said:

"To be precise, the rehydration solutions had been stolen when we arrived. But the Dominican authorities replaced them with equivalents."

Mallock paled. What if Delmont was right? Did Darbier's *brutos* really have arms that long? Just then, as if to confirm him in his most paranoid fears, the electrocardiograph sped up.

"Shit! The heart rate is taking off. We're losing him . . . "

"Ventricular tachycardia," the second doctor said. "I'm going to defibrillate him, you ventilate him. Out of the way, superintendent."

Mallock took two steps backward, then turned around and opened the curtains. The passengers had all turned around toward the place from which the sounds were coming, curious about the drama that was unfolding. Death at work, that always attracts customers.

He gritted his teeth.

Had the great superintendent allowed himself to be had, out of overconfidence, like a rank beginner?

When nothing really counts anymore, nothing has any taste, and barges full of sorrows rip up oceans of purple silk. When one doesn't give a damn about anything and nothing gives a damn about us. Just try telling superintendent so-and-so that it doesn't matter, that tomorrow will be better. Tell him all your bitter platitudes and your rose-tinted nonsense. Promise him swimming pools with children in them.

Under his funereal clouds, Mallock tries to go on living:

"I'm well aware that I shouldn't talk aloud, my dear. I must seem like a senile old man, but I miss you so much . . . "

Today, Thomas would be ten years old. Opening a can of peas, Mallock speaks to him, and his voice resounds, somber and hoarse, in the solitude of the apartment.

"You've never tasted *confit de canard*, my baby? I'm sure you would have liked it. I would have made it with little potatoes cut into cubes and grilled slowly with garlic and parsley. You'd have loved it, my little fellow."

And then there would be a cake with ten candles, and he'd blow them out and laugh.

Mallock talks and Mallock weeps.

Amélie's death reawakened in him the pain of Thomas's. And he was now mourning both of them. In fact, one after the other, in a sad kind of tennis game. When he concentrates to stop thinking about Thomas, he starts thinking about Amélie. And, on the other side of the court, she strikes him in turn. In the street it's the same thing: every child's cry reminds him of his Tom, every woman's skirt reminds him of Amélie. And then, all those faces that resemble theirs! When you lose someone, you see people who look like them everywhere, on every sidewalk. And in filmed crowds as well.

Outside, after having long wallowed in a kind of Indian summer, a substitute for spring, the weather had suddenly rushed without warning into a hard winter, an eternity of frost and ice.

In Mallock, everything is big—his belly and his heart, his hands and his fits of anger. So why would it be different for his sufferings?

His sadness weighs tons.

Heartache, sorrow.

Since his return from the Dominican Republic, Amédée has continued to live and act. To get up, eat, use his brain in service to the community. No revolt and no tears. Show nothing, fool people. Don't forget to respond scrupulously to all these smiles. And then even laugh. Laugh with others. A perfect management of appearances for an existence from which all desire has disappeared. In its place, emptiness and depression.

Ice-cold cotton swab. Shot. Morning, noon, and night, the daily injection of sadness. The coldness of the ether evaporating. Bandage. And the irrepressible desire to weep all his body's tears. To collapse in sobs, to vomit sad stuff. Amédée is well acquainted with sadness. It is a son who wakes up one morning, says, "Hello, Papa!' and then dies.

Mallock wolfs down an enormous potted duck thigh, presented skin side down. A skin lightly cut into squares to make it easier to detach it from its grease. The waterfowl comes from the Dordogne, and was prepared by Jules's mother.

Ten minutes later, he is startled by the ring of the telephone. Picking up the receiver, he says to himself that he really should adjust it. On the other end of the line, a smile is waiting for him. It's Margot Murât, or Queen Margot, as her colleagues call her. A leading journalist, she has been assuming in the meantime the difficult role of the superintendent's companion.

"You okay, teddy bear?"

"Okay," Mallock lies, because he doesn't like to complain.

And then, it's almost true; just hearing her voice makes him feel better. Margot is doubtless the only person who can get him out of his moments of complete helplessness, instantly, by the simple miracle of her voice. How should he interpret that sign?

He decides not to answer that kind of question and instead asks a different one:

"Are you coming back to Paris soon?"

"Do you miss me, Superintendent?"

"Guess."

That's the best Mallock can manage in the way of a declaration of love.

"We can see each other, if you want. I'm landing at Roissy this evening," Margot continues, "at 10:10. I've written a great report and I'm giving myself three days' vacation."

Mallock is happy, but the poor dope, he doesn't show it. On the contrary, he can't help adding an annoying question:

"And your husband?"

"My husband is not your problem."

"You know that isn't true," Amédée insists.

""You want me to get a divorce? When are we getting married?"

"I didn't say that, but . . . "

"This kind of discussion has never gone anywhere."

Margot is right and Mallock knows it. He's acting like a jerk.

"Call me when you're back in Paris," he finally says.

"Maybe. You could also come get me, Mr. Grumpy."

She hangs up without saying goodbye, annoyed. He gets a dial tone. Pensively, Mallock puts down the receiver. He's happy that he heard her voice and that he will soon be able to hold her in his arms. Even if he's sorry she's married. The superintendent has trouble with the adulterous aspect of their relations. He wishes she were free.

"And why not a virgin, too, while you're at it?" Margot would have asked him.

Mallock runs his tongue over an upper right molar.

He thinks he's finished with his past, but his past hasn't finished with him. When you finally understand that your love for your mother isn't mutual, then you decide never to make the same mistake again.

Being normal is too painful.

After returning from his first vacation with Margot a few months before, Mallock had bought the apartment over his. The big bear had decided to enlarge his cavern. He hadn't asked himself why, not for a single minute! He'd had his apartment remodeled, made into a duplex, and at the same time he'd had all the doors reinforced. He'd had his little entry door transformed into a double security door with cameras. All the windows had been fitted with bulletproof panes, and detection systems installed in each room. A second Fort Mallock, so to speak. All that just for himself?

He hadn't been able to protect Amélie.

He'd replaced his little bed with a king-size one two yards wide. Still without suspecting his secret conjugal thoughts.

The new second story, which had been completely renovated, opened out on the courtyard in a semicircle like that of the living room, and across from it, there was another large window looking out to the south on a private garden, Douanier Rousseau style. It was in this vast space that he'd set up the office he'd so long dreamed about: a center for reflec-

tion equipped with a computer and sound and projection systems, his collection of unpublished recordings of the Beatles
and, finally assembled in one place, his personal collection of
books on all the techniques of criminal investigation.

He was standing in front of the latter when the doorbell
rang.

On the security screen, a motorcyclist wearing a helmet
stood outside his door. He identified himself by looking up at
the camera. Mallock let him through the first security door and
then clicked him through the second after going down to the
ground floor. The policeman gave him a big bubble-wrap
envelope. It contained the film that had so much disturbed
Julie's brother and triggered his incredible punitive expedition
to the Dominican Republic.

In the plane, he'd almost died.

Now he seemed to be out of danger. A miracle, the emergency doctor had said. Mallock was no longer concerned
about that. He just wondered how he was going to untangle
the whole affair in a rational way. He thought it was all over,
not suspecting that the worst and most puzzling part was still
to come.

He thanked the motorcyclist, closed the security door, and
went back up to his office. The first report in the program,
which was much older, appeared on the flat screen that covered the west wall of his cave.

Fifteen images per second, black and white, jerky stride and
smiles: a group of explorers was parading, white and tall,
among an army of Haitians, small with dark faces and toothy
smiles. The film seemed to have been restored, but the gray
tones were almost completely absent. The whole thing made
you think of a Corto Maltese comic book. After the introductory scene, the cameraman had immortalized a celebratory
dance, full of feathers and makeup, towering headgear and

grass skirts. And then came a shocking sequence, the dinner. Scrawny little monkeys had been tied up and brought in. The natives attached them to bamboo chairs that they slid under the large table. The tops of their heads poked through holes that had been made in the wood. With blows of a machete, the Haitians attacked the heads and, with a twist of the wrist, sliced the tops of the poor animals' skulls off. With wooden spatulas, the guests could then enjoy their brains while they were still warm.

Mallock gritted his teeth.

He'd seen his share of dead human bodies and horrors, but even he found it impossible to bear seeing animals suffer. Like the sight of a child's body in the bushes, it made him want to kill somebody, to scream and commit suicide all at once.

The desire to be dead, to no longer be there, in any case on this planet.

Amédée remembered the little monkey playing the piano that he'd glimpsed in his dream. He didn't push his reflection any further. It wasn't the first time that such a coincidence had arisen in Dédé-the-Wizard's life.

End of the first segment of the program. The second was in color and Mallock recognized the Dominican Republic, on the other side of the island of Hispaniola.

At the very beginning of the film, women were rolling cigars, or at least, contrary to the caption, the wrappers for them. After removing the central vein of the biggest and most beautiful tobacco leaves, they smoothed out the two parts on their thighs. The film lasted about twenty minutes and in it Mallock relived the atmosphere of the factories. He even thought he caught a glimpse of the strange Zagiõ with his gleaming teeth, sitting at the entrance to a humidification room.

A second part showed a tour of the island to visit the tobacco plantations. The camera moved through villages typical of the Dominican Republic, with their houses made of wooden planks and corrugated metal; some of them were larger and made of reinforced concrete with reinforcing rods pointing toward the sky. Mallock recognized the trees painted mauve and the ads for the local beer, Presidente. Then he came to the part that had triggered everything. In a shot of an almost completely deserted square, he saw a man accompanied by two bodyguards wearing suits. The man's skin was gray and his eyes yellow and bloodshot. Mallock thought again about what he'd been told regarding Darbier's birth. At the end of the shot, he moved out of the frame without his blond eyes having noticed the presence of a camera. Had he realized that he was being filmed, he would probably have seen to it that the video and the journalist were destroyed, and the course of his life, like that of Manu, would have been totally different.

Mallock replayed the sequence several times, trying to discover a clue, a detail, that would help him escape from this enigmatic mire in which he felt he was getting more and more bogged down, swallowed up alive. Nothing! There was nothing to be seen except this bloody old man crossing a bloody square.

Was Mallock blind?

The potted duck was grilled just right.

No more fat and a perfectly crunchy skin.

Amédée put the thigh on three layers of paper towel. Then he put it on a plate before sprinkling on the hot skin a few drops of sherry vinegar, chopped cilantro, ground pepper, and freshly grated ginger.

He sat back down in front of the screen to enjoy his duck.

A cultural channel was showing a very well-documented report on an animal reserve in South Africa. A young blond woman with full lips was explaining in English her strange job: she masturbated white rhinos to harvest their sperm. A new kind of white gold that the country sold at high prices to zoos all over the world. The beautiful woman mimed a mating dance in front of the animal to put him in the mood so that she could proceed to harvest the sperm.

Amédée watched, appalled. He was living in a world reduced to having nymphets in tight jeans jerk off endangered species.

It was better to laugh about it, and that's what he did.

The next morning, Anita rang his doorbell at eight o'clock sharp. Mallock's housekeeper was Mauritanian, and had always been extremely punctual. Small and very buxom, she had a vase-shaped face, a vast black moon. All the good will in the world was reflected in her face. She took care of Mallock's cave as though it were the most precious of palaces, and of Amédée as though he were the last of the Merovingian kings. Sometimes she prepared little dishes "from down there" for him and put them in his freezer, so that he wouldn't die of hunger. She was a gem, a black pearl, a marvel of humanity and kindness. Between Mallock and her a bond of fidelity had been woven that was strengthened by an affection that consisted essentially of silences shared and smiles exchanged.

"Good morning, Superintendent. I hope I didn't wake you up?"

"Well, actually you did; for once I slept like a log," Mallock yawned.

"How was your trip? Not too difficult?"

What answer could he give?

"Let's say that I'm not sorry to be back to my apartment and my Anita."

The Mauritanian woman blushed with pleasure. Or at least Mallock supposed she did. He took advantage of this to return to his bedroom and take out of his suitcase a colored top in size XXXL.

"A little souvenir from over there for my Anita," Amédée announced.

"Monsieur, you're too kind! My God, how beautiful it is!"

Mallock assured her that it wasn't anything much. Nonetheless, he received two big, smacking kisses in gratitude.

"Shall I make you breakfast?"

"Thanks very much, but I've got an appointment on the square with one of my collaborators and a friend."

In fact, Mallock had decided to follow Manuel's trial very closely. He had set only one condition: he would never have anything whatever to do with any lawyer, prosecutor, or judge. Julie and Kiko, Manu's wife, would serve as an interface between him and this world that he'd come to detest.

How had justice managed to become so vague? The lawyers, who were chiefly involved in clientelism, did not know their briefs, judges were subject to influences, and most of the judgments were stained by ideological subjectivity, money, and incompetence. Confusions of genres, confusions of punishments, confusions of minds. The commercial tribunals were a bad joke, and the criminal courts as well. If to that the frenzied influence of the media was added, one arrived at a game that should never be played!

For Mallock, the matter was settled.

The current situation could be a defendant's worst enemy or his best friend. Double-edged sword. If justice was blind, it was unfortunately not deaf to the crowd's cathartic howls, nor to those of demagogues of all kinds. The mote and the beam: things changed their dimensions totally depending on the camp to which one belonged. With the arrival of the twenty-first century, objectivity, common sense, and moderation were no longer more than moribund words. The solution? Accept this unhealthy game for fear of being its victim.

In Manuel's case, they had to find an "angle" that was very

demagogic and politically correct, a single one, and stick to it. Figure out a way to keep the young man from being classified on the "dark" side of the Force. If Tobias Darbier could be qualified as a "fascist" or "Nazi," his killer would automatically acquire every virtue. No matter what he had done, and no matter why.

Money would also be necessary, because it always made the scales of justice tip to the right side.

Let's make it simple: compassion and cash, and the cake is baked.

Amédée was ruminating on these dark thoughts as he left his apartment to meet Julie and Kiko in one of the cafes on the square.

The little esplanade, which gave on the rue de Rivoli, had been made into a pedestrian zone one year after Mallock bought his apartment in the rue Bourg-Tibourg. And for a few months, the superintendent had taken advantage of this to have breakfast there before going to police headquarters. Then, there had been the Visages de Dieu case, and he had stayed away from the place. Because the pharmacy across the way brought back macabre memories.

Today, he was resuming his old habits for the first time.

"Oh my God, I can't believe it. Mooosieur Superintendent!"

The owner of the Paris-Marseille couldn't believe his eyes.

"I thought you must be mad at me, or too famous to deign to continue to eat at my humble little establishment."

"What kind of guy do you take me for, César?"

Mallock had decided to call him by that name. Still his mania for giving people nicknames. César's first name was Gérard, and for Mallock, that didn't really go with his Marseille accent, so thick you could cut it with a knife. Moreover, Gérard bore a certain resemblance to the famous actor who played César in Marcel Pagnol's famous dramatic trilogy. The same generous nose and the same stoutness.

"Wow! Check out those girls," Monsieur Gérard-César exclaimed. "Damn, what lookers!"

Mallock didn't reply. Instead, he walked over to meet Julie and Kiko. He kissed them on both cheeks, at the same time casting a furtive glance at César's astounded face. The great superintendent had known far greater triumphs, but this one was not to be neglected.

Every satisfaction, even minor ones, perhaps especially minor ones, should be seized these days.

It has to be said that Julie was more than pretty in the little blue-eyed brunette way, and Kiko wasn't bad, either. She somewhat resembled Margot, who owed her Asian facial features to her Vietnamese father. In Kiko's case, what was small —her nose, her breasts, and her buttocks—was as appetizing as what was large—her black braid, her mouth, her intelligence, her legs, and her eyes.

Mallock recalled that Julie had told him that Kiko always slept with her glasses on, so that she would see clearly in her dreams! What he didn't know was that she no longer did so since her husband Manu had disappeared. Even without glasses, her nightmares had become only too painfully precise.

All three of them sat down at a round table from which they could look out on the esplanade. Julie ordered a double espresso, Kiko tea with lemon, and Mallock three fried eggs:

"Without fat and with Tabasco, please, César."

"I have only Espelette peppers."

"Then let's have Espelette!"

Mallock would have preferred to wait for the arrival of his eggs. He was already feeling nostalgic about Mister Blue's *cantina*. But Julie began the conversation:

"We've already lost the first round, between the lawyer and

the prosecutor. The issue was whether the procedure should be expedited or preliminary. Although they didn't go into the cases foreseen in the code of criminal procedure, they nonetheless agreed on a flagrant infraction by assimilation. Without our being able to oppose it, the police immediately carried out, not a simple visit to our home, but a compulsory police search. That's why I couldn't show you, as soon as you got back, the video or the prints Manu made from it."

As always, Julie's explanations were particularly precise. Moreover, she had studied law before joining the police's criminal investigation department. She had not come up through the ranks, like her companions, but entered by the high road. Mallock was glad about that. She was not easily fooled.

Julie went on:

"As you might expect, the pressures didn't stop there. Through the intermediary of the Attorney General and the general prosecutor of the appeals court, the Minister of Foreign Affairs sent orders to the magistrates of the court instructing them to see to it that 'everything is done without delay and with the most rigorous objectivity.' I was furious. The result was that Manu was charged the very day he returned, and despite his condition, by a registered letter sent by the prosecutor assigned to the case."

Julie was still angry: "Two days later, when Manu was still in the hospital, the preliminary indictment had already been written and the legal action against him begun."

Since he got back, Mallock had distanced himself from this case that made him uncomfortable. And then, it has to be admitted in his defense that he had to devote time to other investigations. Now he felt a little guilty about that. Julie was dying of worry about her brother and the acceleration of the legal procedure had greatly increased her anxiety. She needed help and support.

"I'm going to return to the case and knock on a few doors.

Darbier had no family. If pressure is being exerted, it's coming from the Ministry of Foreign Affairs. I don't understand why. There may be a trap here somewhere . . . I hope they haven't hidden things from us."

César interrupted them to set their tea, coffee, and fried eggs in front of them:

"Bon appétit, Superintendent. I've also given you a bottle of worecheustèreusôce."

There wasn't time to laugh at his pronunciation of Worcestershire sauce. Julie went on:

"We have to act very quickly, Boss. The warrants were served implacably. I've never seen article 122 applied so swiftly. A warrant for appearance as soon as Manuel landed on French soil, and the committal order yesterday. He's to go to prison tomorrow . . . "

She tried to continue her presentation of the case but a torrent of tears began to flow from Kiko's eyes. And from Julie's as well. The word "prison" used in connection with someone dear to you is one of the most difficult things you can hear. Mallock knew that very well. He felt powerless and a little ridiculous with his fried eggs and two pretty girls weeping at his table. He decided to keep quiet and let them cry all they needed to. A woman full of tears mustn't be pushed too hard. And two of them . . .

When Julie began to speak again, she had recovered her composure and lucidity:

"Fortunately, the judge has been . . . relieved. Now Judioni is handling our case."

Mallock grimaced. That could be good for Manu. But he himself would have difficulty. Jack Judioni was a media hound who would soon end up in politics. On the right or the left, wherever he was made the best offer. Being made a chief candidate in return for services rendered, that was a classic trade.

"And for Manu—where are we?"

"Antoine Ceccaldi, the lawyer my father hired, has been questioning him constantly. But unfortunately he hasn't obtained even the beginning of an explanation. Manu doesn't remember anything. He offers no reason for his act, and swears he knew neither the victim nor anything about his earlier extortions. As for the notorious statements he made when he was arrested, he doesn't understand what they mean, if they mean anything."

"Don't be furious with me, but, uh . . . what about pleading insanity?"

"We thought about it. Ceccaldi had several psychological evaluations made to see to what extent he could in fact plead temporary insanity, or base his defense on an unstable psychological profile. The results came in yesterday. Apart from his fear of the dark, Manuel was declared to be sane and responsible for his acts. And since there's premeditation, even the act itself can't be justified in that way. It's for all these reasons, Boss, that I asked you for this private meeting outside the office. We're worried sick and don't see any way out."

At this precise moment, Kiki glanced furtively at Julie. The ploy couldn't escape Mallock.

Besides, it was probably done on purpose.

"Are you going to tell me what you're hiding from me?"

Kiko drew herself up before she said:

"Well, here it is. Manu has always had terrible headaches. One day, I heard him mention a man in the building who heals using magnetization. Manu wasn't interested, but I insisted."

Looking at her, Mallock guessed that in Kiko's case the meaning of the verb "insist" must be very close to "command." Probably because of that superb mouth with finely-shaped corners and the pretty, jutting chin.

"After about ten sessions," Kiko continued, "Manu, though not totally cured, felt genuine relief. His headaches were less severe and their frequency decreased. The magnetizer explained to us that he owed what knowledge he had to a great master who practiced hypnosis under acupuncture. In fact, he never stopped telling us how much he admired Master Kong Long. According to him, Long was capable of miracles and had specialized in cases of amnesia that Western science could not cure."

"And you think it would be advisable to resort to this person again now?"

Mallock's tone was negative, almost mocking.

Kiko didn't appreciate that:

"If you have a better idea, please tell us what it is! It's easy to criticize when . . . "

Julie laid her hand on Kiko's leg to make her stop talking, and then turned to her superior:

"Boss, what would we be risking? Manu's amnesia is keeping us from getting anywhere. And then there's a good chance the jurors will see it as simple dissimulation."

Mallock had not foreseen this proposal; his plans were different.

"What we have to look for above all is extenuating circumstances. And I don't see where they can be found other than in this Tobias Darbier's past. Not in Manuel's. We have to work with what we have, and if we continue to discover horrible things about Darbier, we can always claim that Manu knew about them and that it was the shock of the killing that erased everything. That may be the truth, moreover!"

Kiko didn't give up:

"But we don't have to choose, we can do both, and we can keep quiet about Master Long's role."

"In a case like this one, with the press following everything, the lawyers, judges, and other scum, it won't be possible to keep anything quiet. They'll be on the scent before the master in question has even passed through the prison doors."

"So you're against consulting him?"

Kiko was restraining her frustration.

Mallock took a big bite of his fried eggs:

"No, I'm for it, Kiko. In our situation, we don't have much to lose, in fact, and we can do both, as you say. And then I think not all the cards in our hand are bad. Gemoni, Antoine Ceccaldi, and Judge Judioni—don't think I'm a fool, that reeks of a lobby, something I detest in general, but I start to love when by chance I can benefit from it. Like everyone else, moreover. But we're going to be walking on eggs. The court's permission to allow us our little table-turning session is going to annoy more than one person."

Her boss's agreement, the expression "table-turning," and the use of the first person plural extracted a smile from Julie.

"So, we go for it?"

"Where do we find this Kong Long?" Mallock concluded simply, wiping up with a piece of bread the last bit of yolk on his plate.

As they came out, the first snowflakes were floating down over the capital city. Mallock smiled. He loved that. He began praying that the snow would continue to fall, harder and harder, for days and days. It was one of the few joys of his childhood. It was as if these showers of cold stars had been engraved at the back of his eyes. As soon as the white flakes fell, he began to wear a silly smile, like a dog drooling before a bone.

His wish was granted. And much more fully than he'd hoped. On the night of December 3, Paris had one of its most violent blizzards ever. Gusts of wind, hail, and heavy snows attacked the capital. The window of his neighbor on the seventh floor fell in pieces into the courtyard, crushing the lovely Christmas tree that the caretaker had just set up. Police and firemen were commandeered for two days to repair or register all the little injuries of a capital that proved very fragile when nature roared a bit.

Mallock loved it.

A t 10:10 P.M., Margot's plane landed at Roissy.

She'd sworn not to look through the crowd.

Hoping that Amédée would have come to meet her was ridiculous. Besides, everything about this business was ridiculous. A big grumpy bear of a superintendent living with a dead fiancée and a son. And she, Margot Murât, a beautiful and talented journalist, who had found nothing better to do than to become infatuated with this old fellow, a sweet and depressive nutcase. *Beautiful but stupid!* she insulted herself. And beautiful, well, everything was relative. When she woke up in the morning, it took her a good quarter of an hour to put back in place everything that had gone down the drain during the night, to regain control of her hair and her eyelashes.

Much more time than she'd needed to fall in love with her superintendent.

It had happened three years earlier, almost at first sight, a sort of *coup de foudre*. Of course, she already knew him, particularly through the media, but that was their first face-to-face meeting for an interview. She'd been struck by his appearance, halfway between the simian look of a King Kong and the elegance of a Kipling, and then by his intelligence, a kind of treasure, an unhoped-for asylum. Yes, the word "asylum" was just right, because there was madness in Mallock. His iconoclastic and "drunken thinker" side could discombobulate sensitive souls.

Since then, she had suffered in silence, awaiting the slightest opportunity to see her bear, to speak with him. When she really thought about it, it wasn't him she was angry with. He had been quite decent, even a little too decent. No, it was herself she was angry with; she was a dolt, a ninny burdened with her heart's insubordinate urges and her pride's tetchiness.

Poor little Margot, she silently moans as she shifts her bag to the other shoulder. Cameras, computer, batteries, all that's a lot for a little reporter to carry. She enters the arrival hall.

Despite the promise she's made to herself, she keeps her head down but looks around a bit, just enough to scan the crowd of people who have come to meet their friends and relatives, but not too much, so that no one sees that she's looking, that she's hoping.

He's not there, she knows it.

And she knows all the reasons, even if that doesn't console her. Does her superintendent really love her? That is, in fact, the only question. She's tortured by the lack of certainty. Because she herself is very well acquainted with this feeling that forces her to lift her eyes in hope.

She frowns, bites her lip, and quickly heads for the closest exit. The automatic doors swing open, lashing her face with snow and wind.

A man turns around, fascinated.

Margot Murât is really very beautiful.

18

Paris, Friday, December 6

T hat morning, the capital awoke covered in snow. After three days of heavy and continuous snowfall, Paris had once again become a white being, a Christo-like folly, a city wrapped in a cocoon. Meteorologists couldn't remember ever seeing such a quantity of snow.

Since the beginning of the week, leaving his old Jaguar in the warmth of his garage, Mallock had happily set out on foot for 36 Quai des Orfèvres early in the morning, wearing a pair of silver Moon Boots, totally ridiculous but very efficient. From the ground to the rooftops, everything, including the balconies, trees, and parked cars, was covered with three to six feet of piled-up snowflakes stuck to one another and determined to stay there. The street maintenance crews were too overburdened with snow removal and salting the streets to be able to deal with the rest. With the exception of access to historical monuments and certain sidewalks with a high tourist or commercial value, the exits from parking garages, and so on.

The preceding evening, Mallock, forgetting for this reason to go pick up Margot at the airport, had done more personal research on hypnosis. On the net, he'd found testimonials that were both disturbing and documented. Particularly in the second issue of the *Annales médico-psychologiques*, where there was a report on the case of a woman treated in 1953, at the Villejuif hospital, whose amnesia had been cured by three of the assistants. A complete erasure of the last twelve years of her life. According to Kiko, Master Kong Long had greatly increased the effectiveness of hypnosis by doing away with its disadvantages, thanks to various techniques drawn from Chinese medicine.

Today, no Moon Boots but instead heavy crepe-soled shoes. Mallock is heading for his garage. He is going to the prison where Manuel Gemoni is being held to attend the first session of hypnosis organized by this Long character. The first in a series of five.

Not one more, the prosecutor had said.

Before leaving his comfortable nest, Mallock took time to download some Desproges, Philip Glass, and Camille onto his iPod, so he could relax. He sticks the white earbuds into his ears. The young woman's voice rises, incongruously: "In bed as in war, we're all foot soldiers."

Mallock begins to smile in a silly way.

At the same moment, an old man is heading for the same place. But he's not smiling. He's walking cautiously. Because of the snow, of course, but also because of his forebodings.

Master Long stopped practicing medicine a good ten years before, and now gives only a few lectures. Since this morning, forgotten visions have come back to him. All the massacres he survived. The genocide he escaped. He alone, while all the others perished.

What he learned about Manuel's victim, that son of a bitch Tobias Darbier, immediately touched him. The young man's declarations awakened echoes from his own past. The same memory of barbarism. All tortures, all slaughters are brothers. They share the same disgusting liturgy, the same ocean of tears. A similar alarm, the same smell of horror.

His own torturer was named Pol Pot. The Khmer Rouge's hysterical cruelty. The raised arm and index finger of child informers. The pyramids of severed heads. And the heads

thrown into plastic sacks. Genocidal socialists and revolution-
aries.

Master Long is not at ease in France. He has always resented
Western intellectuals, Sartre and his dirty hands and his
pathetic imitators gulping down champagne when the Khmer
Rouge entered Hanoi. Lenin, Mao, Stalin: the radiant "past" of
communism consisted of at least a hundred million dead.

Alongside his body, sheltered in his pockets, Master Long's
hands are trembling. Does he really want to hear the horrors
that Manuel Gemoni is going to confide to him? He knows that
whether or not there is a duty to remember, it's all going to start
over.

Rwanda, Srebrenica, everything has already begun again.

The past whispers the future to us, but we never believe it.

A few miles away, in front of the church of the Madeleine,
Julie is trying to find a parking place. The entrance to the parking garage is being cleared, and dozens of cars are already waiting. At the moment when she is just revving up to climb over a
snowbank, Kiko appears at the foot of her building.

Julie leans over to open the door for her:

"It's good of you to have come down."

"No, it's for me to thank you for giving me a ride."

The two sisters-in-law embrace each other.

They've always liked one another, but this test has further
strengthened their friendship. Julie puts the car in second and
heads, at five miles an hour, for the hospital.

Despite the tons of salt already spread on the pavement,
Paris's streets have become traps for overconfident drivers. Last
Sunday, Jules had had brand new snow tires put on the cute
4x4 that Julie's father had given her "to express to you all the
Gemoni clan's pride." He was alluding to the wound and to
Jules and Julie's active participation in the matter of the poi-
soner. But it was also a way of giving Jules, his future son-in-law,

a new car, without Jules taking offense. All the Gemonis had been worried sick when the young man had been hit by a bullet in the middle of his forehead. The miracle of his healing had made him even more popular among his in-laws.

In any event, thanks to her tires and the quality of their traction, Julie performed miracles in this icy Paris, easily passing stalled cars by going up on the sidewalks.

"Do you really think we're right to want to be all present?" Kiko asks.

"It's very important that Mallock be there. He has analytical and synthetic powers that go far beyond anything you can imagine. What Manu is going to tell us is likely to be fragmentary or even unintelligible. And then, it's not without danger . . . "

Kiko looks at her sister-in-law, waiting to hear the rest, worried.

"Mallock has asked that everything be recorded, both sound and image. These recordings will be immediately sequestered and remain at the disposal of the court. It was solely on that condition that the public prosecutor gave his assent. The revelations have to be able to be used by the prosecution, and not only by the defense. Knowing the truth is likely to allow us to do research whose results will be acceptable to the court. Two copies will be made for that purpose, during the hours following each session. Antoine Ceccaldi was furious. In his view, it was unconstitutional and not in conformity with the accused's basic rights But as the adverse party pointed out, our request wasn't either. Mallock finally persuaded Ceccaldi by making him see that since Manu is currently accused of premeditated murder, the risk of aggravating the reason for the indictment was practically nonexistent."

"Practically?" Kiko asks.

Julie no longer has any possible escape hatches.

"Don't get upset, but Ceccaldi and Mallock are not entirely setting aside the possibility of other murders."

"Manu, a killer! That's stupid, ridiculous. How can they believe such a thing? What's their game?"

"Calm down, they are far from believing that. Otherwise they wouldn't have opted for the recording."

"Without asking my opinion or agreement? He's my husband, it was for me to decide, wasn't it?"

Kiko is transforming her fear and her pain into anger, which is much more bearable.

"You're too involved in it," Julie interrupts. "But don't worry, although my opinion doesn't count, even though I'm his sister, 'your' signed agreement will be obligatory before the first session can begin."

"They could have talked to me about it earlier! Especially you!"

Kiko is furious, and her concern has just found a perfect sparring partner. And one who is, moreover, kind, very close to her, and boxing in the same weight class.

"But that's what I'm doing," Julie replied. "Everything was decided yesterday afternoon. Mallock wanted to call you but I persuaded him not to."

"Thanks a lot!"

"You don't understand. I wanted to tell you about it in person."

"And I assume I'm supposed to be grateful to you for that?"

There was a moment of silence between the two sisters-in-law, each of them in the grip of a fear that was the same but took on a different face that matched the nature of their feelings. Then these feelings slowly receded and were replaced by the shadow of a doubt, strengthened by fear, and the same terrifying question:

What if it was discovered that their Manuel was in fact a psychopathic killer?

Inside his cell, Julie's brother had finally asked himself the same question. If he had committed other insane acts, would he remember them? Hadn't he had bouts of amnesia before? How else could he explain how easy it was for him to kill without even trembling or hesitating? Was he simply crazy?

Mallock and his lawyer had put the deal to be cut in his hands. The procedure of a recorded interrogation under hypnosis, though not unprecedented in the annals of the Paris criminal police, was nonetheless exceptional, even extraordinary. It was not without risks, either. Mallock had discussed this with Manu in detail. But Manu had not really hesitated. He wanted to know, whatever the cost, what had really happened and was hidden at the back of his head. He had agreed to be hypnotized and recorded without any reluctance other than that of his modesty. Being laid bare like that before the eyes of his friends and relatives was not so easy to accept. But the stakes were too high. Years in prison without Kiko and his little Maya—that prospect was simply unbearable.

Manuel grimaced. His knees was still in a cast and his shoulder was causing him enormous pain. During the night, he'd had a nightmare. Were his wounds to blame? Or was it these images that had surged up from his past?

He'd dreamed that his hand was armed with a sledgehammer and was trying to smash carcasses. Naked, tortured bodies that he struck methodically in order to break all their limbs, the alveolar, scaphoid, metatarsal bones, the ivory of the teeth. He'd dreamed of sophisticated assemblies of ropes at the ends of which people were screaming. He had dreamed of the rending of flesh, the bloody wrenching away of limbs, the stretching out of nerves and the crack of tendons giving way.

Had he dreamed all this, or did he remember it?

In a few minutes, if all went well, he'd know. He sat up on the edge of the bed, impatient and terrified.

Paris, Prison de la Santé,
Manuel's First Interrogation under Hypnosis

A room had been set up for the occasion in another part of the infirmary. A bed, three videocams covering all the angles, two Nagra tape recorders in parallel and five white plastic chairs with names written on them: Julie Gemoni and Kiko, representing the family, Maître Pierre Parquet, representing the prosecution, Maître Ceccaldi, attorney for the defense, and Mallock.

A police officer, in this case Jules, a bailiff, and two representatives of the prison would be present in the adjoining room, where there was a small control board and three monitors.

Mallock had hesitated to choose Jules rather than Ken to assist him, but then he'd thought about Manuel's possible revelations. Julie would need him near her. It wasn't very professional, but as he grew older Mallock had seen his heart soften to the point that it resembled a big caramel forgotten in the heat of the desert.

Manuel had taken his place on the bed before the little group entered the room. His thin body was still tanned on the arms, the torso, the face, and the feet. His cast and immaculate bandages seemed all the whiter. He turned his head toward Kiko and Julie, smiling sadly at them before closing his eyes again. Mallock had the sudden, striking impression that he was looking at a painting like El Greco's *Pietà* or Caravaggio's *Beheading of John the Baptist*.

Marked by his Christian upbringing, Amédée continued to

wonder about God only out of habit and simple curiosity. If this superior being really existed, he was a God of suffering and not of mercy. An old man who had become, over the centuries, a little cynical and terribly disenchanted in view of the patent failure of his creation, a work that was increasingly contaminated by another force. These days, who except the Devil could lend any credence to the existence of God?

Master Long had often been called upon when judicial institutions throughout the world found themselves confronted by cases of amnesia that posed serious obstacles to the course of justice. Hypnosis in conjunction with acupuncture, as he practiced it, had been developed by his grandfather, who had worked in particular with the famous Charcot at the Salpêtrière. Later, with his son, he had enriched his knowledge by combining acupuncture and hypnotherapy. All his research sought to find a way to increase hypnotic hypermnesia while at the same time avoiding a disqualifying secondary effect: an increase in the memory's potential for fabulation.

The hypnosis Master Long practiced on patients prepared by acupuncture allowed him to bring to the surface the most hidden memories. More reliable than a truth serum or a lie detector, it allowed only actual facts to emerge. Master Long had only rarely failed, and he had always remained discreet. This assured effectiveness and confidentiality had made his reputation.

The old man began his work on Manuel by practicing a kind of *digitopathia* on the principal chakras and meridians. His fingers had a extraordinary power and a sort of autonomous intelligence. Under his hands, Manuel's body changed in form. His muscles relaxed and the expression of his face changed.

Two minutes later, the first sentences Manuel uttered left the audience frozen with fear. Everyone had been expecting to hear hours of incoherent gibberish, even an endless babble about his childhood, random memories in a hesitant language, but when Manuel began to speak it was nothing of the kind:

"I'm naked, lying on skulls, hundreds, thousands of bodies . . . "

His voice was muffled, hoarse. It trembled slightly. And his face had taken on all the signs of suffering . . .

"Tiny skulls. They're birds' heads. Above me, there is a perfect circle, a halo of blue and clouds surrounded by shadows."

Manu's neck twisted around to try to see the sky.

"I see a black triangle in the center of the circle. It seems to be growing larger. No, it's falling toward me! My God!"

Manuel's whole body twisted about.

"My God! I'm sinking into the swallows!"

Master Long, surprised by the craziness of this utterance, remained silent a few seconds before saying:

"And now?"

Manuel's breathing had quickened.

"I smell feathers and blood. I think . . . I think I'm dying. It's nothing, there isn't anything anymore . . . no more pain . . . it's fine . . . "

"Could you go back a few days earlier?"

Master Long hadn't finished. Manu squinted as if to see better. Then he calmed down and smiled.

"I'm at the seaside. The sea . . . It's so beautiful. It's full of gray and blue, the color of oysters in July. It's so perfect."

Manuel's face became tense again:

"There's blond silk in front of my eyes. It's the hair of a little girl in my arms. She's sucking on a strawberry candy. She's wearing a red dress with a big daisy embroidered on it . . . "

"That's perfect, go on. Do you see something else?"

Master Long had now closed his eyes in concentration.

"In front of us, there's a parade of soldiers and Roman chariots. Everyone's smiling . . . Icarus is barking."

"Is Icarus your dog?"

"No, my fiancée's."

Mallock couldn't help sighing. Now the Roman Empire! He saw his worst fears being realized. They were going to get into earlier lives. With a little luck, Manuel would be Caesar and Cleopatra would soon be showing the tip of her pretty nose.

But Master Long kept control of the questioning. He asked calmly:

"Manuel? On what date are these facts occurring, and where are you exactly?"

"We're on the coast of Normandy. There's a parade with people in costume. But we're all a little sad, especially Marie. Instead of marrying her as planned, I have to leave . . . "

"Where are you going?" Master Long continued, without showing the slightest emotion.

It was as if Manuel were drowning in his past. For him, the old professor's regular speech represented the surface of the water.

"Where are you going, please?" Long repeated.

"To Hell," Manuel finally breathed.

When he said this, everything changed. His skin was covered with sweat. He was trembling. Then his hands flew up from the edge of the bed and covered his face.

"I've put shoe polish on my body! I think it's better that way. They mustn't see me."

"Who are they, Manuel?"

"They're the dark and they'll be in the dark! I didn't know that such an obscurity could exist."

His eyes opened wide and he shouted like a madman:

"It's done, de Gaulle is flying off . . . It's terribly cold, I'm falling in the wind."

Master Long was surprised to find himself asking:

"Did you know the general?"

"What general?"

"De Gaulle?"

"Yes, the bird that flies," Manu replied simply.

A minute or two passed. Kiko had kept her hand on her mouth. Julie's lips were pale and tight. Manuel's eyes never stopped moving under his eyelids.

But what was he seeing?

"No, I'm not alone," he finally said. "I'm naked, but around me people are dressed. Very beautiful black suits . . . with glints of light."

"Where are you, Manuel?" Master Long asked again.

"In the forest. I'm in the forest with the men in black . . . I think they haven't seen the pitchfork."

"What pitchfork?"

"I have to sink it into the body of the woman, even if it's the last thing I ever do."

"What woman?"

"Her! The one who's tied up between the two trees. She must be beautiful, but terror has distorted her face. Her thighs are garroted at the groin. The muscles of her legs have been cut with a knife . . . My God! What horror!"

Despite all his efforts to keep his distance, Master Long couldn't help quietly groaning.

Manuel went on:

"I've . . . I've eaten the flesh of that woman! I didn't know. They laughed as they served it to me. Raw meat . . . I liked it. I was so hungry. Now I have to kill her . . . "

Manu's body twisted on the bed.

His legs flailed in the air.

"Fortunately, the pitchfork's tines went into her belly easily. I stuck them in again a little higher, to be sure I'd pierce the heart."

"But who is this woman, Manuel?"

Manuel was over there, confined in his infernal past.

"'K' wanted to prevent me from killing her. So I gave her a violent blow with the handle of the pitchfork and hit her face. Her nose and her mouth exploded . . . "

"Who is 'K'? Who is that woman? Could you be more precise, please?"

Long tried to bring Manuel back toward a purely factual account.

"'K' is the ogre. Triple K is written on his hand: 'KKK.' He's one of the Devil's nine reflections. I'm going to kill him, I have to. Afterward, everything will be over. The pitchfork has sunk into his forehead. Squeaking, it has slipped between his skin and his skull. I'm now pushing with all my strength. I've scalped this bastard."

Manuel smiled. And this smile was terrifying.

"There are pieces of flesh stuck to the tips of the tines of the old pitchfork. But he's still standing. I'd like to hit him again, but a pain is resounding in my back . . . "

Manu's mouth remained wide open, as if frozen by suffering.

"And now, Manuel?" Master Long said after three minutes of silence.

"Afterward? I don't see anything. Unspeakable things are happening. I remember only the moment when I found myself naked, lying on a bed of skulls, thousands of birds' bodies."

Manuel's features, which had been marked by morbid elation, had resumed a look of fear. He'd gone full circle. He began to scream:

"My God, I'm sinking into the swallows!"

Worried, Master Long bent over Manuel to take his main pulses.

"We have to stop for the moment. He's exhausted and he has completed a cycle of revelation. It would be unreasonable to begin another one."

"But isn't that nothing but a horrible nightmare?" Kiko asked.

Her voice was breaking with emotion. Julie was holding her by the shoulders and Jules, behind the two women, had put his hand on Julie's.

"No, I'm quite certain," Master Long said. "With the chakras open and the meridians freed, a man can neither lie nor invent things. So far as I'm concerned, Manuel has experienced what he has just told us about. The reality may be masked by an oneiric coding, as in our dreams. But I'm not sure even about that."

For his part, Mallock was lost and angry. Or rather angry because he was lost. Unjustly he cried in conclusion:

"If we follow you and accept your theories, Kong Long, this is not Manu's first murder. He has already killed, and in the worst of ways! Bravo, the prosecution is going to thank us for this."

The day after the first interrogation, Margot met Mallock for lunch at La Coupole.

Outside, it smelled like exhaust.

The snow and cold were making things hard for cars.

They chose a special oyster platter. He liked the little ones, fat and milky with vinegar and shallots, while she preferred them green and translucent, with lemon. He saw in this still another reason for not expressing his feelings. They were too different, it would never work.

As if people had to be alike in order to love one another!

During lunch, he listened to Margot tell him about her latest travels. She was pretty when she talked. When she listened, too. All the time, in fact. Her mouth was like an incredible animal, a red octopus that sucked and smiled, unveiling white pearls and a pink tongue from which phrases and images departed. A word, a bite, an idea, a mouthful, a burst of laughter. She breathed mental strength and a disturbing physical appearance.

He ate little and did not speak.

He watched her.

He realized that he had never really looked at her. In any case, not like this. Without worrying about the emptiness. Looking at her until they were connected only by their eyes.

His love for Amélie and his feeling of guilt had prevented him from contemplating Margot like that, in all her brilliance.

His fear of happiness as well, probably.

She was magnificent, quite simply magnificent, with her too-bright eyes, her delicate neck and wrists. Her irregular teeth. Her cheekbones, her slightly jutting chin, her wide, slightly downturned mouth. And then her tanned skin that smelled of the open air, the sea foam, and all the suns of the world.

Mallock had a furious desire to eat her up.

Suck on her little ears.

Taste her breasts and her belly.

Spread her legs and enter her.

Ejaculate in her all his joys and sorrows, his love and his infinite desire for her.

And then caress her.

Mallock and Margot reappeared in their respective offices only around 4:30. What their hearts felt during the brief truce their bodies gave one another, neither of them had ever experienced before.

And neither had their skins.

Especially their skins, perhaps.

21

Paris, Sunday, December 8

The second hypnosis session took place on Sunday. After the retranscription of the first interrogation, the prosecution had filed a new charge of "the murder and torture of an unknown person, at an undetermined date, and by means that remain to be clarified." The hypnosis sessions, instead of bringing to light possible extenuating circumstances, were producing further revelations. And, perhaps soon, further murders. But it was no longer possible to go back.

So a second session had been set up. Kiko, Jules, and Julie arrived together. They met again with Maître Pierre Parquet, the representative for the prosecution, and Maître Antoine Ceccaldi.

Master Long took his time preparing this session. He was not really nervous, but he was concerned. The wrinkles on his forehead were tenser and deeper. The first time, he'd been surprised, and he didn't like that.

As he began his questioning, he avoided returning to the episode of the woman's murder:

"Could you go back, please, to the moment when you had the little girl in your arms. You told us: 'It was on the coast of Normandy. There's a parade of people in costume. But we are all sad because I have to leave.' Could you try to find the exact date?"

"July, 1939," Manuel replied without the slightest hesitation.

"Which year?"

"1939," Manuel repeated. "Or 1940 . . . "

"Very good, Manuel. Think carefully. What was the date of the murder of this woman that you found tied to the trees?"

Manuel frowned and went on without stopping as if receiving instructions:

"May, '44."

His voice was thick, but the words were clearly articulated. There was a thirty-second silence.

"In what circumstances did this occur? Try to remember precisely. Where were you?"

Manuel remained silent for three minutes, then began to tell everything. His voice was calm. No more cries or broken-off sentences, he spoke as if he were reading from a book:

"Four difficult years have passed since my last trip to Normandy. It's the month of May. I'm a lieutenant-colonel in the Free French forces. This is not a choice, it's normal, it's my duty. I've just volunteered for a more dangerous mission. I'm not afraid, I'm impatient."

Mallock grimaced. What was he going to tell them now? He couldn't decide how much he should believe these statements, whether regarding their veracity or even the interest they might have. He was beginning to be sorry he hadn't forced everyone to limit themselves to research on Darbier, as he had intended when he returned to France.

Manuel, his eyes wide open, was continuing:

"There aren't many of us. As Frenchmen, we owe it to our country to do well. My unit, ten men, is going to parachute into the interior to prepare for the landing. We are to make contact with the Resistance, assess the enemy's forces, and sabotage two strategic buildings."

Long asked gently:

"Could you give us the names?"

"The Istre bridge and the switchyard at Courcy."

Then Manu resumed his account:

"In fact, at first there were supposed to be two other groups of French forces assigned to the same tasks. But the preparation turned out to be a real hell. It was very important that none of us be able to reveal the imminence of the landing in the event that he was captured. We were attached to the SAS. The English had subjected us to a pitiless training, including torture sessions, and they kept only the twelve best men. Out of a hundred and seventy-seven, half of the men cracked and ten died. They called that 'Operation French Kiss,' British humor. But we weren't the only ones preparing for combat. Over there I met the corvette captain Kieffer and his unit, true heroes, those guys; the French Squadron, placed under Commander Bourgoin's orders; the men of the first air infantry battalion, which was operating in Brittany. Me. Yes, I think it was me. I was wearing boots and standing up straight. I was hungry. Not really scared, but eager to eat. It's hard to be hungry for such a long time!"

Suddenly, like a radio that someone has turned off, Manuel stopped talking. After a minute of silence, Master Long tried to resume the dialogue:

"Manuel, you're thirty-three years old. We're in 2002. The facts you're relating go back more than fifty years. Are you aware that you weren't yet born . . . "

"I was twenty-four at the time I parachuted into France. But my name is not Manuel."

A second of hesitation.

"Who were you?"

"Who am I?"

"Your name, please."

"Jean-François Lafitte, lieutenant in the Free French forces. Serial number 140, 651."

In the room, the silence became much denser. Everyone had received this declaration as a personal challenge. A contradiction of their innermost beliefs, a slap in the face to the rationality inherent in them all. A silence in which madness also had its place, that of a Manu lost forever in a fathomless delirium. For a quarter of an hour, the young man continued to talk about his earlier life.

When the medication began to lose its effect, Master Long stood up and said:

"Thank you very much. It is now 11:21, and we're going to stop this session."

He went up to Manu to remove the needles and begin the process of waking him. Mallock rose and invited Julie and Kiko to an informal meeting at his place. At that precise moment, he had the firm intention of doing everything he could to turn the investigation in a different direction.

He didn't yet know how.

3 P.M., rue du Bourg-Tibourg.

Everything was in perfect order in Mallock's duplex. Anita had once again put in extra hours. A bell rang. The three guests appeared on the screen of the security system's control panel. Amédée began the process of opening the security door. Between the two doors, Julie, Kiko, and Master Long took off their overcoats and the last snowflakes that were still sticking to them.

As she came in, Julie was struck by Mallock's apartment, just as she had been the first time she'd been there. She'd expected something much smaller, barely functional, and especially disorderly. The cliché you always find in crime novels. And on the floors, empty bottles and tattered newspapers. Maybe dirty underwear, if you're lucky. But on the contrary, the place was clean and refined. Few objects. A couple of pieces of furniture. Everything that could be had been built into the walls or put into drawers.

It was a bright, classy, zen kind of place.

When one has, as Mallock did, such a chaos of feelings and memories in one's head, one avoids adding to them. On the other side of his eyes, he needed flat, empty surfaces to counterbalance the tons of dirty, wrinkled stuff that filled his brain. A need for the matte infinity of the walls and the mute brilliance of objects. The garbage cans and ashtrays had to be empty and clean to contrast with the loads of damaged things and sacks of decomposing feelings that filled his belly and his memory.

On the coffee table in the living room, Mallock had made tea in a superb teapot from the late 1930s. The tea service matched, as did moreover the duplex's furnishing, which was entirely *art moderne*.

"Would someone prefer coffee, or something stronger?"

Everyone opted for tea, a house mixture composed of Suchong lightened with a classic "breakfast tea."

Mallock:

"My intention in inviting all three of you here was to persuade you to change direction. To re-center and concentrate on Tobias Darbier, to work, I repeat, on everything that might be used as extenuating circumstances."

Julie, Kiko, and Master Long drank their tea as one takes a drug. Hoping for immediate relief. They were still stunned by the morning session.

"I also wanted to suggest that we stop the hypnosis sessions," Mallock went on. "I found them too dangerous for Manu, and difficult for us who love him. But then during the lunch break I took the time to check certain aspects of his . . . revelations with two historian friends of mine."

Long didn't even look up toward the superintendent. He stirred his tea and seemed to be elsewhere.

"The names Manu gave us—the corvette captain Kieffer and his unit, the French Squadron, Commander Bourgoin, the first air infantry battalion—are all part of history. As for the Istre bridge and the switchyard at Courcy, these two sites were in fact dynamited before the landing by an unidentified commando unit."

All three of the guests put down their teacups. Mallock had caught their attention.

"And there's something else that is even more astonishing. His story of the parade of chariots on the Norman coast deeply disturbed me. Annoyed me in fact. But I found on the net a poster for the 1939 parade in Roman garb. It actually took place in various villages on the Côte de Nacre, notably in Saint-Aubin-sur-Mer. Part of the last recreational activities intended to help people forget about the phony war and say farewell to the 1930s."

Julie and Kiko sat there with their mouths open. Mallock even felt obliged to add:

"Now, if I've been able to find this information, Manuel could easily have known about it earlier."

"He'd have to have planned this incredible scenario from the beginning. And he'd have to have guessed what it would occur to us to ask him under hypnosis. That's impossible," Julie grumbled.

A silence fell over the apartment. They were all reflecting on what they knew, what they felt. Not sure what to think, they kept quiet.

Finally, suspecting that it was up to him to speak, Master Long took a deep breath, like an athlete about to lift a great weight:

"In the hope that it might help you, I'm going to tell you about my experience. But be careful to keep an open, critical mind."

He poured himself another cup of tea before beginning.

"All my father's knowledge, his works, like mine, led to certain lines of inquiry: life, death, God, reincarnation, our mental structure, what is acquired, what is innate, etc. Given the scientific quality of our approach and the number of cases analyzed, we could have transformed these lines of inquiry into a theory, even a dogma. We always refused to do so. Everyone has a right to his own convictions, his own beliefs. Ideologies, like religions, cruelly impose their certitudes. In fact, the only outcome is war. That is why we've never revealed our results. We talk about our methods, we train a few initiates, and we stop there. We do not wish our work to trouble the minds of the millions of people who believe, for instance, in reincarnation, or who reject it. What I can tell you, just between us, is that a tiny number of our patients have regressed toward an earlier life and have been able to describe it with precision. But for all that, without being able to provide us with incontestable proof. On the other hand, what proof do we have of the existence of God, of the resurrection of Christ, or the survival of the soul?"

Everyone was hanging on the Master's words.

He put four sugar cubes in his cup, stirred the liquid, and continued without having drunk any:

"Let's look at the side of the supporters of regressions. Over several hundred years, there has never been any scientific proof that can be considered . . . unchallengeable. It's a little as if the phenomenon were protecting itself against its revelation. Perhaps to keep its status as a belief? I don't know, but it's strange. If you think about it, it should be rather easy to provide this proof. You were a pharaoh? Then speak Egyptian to me. You were Marilyn Monroe? Were you murdered? By whom? Why? You were Caesar? Fine, speak to me in Latin."

Master Long turned to Kiko and Julie:

"The way Manuel spoke to us this morning disturbed me, too. Out of curiosity, has he always had this fascination for history and war in particular?"

The two sisters-in-law looked at each other in silence and then replied in unison: "No." Kiko went on: "On the contrary, you could never get him to read or watch anything that had to do with weapons."

"He can't stand war films and hates uniforms," Julie confirmed. "A phobia that can be connected with his fear of the dark and forests. He specialized in ancient Egypt. It's on that terrain that he might have wanted to 'play at' reincarnations."

Long sighed. He was familiar with all the resistance he was going to have to confront. So he took the time to taste his sweetened tea:

"Well, then, since one of us had to begin. After all the reservations I've just expressed, I have to tell you all that this morning's session, as well as the facts you discovered, Superintendent, leave me few doubts regarding what happened to Manuel Gemoni."

Silence in the apartment.

"I'm able to state that Manuel cannot lie when he is under a hypnotic process combining ayurvedic techniques and neurostimulation. And he could absolutely not remember anything other than his actual life, or else another one of his lives, even if that is, as I told you, extremely rare."

"Meaning?"

Mallock was getting impatient. Master Long hesitated.

"It's difficult to have complete certainty."

"A certainty will be good enough," Amédée said.

Kiko and Julie were looking at Master Long as if petrified by the expectation of a diagnosis of life or death.

Long finally said, apparently regretfully:

"I believe Manuel Gemoni did in fact live an earlier incarnation, in which his name was Jean-François Lafitte."

Mallock took a deep breath, looked at the two young women, and concluded:

"So even if I don't much like it, our only choice is to continue to plunge into the unknown!"

22

S mall electric heaters had been installed in the prison. The snow had almost filled all the internal courtyards, and the central heating system needed help to cope with the cold. In the medical room set up for the purpose, a third interrogation, not foreseen in the program, was about to begin.

Two days had passed since the four people had met at Mallock's apartment. Two days and two nights that had tested everyone's nerves. At 3 P.M., a new time imposed by the prison's administration, the tension in the infirmary was at its height.

What further horrors was Manuel/Jean-François going to unveil to them?

Kiko and Julie had the same downcast air. Mallock too. He really no longer knew what to do. And that was an unprecedented situation for him. Few circumstances could escape his powers of deduction and synthesis that way. Understanding and then making rapid, unhesitating decisions had become second nature for him. But here, he had to deal with a complex enigma that offered no irregularity, no crack through which he could penetrate it. And what an enigma! Gentle Manu's killing of a monster, a woman devoured alive, the landing in June '44 . . . And the KKK, Ku Klux Klan?

In fact, there would have been only one way to emerge from this impossible rebus: decide to question Master Long's techniques and start over from zero: "Stop! I'm not playing this game anymore, enough nonsense, everybody out!" But Mallock wanted to move ahead, to push further this unthinkable hypothesis of reincarnation. Driven by a somewhat morbid fascination, but also by the desire to clear things up. If he backed off now, he'd never know. Sooner or later, it would all fall apart, without his having to intervene. Or so he thought!

Master Long, who could not be unaware of Mallock's doubts, spent half an hour more preparing Manuel. He wanted to be sure that the whole process of freeing up the meridians and the chakras was performed perfectly. For him as well, the age of doubt had come.

After a long telephone conversation the day before, they had decided that the superintendent would ask the questions from now on. On the one hand, to eliminate any suspicion of manipulation, but especially because they were now entering a domain that was primarily that of the police.

They were dealing with the torture and murder of a woman.

Mallock began his questioning by identifying the suspect. A classic method: the policeman, a cigarette hanging out of his mouth, makes a little pile of papers separated by carbon copies, taps them horizontally and then vertically on his desk to square them up, then slips them into his typewriter. After rotating the platen, he puts his hands on the keys, lifts his eyes, and asks: "Last name, first name, date of birth?"

But Mallock addressed the recording system:

"December 10, 2002, 3 P.M., interrogation of the accused, Manuel Gemoni, by Superintendent Amédée Mallock, in the presence of the persons registered in the log."

Then without further ado, he asked Manuel:

"Your name, age, and occupation?"

"Jean-François Lafitte, twenty-four years old, lieutenant in the Free French forces, serial number 140, 651."

"Why did you execute an old man named Tobias Darbier in the Dominican Republic?"

"He had tortured and murdered me."

Mallock felt this sentence like a slap in the face and wanted to counterattack:

"And this woman, the woman you tortured and killed with a pitchfork, what had she done to you?"

"I didn't torture her . . . I put an end to her suffering."

"You told us you had eaten her flesh. Do you confirm that?"

Manuel's face twisted with disgust:

"I didn't know that it was human flesh . . . 'K' had told us that he would grant us a meal as a favor, and then we were so hungry . . . "

"Who was that man? A member of the Ku Klux Klan?"

Manuel grimaced, astonished by this suggestion.

"No, he was an SS-man, an *Oberleutnant* . . . A monster, an . . . ogre."

"Why these three K's? Are they initials?"

Manuel frowned with repugnance. He spoke calmly and without hesitating, but he left a short pause between each sentence.

"He had a double signet ring connecting the index finger and middle finger on his right hand. It was with that that he began to hit us before bringing out the hammers and setting up his system of ropes. Across the width of his ring, three 'K's' were engraved. He never told us his real name. So we called him that among us."

"Do you remember the number that was on his uniform?" Amédée was determined to obtain as many concrete facts as possible from this further interrogation.

"I did everything I could to memorize it in case I survived."

"So what was the serial number?"

"OL 876, 482."

"Not the slightest hesitation. Mallock was a little unsettled, but he didn't show it. Despite the recording, he took the time to write down the serial number on a piece of paper. Then he picked up the packet of transcriptions typed up after each interrogation. In this case, the second one.

"I summarize: 'Four years after my last day in Normandy. I was a lieutenant-colonel in the Free French forces. I was assigned to a suicide mission. My twelve-man unit was supposed to parachute into the interior to prepare for the landing. Make contact with the Resistance, assess the enemy forces, and sabotage two strategic targets.' What happened afterward?"

Manuel's face froze into an expression of concentration, as if he were gathering together his memories.

"We jumped in the middle of the night, fear in our bellies and our faces covered with shoe polish. Not without a feeling of excitement, impatient to return to French soil. It was terribly cold, and the mission had gotten off to a bad start. The youngest of our comrades, not even seventeen years old, had crashed on the ground. We saw his parachute go up in flames. It was too dark, and we couldn't find him. There were now only eleven of us, without little Gavroche, and we had three days to accomplish as much as we could before the landing."

"Take your time. Tell me about those days in detail," Mallock said.

"The first day, everything went well, and we destroyed two objectives, a bridge and a switchyard, then we sent in a first series of intelligence data. We were proud of ourselves, excited, happy. If we'd been able to guess . . . Around six P.M. on the second day, when we were about to blow up a coastal battery in Saint-Jean, they fell on us."

"Who was that?"

"An SS unit of about thirty hardened and completely insane men. At their head was that officer with his signet ring."

"Can you describe him more precisely?"

Manu retched and then his whole body slackened. A tear began to form in the corner of his right eye.

"He was strange and very handsome, with an almost

unhealthy regularity of features. He had brown hair combed back, full, well-defined lips, a perfect nose, and not the slightest trace of humanity. I'm happy to have been able to disfigure him before he put an end to my life."

"Did your men survive?"

"They all died, massacred long before I was!"

"Could you be more precise regarding the way in which they were killed, and give us names and details?"

Mallock felt a little ashamed. He was focusing on what caused pain, like a journalist trying to make the person he's interviewing crack and thus win a bigger audience.

A tragic smile illuminated Manuel's face:

"Thibaut Trabesse, a marvelous friend, was the first one. They caught him and 'K' hit him with his signet ring until there was no longer the slightest human feature on his face. Thibaut was still alive, but he no longer had any ears, any eyes, teeth, jaws, or mouth, nothing but a mass of flesh, ligaments, and bones, his tormentor had spared his nose only to allow him to continue to breathe. And then—"

"And then?" Mallock asked.

"The bastard licked his fingers before ordering his men to hang Trabesse up by his feet. When that had been done, he went up to the body and opened up his abdomen with a bayonet. He finished his work by cutting off Thibaut's genitals. It took him half an hour to die, drowned in his own blood."

Silently, tears were running down Julie's and Kiko's cheeks. Mallock heard only the sound of the words, with just one question in his head. Was it imagination or delirium, fabulation or truth? Manuel's rapid delivery bothered him. Only honest people can talk that way without having to think too much, without lies that have to be monitored. But a few criminals can do it, too, when they've learned their story by heart.

Manuel went on:

"Afterward, he dealt with the others. I remember Gaël Guennec and Lucien de Marsac. Their courage, their terror, and their pride. The most abominable thing is that the monster was no longer really trying to make them talk. For two days, he massacred my men, one by one, with a minuteness and a persistence that left us not the slightest glimmer of hope, not even that of being shot after having confessed everything we knew. Some of them did that, but he continued to torture them as if the information had no value for him. At the end of the second day, he had a grave dug in the middle of the clearing and all the bodies were thrown into it. Only then did he begin to deal with me."

A delirious smile then appeared on Manuel's face.

"That was the moment I'd been waiting for. I'd found a pitchfork buried in the earth. Looking up toward the heavens I'd seen, like a sign from God, above the trees, a pair of luminous, almost violet eyes, those of Gavroche, the first to die in this doomed expedition. It was he who gave me the strength to make my attack. I finished off the woman they'd captured and then spun around to attack the ogre with tremendous blows of my pitchfork."

"But you were alone against thirty men, right?"

"Maybe more, I didn't count them. I received some unexpected help: his own dogs, a couple of rather terrifying Dobermans. They were enormous, with different-colored eyes and a spot of blond on top of their heads, like a third eye. Incredibly enough, they attacked him and bit everyone who came toward me, including 'K,' while I was trying to kill him. Unfortunately, he survived the attack and took his revenge on me. And on the dogs, too, moreover."

Then Manuel began to describe with terrifying precision all the details of the tortures that were inflicted on him. In the room, people's throats were tight, their jaws clenched. He depicted each blow, each fractured bone, each amputation, as well as what he had felt at each stage. Mallock hesitated to interrupt his account even to let Kiko and Julie leave.

"But he stopped after a few hours, probably because he was no longer strong enough. He had lost a great deal of blood. I lay along a tree, a chestnut, I think, while he recuperated. There, I no longer really remember. I believe the dogs attacked me, and then I don't know anymore. When he came back out, he ordered his men to take me to the well and throw me in. But instead of crashing on the bottom or being drowned, I landed on something soft, rather like a mattress. Night had not yet fallen, and I could see a circle of blue sky above me. I turned my head and realized that I had landed on a multitude of dead birds. By their wings, I identified them as swallows. There were thousands of them, little skeletons, skulls, and feathers. Lifting my head to see the sky again one last time, I saw a black triangle appear, probably a stone held by four arms They threw it on me, and I believe I died at that moment."

"Where was this clearing?" Mallock asked, intrigued.

Wells and swallows? These two words were both present and coded in his head. Another one of his intuitions?

"In the forest of Biellanie, in the middle of the Pays d'Auge. Practically equidistant between Saint-Lyon and a hamlet just outside Vignon."

"How can you be so precise?"

"I was in charge of the maps. It was part of my role as lieutenant to always know exactly where I was leading my men. This time, I led them directly into Hell."

At that moment, Mallock prepared to leap.

He asked the question that had been burning his lips for such a long time:

"What is the relation between what you have just told us and your misadventure in the Dominican Republic, sixty years later?"

Manu didn't hesitate a second:

"It's obvious: 'K,' the ogre! He's the one I shot on the square. I killed Tobias Darbier because he killed me . . . and because he murdered all my men."

Mallock sighed. In the end, at least there had been a kind of logic in Manu's delirium. But that wasn't going to help him. How could he construct a defense on that basis?

Amédée gave a hard look at the professor, who approved this silent request. It was time to put an end to this third session. Manuel was covered with sweat and his heart was pounding. The other people present were in no better condition. They all seemed to be awakening from the most grueling of nightmares. As he had earlier, Jules was trying to console Julie and Kiko. The lawyer put his papers in his briefcase, taking long enough to regain his composure and make his hands stop trembling.

"3:57 P.M., end of the third interrogation of Manuel Gemoni, conducted by Superintendent Amédée Mallock," the latter said for the recording equipment.

A technician stopped the recording and the participants in this difficult session left the room without saying a word.

Outside, snow was falling in tiny, scattered flakes. Mallock had decided to go home on foot. It was quite a long walk, but he needed time to think with his head in the cool, fresh air. He'd hesitated to take a taxi that morning. For three days his car, buried in his parking garage, had been inaccessible. The ramp was frozen. So for the trek home he'd taken along a heavy overcoat and crepe-soled shoes.

Mallock had taken Julie aside and asked her to check this story about the forest of Biellanie, and, if it existed, suggested that they go there together to have a look at it. Then, the whole little group had furtively said goodbye, without looking at each other too much. Hope was no longer in their camp, and none of them had the strength or the desire to talk about it. Mallock began his long march a little too fast, as if to drive it all away. He fell flat on the sidewalk and took the opportunity to swear a bit. For several days he'd been looking for a pretext to do that.

Alone, under the falling snow, he screamed:

"Goddamned son of a bitch of a stupid shitty snow!"

His oaths didn't resound strongly enough to satisfy him. The streets of Paris were muffled, soundproofed by the accumulation of billions of crystals on the buildings and pavement. With all the strength of his lungs he shouted: "Shiiiiiiit!"— which did not resound much more than his first effort.

He got up and resumed his walk, angrily brushing off the snow that had adhered to his overcoat. It was not only his inability to help Manuel that had put him in such a state, nor even his sadness about Julie and Kiko. There was something else. He was experiencing, without being able to defend himself against it, a regular attack by the most militant irrationality. His world of deduction and synthesis could handle intuitions and even visions without too much difficulty, but no more. And here he had to cope with something quite different. What troubled him the most was the perfect coherence of Manuel's remarks and the precision of the details he'd given. He hadn't yet checked them, but he knew that a liar always uses the vaguest possible words and approximations.

He'd had the Calmel sisters, semiologists and friends of his, listen to the transcription of the first two interviews. They had been clear: "So far as we're concerned, your guy is not lying."

Trained as psychiatrists, the two semiologists had gone together to the United States to study and write an essay on the semantics of criminal discourse and thus create a new profession, a new weapon to be used against murderers. How, for example, could the criminal's real intentions be deciphered? They proposed to carry out linguistic analyses, such as the

"pronominalization of discourse" or its "cognitive dissonances."
And to find the "point of congruence" that would allow them
to put an end, for instance, to a hostage situation. These same
exercises were also intended to study the messages left or sent
by serial killers, as well as telephone conversations among
criminals. A special unit using these techniques to arrest criminals had just been set up in the United States, thanks in large
part to their work. In return, when Karyn, the elder sister, was
making this transfer of competence, Clémence had taken
advantage of it to increase her knowledge of behavioral psy-
chomorphology.

The latter took into account not only discourse, but everything else: facial expressions, micro-tics, heartbeats, sweating,
movements of the body, fingers, hands, legs, shoulders, and so
on. Together, the two sisters quietly developed the absolute
weapon against liars. Mallock had been watching them from a
distance, determined to ask them to join his team and be part
of the Fort. Two women of that type were well worth three
men of normal stature.

And even more, Amédée smiled as he thought about them
again.

In Manu's case, Karyn and Clémence had been categorical.
For them, an inventor of tall tales, especially in such a case,
would speak using signifiers that were more general and had
multiple signifieds. He would play on the ambiguity of meaning and use broad paradigms, highly dispersed syntagmatic
sequences. He would use and abuse ruses at different levels of
pronominalization. As for gestures and facial movements,
there was no objection. Micro-expressions that they called
"micro-tics" corresponded to the emotions conveyed by the
discourse. No grimace of shame or fear, except when he was
talking about the murder itself, and then only with a shudder
of disgust, even though he claimed to have taken pleasure in it.
His fingers were at rest, his legs heavy and motionless. Karyn

and Clémence had arrived at an unambiguous diagnosis. In their humble opinion, the man was not lying.

For his part, Mallock, who had been in the trade for thirty years, limited himself to listening to music. Without even having to undertake a textual analysis, the truth resounded in a certain way on his eardrums. And today, his thirty years of experience constantly confirmed the Calmel sisters' convictions. Manuel was telling the truth, even though that truth was implausible.

As he was ruminating Mallock had been walking alongside the gardens of the Observatory. The ground was covered with a mixture of fresh snow and melted ice. His efforts to keep from slipping were beginning to make his back hurt again. Passing in front of the Port-Royal metro station, he hesitated a few seconds. But the snow started to fall heavily in big flakes, slow and vertical. Since he loved that, he resumed his walk, wondering whether he was going to go directly home or stop off at headquarters.

Malloc realized that there was now a kind of incontestable coherence in what Manuel was saying. This story of fighting with a pitchfork could explain part of the mystery. The first blow could very well have given Darbier's nose and mouth their postwar form. The second might have caused the strange scars on his skull, which were certainly not due to his mother's teeth, as the legend claimed. Moreover, this incident removed another implausibility: the fact that no one, including the Israelis, had found this war criminal. Disfigured in this way, he had been able to escape every attempt to find him. Especially if his hair had grown back in another color, probably white, and then been dyed yellow. However, this bastard in uniform had to have actually existed. But there again, Manuel had come through. He had given "KKK's" serial number. As he had for his alter ego, Jean-François Lafitte. There was now just one priority: checking the validity of the numbers and the names given. Seeing if they corresponded to something that actually existed or had existed. Afterward, there would still be time to construct risky hypotheses or die laughing.

It was in fact to eliminate the first possibility that he went by the office to assign Ken to do this research. Which was not without irony, since the latter's complete name was Ken Kô Kuroda: KKK, as he initialed his files. A mere coincidence but one that would leave a disagreeable taste in Ken's mouth.

As for Mallock, he would never have admitted it, but he was afraid of looking into it himself, for fear of coming upon these numbers and these names, fear of seeing Manu's wild ideas in black and white in the memory of history, fear of feeling all the madness, the terror, and the fear of being alone at that moment!

That was undoubtedly why he was so gentle in giving his orders:

"I have to have all that tomorrow at noon!"

"To put it politely, Boss, I'm totally wiped out."

"I don't give a damn, you can sleep tomorrow when you're dead."

Amédée knew how to be agreeable.

He left for home without offering further explanation, entirely aware of what he had done and feeling guilty and embarrassed about having taken out his frustration on his assistant in that way. He stayed angry at himself until he got home and swallowed a double dose of sixteen-year-old Lagavulin, neat, standing in the middle of his living room, the back of his overcoat still soaked and his boots covered with snow.

23

The next day, it was a very irritated Mallock who awoke at 4 A.M. He sat down in front of his computer with a café-crème and a corona, which was also a double. It was high time for him to form an opinion regarding these stories of "reincarnation." The first step was a Google search. Four other key words: renaissance, metempsychosis, transmigration, and palingenesis.

Mallock didn't like superstitions, or religions. Believing was not his thing, not in the Lord, nor in Man, nor in all the prostrate contortions people went through to forget time, corruption, and worms. Although he had finally adopted and cherished the values of Christianity, he hadn't adopted either its deacons or its god.

Whatever trials he might have passed through, Amédée had decided that his despair would have no Church.

A 8 A.M., Mallock finally let go of his mouse, not converted, but annoyed.

Concerning the theory based on the belief in the immortality of a soul that left the body only to reappear in an animal, vegetable, or human form, he had found everything and its opposite. As many versions as there were peoples and religions.

Reincarnation had been a favorite notion among believers in every age, well before the arrival of a providential man on Earth. It was found everywhere, from Africa to Asia, by way of Dorsetshire and Bengal. An incredible muddle that each person appropriated, adopted, and adapted in accord with his ritual or spiritual ideology.

As for the accounts, proofs, and testimonies, of which there should have been a plethora, they seemed to be poor relations. Nothing serious to get your teeth into, and only one researcher worthy of the name, a certain Stevenson. This psychiatrist had made searching for clues relating to reincarnation his specialty. All that to end up saying, eleven years after the first publication of his work: "Whether they are taken individually or as a group, these examples do not constitute even the beginning of a proof of reincarnation." Even if, in most of the cases studied, "Metempsychosis remains the most plausible explanation."

Xenoglossia, the ability to speak or write in a language one has not learned, had seemed to Mallock an interesting lead. If someone wakes up one day with such an aptitude, something bizarre must have happened. But there again, not a single proven case, nothing, zero, zilch, diddly-squat, except perhaps the gift of certain prophets or disciples of God speaking, in the Old Testament, unknown languages they had not learned. And there, it was even worse, since it was not a matter of xenoglossia but of glossolalia, an amusing variety of the phenomenon, because if the subject in fact started to speak a language unknown to those around him, it was also unknown to any human person, only God being capable of understanding it. A little facile as a sleight-of-hand.

As a last resort, around 9 A.M., Amédée decided to call his old pal Léon. Léon had read everything, and he might have learned something interesting. And Mallock trusted him without reservation.

"Listen, Amédée, I'm going to send you a list of the best works, but I can tell you there's nothing transcendent. Either it's written by groupies of this paranormal stuff, and then it's anything goes, or by skeptical-scientific types, and then it's the reverse certainty, and no more objective."

"And you, what do you think?"

Long silence.

"Hello, you still there?"

"Yeah, I'm thinking . . . I don't have anything that resembles a proof in any way."

"You don't believe in it, right?"

"Uh . . . yes, I do. In fact I should believe in it, or rather . . . Wait . . . "

Then it was Mallock's turn to fall silent. He was both astonished by his friend's statement and aware that he had to give him time.

When Léon began talking again, his voice was different. The ironic tone that distinguished it from any other had disappeared. As it had on the day when he'd told Mallock his story, about the camps and his terrible journey.

"Back then, I almost died more than once, I already told you about that, and I'm not going to start complaining again. But one morning I simply didn't wake up. They thought I was dead and threw me into a grave that I myself had started digging the day before. In fact, I was in a coma . . . At least, that's the most plausible hypothesis."

The sound of a lighter. Léon was lighting a cigarette, a cornhusk Gitane at the end of an ivory holder.

"During my . . . absence, I dreamed. A helluva dream. Much more real than life. I had the feeling that several years had passed. In that other existence, I was an astronomer. My name was Domenico and I worked in Bologna. A comet occupied most of my time, that and the construction of a meridian in a church. I had a friend, Giuseppe, who was a lens grinder."

Mallock, who had looked everywhere for testimonies, particularly to xenoglossia, was not expecting to find one associated with his friend. However, with Léon, he should have been prepared for anything.

"When I woke up, it was dark and the smell was awful."

"Could you speak Italian?"

"No, not really. In fact, I don't know, I already spoke Italian earlier. My grandmother was Italian. No, I didn't notice any change in that regard."

"Too bad, I would have believed you. So, why do you believe in reincarnation?"

Another silence.

"In fact, I didn't notice anything at all unusual at the time, it was only later that I began to realize that something had happened."

Léon liked to maintain suspense. Mallock played along and waited.

"When I woke up, there were thousands of stars over me."

"So? They were already there before!" Amédée tried to joke.

"Yes, of course, but there you are. Without having learned anything about astronomy, I knew their exact placement. And better yet, I knew the exact name of each of those little pearls in the sky!"

At 11 A.M., Ken came into Mallock's office. His eyes were narrowed and swollen, even for a Sino-Pole, and he moved in a tired way.

"The baby?" asked Mallock, who had just come in.

"A hellish night. Nina had an acute earache and we kept her in our bed all night. Ninon is going to take her to the Children's Hospital at 2 P.M. to see an eye-ear-nose-and-throat man."

The little girl had barely escaped the name Ken had absolutely wanted to give her: Niwi. With a wife named Ninon, that seemed to him an obvious choice. They had compromised on Nina.

"She's seven months old, if I remember correctly? Tom had the same thing when he was a year old."

Ken's mouth hung open. It was the first time the boss had alluded to his son since the boy had died. It was a taboo subject, a national security secret. The pain the superintendent had felt when his little Tom died was engraved on everyone's mind. A typhoon carrying off a butterfly. A two hundred and twenty pound sphinx full of tears. His return to police headquarters had surprised everyone. They had thought he would never hunt down criminals again. No one, not even Dublin, had ever dared mention Thomas to him again. Ken, worried, went on:

"I wanted to know if . . . "

"Of course, you big dope," Mallock interrupted, seeing in this a way of redeeming his behavior the day before, "if the doc has to drain the ear, the poor little girl is going to have a painful quarter of an hour. Don't leave them alone, the two of them. We can get along without you. And what about my results? Did you have the time, anyway?"

"My superintendent's desires are orders. The number Manu gave you matches up. After reaching the ministry's offices on the telephone, I spoke to an official who confirmed it for me: the serial number corresponds to a certain Lieutenant Lafitte, Jean-François Lafitte. It seems that he was reported missing in '44. But they don't know exactly when or where. In fact, they seemed reluctant to tell me more about it on the phone. So I went there early this morning and snooped around. Being very persistent and using all my charm."

"I'll bet. I know you. Seducer and snoop, that sums you up pretty well."

"Go ahead, make fun of me, but thanks to my physique and my handsome face, I was able to make them tell me a lot more. This Lieutenant Lafitte is supposed to have parachuted into the interior before the landing, at the head of a unit of French soldiers with an English carrier pigeon, "Lord de Gaulle." I swear, I'm not making this up. The bird was one of 7,000 pigeons who took part in D-Day. The other names you gave me, Thibaut Trabesse, Gaël Guennec, and Lucien de Marsac are those of soldiers who were also part of this mission. It was a catastrophe, because no one came back. Worse yet, none of the bodies are supposed to have been found. They promised me a written confirmation, and maybe more details, within forty-eight hours, if we send them an official request signed by the big boss. As for the other number, it is in fact the serial number of a member of the Waffen-SS, Oberleutnant Klaus Krinkel. By an odd coincidence, he is also said to have disappeared in '44, and on French soil. It is assumed that he was killed during the landing. Nothing more! That's already pretty good, isn't it? So is that good or bad news for you? You're making a strange face."

Something was trembling in Amédée's body.

His bones and his certainties had started to crack like the beams of a ship caught in a tidal wave. A slight whistling had begun in his ears and his throat dried out in a few seconds. "Good God, for shit's sake," was the only idea of which he was still capable. KKK, Klaus KrinKle. "Good God, for shit's sake," his mind repeated to him, decidedly very inspired.

Ken continued:

"This information has never been made public. I had to really lean on them to get it. Where did you learn about it? Is it connected with Julie's brother's case?"

Mallock did not reply. He preferred to take refuge in silence.

Ken made up his mind:

"Boss, if you told me what this is all about, I'd look less like a dolt and who knows, I might even be able to help you. Even a big ship needs a bell!"

Distracted, Mallock looked at him. This last sentence

deserved at least a smile or a word of encouragement. But he preferred to end the moment of silence he'd begun in honor of his convictions that had died on rationality's field of horror.

"I don't know what's going on, Ken. And so far as the bell is concerned, as Shakespeare said, 'If a man do not erect in this age his own tomb ere he dies, he shall live no longer in monument than the bell rings and the widow weeps.'"

Ken looked at his boss.

"OK, if you say so, but what's the connection, Boss?"

"There isn't one, Ken. Just an association of ideas. Do you have anything else for me?"

"Yes, I do! Regarding hiring. Do you remember Jo?"

"Jo? The guy who slipped through our fingers in the case of Nadine's murder?"

"No, Jo, the person who worked for us on the poisoner case. Marie-Joséphine Maêcka Demaya, the big woman from Martinique?"

"Ah! Yes, the wonderful computer-criminologist and so on and so on."

Ken smiled.

"Sort of. Well, she's supposed to be available for another assignment with us, but I don't know what you want to do about it, or if we have the funds to bring her in . . . "

Mallock took only a few seconds to respond:

"So far as her professional profile goes, it's more than acceptable. But I haven't yet formed an opinion about her. Send her to me as soon as you can, I'll use my famous talents as a psychologist. You know, the ones that served me so well with Frank."

Ken risked a slightly sly smile of complicity.

"No problem, Marie-Joséphine is reliable. Very intelligent, even brilliant. Her competencies would be useful to us all, to the group."

For a second, Mallock thought about his "major," a post that had remained vacant.

"It's been quite a while since Frank was let go," Ken continued. "Even if he really screwed up, he did his part of the work. Given the whole raft of diplomas Jo has racked up in the area of legal experience, plus her competence in computer science, her sense of humor, and her reputation for hard work—"

"Okay, that's enough. Bring her in, then. Friday morning would be good. In the afternoon I've got the fourth interrogation with Manu and Kong Long, starting at 3 P.M. So, let's say morning . . . "

Mallock was already staring into space. Ken left his superintendent to his thoughts. He would have bet that he was already working on one of the crazy hypotheses he was so good at weaving.

He would have been wrong.

Amédée was simply wondering how to get to the forest of Biellanie. The streets of Paris were more snowed in than a mountain village. As for the suburbs and the main thoroughfares, the officials in charge of street maintenance and the management of the autoroutes had either resigned or hanged themselves. In this kind of weather, the little trip he planned to take was like an expedition to the Antarctic.

Then he remembered seeing a big, luxurious 4x4 under a blue tarp. It had been parked for several weeks in the third subsurface level of the parking lot reserved for police headquarters.

War booty, Dublin had called it. Well, he was fully at war. He decided unilaterally to requisition the vehicle. It would be his personal car from then on.

24

Forest of Biellanie, Wednesday, December 11

Amédée had decided to skip lunch. He'd gone to pick up Julie. At noon, they were both in the coveted vehicle, a big mustard-colored Toyota with snow tires and a ridiculous bull-bar. They were headed for the forest of Biellanie, in the middle of the Pays d'Auge.

Mallock took advantage of the situation to bring his assistant up to date on the latest information, particularly the information Ken had provided regarding the names mentioned and the military men's serial numbers. They agreed in thinking that this was not enough. It was, to be sure, very strange, and it could offer the beginning of a proof, but no more than that. Even though this glorious event had remained unknown to the general public, since Ken had found the information, Manu could have learned about it through a combination of circumstances. On the other hand, if they found something in the forest of Biellanie that had a direct connection with the revelations he had just made, they would be confronted by a very different situation.

As implausible as the facts might appear, Mallock had decided to have done, once and for all, with this nonsense about wells, Nazis, and swallows. Even if Léon's testimony had perturbed him, it was not enough to lead him to make a religion out of it. It has to be said that it took a lot to have any hope of converting a Mallock.

"In a mile and a half, you have to turn right. We're almost there."

Julie smelled good, and just for good measure she also read maps very well. Or, on the contrary, she knew how to use maps, and it was just for good measure that she smelled good.

In any case, it was a stroke of luck for Mallock. Without a GPS, but with a pretty Julie: he had a winner. The superintendent had never known how to use Michelin maps, with their complicated system of folding and their illegible hieroglyphs. This was a failing, or worse, a defect. "Look at the map before you leave" was an integral part of the complete panoply of the basic male, along with knowing how to light a barbecue, carve the Sunday leg of lamb, and knock back beers while watching soccer on television.

Julie said in a loud voice:

"We're coming into Saint-Lyon, the village closest to the forest. But the forest of Biellanie covers more than 1,500 acres. We'll have to find someone to tell us where to go."

They entered the village at 3 P.M.

It was silent under the snow.

The flakes were falling, heavy and slow, orange in the streets where the electric lamps were helping out the sky, which was now failing to do the job. Elsewhere, everything was blue. Julie and Mallock got out of their rolling fortress and ploughed their way down the main street. For the first time since the beginning of the investigation, luck was on their side. At the third house they came to, they found an old couple who said they knew the forest well.

"So far as it can be known, that place," the man said, insinuating much more.

The woman had been going into the forest for years to gather herbs, but not everywhere and never at night.

"It's not a forest where you go for walks. There are even areas where you can't go!" she explained in what was almost French.

Stirring a horrible substitute for coffee, Julie and Mallock learned a little more about the Coudret couple. After having poached for twenty years, the husband had been named game warden by the commune's mayor. He'd really had no choice, since no one but Charles Coudret dared enter into what had become a foul and inextricable jungle.

The former poacher, who was now on the right side of the law, took loving care of the forest's flora and fauna, in exchange for authorization to do a little hunting solely for his personal use.

"A well, you say?"

Mallock's first question had been direct.

"There is in fact one, but it has been centuries since it has had any water in it. It's not only filled in but practically invisible now. There must be not more than three of us in the village who know it exists. Who could have mentioned it to you?"

"A fellow who died and has been buried in it for half a century," Amédée couldn't keep from replying.

Julie went pale, whereas the man broke into laughter.

"OK, OK, it's secret, I understand! Would you like a little Calvados?"

After an undrinkable coffee whose disgusting bitterness had stuck to the insides of their mouths, Mallock and Julie accepted his offer. That might go down better. At worst, it would serve as a mouthwash and a disinfectant.

The Calvados was pink. Pink candy!

"My husband makes it," the old woman explained. "This year, the big lout used an old wine barrel. That colored it and as a result we're having trouble selling it, but . . . "

The husband, who obviously didn't like his wife to discuss this thorny subject with strangers, interrupted her:

"This business of the well reminds me of the old legend of the cemetery of the swallows."

Mallock and Julie were stunned. The nightmare persisted. Without realizing the effect that his words had had on his listeners, the repentant poacher went on:

"My grandmother told me that swallows used to come to drink at that well. They flew by and dipped up a little water. Then there was less and less water, so it was deeper in the well. One day, a swallow who couldn't fly back up drowned. Then another, and another, until they completely covered the surface of the water. The birds made this well a cemetery. When one of them was sick, it went to the well to die. I resolved to check out that legend, but I always hesitated to do it, I don't know why. The fear of being disappointed, maybe. And then it's in the middle of the forest. I avoid going there because it's a little dangerous."

"Dangerous?" Mallock asked.

"There've been wild dogs around there for years. People have even talked about wolves, but it seems that's not possible. In the 1950s, well before the forest was fenced off and entrusted to my care, there were deaths. That much is certain. At the time, hunts were organized, but they didn't catch anything except for some lousy wild pigs."

He poured more Calvados for himself, and didn't forget Mallock and Julie. In return, they gave him timid gestures of gratitude.

"If you want, I'll take you to the well. You'll never find it by yourselves. What do you say? Are you armed?"

Pick and shovel in hand, and equipped with yellow waxed coats lent by the couple, Mallock and Julie plunged into the forest, following a resolute Charles Coudret, who was carrying a wooden ladder and a hunting rifle.

The whole forest was surrounded by a barbed-wire fence and no-trespassing signs. A genuine barrier. The only practicable entry was itself barred by an enormous gate with three padlocks that the former poacher opened and then closed again after him.

Inside, the forest was in a state of complete abandonment. Trees had fallen and others had grown, intertwining with each other. Only the little trail Coudret had blazed and maintained made it possible to penetrate this wall of vegetation. More recently, the great storm that had marked the end of the last millennium had uprooted the oldest trees. In each overturned stump little frozen lakes had formed in which the roots of the dethroned kings of the forest were reflected.

"You haven't yet cleaned up after the storm?"

"It hasn't been maintained for years. Explosives would have to be used to clear out the biggest stuff, and then you'd have to go in with a bulldozer. Besides, I don't have anyone to help me!" He paused. "You've chosen your day well. People no longer know how to dress . . . "

They heard three howls in the distance. Coudret pretended he hadn't heard anything, unless it was just habit.

"Not too cold today," he went on. "Have to say that with the snow that's falling, it must be around freezing."

Julie, with a twinkle in her eye, offered a lovely climatic joke in turn:

"Still, we little old ladies don't mind wearing gloves!"

At any other time, Mallock would have smiled at this, but the place was too sinister. Like this whole investigation, in fact. Like the forest, it was inextricable and full of claws.

Charles Coudret seemed to know what he was doing. He slipped his hunting rifle under his right arm and, turning around, reassured Julie:

"Another eight minutes and we'll be there!"

But it was Mallock's painful back that received that news with the gratitude it deserved.

In fact, it was at least another quarter of an hour before they reached the clearing. Two trees had fallen across the path since Coudret's last visit.

"I'll come back with my chainsaw," he grumbled as he helped Julie climb over the obstacle.

The clearing where the well was looked different from the rest of the forest. There was practically no snow in this forgotten place, just a thick layer of muddy clay, smooth and oily. Patches of moss, greenish crusts, covered parts of this diseased skin. The whole of the leprous surface must have covered some five hundred square yards, and one really had to know the place to locate what remained of the well. A granite mouth screaming at the stars, the circle of stone hardly projected from the ground. The circumference of its teeth was six to seven yards.

Their impatience to find out what was there and the imminence of nightfall made Julie and her two companions go to work immediately, without even having agreed to do so.

With their shovels scraping and the pick screeching, they dug for a good hour without saying a word. The soil was friable and the work went fast. Around the edges of the clearing, while the sun was struggling to help the three workers see what they were doing, other howls resounded.

Coudret grabbed his rifle:

"Those are the wild dogs I told you about. We're right in the middle of their territory. Watch out, they're dangerous."

At the same moment, Mallock, who had continued to dig, grumbled:

"I think we're there."

Without worrying about the state of his suit, he got down on all fours in the mud to dig at the earth with his big superintendent's paws. Julie caught herself smiling as she watched him. One really didn't know what he was going to do next. Mallock was unpredictable, and without her knowing quite why, that made her happy.

Amédée turned around:

"Pass me two or three sample bags, the plastic ones, quick."

The young woman did as she was told, impatient. What had he unearthed? When he handed the bag back to her, she shined her flashlight on it to see better. The bag was full of birds' bodies, swallows, to judge by the shape of the wings. Weren't these little skeletons the proof that the legend of the forest and Manu's wild imaginings intersected in a single reality? Night smells were beginning to invade the clearing. Mallock and Julie looked at one another. They were going to have to take Manu's statements into consideration, and that was the problem. Where could all this lead them?

Night was beginning to fall on the clearing when they found a large stone. They spent a good half hour removing all the earth and uncovering the first layer of birds. Mallock felt a shock when he discovered a perfectly triangular form. He remembered the exact words Manu had used three days earlier: "I see a black triangle in the center of the circle. It seems to be growing larger. No, it's falling toward me! My God!"

Amédée no longer knew whether he should be glad or frightened. He felt a mixture of exasperation and excitement. He rejected the second feeling, preferring to mope in a frustrated rationalism that was more in keeping with his status as one of the Republic's main cops.

"Goddamn puzzle, what is this mess?"

A quarter of an hour passed.

No one had tried to answer the superintendent's question. Having raised and set aside the notorious stone, helped by Coudret's strong arms and the ladder he had been smart enough to bring along, Mallock had started digging again in the bird skeletons and mud. Above him, the full moon cast an almost violent light on the crumbling stones forming the edge of the well. A strong feeling mixed of unreality and earth had overtaken Amédée. He was in the swallows' well, in the midst of Manuel Gemoni's delirium.

Up above, Julie, kneeling at the edge of the hole, stared into the obscurity that covered the bottom of the excavation like blind asphalt. Mallock was no longer the eager beaver who had attacked the job without hesitation three hours earlier. He was now acting like a gravedigger or an archaeologist. No more big vertical blows of his foot on the edge of the spade. Mallock was now digging on a horizontal plane and bringing up much smaller quantities of birds and earth. He was taking precautions to avoid damaging Lieutenant Lafitte's body.

"But there's nothing down there, you fool," he murmured as he thrust the shovel into the ground.

Then the spade struck an object that for Mallock, at that moment, could only be a human bone. Julie, perhaps because she had realized the state in which her superintendent found himself, climbed down into the hole to take over:

"We have to go more slowly now. Let me do it."

In the darkness, she started disengaging the buried object. She spent ten minutes achieving her goal. A flashlight shone down from the surface: it was neither a femur nor a skull, but a cross laid horizontally, at the exact center of the circle. A cross of light-colored wood, carved and varnished. They all three looked at one another, incredulous. Two of them already knew what they were going to find underneath. Mallock took Julie's place at the bottom of the well to observe the object more closely. Although he was profoundly troubled and impatient, he decided to halt the excavation.

His voice was toneless:

"We'll come back as soon as possible, but with Judge Judioni, the forensic police, excavators, the whole show. Above all, we have to avoid procedural errors."

And it was at the very moment when he put his hands on the edge of the hole to pull himself out that the attack took place.

Bounding out of the north side of the clearing, four huge dogs were running toward the little group. Taken by surprise, Coudret had only time to put his arm up to protect himself.

The first dog sank his teeth into it. The game warden howled with pain. Amédée took advantage of this to leap back into the hole and grab his shovel. A second hound hesitated a moment at the edge of the hole and Mallock had time to aim his blow to strike the beast.

Julie shouted to Coudret:

"Try to keep him from moving!"

Seeing Julie's revolver, the game warden, his eyes closed, stopped struggling. Julie's Manurhin Police Special F1 was loaded with special .357 magnum bullets; they were much more powerful than the .38 cartridges normally provided. The young woman fired only once. A roar of gunpowder, a spurt of blood, the animal let go of the guard, shrieking shrilly before collapsing like a sack. With one beast stunned, another dead, the remaining two retreated.

"Are you all right?" Mallock asked Coudret.

"Fortunately, I had my overcoat. But with these rabid beasts, I'll have to have a shot in the ass and a few stitches."

Then he turned with a smile to Julie:

"In any case, bravo and thank you, miss. Nice shot!"

Julie smiled, but she was still very pale. The unexpected violence of the attack was now making itself felt in her veins. She'd reacted well but she'd been very scared. And then killing a dog, that was a first for her. Very unpleasant. Like her superintendent, she loved animals, and dogs in particular.

Mallock turned his flashlight on the beast's cadaver. Then he bent down to examine it. As he stood back up he growled like a bear.

"What is it, Boss?"

"A black Doberman with a yellow spot on top of his head and different-colored eyes, does that remind you of anything?"

"Good lord!" Julie's pretty mouth swore.

When he got back to Paris, Mallock found a message waiting for him:

"It's been four days, Superintendent . . . Am I the one who's a dummy, or are you a triple idiot?"

The tone was bitter. Queen Margot was going to be thirty-seven years old, and before she met Amédée, she'd often been loved, even adored. She had sometimes loved in return. But she accepted less and less the idea of a couple, and still less that of marriage. To be reduced to the status of a man's woman, his other half, what a horror! And then, she'd already made her contribution.

She expected a lot out of life, but from men she expected too much. Everything and its contrary. Like many liberated women. She wanted a knight in shining armor who also did dishes, a fearless explorer who stayed at home, something half pale, half male covered with hair, half Chanel, half diesel.

Margot was much too intelligent not to see the trap into which generations of men and women had led her. But knowing about something is not always enough, and her requirements seemed to have doomed her to never being satisfied. So she'd ended up deciding to marry Mathieu, Count of Mas de Plaissac. Maybe because he used only the name Dumas and kept both his blue blood and his fortune to himself. And then because he was tender and paid attention to her. She had accepted his proposal with tempered passion! And she'd been happy with him. But she was not in love with him enough to abandon her career as a journalist and start giving him children. She was proud, and rightly so, of standing on her own two legs. A position that few women succeeded in taking and keeping in a world in which the great gravity of things, like the burden of conventions, often required men's powerful muscles and lightweight brains.

Gradually, the gap between the cruel realities of her trips into minefield territories and her chateau life, all Angevin sweetness, had a devastating effect on her. She had tried to convince herself that she'd get used to it. The exact opposite happened. The repeated shock, each time and at the same place, right in the heart, had ended up forming the most painful of gashes. You don't move, in a few hours, from a white-wine tasting in the darkness of a cellar to a child massacred with a machete in broad daylight, without blinking and developing a terrible anger. In Margot, and perhaps because she'd tried to deny it, this rage had grown and transformed itself into a resentment against the human race in general and against her husband in particular. Against herself. She, who considered herself the most guilty of all, like a kind of double agent, a traitor to both sides.

Margot and Mallock suffered from the same malady, lucid integrity. Toward life, as toward themselves. There was the same strange emulsion in their eyes, oil and water, execration and tenderness. Disabused, but still on a war footing, she shared with the superintendent the same despairing misanthropy.

They had begun to see each other, from time to time, when she could and when he wanted. They took from one another what they wanted, a mouth, a skin, strength, reflections of themselves, phrases, and great stretches of solitude. But the little adventure had lasted. And they'd exchanged more objects, tender feelings, verbs in the future tense, and even vacations with a view of the sea. Then one day her little female brain hadn't been able to keep from saying out loud what she was thinking to herself: "Girl, you're going to have to get used to it, this tender brute with his fifty years, this weird half-bear, half-tiger, is the love of your life."

For Queen Margot, the superintendent's green eyes and astonishing humanity seemed to be a remedy for all her ills, or at least a marvelous balm. Everything in that man was too big for her to be able to resist: his heart, his suits, his hands, his angers, his mind, his nose, and his sadness, his damned character. He was like a hundred-year-old oak, still green, with enigmatic branches and big leaves full of shadows. No guy had ever had the effect on her that Mallock had. When she was near him, she was finally willing to be fragile, protected, mortal, and warm, sheltered from things that cut. She loved his compassion and the fact that he was fundamentally and forever . . . inconsolable!

That evening, Mallock didn't call her back. The incorrigible homebody won out over the lover.

And Margot remained alone.

After taking off his icy clothes, Mallock began to draw a bath before he went upstairs to send an e-mail. He wrote a nice note to Margot to explain his weariness, the late hour, and the mud that covered both his boots and his every thought. He ended with a "*Je t'embrasse,*" which, for an introverted bear like himself, represented an exceptional proclamation of fondness. "I love you" was out of the question; he could never have written that. And besides, that was a declaration that Thomas had tattooed on his heart and that Amédée reserved for him, to repeat to him every night before going to sleep. The superintendent had a heart as big as a castle, but his son and the memory of Amélie still occupied most of the rooms.

The bathtub probably was still not full.

Mallock took advantage of this to glance at the digital photographs he'd taken in the clearing. He took the card out of his camera and slipped it into his cell phone, which was connected to his Mac. Thanks to his computer-savvy friends who kept an eye on developments for him, he always had the most reliable and effective devices on the market. That's indispensable when one is, like Mallock, scared of the mouse.

Amédée opened his pictures in raw form the better to view and optimize the images taken a few hours earlier: the clearing, the well, the swallows, the dead dog, and the cross. For all the visuals together, he had only to boost the definition, the clarity, and the color, while at the same time bringing out the dark parts. Without waiting, he started printing these photos in the background. He had set aside the last photos, particularly one that was much less legible than the others. He had to do some work on that one. Taken as night was falling and in the depth of the hole, despite being illuminated by the two flashlights, the cross and the soil on which it was lying were lost in the same bunch of dark pixels. Mallock almost gave up. His bath would soon start running over, and he could photograph the object again the next day, in broad daylight.

By zooming in on the cross, he saw what seemed to be letters on it. There seemed to be three of them. At first he thought they read "8bw." The shape of the W was strange. Suddenly he swore: "What a moron!" He rotated the image 180° and read it again. Once it was right-side-up, he could read "MPF." Thus these were not Jean-François Lafitte's initials, which were what he secretly expected to find. But in any case, what would he have done with such a discovery? Other than wade still further into the irrational?

As he was going downstairs to turn off the bathwater, a signal appeared on his screen indicating that he had a call. He hesitated to respond. It was Margot.

"Did you get my message?" he asked.

"Yes, Mr. Superintendent, but I wanted to see you, tonight."

The queen didn't beat around the bush. Mallock did.

"I'm just about to take a bath. I'm covered with mud because—"

"I know, you explained that to me. By the time I get there, maybe my teddy bear will have had time to dry all his fur?"

"That could be," Mallock replied, smiling.

Seeing her so pretty, in the little window on screen, he felt his desire to see her in person, to touch her, being rekindled, And that desire was far stronger than his desire for solitude.

"Fine, I'll expect you," he concluded before hurrying downstairs to turn off the faucets in the bathroom at the last minute.

After his bath, wearing a white bathrobe and armed with three inches of whiskey, the damp bear went back upstairs to check his e-mail one last time. Ken had sent him a new report.

In sum and as expected, he'd received confirmations from the British Foreign Office and the Veterans' Association.

Both Klaus Krinkel and Jean-François Lafitte had in fact been in France in June, 1944! The French lieutenant had disappeared without a trace at that time. For his part, Krinkel, considered one of the "craziest" of the officers, belonged to one of the SS divisions. And God knows the latter had included some amazing psychopaths. But despite his charm, Ken had not been able to acquire many further details. He'd concluded that his interlocutors didn't know them, either, and proposed to contact the German authorities. To dig around in the files assembled by Serge Klarsfeld's Nazi-hunting organization. So far as Jean-François Lafitte was concerned, Ken had been able to find the young lieutenant's sister. On the telephone, she'd told him that she didn't know much, but she had given him the name and phone number of her brother's fiancée at the time of the tragedy, a certain Marie Dutin. Finally, he told Mallock that at 10 A.M. the next day the judge, the forensic team, and the rest would be waiting for him at the southern edge of the forest.

Ken wound up his report by saying: "You'll find the basics of what I dug up in the attachments. Good night, Boss. Everything's O.K." Smiling, Amédée opened the two images attached to the message.

His smile froze on his face.

Krinkel's identity card, showing his face and chest, dressed in an SS uniform, that was quite a sight! Mallock immediately felt uneasy. It took him a few seconds to recognize the nature of the impression that had gripped his guts: it was an irrational fear.

This face of a killer with slicked-back hair, close-shaven cheeks, the imaginary odor of soap that emerged from them and even the absence of the slightest whisker, and of the slightest humanity, were obscene. The impeccable creases of his uniform, the perfect seams, the signs, insignias, and symbols, each detail screamed his hatred. Each external perfection clashed with the infernal chaos that could be divined inside him. The starched collar and the ironing concealed a crumpled soul. The rampart of cleanliness was opposed to the dirtiness of the urges still retained. He was like a peaceful lake in a volcano before it erupts, like impeccable order in the service of the Devil.

What Mallock had before his eyes was nothing less than a new race of psycho killers, different from the ones he had fought up to this point. A psychopath nourished, lodged, and exonerated by a government, a fucking bastard authorized to give free rein to his most demonic instincts. The two kinds of trash in a country, the bureaucrat and the psychopath, combined in one and the same person.

Mallock had a hard time getting back to his investigation and the one question he had to ask. Was this Krinkel, whom he was gazing at in disgust, the same person as the infamous Darbier, the old man Manuel had killed? For the moment, it was hard to draw that conclusion, but it was not impossible. As for the second photo, that of Jean-François Lafitte, it left him speechless. Beyond all reason and against all logic, the young soldier who died in 1944 exactly resembled Manuel Gemoni.

The security phone's ring made him jump.

Forest of Biellanie, Excavations Conducted
Thursday, December 12

T he day before, the doorbell had surprised Mallock as he was staring incredulously at Lieutenant Lafitte's face on his screen.

It was Margot.

He'd gone downstairs to open the door. An hour later, they were sleeping beside one another. Mallock wondered how he managed to forget, each time, the happiness he felt in holding her in his arms. When he woke up, the queen was gone. He looked for the little note she always left in such cases. He searched the living room but found nothing. Disappointed, the big teddy bear deprived of honey stubbornly looked around in all the other rooms, even though everyone was waiting for him at the edge of the forest of Biellanie.

Since she hadn't left a note, he decided to write one. He opened his e-mail and typed: "Since you're constantly asking me if I miss you, I'm telling you once and for all: I always miss you!"

Then he thought for a few seconds and added, smiling:

" . . . even when I'm with you."

Once he was on the autoroute, he drove the 4x4 as fast as he could, but wasn't able to make up for his late start. Too many trucks and too much snow. He arrived twenty minutes after the time that had been set. Mallock, the punctuality maniac, the person with a clock phobia!

A little crowd was impatiently awaiting him. From Judge

Judioni to the excavator Dugnoux, from the well surrounded by earth to the dog's body. Without hesitating, Mallock blamed his lateness on the numerous toll plazas that segmented the autoroute. It was out of the question to admit to them that he had wasted time looking for a love note, and then, disappointed, writing one himself. But he had the unpleasant impression that they all knew! Otherwise, why would they be smirking? Fortunately, as a diversion, he spotted Charles Coudret's face.

His right hand was bandaged and his arm was in a sling.

"So, is it any better?" Mallock asked him, without bothering to greet the judge and his consorts.

"It'll take more than a Doberman, even if he comes out of Hell, to defeat an old warhorse like me," he smiled.

"So much the better. We're still going to need old nags today," Mallock said.

Coudret laughed.

"At your service, Superintendent!"

Mallock greeted everyone. The judge, wrinkled and emaciated, with an eternal smile pasted on his tanned face, responded with a pitiful:

"It's nice of you to have deigned to join us."

To which Amédée replied:

"The lofty magistracy before the lowly constabulary, Your Honor, it's a matter of respect."

Judioni grimaced. He didn't like it when people stood up to him and even less when they mocked him to his face. But knowing Mallock's reputation, and in conformity with his own, he preferred to give way at the beginning, the better to regain control later on.

"Okay, let's go," he yelled, his arm in the air like Alexander the Great ordering his elephants to invade a sandbox.

Mallock had no difficulty finding the footprints he'd found in the mud the day before.

"Don't worry, the clearing isn't too far away," he said, noting the delicate city shoes the judge was wearing.

"What are we looking for?" the latter asked.

"If you had time to read my memo, you must have realized that we're playing it by ear in this case. I don't like that, but I can't do anything about it."

"But still, Superintendent? Although I may be able to put up with your usual charming artistic vagueness, my superiors won't."

Goddamn viper, Mallock thought.

"Let's say, to make things simple, that one of the leads in the investigation brought me to this forest. And that whatever my doubts about the usefulness of this line of inquiry, I have to take it all the way. At least in order to be sure."

"Sure about what? If you don't mind my asking, Mallock."

About what a fucking asshole you are, Mallock decided not to say, replacing it with a simple rectification:

"I'd prefer 'Superintendent,' if that's okay with you, Judge."

Judioni let a few seconds pass.

"According to your report, we owe this chance to wade through mud at the crack of dawn to your channeling séances. Whereas no new evidence has corroborated the statements made by your Manuel Gemoni. I hope you're not leading me on a fool's errand. It would be a mistake, Superintendent, to take me for I'm something I'm not."

"Don't worry about that, Judge, I take you for exactly what you are," Mallock retorted, all smiles. "You're not risking anything in that regard. And so far as this . . . 'errand' is concerned, let's just say that in my view the very existence of this clearing, as well as the presence of a well full of swallows, are facts disturbing enough to continue to dig into this, in the literal as well as the figurative senses."

They looked at each other. Predatory smiles. No love lost between these two.

The judge looked away first, on the pretext of the roughness of the terrain.

"You're giving us a hard time, Superintendent."

"Trekking in search of the truth is motivating, isn't it? And then it's a change for you."

The attack was perverse.

Judioni preferred to talk about something else.

"To sum up, if I understand correctly, it's the young woman that your Manuel is supposed to have killed that we're looking for today?"

Mallock gulped.

How could he tell him that it was not the body of the victim but that of the murderer, imprisoned and alive in Paris, that he hoped to find at the bottom of the well?

He himself didn't dare believe it, or at least he didn't dare express the matter so crudely. He was perfectly aware that without having experienced the extraordinary sequence of events that had led him to this point, no one could understand the decisions he was now making. It was in total contradiction with logic and the long rationalist tradition of the criminal police in the French Republic. But on the other hand, you didn't lie to a judge. Especially since his threats were not empty. He knew the man. Maybe it was better to evade the issue, to delay, to be ambiguous and equivocal, indulge in vagueness, anacoluthon, and amphiboly?

Since the beginning of this case, Mallock had been very lucky and enjoyed great freedom. He had taken advantage of his notoriety to lead the investigation down paths that others would not have been allowed to follow. In normal times, with a normal superintendent, a normal judge would not have let himself be mystified this way without demanding an explanation from the cop in charge.

But after all, a guy like that doesn't deserve the truth, Mallock decided, giving one last glance at the judge's hesitant steps in his fancy shoes. He wouldn't know what to do with it. Not used to it. So after having thought about it, and in total contradiction of his good intentions, Mallock decided to lie.

"Absolutely, Judge, it's the young woman in question."

Sometimes you have to know how to make it simple.

Ten minutes' walk and a few acerbic exchanges later, the whole group arrived at the clearing. In the full sunlight, the place, though it did not have the disturbing appearance it had had the day before, still retained a good share of its mystery.

The ruined well, the hundreds of swallow skeletons, the triangular stone, and the dead dog made up a strange picture, half rebus, half enigma. "You'll never discover the secret of the swallows' cemetery!" the clearing seemed to say to the new arrivals.

After having noted the exact placement of the cross, the forensic team set it outside the well and began digging. Mallock restrained his desire to get down in the well and dig along with them. He waited, smoking a cigar, one of the *robustos* he'd brought back from the Dominican Republic. He took the opportunity to photograph the scene and to examine the cross more closely. It was in fact the initials MPF that were carved on it. And the wood had been varnished, at least three coats. At its tips there were four ornaments in gilt bronze, in the form of leaves. The work was professional, not something done hastily. On the wood one could also see, despite the time passed, what might be the remains of fingerprints, though much too faint. Then Mallock had an idea. Using a screwdriver, he started detaching the bronze tips. The metal leaves yielded easily, and the nails, though rusty, were too small to offer much resistance. Under the central leaf at the bottom of the cross, a clear thumbprint had survived. Mallock signaled to one of the forensic men and asked him to take the print. Pointless? Probably.

But in this case, everything seemed pointless confronted by a truth that escaped all discernment.

An hour and a half later, logic reminded Mallock's memories of its presence. One of the shovels made a metallic sound. It had just hit a stone. Continuing to dig carefully, one of the specialists uncovered the top of the stone. Then another stone next to it. But nothing was ever to be simple in this case. They were all expecting a new discovery. Further down, it was the rational that was waiting for them. They had arrived at the bottom of the well, and there was no body of either a man or a woman.

Hiding both his disappointment and his profound perplexity, Mallock ordered soil samples taken at different depths before slipping away to escape Judge Judioni's possible, and very legitimate, questions.

It took him barely a quarter of an hour, walking in the reverse direction, to reach his car. A tiny, lonely cloud in the form of an inkblot passed in front of the sun. Mallock shivered. In relation to Manuel's statements, he had one more cross and one less body. What the devil was he going to do with an equation like that?

A cold, platinum-colored sunlight was reflecting off all the chromed parts of his car. Since he'd come out of the forest, Mallock hadn't stopped thinking. He threw three coins in the basket at the toll plaza and swore as he floored the accelerator. He'd made up his mind. Since it seemed increasingly evident that he couldn't control events, he was going to speed them up; from now on, he was going to be the one who struck the blows. Head-butts, straight to the solar plexus.

Mallock knew how to do that.

But one question remained.

Who was the enemy here? Who was the man to bring

down? A dead Krinkel, a living Manu, or a phantasmal Lafitte? Was he going to have to plunge into the depths of the irrational or return to the shore, get out of the water, stand on terra firma, and see Manuel Gemoni for what he probably was, a deranged killer?

Amédée was well aware that had Manu not been Julie's brother, that's exactly what he would have thought and done. Wasn't it time for him to regain his spirits and follow, with his complete divisional superintendent's panoply, his favorite recipe: first an investigation, a carbon copy, then an interrogation, another carbon copy, and then bam! Incarceration? But that was just it: Julie was involved, and he couldn't let her down.

Although . . . a little part of Amédée began to murmur down deep in the great Mallock.

A flash suddenly returned his attention to the road. He let up on the accelerator, slowing the car. Too late, there was a damned radar!

What was it with this shitty society, Mallock began to grumble, in which you can no longer drive, eat, smoke, or work as much as you can, or tell the truth to anyone you want, in the words that come to you? What was this fucking purgatory in which men, reduced to the lowest common denominator, lived only emasculated, assisted, insured, Botoxed, lobotomized, obsessed with lotteries, liposuctioned, and snagged by radars? Goddamn soft life, in which people went with their tails between their legs, self-censored, and with careful steps, to pick up their registered mail or the results, duly reimbursed, of their colonoscopies!

When he arrived in Paris, Amédée was still grumbling. The sun had set, and as dark fell snow began to fall on the capital again.

So far as the case was concerned, Amédée's brain had continued to work in the background, and his mind was made up. There was only one place to dig now, and much more deeply than in the clearing: Manu's head! If the truth was to emerge, it wouldn't be from the well, but from his damned noggin. Mallock simply had to be sure that it was the whole truth and nothing but the truth, as the phrase went.

He had an idea of how to do that.

He parked his car on a sidewalk near police headquarters on the Quai des Orfèvres by ramming into a kind of mountain of dirty snow and immaculate new flakes. When he got to his office, he immediately dialed Master Long's number. Long, who wanted to do some Christmas shopping near Châtelet, suggested they meet in Mallock's cavern: the offices of the criminal police.

"It would give me great pleasure to visit Maigret's lair," he said.

"In half an hour?" Amédée proposed, only too happy not to have to go out.

"Let's say in two hours. I have sixteen grandchildren." Kong Long hung up with a laugh.

While he waited, Mallock opened the report Daranne had just deposited on his desk. The work he'd asked for when he was still in the Dominican Republic. It was, as always, solid investigative work done the old-fashioned way. Bob had looked into what Manuel Gemoni knew. Sixty typed pages, poorly presented and a pain to read, but apparently exhaustive.

The upshot was that nothing connected Manu directly with the Dominican Republic, Darbier, or any Israeli activists. Only the very insular personalities of Julie's and Manu's two grandfathers might offer something to look into. The stories told about the two old men were full of superlatives. They knew the whole world, they had defeated the Nazis practically single-handed, and they had hung out with all the godfathers of all the mafias of Italy and of the universe.

But what could he do with this information?

A single, very complicated hypothesis occurred to Mallock: the idea of a contract put out on Darbier that Manu had agreed to carry out in exchange for a small fortune or a family clan's eternal gratitude. Unless he'd been brainwashed to force him to accomplish this mission? But then why choose Manu, when there were plenty of professional killers? The whole thing just didn't make sense, and Mallock decided to drop it.

He immediately moved on to another hypothesis.

Amédée worked without stopping, and never ceased to learn things. During each investigation, no matter how modest, he analyzed every hypothesis, whether impossible or probable, with the same energy, and never failed to examine systematically all the dead ends and byways. Mallock wasn't always right, but very often he was. Too often, for those who were jealous of him. They were wrong; Mallock didn't compare himself with anyone, he assessed, tested, and challenged himself. For him, the point was not to be better than others, but simply to try to become better than he was, and never to stop trying.

Master Long came into Mallock's office carrying big bags filled with presents from the Samaritaine department store. A few pieces of confetti adhering to his goatee showed that he had come by way of the Christmas festivities and display windows. Amédée closed Bob's report and gave the professor a warm welcome. Then, without wasting any time, he began. What he had to say wouldn't please the old man, and Mallock didn't like wounding people unnecessarily.

"As you know, Master, we have obtained authorization for only five interrogations. I want to make them as advantageous as possible for our side. To ensure that, I would like the next interrogation, the fourth, to be conducted after Manu has been injected with benzodiazepines."

There was a silence that Mallock respected. Each one in his turn.

Now it was for Long to counterattack:

"Have you lost confidence in me?"

"That's not the problem. By combining your procedure with one that is, shall we say, more Western, I could make what Manuel says more credible. That's where we are at this point. We can't worry about personal sensitivities any longer. Believe me, mine have already suffered a great deal!"

Mallock realized he wouldn't have the patience to negotiate at length.

"My reticence is not a matter of defending my . . . procedures," Long replied. "You know, if hypnosis is the embarrassing past of psychoanalysis, it is also its future. Time is on my side."

"So what are your objections?"

Long made a doubtful face accentuated by his goatee. Finally he said:

"Well, apart from the fact that I don't much like chemical substances, I don't really have any."

"So we agree to use benzodiazepine to be sure?"

"What exactly do you want to inject into him? A truth serum?"

Mallock scratched his index finger and the tip of his thumb. In the bottom of the well, a spider must have bitten his fingers, because they were now itching terribly.

"I'm fortunate enough to know a specialist who has devoted his whole life to exploring the concept of reality. Raymond-Roger de Trencavel. This guy has a kind of personal obsession: truth. After thirty years of experimentation and research, he knows everything about his subject, from the precise reliability of the different types of lie detectors to the effects of LSD. Benzodiazepines, used in the dosages he has determined, produce remarkable results, but their use remains illegal, and under normal circumstances I wouldn't resort to him. Here, it's different, and we have the full permission of Manuel, his family, and his lawyer. Just between us, it would be stupid to deprive ourselves of his services. Besides, Trencavel told me that he had heard of your work. He's eager to meet you. When would that be convenient for you?"

"You have a funny way of asking people's opinions," Long said, shaking his head.

Mallock nobly concealed his personal victory behind a smile of boundless gratitude. He even saw Kong Long out of the building and helped him load all his presents into the taxi.

Nice, no?

Marie-Joséphine Maêcka Demaya breathed health and good humor through every pore of her body. She was pretty as a picture and had come to introduce herself, hoping that Commander Mallock would offer her a job connected with the Fort.

"I'm not picky, Superintendent. A little place in a corner somewhere."

Mallock couldn't help smiling. A woman like her, with such a physical appearance and an admirable mind, makes an impression. Couldn't fool him. Mallock had before him a strong personality who would never be content with a back seat. At least not for too long. That was just as well; there wasn't a single empty position at the Fort. And then Mallock didn't like back seats. Not for himself, and not for others.

On the other hand, since the sudden departure of Francis, a.k.a. Frank, there had been a chair in the royal box, the vacant place of Mallock's lieutenant, part of his "blood brotherhood," also called his "right hand," an indispensable metaphor in the limited circle of the Fort.

A hand of which Ken was the thumb, because he was always ready to participate, always smiling, and gave his "OK" in a flash. Julie, of course, was the little finger. She had the morphology and was capable of digging up the most hidden information. To her companion, Jules, Mallock had attributed the position of the ring finger. Fidelity was inherent in his every fiber. Upright and rigorous, he moved forward without asking any narrow-minded questions about life. He loved duty and work well done. His intellect, though a bit elementary, was brilliant and of the first order. But the twists and turns of the human mind, its calculations and manipulations, were not his thing. And then the index finger was Bob, Robert Daranne.

At the very beginning of Mallock's career, the old inspector, as they were called at the time, had shown him the obstacles, the hidden corners, as well as the vocabulary and the lingo that make a policeman. It was Bob who had pointed out, always with his index finger, the traps to be avoided, the ideas to be kept quiet, the men to fight or get around. Although he was irritable and brusque, there was no real brutality in Bob; instead, there was a great awkwardness, both psychological and physiological, that he had inherited from the 1950s and parents who were probably still more obtuse than he was. He wasn't very bright; his intelligence was more a matter of shrewdness and experience, or more prosaically, memory. In fact, at this point he was no longer anything but that, an old hard disk chock-full of data as precise as it was useless; everything depended on the moment and what others were doing. For a long time, he'd liked playing this role as the living memory of police headquarters. Then, slowly, he'd grown tired of it to the point of feeling as much bitterness toward those who made use of him as he felt resentment of others who thought him superfluous, even for this simple purpose. Bob was a good man who was up against what others thought of him, because he was incapable of seeing himself otherwise than as useful or useless, fit for service or not, on or off.

He was the tired but affectionate index finger of Mallock's big hand.

Seeing Joséphine come into his office, Mallock couldn't help thinking of the "middle finger," the last finger that still remained free on this hand that was virtual, to be sure, but essential for him. Jo had the imposing stature and haughty presence. He surprised himself by smiling. She would know how to stand up to adversity, how to tell people to fuck off when Mallock wasn't there. His group mustn't depend on him too much. It had to be able to exist and resist alone, and never let itself be walked all over. *Even by him*, he thought. His group was not a prosthesis at the end of his arm, but an additional strength. Fort Mallock was him, but him multiplied by five. By them. Something that Mallock wished to be, if not invincible, at least optimized for its mission: hunting down monsters.

Before she arrived, Mallock had glanced at Jo's file. As Ken had explained to him, her training had been, in fact, very extensive, a perfect complement to that of his present collaborators.

"I have trouble understanding. How did you happen to study criminology and computer science? Was there a little voice inside you? Can you tell me a bit about all that?"

Josephine took a deep breath and began:

"My full name is Marie-Joséphine Maêcka Demaya. I'm called 'Jo,' which you'll have to admit is a serious diminutive."

Big, brilliant smile.

"I'm now an investigator specialized in computer-aided criminology, an operational member of the Office of Anti-Crime Technology. My background? After two years of graduate study, I took the examination to qualify as a secretary of information and communication systems. An examination that I passed, if I may say so, with flying colors."

"So information and communication technology no longer has any secrets for you?"

"If I make a serious attempt to keep up with the field. Things move very fast in this area."

Mallock started scratching his thumb again. Damned spider.

Jo continued the description of her CV:

"One year later, I passed the exam to qualify as an engineer in the technical and scientific police. Then I was at Rosny-sous-Bois, at the National Institute for Criminological Research. There, I joined the division of computer criminology. That helped me perfect my knowledge in the domain of networks and cyber-criminology."

"You don't have training in the biological or ballistic aspect. Ken—"

"Yes, I do. I studied explosives, ballistics, biology, and microanalysis in the division of physical and chemical criminology. And then I studied drugs and toxicology with your neighbors in the Prefecture of Police's labs. I finished my training by being admitted to the last criminological division, that of human identification."

"Entomology, biology, fingerprints . . . "

"Yes, and anthropology, thanatology-odontology, and trace documents."

"Is that all?" Mallock cried, laughing.

"No. I completed a specialized program at the International Association of Bloodstain Pattern Analysts in Aylmer, Ontario, where I learned to read and reconstitute a murder by analyzing bloodstains. I then spent six weeks working for Professor Mordome and three months in the laboratory for the analysis and processing of acoustic and visual signals, at Écully, outside of Lyon. All the questions of noise reduction, voice identification, etc. My knowledge of computer science has been useful to me."

"It's true that we spent a fascinating hour together in the monitoring room during the case of the poisoner."

Jo gave him a big smile.

"I'm so happy that you remember that."

"The honor is all mine. An amazing career, little Jo!"

The adjective "little" had the excuse of being affectionate.

At 5'11", she was almost as tall as Mallock. He was impressed. He didn't know anyone with such broad training.

"To be honest, I was very lucky. I've always been encouraged and I benefited from a little . . . string-pulling."

"Tell me more about that."

"My father and mother are very important people in Martinique. That helps."

Mallock got to the point.

"What would you think of working in my office?"

So this was it. Josephine was up against the wall. "Above all, don't cheat," Ken had advised her. "Don't try to manipulate Mallock, he'll know what you're doing and he hates it. Be frank. Tell him what you want."

So Josephine said:

"Ever since your last investigation, everybody wants to join the Fort. For my part, to be perfectly honest, I want more than that: I want to be part of your team, your blood brotherhood. They've told me that there might be a position since the departure of one of their number, and that's the job I'm dreaming about. It's the only reason that I wanted to move from the gendarmes to the police."

Mallock reflected for a moment.

"You do realize that I couldn't offer you the salary level you could get elsewhere?"

"That's not the most important factor for me. My parents support me and I have . . . how to put it? another source of income."

Mallock didn't immediately pick up on this last statement.

"What is the most important factor for you?"

"Solving cases. And working with the best people in the best possible climate."

Mallock smiled. That had the merit of being clear. Ken must have briefed her.

"And what do you really not want to do?"

"Hold a position 'in' the police. Otherwise I would have remained a soldier in the gendarmerie. That is a great and wonderful body, full of highly motivated people and values. I want to use what I've learned to . . . "

"To be useful to others?"

"No, just to be useful. I want to put harmful people out of action and help victims. For my personal satisfaction. If that benefits the community, as I assume it does, so much the better."

Altruistic, but not otherworldly. That pleased Mallock enormously.

"You should come in at the rank of captain, but you know that most of your career has been in the gendarmerie, and the equivalences have not yet been clearly established. Second lieutenant at 2,300 euros a month is the best I can offer you at the moment. You would be working under Ken, on the computer side, and you'd also be wearing a second hat—the Fort's expert on criminology and its interface with the laboratory of the forensic police on the ground floor. You know them already, that will be a plus. But there are no elevators, and you'll need good legs to get from one to the other. Does that suit you?"

In these last sentences, Mallock finally stopped using the conditional.

"When do I start?" was Josephine's only response.

Exactly the reply Mallock was expecting. Marie-Josephine Maêcka Demaya had just taken the position left vacant by Francis, alias Blockhead. Mallock gained by this change, and it was going to be very important for him.

Just as Jo was about to leave his office, Mallock said:

"Ah, I almost forgot. What is the other means of subsistence you mentioned?"

Marie-Joséphine Maêcka Demaya explained it to him in all honesty, and Amédée found himself unable to react. Was there a precedent? He doubted it. Was it compatible with being a cop in the criminal division? He doubted that, too. On the other hand, he didn't feel it was for him to forbid her to supplement a salary that would be modest in view of her skills.

As a second lieutenant of the criminal police in Mallock's office, and a model at Gaultier and Lagerfeld, Jo could at least claim to be atypical.

The fourth interrogation took place without Jules or Julie, who had both been replaced by Trencavel. Mallock was tense, stressed-out. This was now serious. The patience of the judge and the authorities had its limits, and there was no longer any question of being satisfied with hypotheses.

When Manu resumed his account, this time under the twofold control of acupuncture needles and chemistry, he went to the heart of the matter.

"They're urinating on the bodies of my men. The bastards! God, they're grotesque, standing around the grave in their uniforms with their pants down. The sons-of-bitches are laughing their heads off. I'd like to be able to kill them all, but I can't even move my hands."

"Can you tell us exactly where you are?"

To make up for imposing Trencavel's presence, Mallock had diplomatically asked Master Long to conduct the interrogation.

"I don't know. I'm covered with blood. My body is alien to me, it no longer belongs to me. It's . . . it's . . . like a pile of flesh humming around me. Krinkel took revenge for my attack by tearing off my ear with his teeth. He ripped the hair and the skin from my head, too, with a bayonet. My whole body is vibrating with pain."

In the room, there were five horrified men—Antoine Ceccaldi, Kong Long, Pierre Parquet, the prosecutor's representative, Mallock, and Professor Raymond-Roger de Trencavel.

White-haired, blue-eyed, 5'2", tanned, all dried-up, with a nose like a wedge of Brie, he normally wore a perpetual smile engraved on his overly-large jaw. An heir to the Cathars and their memory, Trencavel was a direct descendant of Tédéric de Trencavel. For him, the massacre of the Cathars was not something abstract but a living trauma that had marked his heart and shaped his mind forever. For the Trencavel of today, Innocent III, Archbishop Arnaud Amaury, and Simon de Montfort were monsters on the same level as Hitler or this Krinkel. His ancestor Tédéric de Trencavel had been killed at the age of twenty-four but left a son, and his descendants regarded it as their duty never to forget. That morning it was the great-great-great-grandson of Tédéric's great-great-great grandson who had just injected his truth serum into Manuel Gemoni's veins.

He was stunned by Manu's words.

"They've set aside the body of Charles, a big blond Lorrain, at the edge of the forest, and they're playing with it . . . My God, they're . . . I can't remember any more . . . "

Manu's eyes were full of tears. Under the double control of Kong Long and Trencavel, he was theoretically incapable of lying. And for Mallock, it was the nightmare that was continuing. He had to hang on, wait for his time to come. A single, simple clue provided by Manuel would suffice to allow the investigation to finally take an acceptable direction. But in the meantime he was obliged to follow the young man, without questioning, without balking, straight ahead and farther and farther, step after step, to the very bottom of his mad fancies. He was obstinate and wouldn't omit anything. The truth still had hundreds of possible faces. They had to start over on firm ground, dig at ground level, smooth it out down to the last fact, and take samples of everything to be sorted out later. The legitimate defense of a superintendent in distress.

Then Mallock tried to trap him:

"So they threw this Charles's body in the well?"

But Manu didn't hear him. This time, he would respond only to Master Long's voice.

The latter therefore asked the superintendent's question again:

"Could you tell us, please, if they threw the remains of your friend Charles into the well?"

Manu's eyes were red with sadness and anger.

"No, not him, nor the others . . . They dug a grave in the middle of the clearing . . . That's where they finally put the Lorrainer's body . . . his body and those of all my men . . . Yes, in a big cavity, right in the middle . . . I'm the only one who died in the well, I think . . . "

"You're talking nonsense, Manu," Mallock started to roar. "There isn't anything in that damned well."

Master Long put his hand on Mallock's shoulder:

"Please, Superintendent, let me run the session."

He then reformulated, in the form of a question, Mallock's untimely interjection:

"No body has been found in the well. Are you sure that you . . . died in that place?"

Even Kong Long was stumbling over his words. Manu, for his part, seemed to be thinking before he replied. It was the first time he had done so.

"There was a circular opening above me . . . yes, a little circle of stars . . . so I must have been in the well when the triangle crushed me."

Manu had remained calm, as if impervious to Mallock's attack. Had he even heard it?

"Just before I was pushed into the well," he added, "I managed to save Marie's gift . . . it was the most important thing for me, then . . . "

"What gift are you talking about?"

"A heart, it was a heart of gold that played an air of Satie's when you opened it . . . a *Gnossienne*, I think . . . yes, a little heart with our photos inside it."

Mallock froze. Once again that feeling of déjà-vu. He'd been told about that music. It was already connected with this case. But where and when?

Forgetting again that he couldn't question Manu directly, he asked:

"How did you hide it?"

If he succeeded in finding such an object, it would finally be a proof. But of what? To do what? To deduce what?

"I had no choice, I took off the chain and I swallowed the little jewel!"

No body, so no music box. It seemed as if nothing could intersect.

But Mallock persisted:

"And what did you do with the chain?"

Amédée hadn't realized that Manu had just answered him without passing through Master Long.

"I wouldn't have been able to swallow everything, so I threw it on the ground and stepped on it so that they wouldn't find it . . . It must still be there."

Mallock tried to reassure himself a little. Between the alleged common grave and the golden chain, there would be enough evidence to justify one last investigation around the well. But if he came up empty-handed this time . . .

Manu was now beginning to speak on his own, leaving his audience stupefied.

"You know, Superintendent, I saw the ogre . . . the bastard was eating children's fingers . . . "

The macabre detail was horrifying.

"There was a blazing fire on the hearth and the walls were shining like amber," Manuel added. "It's not possible, what I saw . . . not possible . . . It's impossible . . . my God . . . impossible . . . what I did . . . "

Then he began to laugh like a madman.

Mallock and Long had enormous difficulty in regaining their composure and ordering the session stopped in order to take care of Manu. What they had felt this time was an irrational fear, a God-awful terror. The anxiety in which Manuel was immersed had spread to the whole room, and the participants in the interrogation all had pale lips and hoarse voices.

"It's dreadful," Trencavel summed up, closing his instrument case. His hands were trembling so much that Mallock had to help him. "It was as if he'd brought Lucifer into the room with him. In my opinion, this man is not hiding anything. As terrifying as it may seem, what he's telling us is, at least for him, the truth," Trencavel added.

"I no longer know what to say," Master Long remarked. "It's strange that he spoke to you directly, but it's not impossible. You questioned him the last time and your voice has remained in his subconscious."

"In any case, we mustn't take him so far. It's really becoming too dangerous, and then it's useless, isn't it?" Mallock said.

But Long contradicted him:

"On the contrary, Superintendent. Manu is clearly confronting a traumatic event. I don't know how, but we have to allow him to . . . get past this moment, express it out loud, articulate it. That may be the key. If not for your case, at least for a possible cure for him."

They parted, saying they would think about it and call each other.

Outside, what was going on in Paris—wind and snowflakes blowing furiously around—was resembling more and more the kind of snowstorm encountered in the Alps or the Juras. The streets, which cars had abandoned, were full of bundled-up people walking with their heads down. They were battling cold, blindness, and loss of balance, especially when a big gust of snow caught them from behind.

Back home, Mallock ate a quick supper and then stretched out on the couch in his office. After carefully lighting his favorite opium pipe, he closed his eyes and commanded his mind to replay, in a private show, the slightest details of the events that had taken place in the gloomy swamps of the Dominican Republic.

He had the odd impression that he'd forgotten something back there, a word, a smell, or a sound, some fact that he now urgently needed. Breathing in the poppy and the coursing of the opiate through his veins might help him free up his imagination.

For inconceivable things were still hidden, horrors that even Mallock, in his normal state, would have been incapable of guessing.

29.
Saturday Morning, December 14

After his attempt, Mallock had collapsed from fatigue, leaving the opium pipe at his feet. He'd hardly fallen asleep before finding himself embedded in a tree, wood and flesh coalesced, with Thomas in front of him, howling with fear.

The shadow of a creature was turning around his son at great speed, as if in an accelerated film. This vision alone was terrifying in itself, but afterward, it grew much worse. The shadow suddenly stopped, bent over Thomas, and broke one of his fingers. Then it attacked his limbs, one after the other, meticulously. Between each offensive, it began to revolve around him again with a shrill whistling. A sound of crinkling. Of rattling. Something midway between wind passing through a narrow passage and the cry of a swallow. Tom was calling to his father, screaming with pain, and begging him to help him. Mallock would have unhesitatingly uprooted his muscles and dislocated his body if only he'd been able to. But he was fused with the tree. After playing at length with Thomas's bones, the shadow sprinkled his torso with white spirit. Then it lit a match. Then Amédée had to watch his son burn for what seemed to him an eternity before he could finally wake up.

Wake up.

Headache.

"Serves me right," Mallock grumbled.

Three puffs of opium in a moth-eaten bear's body—that may calm pain for a while, but at a price. Raising his head, he saw the date and time on his computer screen: Saturday, December 14, 7:55. In three hours he had a meeting with his team at the Fort.

He lay back to assess his adventure in the mangroves. The opium had taken him back there. He remembered almost everything, and other things as well. The serpent, the DNA, the little hairless monkey, Satie's music, the Caribs devouring the Arawaks, the bonfires of children's arms, the mountains of teeth, the swallows, the dogs, the well, the flag, the flame . . .

Apart from a splitting headache, the opium seemed to have left no trace. He suddenly sat up on his couch, without even knowing why. That happened to him often, as when he went to open the door or answer the telephone before he'd even heard them ring. What he called his everyday clairvoyance. Once he was up, he remembered the vial the old shaman had given him. He must have gotten up for that reason. Unless he'd been thinking about his headache and the precious tablets. He went to look for the piece of amber. As he passed in front of the bar, he served himself a single malt, straight from the cask. And—this was a heinous crime—drowned it in Perrier. In a second infamy, he gulped down three mouthfuls to make the pills go down and to calm his heart a little; his blood was pulsing in his head.

Then he moved on to serious things.

He had a little goldsmith's polisher, confiscated during the somber case involving jewelry fencing. He settled himself comfortably near the window that looked out on the garden and turned on the array of spotlights he'd had installed there. They projected an even white light, as warm as that of the midday sun. Thus the colors of the objects or photos he was examining were respected. He turned on the polisher and, as he'd seen Mister Blue do, carefully began to polish the piece of amber. He took care not to touch the silver stopper. He put on a pair of magnifying glasses, confiscated from the same jeweler, licked the surfaces of the stone, and raised his arm toward the light.

The landscape was sublime.

Suspended immobile inside the stone, tiny gnats several million years old were floating in a whiskey-colored sky. If Mister Blue had seen that, he'd have had a heart attack. He had some nice pieces, too, but none that was cut and hollowed-out like that. After having fiddled with it, Amédée managed to open the tiny silver catch. The smell of the fluid filled the room.

"Good Lord!"

In a flash, Mallock saw the smile of the old woman, handing him the vial.

And he knew what he had to do.

At 11 A.M., his clothes all wrinkled, he arrived at the Fort. Julie, Ken, and Jules were laughing.

"Where's Daranne?" he asked.

His assistants looked at one another. Amédée didn't like it at all when he felt they were like that, both embarrassed and in league against him.

Julie finally said:

"He's probably still doing research on Manuel and the Gemoni family, putting on great airs of being a sneaky conspirator. Haven't you had his report yet?"

Julie had not appreciated Mallock acting behind her back. On reflection, she wasn't wrong.

"Well, yes, I have," Mallock said. "But don't take it that way, Julie, I always intended to keep you informed."

"The way you've explained the inside story on this case?" Ken asked. "We're completely in the dark. You give us research to do, but we don't have the right to know anything more."

"I also have to say, Boss," Jules added, "that we're swamped with work here. And we don't see you very much."

Amédée didn't reply for a few seconds, He hadn't been expecting such an uprising.

"What is this, a revolution?"

"No, Sire," Ken retorted, "a simple revolt. You'll have to wait for July 14 for the rest."

Which made everyone laugh and had the enormous advantage of relaxing the atmosphere.

"So, what have I done this time?" Mallock asked, giving the signal for the free-for-all.

And he wasn't disappointed.

Obviously, his absences from the Fort had been taken very badly, as had the obvious lack of explanations. He could have tried deception: "That was precisely the reason for this morning's meeting." But that wasn't his thing. And then, honestly, he deserved these reprimands. The fantastic complexity of the case and the wave of depression that had struck him since his return from the Dominican Republic had made him a zombie superintendent, leaving the Fort without any real command.

"That's enough, kids, the cup is full. I agree and I offer you my most inadequate excuses. Where do you want to begin?"

The meeting lasted four hours, without even a short pause for lunch. Since he was the accused, Mallock didn't dare complain too much. As a result, it was past 3 P.M. when his assistants finally decided they'd heard enough.

"No more questions? Are you going to let me go, or should I consider myself held hostage for the whole weekend? If that's the case, I remind you that I have a right to a telephone call and a sausage and butter sandwich."

"Hmmm . . . now that you mention it, I think it smells like fish in here, doesn't it?" remarked Julie, who had a delicate sense of smell.

Mallock took offense and thundered:

"It's I, demoiselle! I stopped by my fishmonger on the way

in, where I bought, for a great deal of money, a sublime little sea bass whose bright eyes and ruddy gills, as well as its cadaveric rigidity, can only emit exquisite ocean fragrances."

This was followed by general laughter. They all needed to relax and make peace after the verbal assault made early that morning. At the same moment, Daranne came into Mallock's office.

He was wearing an imbecilic smile under his dachshund's mustache.

"What are you all doing here? Did I miss something?"

"We've sequestered the boss," Ken replied with a grim face. "Where can we hold him until Monday? Do you have room at your place? And by the way, don't you smell it?"

"What?"

"The fish."

"Ah! Yeah, it stinks. What is it?"

"We've bought a fish for the prisoner so that he doesn't die of hunger during his detention. You wouldn't happen to have salt and olive oil on you?"

Daranne's flabbergasted look was a kind of compensation for all of them and a great moment of loneliness for him.

Half an hour later, a smile on his lips, Mallock took home four photographs, one of Darbier, one of Krinkel, one of Jean-François Lafitte, and one of Manu, taken on the day of his daughter's baptism.

At the back of the room that served as his studio, library, and office, Mallock had installed two 30-inch flat screens. On the right was a computer and a hard disk for backups. On the left was a scanner for negatives and another for opaque documents, a printer, and a 17-inch laptop. Everything was networked and connected by cable.

Although he had always been a passionate amateur photographer, Mallock had only recently gotten into digital retouching. But he'd spent his vacations boning up on various programs, including the indispensable Photoshop. At police headquarters, he let Ken, and earlier Francis alias Frank, use the equipment, without ever getting very involved with it himself. It was only at home that he touched the keyboard.

"Computers are even better when you don't have to use them," he'd been told by Vincent, his friend Jean-Claude's right hand and the official installer of the Mac'llocks, as they called them.

Around 7 P.M., Amédée decided to prepare his bass.

He cleaned the fish and filled it with sprigs of fennel, peppercorns, and salt before frying it on both sides. Then he wrapped it in foil and let it cook while he opened a bottle of Pouilly-Fumé. After taking off its aluminum carapace, he sprinkled the fish with a mixture of vinegar, finely sliced pepper, olive oil, and sea salt. On the news, as usual since the snow had begun falling, there was a series of idiots, corporations, and opposition politicians denouncing the negligence of the government and the street maintenance services. Mallock decided to eat his dinner without listening to them blab and instead to watch, for the fifteenth time, the DVD bonus of the Beatles video anthology. Paul and George, accompanying themselves on ukuleles, were singing as they sat on a bench. Ringo was marking the time by tapping on his thighs. Simple genius gathered under the banner of friendship and melancholy. Mallock swore. He would have given his right ball to be able to discover a previously unrecorded song by the Fab Four.

An hour later, regretfully, but with his balls intact, he got down to business. He sometimes brought work home. Today, he had relieved Ken of a job that he could do himself, and what was more, amused him.

He began by running the negatives of Manu and Darbier

through the slide scanner, then digitalized the photos of Krinkel and Jean-François, which were on paper, using a different device.

Half an hour later, he had the four photos lined up on the left-hand screen of his computer, and on the other screen, well-arranged, the different palettes and tools necessary for the job of retouching the images. And there was work to be done. The two prints had suffered from age, traces of stamps, and much handling. Mallock worked for a good hour on cleaning up the proofs. Once he was satisfied, two whiskies later, he took ten minutes to calmly compare the faces of the four men, playing with overlays and transparencies.

The results were clear. Although the two faces were apparently different at first glance, Krinkel's features, dark and handsome, and those of Darbier, blond and disfigured, corresponded perfectly once one made a meticulous comparison of them. The same distance between the eyes, the same high-set ears with respect to the nose, the same jaw within a millimeter or two. For Mallock, the identity of the two was not in doubt:

Darbier was Krinkel. They were dealing with one and the same person.

He'd done the same for the lieutenant and Manu, superimposing the images after having put them on the same scale. Here despite a strong resemblance, the morphology of the two skulls also disconfirmed the first impression. They did not correspond. There were a few similarities in the height of the forehead and the breadth of the mouth, but there was no doubt that it was not the same man.

Mallock swore.

Obviously! It wasn't the same person. That was impossible. What a dimwit! How could he have allowed himself to be drawn into such nonsense? In Krinkel's case, there was a logic. The former Nazi had simply taken refuge in the Dominican Republic. His age, like the rest, corresponded.

But for Manu and the lieutenant, it was simply . . . impossible.

And yet, despite that, or maybe because of it and that word "impossible," just to clarify matters and finally rule out the far-fetched hypothesis that was ruining his life, the next day Mallock found himself roaring down the road in pursuit of the fiancée of a goddamn phantom.

30.
Sunday, December 15, Visit to Marie Dutin

9:12 A.M.
Mallock is driving on the autoroute du Sud. Or at least what remains of it. After two weeks of uninterrupted snowfall, there is a seven-foot-high snowbank between the north and south traffic lanes. At the sides of the road, a kind of white, beige, and black hill now accompanies the cars.

Enclosed in this icy basin, Mallock is driving fast, much too fast. Simply because he's sick of not understanding anything, and because he's also afraid of being late for his rendezvous. You don't make an old lady wait who has agreed to meet you without even knowing you. He's always been afraid of not arriving on time. That's the way it is. Being late for the last excavation in the forest didn't help matters. He feels the fear growing and getting more elaborate, to the point of taking his breath away. Like all those who have been late one time when it was too, too serious, irredeemable. The time, for instance, when he found his mother at the end of a rope.

Amédée runs his tongue over his upper left molars, clears his throat, looks to the left, then to the right, like a windshield wiper.

In one short hour, he has a rendezvous with Marie Dutin, the lieutenant's fiancée. "I'll have to send you on your way at 11 A.M.," she told him, "it's Sunday." Mallock didn't understand at first. Now he does. The old lady undoubtedly goes to Sunday mass. How many prayers and genuflections has she made in sixty years of mourning? How many loads of tears and regrets all tied up in little packages? How many candles lit, her eyes shining?

Take the exit, the third little town, and, after the bakery, a dead-end street to the right with the sweet name of Ampélopsis.

In front of Mallock is a modest house with a blue roof. He adjusts his tie before ringing the bell. The door opens with a squeak like a cat's meow. Behind it, a little body less than five feet tall appears. The old lady standing before him is very cute, with a charming smile and a carefully made-up face. Powder, two circles of rouge on her cheeks, and mauve, almost fluorescent mascara.

"Please come in, Superintendent. You didn't have too much trouble finding me? It's not easy with all the twists and turns. But no, of course, how stupid I am! You took the autoroute. I hope you're not too tired? Oh! but you must be. It's a long way, after all. Can I make you a cup of tea? Milk or lemon? Did I tell you about the mass? At 11 o'clock sharp I'll have to leave."

As often happens with people living alone, Marie Dutin was making up for her thousands of hours of silence by asking the questions and also giving the answers.

Mallock limited himself to smiling at her and saying:

"This is really a very pretty place you have here."

That always pleases people. And then he wasn't lying, not really. "Pretty" isn't the appropriate adjective. In fact, the home of the lieutenant's fiancée is clean and tidy. Spick and span. Once you've crossed the threshold, you're suddenly transported into the prewar period. Inside, time has stopped, frozen in the furniture polish.

Everything in Marie's home is period. Her furniture, her radio, her clothes, and her makeup.

Her sadness, too.

Her Jean-François loved her like that, so she has remained

that way. Plucked and redrawn eyebrows, powder and Guerlain foundation in generous layers, mauve eye shadow, like her eyes, and a bright scarlet mouth whose redness age has caused to wander into the vertical wrinkles of her upper lip.

Everything is old-fashioned here, even the beige memorial plaques surrounded by red ribbons and lace.

The walls are hung only with the past, as well.

Photos of relatives, dead friends, and, of course, her fiancé. A handsome young man in black and white, enlarged and retouched, embellished like his memory. Frozen on the ramparts of memory, there he is in civilian clothing, in a tennis outfit, in a dinner jacket too big for him, and in uniform, with a white scarf around his neck.

Nothing but him and no more than him for a whole wretched life of tears and sorrow.

Mallock comprehends and Mallock has compassion.

He feels even more awkward than usual with his big clumping shoes planted right in the middle of this doll house. So he hesitates. Why not simply drink his tea and leave, excusing himself for having bothered her? But once a cop, always a cop. And then he absolutely needs to stock up new facts, whether to corroborate Manu's crazy ideas or to find something to confound him.

Once he is seated in an armchair as old as it is uncomfortable, he asks Marie's permission to record their conversation. She agrees with a nod of her head. Her gray hair, perfectly lacquered, does not budge by a millimeter. Mallock thanks her and turns on the little digital recorder that he always carries with him. He taps the microphone, looking at the needles of the meter. Finally something that works in this damned case.

He sets it carefully on a lace doily in the center of a pedestal table surrounded by a gilt railing. Then he says:

"Sunday, December 15, 10:17. Interrogation of Mada . . . Mademoiselle Marie Dutin. Recording made with her authorization."

He clears his throat.

"Dear Mademoiselle, please excuse in advance the involuntary coarseness of some of my questions. I am probably going to stir up some very cruel memories, but—"

"Oh! I'm failing in all my duties. I believe I promised you some tea, did I not?" Marie asks, hanging her head.

"That's very kind of you, but if you have no objection, I'd prefer to tell you first what brings me here."

Marie waits silently. Something she knows how to do marvelously well. That and tea, like a kind of compulsory vocation.

Mallock finally begins:

"I was very mysterious on the telephone and I beg you to pardon me for that."

Marie smiles at him, her two hands folded on her flowered dress.

"In the framework of a police investigation, I have come to know of the existence of your fiancé, Lieutenant Jean-François Lafitte. The circumstances of his tragic death, which remain rather obscure for me, could perhaps help me understand better another event . . . that concerns . . . It's really very hard to explain. How can I tell you?"

"Ask me your questions, Superintendent. I'm not made of porcelain."

Mallock smiled gently before saying:

"So far as you know, was Lieutenant Lafitte actually buried?"

Because the superintendent thought he'd received authorization to handle the porcelain a little, he's surprised to see the old maid's eyes fill with tears. But those little pearls were never far away, and knew the way to the outside only too well. Tears share the same memory with the soul. And some of them are able to reach the ocean, like so many baby turtles, with their eyes closed.

Feeling sorry for her, he leaves her all the time she needs to regain her composure.

"We didn't even find him, Superintendent. His family and I would have so much liked to give him a decent burial, but that was not possible."

She then takes out a microscopic handkerchief to dry her eyes. This tiny bit of lace, delicately folded into a triangle, is gently placed to drink up the little lake that has formed on the inside of her eyelid.

Mallock, unflinchingly assuming the thankless role of the big workhorse, perseveres:

"A well in the middle of a clearing, or the forest of Biellanie, do those mean anything to you?"

"No, nothing at all, but why do you ask me that?"

"It's much too complicated for me to bore you with that story. Let's just say that I, too, would have liked to find Jean-François's body."

"After such a long time? You know," she went on, "no matter what your reasons or your means, you won't find it. We tried everything at the time. Despite all our persistence, we received no response from his superiors. As for his companions in arms, Lucien de Marsac, his second-in-command, and the youngest of the group, Gaston Wrochet, called Gavroche, they both disappeared at the same time he did. For our misfortune, their mission was classified as secret and it long remained so once the war was over. We ran into a twofold wall, that of the administration and that of the military."

Something strikes Mallock's attention, but it's too furtive and he can't quite tell exactly what it is. At the same moment, a jet plane passes overhead, making the windows vibrate.

"There's a military base four miles from the village," Marie explains.

She conscientiously smoothes out her dress with her hands before going on:

"According to what I understood at the time, the French battalion's mission was considered a failure. Especially the intelligence-gathering phase, as well as the non-destruction of an important strategic objective. But whatever anyone says, it was an act of bravery, nothing of which the army could be ashamed. However, they decided to erase it from the official history. And I've never been able to get Jean-François's body back, or any of his effects. I have had only my own heart to remind me of him."

Looking around him, Mallock notes that except for the photos and a lock of hair, there is no object that belonged to her fiancé. If that had been the case she would have put it in a velvet case or protected it under a glass globe.

"It was only in 1951," Marie continues, "that we were finally officially notified of Jean-François's death, along with that of all his men. By persevering, we finally learned that they'd parachuted onto French territory in late May, 1944, but we were told nothing more except that their mission was to gather intelligence and probably organize acts of sabotage. As for my fiancé's body, according to them there were only two possibilities. Either Jean is buried somewhere on the French soil he loved so much, or he was deported to Germany and died in a prisoner of war camp. I'd so much like to know! But I no longer have any illusions."

Mallock, aware that it's pointless to continue to torture the old lady, turns off his recorder.

But after having discreetly blown her nose, Marie Dutin picks up the thread of her memories, this time in a confidential tone:

"I remember everything, the smallest moment I spent with him. Every morning and every night. One day in particular, for many reasons. It was the day before he left for London, and then . . . "

Marie blushed like a young girl.

In reality, Mallock sensed the blush more than he saw it. There was too much powder on the old maid's face.

"We'd gone to spend the day in Normandy, in a little village at the seaside, Saint-Aubin."

Mallock jumped. Was that a coincidence? That village on the Côte de Nacre was very much in fashion at the time. Whence the fine dike and the city's gas system. Who had not spent a summer, at least once in his life, at Saint-Aubin-sur-Mer?

"My Jean-François had a little three-year-old sister, Marguérite, whom he carried lovingly in his arms. I had my dog, Icarus, with me. On that day there was, I don't know why, a parade on the dike, a whole crowd of young people dressed up as Romans riding on pasteboard chariots. The weather was wonderful. It was a last moment of happiness for me, and for so many others . . . But we didn't know it then."

A stupefied silence, on Mallock's part.

Stunned.

He stares into space, wondering if he's dreaming or if he has really heard it. Especially these four words: Marguérite, Icarus, chariots, Romans? Words that sank into the wall like nails to attach a mysterious cross to it. Was it the cross from the well?

How the devil could Manu have known about that? His voice and his words resound in Amédée's bewildered brain: "There's blond silk in front of my eyes. It's the hair of a little girl in my arms. She's sucking on a strawberry candy. She's wearing a red dress with a big daisy embroidered on it . . . In front of us, there's a parade of soldiers and Roman chariots. Everyone's smiling . . . Icarus is barking."

Mallock is still sitting there with his mouth open, frowning. The ticking of a clock punctuates the silence.

Marie's index finger, extended under the white handkerchief, touches the inner corner of her right eye. The tears take refuge in it and make it transparent.

After a discreet little sniff, Marie goes on:

"I believe one should never complain. We just have to take what life gives us and put up with what it makes us endure. On that day, it brought me a great deal. Everything, in fact. All at once. What a marvelous day."

How many times had Marie relived that day?

"In the late afternoon, we found ourselves all alone on the cliff. We had even succeeded in getting away from Gavroche . . . "

She laughed.

"I was beginning to get cold. Jean-François wrapped his white scarf around my neck and told me that he loved me. That was when I noticed the scar from his wound."

"What wound?"

Manu had never mentioned it. Maybe here he had a detail that could confound him?

"He'd been shot under the jaw during the Phony War. The military doctors had not been able to extract the bullet because it was too close to his spinal column, between the first and second vertebrae . . . "

"Atlas and axis," Mallock murmurs, almost automatically.

The research he'd done in entomology had also led him to perfect his knowledge of the human body. And then he'd found the names pretty.

Undisturbed, Marie Dutin continues:

"He was supposed to be discharged because of that, but the armistice came. And then there was General de Gaulle's appeal to the French. His friend Lucien who telephoned him just at the time when . . . Well! It was destiny, I suppose . . . "

Marie Dutin heaves a deep sigh.

That's the effect destiny has on people, Mallock thinks. It makes them sigh, often because they're powerless. It suffocates them, wears them out. It blows over the human race, objects, and even the wind. An idiotic clown playing blindman's bluff, it strikes at random, by chance, or even on the off-chance. Like a child pulling off an insect's leg, destiny amputates human beings. Never maliciously, but often suddenly. A sudden blow in the solar plexus: the man pales, the woman collapses on the spot, a sad little heap of rags and skirts in tears.

But the old maid is like Mallock, she accepts sadness and melancholy, but not pity.

She smiles.

"In any case, on that day we made the most of being together. We made love to each other for the first time. It was marvelous. Before we separated, he gave me a little jewel he'd kept hidden in his pocket."

Mallock held his breath. What was she talking about?

The old lady continued her story without saying what the jewel was:

"In time, and by remembering these moments, the colors have faded but not the feelings, the wind and love, the little blue jewel box, the smell of the grass and his cologne, like a single material that enveloped us. I wish all people could have such an experience. That and the birth of a child, no doubt."

Another flight of the handkerchief toward the old lady's blue eyes.

Mallock wondered for an instant whether he really wanted to know what was in that box. He told himself that if Amédée didn't absolutely insist on it, the superintendent, Mallock, had to ask the question.

"It was a heart made of gold that opened up," she answered without realizing how much she was disturbing Mallock. "Inside were our two photos. And it was also a music box. It played a melody that was sad but adorable . . . "

"A piece by Erik Satie?" Mallock asked, in spite of himself.

"The third *Gnossienne*," the old maid said. "How did you know that?"

"A lucky guess," Mallock stammered. 'Sad but adorable' made me think of it. Who else better deserves those two adjectives? But I suppose you still have it?"

"No, unfortunately, I'd so much love to have it. I often dream about it. I believe that it would console me more than anything. Well! You know that we . . . saw each other again, during the four years of the war. Six times in fact, on each of his missions in France. During our last meeting, I gave him back his gift as a talisman. He was supposed to give it back to me on his next visit. That was the last time that we would be separated, he was sure of that. He didn't tell me about the landing but he made me understand it. I was very frightened. But after all this back and forth right in the middle of the war, I'd ended up thinking he was invincible, my Jean-François."

Another point for Manu. And a huge one. How could he have guessed this romantic story? It's almost eleven o'clock. Mallock doesn't want to make the old lady late for Sunday mass, so he decides to wind up the interview:

"I'm going take the liberty of sending you a bailiff and one of my men to officially record your statement. Don't hesitate to give them as many details as possible. They will take the opportunity to borrow a few samples of your fiancé's hair. That is a lock of his hair that I see in the frame with the miniatures of the Croix de Guerre and Legion of Honor medal, isn't it?"

"Yes, that's his hair, from his childhood, to be exact. His mother gave it to me much later on. She took it out of a silver powder box and counted the strands out one by one. She wanted to give me half of it. Since there was an uneven number of hairs, she gave me one more. That was silly, but it's the kindest thing anyone has ever done for me, you know."

Mallock understands very well, and he feels tears welling up in his eyes as he listens to her. He goes on:

"I have to warn you that we may not be able to return them all to you. The analyses and manipulations . . . "

She hesitates, then smiles.

"Do the best you can. It's very nice of you to concern yourself with this."

"So he did receive honors, then?" Mallock asks as he gets up.

"In June, 1956. We waited twelve years. Well, better late than never, as people say. And they're right. Never is terrible, you know."

Mallock agreed.

He knew.

31.
Monday, December 16

Ever since the beginning of the investigation, and contrary to his habits, in order to balance things out when he was confronted by the irrationality of the situations and the surplus of fantastic facts, Mallock had taken the side of rationality. To make up for the excessive role played by the paranormal, he'd silenced the little magical chatter on which he usually relied. The magic that constituted all his charm, Margot would have said. It was a matter of balancing the vessel, the way one leans to port when the boat lists to starboard.

Only his dreams, by escaping the general censorship he had imposed on himself, had sent up their lucid bubbles here and there. In addition to them, since the beginning of the case there had also been the ayahuasca of Oba, the weeping flower, which had generated truly pertinent visions.

The *yague*, the death vine, was part of the potion the old shaman had made him drink. He suspected that it contained, in addition to harmaline, both ibogaine and peyote. All these psychotropic drugs had been used in the 1960s to produce "modified states of consciousness" that led to a re-evaluation of the subject's spiritual quotient. Ayahuasca was a dangerous product that the shamans prepared only for selected persons, whom they supervised during the whole course of the ceremony. In the middle of "the devil's space," the name given the circle formed by the shamans, the initiates were monitored and aided. Ayahuasca of Oba was still more powerful. But it was not without risk, because the initiate could pass through phases in which death was imminent.

By means of this potion, Mallock had been able to catch a glimpse of the well, the swallows, and the dogs. He'd heard the music and smelled the odors of flesh. Dozens of details had then reappeared, here and there, in Manuel Gemoni's insane narrative.

If he couldn't transfer his . . . gift to Manu, he could at least give him the divinatory drug. For it was in fact a concentrate of ayahuasca that was in the little amber vial the old shaman had given him. Niyashiika had called it the vine of the dead, and had referred to lives, in the plural. If she had preferred to say nothing, that was no doubt because she knew Mallock wouldn't have believed a word of what she said. She had to make him travel the royal road to prove its existence to him. On reflection, hadn't she spoken to him about it while he was under the influence of the drug?

Now Amédée had enough motives, indeed motivations, to request a second excavation. He hoped to be able to find several things, or confirm their absence: the common grave in the middle of the clearing, the tortured bodies of Lieutenant Jean-François Lafitte's men, and the gold chain that according to Manuel should be found at the edge of the well.

Even if he was not yet ready to acknowledge it, even if he did not understand how, after his visit to Marie Dutin, Mallock now believed in the authenticity of Manu's stories. The day before, he'd been convinced of Julie's brother's honesty. Now he knew that what he was recounting during the sessions of hypnosis corresponded, if not to reality, at least to a truth. He was beginning to understand that Manu's misadventure could take on meaning only if it was admitted that reincarnation could actually exist. And that was the real problem: by succeeding in proving Manu's innocence, he would also be proving, in a way, the reality of metempsychosis. The two demonstrations now seemed to be intimately connected. And the stakes were becoming all the higher.

The implications were incalculable.

Thus he would need many more arguments, more incontestable facts, more unexplained but proven similarities to shake up the edifice of justice. If by a miracle he found all the bodies of the men in Lafitte's unit, and if moreover he was able to recuperate that of Jean-François with a golden heart inside him, no one could any longer doubt that something totally extraordinary had happened to Manuel Gemoni, requiring an equally extraordinary judgment.

It was for this reason, seeking still more . . . coincidences and bolts from the blue, that he'd decided to encourage Manu to drink the ayahuasca given him by Niyashiika.

9:07 A.M.: when his computer system connected with the Fort, a rumble resounded, making his whole apartment vibrate.

A powerful lightning bolt. Thunder. A winter storm.

"There really are no seasons anymore!" Ken's face said when it appeared at the top of his screen.

Behind him, Mallock spotted Jo, with a big, amused smile on her lips. It was he, helped by Jean-Claude's and Vincent's men, who had configured the various terminals so that they would be connected to the high-speed Wi-Fi network and could set up conference calls. Each member of the Fort—except Daranne, who was allergic to any kind of modernity—had not only a personal desktop computer but also a laptop with a built-in videocam that he carried along with him when he traveled.

On Mallock's monitor, in conference mode, Jules's and Julie's faces appeared in turn.

"Hi, kids. To follow up on the good resolutions I made on Saturday, I'm going to give you a little talk about what I learned over the weekend."

"Were you able to meet with the lieutenant's fiancée?" Julie interrupted impatiently.

"Yes, and the result is very . . . upsetting."

A second thunderclap made the light flicker.

"Okay, listen carefully, I've got two or three bits of information to give you and I want to ask your opinion."

Mallock began his account. Thirty minutes later, after saying, "See you in a minute," to Jules and Julie, he shut down his computer. Even though it was well-equipped with surge protectors, he mustn't tempt fate too much. Without any respect for the status of the commander of the Fort, the thunderstorm could take his equipment as its target.

Two of Mallock's lieutenants, who were in fact captains, consented to the use of the ayahuasca. Jo opposed it, without daring to insist too much:

"I've just arrived, but everything connected with drugs scares me."

And Ken had declared himself incompetent:

"Sorry, I have no opinion."

Another proof, if one were needed, of his intelligence.

Coffee break.

Mallock spent more than a quarter of an hour trying to reach Mordome and Léon Galène in order to propose a teleconference meeting the next day at the same hour. As he hung up, he glanced worriedly at the clock. At 10 A.M. he had a meeting with Manu. Jules and Julie were supposed to meet them there. Julie had insisted on taking part in Manuel's last interrogation, under the influence of the giant jungle vine *Banisteriopsis caapi*.

"I'm willing to proceed with Manu's permission and not rush off to inform Kiko, but only if I'm present."

This amounted to a kind of blackmail, but after all, the presence and permission of a member of the family wouldn't be a bad thing. Mallock had complied.

Around 9:30, Mallock went down to the living room. After a slight guilty hesitation, he served himself a slug of whiskey before donning a transparent plastic raincoat over a red and mauve striped shirt, itself pulled over a yellow T-shirt. According to Mallock, elegance sometimes flirted with eccentricity when his inner carnival showed its branches and flowers, a colorful camouflage covering the drab grayness of his heart.

Outside, Paris seemed to have been attacked by an invisible army whose artillery, still stationed outside the walls, was carrying out the traditional barrage before the assault. The icy rain had made the gutters overflow. It was running down the streets, carrying off clumps of dirty snow that looked like small, dingy icebergs.

Mallock went into the storm without hesitating an instant. Heavy drops struck his face and a lightning bolt made his eyelids flutter. Thunder. Amédée loved it. It reminded him of the walks in the rain he'd taken on the deserted beach at Andernos when he had the opportunity. The showers and lightning followed one another round the basin with enormous rumblings, and he was walking along with a smile on his lips and his face turned up to the sky, looking completely out of his mind but happy. Practiced properly, this Mallockian sport recharged him with brilliant ideas and incinerated the last sad aftereffects of his life in the world.

When he arrived at the prison, soaked to the bone, Jules and Julie were waiting for him. They looked at their boss's clothes with a worried air. Either he always wore the same gray suit, chic but too big, or he let himself go, putting on anything at all, whatever his mood of the day suggested. On that day, he'd outdone himself, a plastic raincoat over a Hawaiian shirt!

They went into Manuel's cell to explain their plan to him.

Julie's brother didn't hesitate a second.

"Anything, I'll do anything to get out of this nightmare."

"It's not without risks," Mallock insisted. "It will be just us, no medical assistants and no recording camera."

"We'll stay here with you in your cell, but you've understood that it's not without risks, haven't you, my little Gandhi?"

Manu smiled broadly when he heard his old nickname.

"Yes, little sister, I've understood it all very well and I'm ready."

In that cell, only Mallock could have disabused him. Convinced him. We are never really ready to confront ayahuasca and all the substances that compose it: harmine, harmaline, tetrahydroharmine, harmol, harmalol, dimethyltryptamine . . .

But he decided to keep quiet.

It was better not to know, so as not to be frightened.

And not be frightened so as not to die.

Or in order to die?

BOOK 3

32.
The Forest of Biellanie, June, 1944
Jean-François Lafitte's Story

God is with them, they say, but they're wrong, it's the Devil. Jean-François tries not to lose consciousness. His men have been thrown into the mass grave dug in the middle of the clearing. Now night has fallen, he has just disfigured "K," and he's waiting for death to come . . .

From the old house on my right, south of the well, I hear the howls of a wounded animal. And there, covered with blood, leaning against my tree, I ask God to grant me a favor: to see the SS leave carrying their leader's lifeless body. If he dies, nothing else matters to me! I want to see his stinking corpse return to the mud from which it should never have emerged. Let him die, so that Heaven may be avenged, so that the earth may be cleansed of his existence. Let him die screaming insanities at God, so that I can once again believe that the Devil is not the stronger party. So that everything is not hopeless.

An hour has gone by, the screams have died down, but I still hear his voice. "K" is shouting orders and the words he is uttering resound like scraping metal. I also hear a child crying. The blow from the bayonet that I received in my back is causing me to suffer horribly. But it's nothing in comparison to the pain I have in my mouth. My teeth were broken by "K's" triple signet ring.

On my left, the bastards have just set fire to the Canadian uniforms we were wearing. They've thrown in the remains of the woman I finished off.

The wind is driving these execrable odors toward me.

From the house's chimney, another kind of smoke is rising.

The first stars are appearing in the sky. They are like friends, and I start counting them, trying to forget everything. But I will have no respite. The dogs have come closer. I'm trying to make myself faint by banging my injured back against the tree. It's impossible, I no longer have the strength.

I will never see Marie again.

A squeaking noise; the door of the old house opens and a black silhouette comes out. It approaches me, yelling at the dogs. The animals retreat, regretfully leaving their prey. It's he. The bloody face of "K" appears in the firelight. Alive. And holding something. A piece of meat that he gnaws on one last time before throwing it to the dogs. It's hard for me to identify the object that falls at my feet with a wet sound.

Suddenly the fire flares up and illuminates the nearby undergrowth. I don't understand at first. Or don't want to understand.

It's a tiny human torso, the size of a doll, with its head blackened by fire and a largely devoured arm. The dogs rush toward it. In a few seconds, the remains have been divided up and swallowed.

But the animals are not satisfied.

They begin to lick me, all over my body, where my blood has coagulated. Their different-colored eyes shine like firebrands. I know that any moment now they are going to begin. Only a feeling of unreality allows me not to sink into madness. It isn't possible. What I've seen, what I'm seeing. None of it is true! Once upon a time . . .

"K" is leaning over me. "You can escape my dogs and die quickly. Do you want that?" He smiles at me, so I say: "Yes." I'm ashamed, but I add, cravenly: "Please." I'm already grateful to him. "But first you have to do something for me." My eyes ask him what it is and he explains: "Take communion, take communion with me, for the glory of Jesus and Lucifer, those two

rival brothers!" Then he hands me a bit of meat: "Eat this." The bastard smiles: "Because this is my body, human flesh, the Eucharist!" I understand and close my mouth, horrified. "Do you think it's cannibalism? No, my God, what an ugly name: it's communion, my son, communion!" Then he explains to me, as I feel myself slipping away: "It's a choice morsel, very delicate, a child's cheek, and suckling child. You're going to love it."

When I finally wake up I'm being carried by four men in black uniforms. Then I begin to vomit when I realize that my legs have been partly devoured by the dogs. Only a series of leather garrotes keeps what blood I still have from flowing away. "K" has just brought me back to consciousness by giving me smelling salts.

The Nazi's skull is covered with bandages. He's shouting and laughing. The ogre has me in his hands, in his teeth. The monster hasn't finished with me. He has put his metal teeth back in his mouth before leaning over my litter. Suddenly, still wearing his gloves, he approaches me and, God have pity, begins to devour me!

I've regained consciousness for the third and last time. My body is no longer mine. It has secreted all the endorphins it contained, and I am no more than a scrap of brain with bones wrapped in cotton and bandages saturated with blood. "K" has finally given the order to throw me into the well. Before I fall, I think I see two violet-colored eyes hidden in the trees, at the edge of the clearing, two eyes that are weeping.

Lying on the ground, which is covered with swallows' bodies, I feel almost happy. "K" will not follow me into this abyss. The bogeyman is done with me. I'm like a dismembered mouse the cat has left behind. God be praised, I can finally go to sleep looking at the sky.

But was I going to see Marie again someday?

I don't have time to answer that question. I perceive a regular figure standing out against the starry circle formed by the edge of the well: a triangle that begins to grow rapidly until it covers me with a complete obscurity.

It is at that moment, and only then, that I am finally able to forget my sufferings and the bit of flesh that I swallowed in the hope of escaping the ogre's dogs.

May God pardon me!

33.
Tuesday, December 17

The doorbell awoke a very crumpled Mallock. Whereas Manu's account had touched his heart the day before, now the rest of his body was reacting. He glanced at the video monitor. Friend or foe? Friend, it was Anita coming to take care of her superintendent.

"Hello, I'll open the door for you. Could you pick up my mail, please?"

"Of course, Superintendent."

There was nothing to do about it. He would never get his dear Anita to call him Amédée or even just Sir. After all, maybe she was right. Her big, bright smile when she handed him his pile of newspapers and mail calmed Mallock for a time. But not long. Reading the papers took his appetite away again.

"One question remains unanswered: between the superintendent and the old man's killer, who is the more insane?"

That was how the first really complete article on the Gemoni case ended. A scoop for *Le Figaro*, which had put the story on the front page and given it a whole inside right page. The headline, "Mallock and His Ghost," alluded to one of Maigret's cases. In the introductory paragraph, the journalist asked: "What is craziest in this case, Gemoni's earlier lives or Mallock's methods?" The rest of the article revealed the whole chronicle of the case, from the day the young man set out to kill a former member of the Waffen-SS to the recent sessions of hypnosis Mallock had organized. All the details were there, including the names—misspelled, of course—of the main actors. Amédée was not really surprised. For two weeks, he and his men, as well as the judicial system, which was notoriously leaky, had managed to keep most of this case secret. What bothered him was that the journalist wrote in detail about the sensational hypnosis sessions. Who had leaked that information?

He tried to reassure himself by saying out loud:

"In any case, it doesn't come from the Fort."

The silence of his apartment and Anita, who was already fully involved in cleaning up, had the courtesy to avoid contradicting him. There had been a painful precedent, and Mallock had fired the person responsible. He didn't want to consider the possibility that a member of his current team might have been tempted again.

The article was complemented by two boxes.

The first was nicely titled: "Mallock Talks Rubbish." Some hack violently attacked the now famous divisional superintendent. That was normal; people like nothing better than to lapidate those whom yesterday they adored and praised to the skies. By practicing the same lack of discernment and sense of proportion.

The second box was a brief interview with Serge Klarsfeld. He skillfully ducked the issue, but one could read between the lines that before Manuel Gemoni's revelations, he hadn't known anything about this Darbier who had taken refuge on an island.

What exasperated Mallock most of all was the fact that for once, the journalists weren't wrong. Who was the crazier? Manuel and his macabre stories or Mallock, who listened to, and worse yet, encouraged him?

He hesitated in front of the bar. It wasn't even 10 A.M. Don't go off the deep end, Mallock! You're not going to let malicious scribblers force you to drink? Have a cup of coffee.

For once, he listened to his little inner voice. The coffee machine was still groaning and spitting out the last drops when the signal on his Mac sounded.

"Anita! Can you keep an eye on my coffee and bring it up to my office, please? I'm being called on the computer," Mallock said to justify himself.

"Yes, of course, Mr. Superintendent. I'll take care of it."

A minute later he was in front of his monitor. Mordome had started a videoconference and appeared in a white shirt in the upper left corner of the screen. With two clicks, Amédée authorized the call. His face appeared in a rectangle alongside that of his friend, whose full name was Bernard-Barnabé Mordome. Mallock realized that his hair was unkempt and ran his fingers through it.

"You're looking good this morning," the medical examiner laughed.

Amédée smiled.

"And how are you?"

"My vanity is slightly wounded. I would point out that you haven't called upon me at all in this reincarnation business."

For the great professor Mordome, who was usually so severe and abrupt, this was more than familiar, even affectionate. The two investigations in which he had participated with Mallock had made the two men friends. Even if the superintendent had not yet fully realized that fact.

"I would point out," Mallock said in his own defense, "that I haven't had a cadaver to give you to work on. Otherwise, of course . . . Anyway, I hope the situation is going to change very soon."

"Tell me about it."

"No, first, we have to wait for my friend Léon to join us. I'm not going to tell you all about it twice."

"Léon? The old queen you introduced me to last year?"

"Be nice, please, he's my friend."

"Oh, excuse me, I'll rephrase: 'the elderly Uranist to whom you introduced me last year?' You're the one who told me about his various sexual escapades. You know, if we go on calling the blind 'visually handicapped' and the deaf 'acoustically challenged,' we're going to have to call fools 'non-understanders' and heterosexuals 'non-sodomists,' and why shouldn't Blacks be called 'non-Whites'?"

Mallock came up with no pertinent retort. The politically correct language of the early twenty-first century exasperated and disturbed him as much as it did his friend the medical examiner.

He just changed the subject by asking:

"When are you coming back?"

Bernard-Barnabé Mordome had been in New York for a week. He'd been asked to go to the land of serial killers and nutcases, the land of experts, as a specialist in the dissection of corpses. A form of recognition, so to speak.

"Tomorrow. With the time difference, I should be landing at Orly about 8 A.M. Why?"

"I'm organizing a second excavation near Paris in connection with this case. Orly isn't exactly on the way there, but . . . "

"Would you be able to come pick me up?"

"If that's okay with you, and if it wouldn't tire you too much, I could swing by the airport."

Mordome seemed to be reflecting. He had to consult the appointment book he carried in his head.

"Okay, let's do that. I'll sleep in the plane and go straight on with you. That's better in relation to the time difference."

Just as Mallock was about to thank his friend, Anita carefully set the hot coffee next to the keyboard.

"Drink it while it's hot, it's better that way."

"Thanks, Anita. Don't hesitate to make a cup for yourself . . . "

He always said that and she always replied:

"I love coffee, but the doctor advises against it because of my stomach."

Mordome interrupted this acute dialogue.

"Your conversation is fascinating, but I don't have all day. Where is this joker of yours?"

"Léon?"

A groan of confirmation.

"He's near Angers, at the home of some friends. But so far as I can understand, his hosts have access to the net."

Mordome made a face.

"Do me a favor: get in contact with him and call me later. I have to give an introduction and start a slide show, and then I'll come back up. The conference is taking place in the main meeting room of my hotel. O.K.? I have to say that the name of your friend—Galène, if I remember correctly—doesn't suggest that he would be up-to-date in matters of communication by Internet."

He wasn't wrong about that.

It was almost noon by the time the three men were finally lined up on their respective screens.

Far from being useless, the videoconference validated his procedure. Even though they had brilliant minds, they, too, felt lost, and concluded that it was necessary to pursue the investigation of Darbier and the theory of reincarnation.

"I understand why you're concerned, Amédée, but go ahead. I've cut up my fellow humans lengthwise, sidewise, and every which way too long to believe this nonsense, or anything else, for that matter. But you have to follow your reasoning to its endpoint. One never knows. All religions flirt with the notion of life after death. Billions of humans believe in it. Whether redemption, reincarnation, or resurrection, it takes different forms but it's basically the same thing. Paradise or a new life, that's how religions retain believers, it's the carrot and the stick at the same time. They all propose their version of the remedy for the same damned lethal malady, life."

Mallock addressed his friend:

"You're really nothing but an infidel, you don't believe in anything!"

"What about you? You're a fine one to talk! You know, old man, that I've opened up bodies and I'd have really liked to find a little creature wrapped around a vesicle, a bit of soul that has remained stuck between two teeth, a diamond that's still beating, embedded in a bone, but there isn't anything inside. It's obvious that religion and the idea of a life after all this shit has been invented. Besides, an amazing bunch of crooks has made a fortune out of all that. But you know, even I would be very happy if you could provide us with a proof. If metempsychosis is proven to us by His Majesty Amédée, I'll already make my choice. I want to come back as a castrated Abyssinian cat, please."

"Castrated?"

"Yes. No more females. Good meals and lots of cushions. What about you, dear Monsieur Galène? A bonobo?"

Léon and Amédée broke into laughter.

Léon had been called Galène only since 1937, the date at which his family, who were Polish Jews, decided to emigrate and change their name. Leonid Scheinberg became Léon Galène, named after the galena crystal used in the radio technology that was his father's favorite pastime until he had a heart attack while listening, on a device he had constructed himself, to one of Hitler's first speeches. When Léon reported his father's death, he did so in the form of a quip: "It could be said that the Führer's words were very successful; they went straight to my father's heart."

Three years later, Léon had been deported to Maïdanek along with his mother, his brother, and two French resistance fighters and all the members of the Christian family that had taken them in. He told the rest of the story to Mallock only once, on a day of despair. Over there, where everyone was made to do forced labor, his beauty had made him a child prostitute. He was passed from one camp to another from Oranienburg-Sachsenhausen to Dora, and then to Ravensbrück.

For a long time, he had remained prostrate, devoured by shame and horror, incapable even of anger, except against himself. How could he have explained that he felt cowardly and complicitous, that these millions of dead were his mother and that the tormentors all and collectively bore the image of his father? How could he say that he felt himself to be the child of this terrifying physical struggle? A monstrous, incestuous child? A consenting object who had played with these monsters' fat penises? How could he explain that one can survive that? Whom would he tell? And why?

Then he had decided to devour life: "at both ends," he often said to express the diversity of his sexual choices.

Now he expressed himself simply and gravely:

"This genocide is my childhood, Amédée, my hatred and my guilt. Tomorrow I'm going to help you find out as much as possible about this Krinkel, because it's my duty and because there is nothing more important."

It was difficult to find something to say after that, especially coming from someone who had made nonseriousness his ultimate and definitive religion.

However, Mallock replied:

"So much the better, Léon. You're the only one who can dig up these documents for me, and I'm sure that there are still answers to be found in your old papers. But I wouldn't want all this pointless research to upset you all over again. I can make do with—"

"It's all right, Amédée. I've been infinitely and irremediably upset for a long time. Even you, my darling, have no idea how upset I am! But you're kind to worry about your old Jewish queen."

Mallock smiled as he thought about what Mordome had called him.

Then they talked about what each of them could do to help Amédée. At 1 P.M. sharp the friends ended their conversation, agreeing to meet. Mallock felt greatly relieved. There was no doubt that the news was good for his tired brain, which appreciated these reinforcements.

But it was equally sweet for his heart.

34.
Wednesday, December 18

The sun and ice, the mist and light of the early morning, were making it difficult to see out the windshield. Mallock adjusted the heat to try to clear his view. Two days of storms, snowfall, and rain had changed the landscape. The white walls bordering the autoroute had been replaced by cliffs of ice formed of gigantic stalagmites shining like glass in the sun. One jarring detail in this impressive setting: the super-intendent was whistling. Very rare for Mallock.

It was probably the optimism that this winter sun and the arrival of his friends produced. Thirty minutes to get to Orly. He turned on his iPod: J. J. Cale, Arcade Fire, Bach, Evora, Taj Mahal, Stan Getz, Camille, Bebo Valdez, Brel, Trotignon, Poulenc, Robert Wyatt, Mozart, Grandaddy, Big Soul, Brassens, Calas, Delerue, Shakira, Andrews Sisters, Monk, Sonny & Cher, Divine Comedy, Coltrane, Brel, Carlos Gardel, David Bowie, Calogero, Zappa, Laurie Anderson… An endless list, and a personal compilation made with the same eclecticism as his melancholic, greedy bear's brain. In the company of so much talent, time passed almost too fast, despite the beginning of a traffic jam at the juncture of the ring road and the autoroute. Mallock arrived five minutes late, but he wasn't too upset about that. Mordome was waiting for him at arrivals. The two friends embraced one another and Mallock opened the car's trunk for him.

"Did you sleep well?"

"Like a stone. But I'm still a little dull. And then I forgot one important detail: I don't have my torture instruments. I hadn't foreseen . . . "

"Don't worry, I've asked my new collaborator to bring her personal toolkit, and the guys from the Judicial Identity Office will also be there."

"And even bodies?"

"As for that, I warned you. We're not sure of anything. But at least we'll have the pleasure of talking to one another."

They smiled. The two friends were happy to see each other and to be working together again. Too bad they had to wait for the first gray hairs to realize that.

"By the way, do you know that you're making headlines throughout the world?"

"With what? I'm working only on the Darbier case at the moment."

"Yes, precisely! I flipped through various foreign rags in the plane. They talk about you and your mysterious investigation. Since the case with the poisoner, you're a star, old man. And then this present 'case' is far from banal. The reincarnation business fascinates everyone."

Mallock wasn't surprised. Just worried. It was never good to be in the spotlight, and worse when it became international. The press, in any country, now had only three angles: polemics, coronation, and lynching. It wasn't good, not good at all, more and more just show, beneath all these Klieg lights. How many pretty butterflies or vain thespians had burned their wings on them?

"What do they say about it?"

Mordome hesitated, searching for words, before he began. He knew that Mallock was sensitive to attacks:

"Honestly, they aren't going easy on you. Since they showered you with praise during your last investigation, they're going for the simplest thing: they're questioning your abilities, especially your mental abilities. The English are talking about the 'lunatic Inspector Mallock.' I hate to be the bearer of bad news, but I think it's better for you to know. Note that it hasn't all been critical, you also have numerous admirers who—"

"Don't bother, Barnabé. Anyway, I deserve some of the criticism. I've had problems from the beginning, and stuck my head in the sand like an ostrich. Though they'd spit out their venom even if I hadn't!"

Three minutes of silence before Mordome went on:

"One thing surprised me, all the same. They seem damn well informed. They know everything: the hypnosis sessions, the theory of reincarnation, the existence of this Lieutenant Lafitte, Krinkel, everything. Are you sure you can trust your men and your communication networks?"

"Absolutely, they're protected to death, Barnabé. Nothing comes out of the Fort. If there are leaks, they're elsewhere."

With this disturbing observation, silence fell again. It lasted until the arrival at the edge of the Forest of Biellanie. Mallock needed to think and Mordome needed to sleep a little.

The forest was crawling with people. And Mallock had to identify himself three times in order to come within five hundred yards of the well, where a kind of parking lot had been improvised.

He turned to Mordome:

"I put two pairs of boots in the trunk, one for you and one for me, but with the cold and the rain that has fallen, the ground is frozen. The rubber soles slip too much. Might as well keep our shoes on. I saw that you had . . . "

It's not only other people who talk without saying anything, his always vigilant little inner voice pointed out.

At the same moment, Jo and Julie came up to them.

"Marie-Joséphine, what a pleasant surprise!" Mordome exclaimed.

He took Jo in his arms and gave her a big kiss. Mallock looked at him, astonished.

"I did an internship of a month and a half with Professor Mordome, Superintendent, and that creates ties. I did mention it to you," Jo said, turning toward her new boss.

"For me, they were six weeks of great satisfaction with this pupil, I have to admit," Mordome added with a big smile. "So you're the famous new recruit who was supposed to be bringing me an instrument case?"

"Exactly, Professor. I don't have everything, but almost."

Jo handed Mordome a good-sized steel pilot case.

"If you need anything else, just ask the crime scene technician over there by the well. He has a whole panoply of instruments in his van."

"Thanks, Jo," Mallock said. "Could you take a series of soil samples all around and on the triangular stone? If there is in fact a cadaver under there, at least some hair must have survived. For the rest, where are we?"

"At 7 A.M. the specialized team began scanning the soil. And they found several interesting things. But when it comes to digging, that's another matter. The earth is like permafrost and they had to use heavy-duty equipment."

At the same moment an officer who had recognized Mallock came up to the group with a friendly smile:

"Hello, Superintendent. I believe I have good news."

His team of technicians had been working since dawn.

"Southwest of the well, at a distance of about thirty yards, we discovered that the soil didn't have the same composition, and that this extended over a regular surface three yards by five."

Captain Jean-Marie Mireille was a tall, husky man with a combination of mustache, nose, and glasses that seemed to be all of a piece, like the pasteboard masks people put on to disguise themselves.

"Let me tell you. At first, we thought we'd found a pile of stones," the gendarme went on. "It could be the walls of what used to be a house. That's usually what we find in this area. With the Gauls, the Merovingians, and the Romans, not to mention still older constructions, the soil of our lovely country is a genuine museum. Sometimes there are even several layers of successive habitation. I remember having found one site that went back more than ten thousand years."

Mallock's frown, followed by a clenching of his jaw, gave Mireille the hint. Maybe he shouldn't go too much into history and get on with it.

"To come to the point, we ran all this data through our imaging programs and I can tell you right now that we are, *a priori*, above a tomb or an ossuary. We have identified at least three human skulls, for the moment, and what seem to be military helmets. Is that what you're looking for?"

Following the instructions Mallock had given, neither Jo nor Julie had said what the precise and final goal of these excavations was. But everyone—even gendarmes, Daranne would have said, like a good cop but a bad comrade—knows how to read. The case had been in all the newspapers, along with Amédée Mallock's . . . divagations and fanciful ideas. Another reason for the Mallock in question to be a little careful, for once, about what he said:

"It was one of the possibilities. In any case, you've done a good job."

The gendarme gave him a big smile. Amédée was reassured to note that there was in fact a row of real teeth and a very pink tongue hidden under the cardboard nose and his mustache's brush of black whiskers.

He asked politely:

"When do you think you'll have finished excavating the grave, Captain?"

The war between the police forces was real, and between the two ethnic groups you had to mediate gently and use kid gloves.

"My men have just begun. The ground is frozen. We'll need a good two hours to reach the right level, Superintendent."

Charles Coudret appeared behind him. The gamekeeper seemed astonished to see Mallock again:

"I thought you'd finished with my clearing after the session last week. You didn't find anything, did you?"

Amused by Coudret's use of the possessive, Mallock smiled at the good man:

"That was another reason to come back. I'm tenacious, some would say stubborn. How is your bite?"

Coudret lifted his forearm and held it horizontal.

"I'm getting the stitches taken out the day after tomorrow. Afterward I'll be as good as new. Can I stay and watch, without bothering you?"

"Of course, this is your land, isn't it?"

"That's kind of you. Would you like some chestnuts, Superintendent?" the gamekeeper asked.

Just then the judge's car arrived at the site and Jack Judioni got out with great pomp. Mallock greeted him vaguely and from a distance, amused to see him coming equipped with big yellow boots and a fluorescent orange hard hat.

Busy taking photos of the site a few yards away, Jo looked at Mallock. Instead of attending to the judge and trying to win over the officials who were growing more numerous with each new search, there he was hanging out with the local forest warden. Her divisional superintendent's sympathies and priorities were as disconcerting as he himself was.

But the judge was a good-looking man, she decided, like a true female.

Around 1 P.M., something changed.

Mallock was still peeling and eating the chestnuts Coudret had brought him after grilling them in his fireplace, but he had understood. They still heard the sounds of the shovels, but the metallic concert was now dominated by the sound of rakes and spatulas scraping the earth. The two teams of excavators were talking less loudly. Some of them had fallen silent, while others were murmuring.

There was no doubt; they'd found bodies.

Mallock waited another good quarter of an hour, long enough to finish off the last four stubborn chestnuts, and then got up. Captain Mireille was coming to see him.

"We're there. It is in fact a grave. We've found ten skeletons."

"There should be eleven," Mallock grumbled.

The gendarme looked at him, astonished. Nonetheless, he had been warned. Mallock, alias Dédé-the-Wizard, lived in another world, with his own certitudes and information that came from no one knew where. But from that to divining the number of bodies in a grave that no one even knew existed two hours earlier?

He accompanied the Parisian superintendent as far as the grave, with a mixture of respect and fear. Mordome was already there, on all fours, brushing soil from the skull of the eleventh skeleton that he had just discovered underneath number three.

He got up when Mallock arrived.

"Stop right there. I can't tell you their first or last names. Let's say that they have been there for more than fifty years and less than eighty. On the other hand, six of them have been severely tortured."

"Severely?" Mallock asked.

"We can say that. For example, in one case all the bones of the head have been fractured. Whoever did it was really relentless. In some cases the legs and feet have been crushed by blows from a sledgehammer. Also *in vivo*."

That was Tobias Darbier's signature. Mallock remembered what he had been told by both Doctor Barride, in the Dominican Republic, and Manuel, during his first interrogation: the terrible death of his friend Thibaut Trabesse, massacred by Oberleutnant Klaus Krinkel. Were all the horrors he'd heard during these last weeks true, then? Mallock suddenly felt sick. The sight of these broken bones covered with earth had just overwhelmed him. Up to that point, the whole story had remained imaginary. The ogre was only a virtual bogeyman, a fairy-tale character who had emerged from Manuel's nightmares. And Mallock had been only a lost superintendent, trying to find his way back to the path of reason.

These bones crushed by human brutality, these fractured tibias and teeth rising, like white cries, out of their gangue, had just made the scale's needle swing toward Manu and his incredible revelations.

Mallock climbed down into the grave and knelt down, both to avoid falling and to be at the right height to pick up a bit of bone. He chose a jaw fragment. He put it on the index and middle fingers of his right hand and caressed it slowly with his thumb.

"What are you doing, Amédée?"

Mordome, who knew him well, had noticed his friend's state of mind.

"Barbarism, you have to actually touch it for it to touch you, Barnabé. See it to know it. Damn and double damn!"

Mallock put the fragment of a jaw back exactly where he'd found it, and then added:

"There is so much passion in these bones, you understand?"

"If you say so."

Mordome hated sentimentality, especially concerning his daily lot: the bodies of people murdered by his fellows. There's nobody in a dead body, he kept telling his students. Even if, paradoxically, he inculcated respect for the victims in them.

"Eleven bodies," Mallock repeated, without taking offense

at the apparent insensitivity of his friend. "Except for the youngest member of the unit, Gaston Wrochet, they're all there. Though we still have to prove that they're soldiers."

Jo, who had come over to them, interrupted him:

"That's no problem. Not far from the well, the second team has just found the remains of a fire. In them they identified several partly melted pieces of metal: military insignias and uniform buttons. For the moment, they haven't been able to determine their exact origin, but they'll get there."

At the same moment, Julie joined them.

"Boss? Isn't Lieutenant Lafitte supposed to have buried a chain? The one that held the famous heart?"

"According to Manu, yes. You know that as well as I do."

"No, it was during the interrogation on Friday, the one with Long and Trencavel, that he's supposed to have told you that. I wasn't there. But I heard something about it."

"Ah! Right, in fact. Well, he told me that he'd taken the heart off the chain so that he could swallow it, and then he threw the chain on the ground. He said he stepped on it so that the Germans wouldn't find it. You'll need to look for it near the . . . "

Without saying a word, Julie slowly opened her hand. In it there was soil and, shining as on its first day, a golden chain.

Of course, Mallock didn't react as his collaborators expected him to. No sign of satisfaction, or even of astonishment. He turned to the gendarmerie captain and gave him an order that no one understood at the moment:

"Halt the search in the grave and around the well, Captain. We have what we need. A hundred yards to the south, you'll find the remains of a house. I would like you and the guys from Judicial Identity to dig around it. But carefully."

"We'll get on it right away, Superintendent."

Jean-Marie Mireille seemed to have adjusted to the situation. With someone like Mallock, you had to not try too hard to understand. And then one of the great joys of the soldier's profession is clicking his heels and obeying blindly, even stupidly. Only those who have never practiced this sport will scorn its frank and subtle pleasure. However, Mallock detained the captain and the head of the crime scene squad before they climbed out of the grave.

He searched for words and then said:

"We're looking for bones that have been burned and perhaps gnawed. Little bones . . . "

"What do you mean by 'little'?"

A deep sigh from Mallock.

"Bones of children, maybe even babies."

Apart from Julie, who had been there when Manuel made his latest revelations, everyone present looked at Mallock as if he had finally lost all common sense.

Then he finished:

"What we're looking for is in fact the remains of a meal."

Captain Mireille and the other witnesses took several seconds to accept the relation between the words "meal" and "babies." When they understood, a new stage was reached in silence. As they moved away to mark out a new search zone, an immense wave of cold bore down on the clearing. The vanguard of a storm that was still gathering strength in the icy upper spheres of the Arctic.

At nightfall, the first little skeletons were found. Charles Coudret decided it was high time for him to go home. His wife must be waiting for him, and now he no longer had any forest. His woods were cursed from now on, forever contaminated. My God, babies eaten! Overwhelmed by what had happened in his forest, he left without saying farewell to his friend the superintendent.

There are times like that, when one doesn't dare look any more, ashamed simply to be a human being.

As the last bits of sky were melting among the branches, Mallock finally understood what there was at night in addition to everything you could see during the day. What terrorized Manu when he was young. The extra thing that was in his room.

This monster that came when night fell, the mysterious element that disappeared when the sun returned, was obscurity.

T homas and two other children were in the courtyard outside the studio when the block of marble was delivered. Several tons of beige stone veined with traces of crimson. In his dream, Mallock began to work that same day. It was urgent. A commission from a Venetian prince. Naked women begging. He had a free hand as to the number and position of these figures. In the dream, days and nights passed and he, sweating, exhausted, worked on. Worked. Again and again. On his hands, hundreds of bruises, blisters, and cuts appeared without any pain weakening his determination. Sometimes he stopped for a few minutes to drink or urinate, before returning to work even harder. He slept little and ate at random.

Six months later, his statue was finally finished. Outside, autumn was turning everything orange. Mallock-the-sculptor had reopened the doors of his studio as he waited for the transporters. Soon these men would take his work all the way south, to the right of the Italian boot.

He felt both pride and sadness. They were going to leave.

As he was going back into the courtyard to look at his work one last time, Thomas came up to him. He had not seen the stone again since the day it had arrived. Putting his soft little hand in his father's bloody paw, he asked him solemnly:

"The ladies must have been imprisoned for a long time in the big stone. See, they're very thin."

Mallock smiled at what he took to be a simple child's

notion. It was a beautiful image, already-sculpted women waiting to be delivered from their gangue of stone. Then his mind shifted to another interpretation that was far more painful.

What if he was right? What if these figures were already there, determined by the veins and cracks in the marble. Hadn't he worked around all the weaknesses until he'd found his subject? And what about the urgency he'd felt? Like a rescue worker scraping the ground after an avalanche. What if everything was already written? Already sculpted? What if we were on Earth only to place our feet between the dotted lines, to follow the arrows in ascending order and unearth the clues to this kind of obstacle course that life was? What if we couldn't do anything about it? Neither the tragedies nor the happiness.

My God! What if even the dignity of choice was denied us?

As Mallock slowly emerged from his dream, he realized that someone was crying inside his apartment. He leapt to his feet and grabbed the revolver that he hid under the bed. He listened, feeling a little silly. The moans seemed to be coming from all over. Very close, like murmurs. He went into the bathroom. In front of him, the mirror revealed the truth to him, a face with puffy eyes full of tears: his face.

He set the gun on the soap dish and resting his arms on the two sides of the sink, facing the mirror, he violently closed his eyes. As if engraved under his eyelids, in the dark, he glimpsed the form of a cross. He was too used to these visions not to recognize the signs. Dry mouth, vibration in the ears, loss of balance. This one was rapid. Light, like the back of a cuttlefish surfing like a cork on the salt sea.

Mallock got dressed and went up to his office. He sent the photograph he'd taken of the cross, along with the reworked segment on which the inscription "MPF" could be seen, to three people, three historian friends, including Léon Galène.

This crucifix was part of the solution, but in what way? Mallock preferred to leave his vision untouched by any mental manipulation. Intelligence not only straightens things out but also twists them.

By reflex, he turned on the television as he went back downstairs to make himself coffee. Captain Jean-Marie Mireille appeared on the screen, lit by flashlights. To his right, the inevitable judge. That must have been recorded the preceding evening, after Mallock's departure. Who had informed the television team? Mallock would have answered: "Who benefits from the crime?" Very handsome in his gray suit with a Mao collar, Judioni had adopted a hoarse voice:

"I've just spent the whole day and part of the night with these men (a little movement of the arm to let the camera make a quick panorama), digging up the earth on the urgent orders of Superintendent Mallock. It's exhausting work!"

So this was the reason for the yellow boots and the orange hard hat, the outfit of an experienced man who has sweat on his back.

"To avoid any new rumors, I want to state that although we have in fact found various . . . things, there is absolutely nothing that directly concerns the Gemoni case."

Then, after a hesitant silence:

"And still less the body of a lieutenant from the Second World War that was supposed to be sought in the context of this case, as some of your colleagues have claimed."

Having said this, the judge raised his right hand, spreading his fingers to signal that he would not answer any questions.

Now broadcasting live in the news channel's studio, the journalist, Jacob Callas, introduced his guest. The same judge, him again. Judioni hadn't lost any time. Being on television was the second thing he'd thought about when he woke up that morning. The third was to smile and the first was to groom himself down to the last hair. Judioni, who had been careful, for once, not to shave and even to set the famous hard hat within sight on the table, began by offering a caveat:

"I won't pretend not to be a little tired. If I have agreed to your request to spend a few minutes with you this morning, it is because I have the greatest respect for journalists in general and for you in particular, Monsieur Callas. But I cannot emphasize too much that my duty is to remain discreet and to scrupulously respect the secrecy of the investigation."

"But what can you tell us, then? What did you discover? There has been talk of infants' skeletons."

Contrary to what he had just said, the interview had been arranged on the magistrate's initiative. Jacob Callas was hoping the judge had come to unveil something.

"I'm only a citizen like others. A great deal of information is already publicly available and I understand very well why it raises so many questions. I also think that the French people are once again showing great wisdom in following, and in such detail, what is happening in our country. Personally, I think they are not given a sufficient voice."

A short silence. A clearing of the throat in the back and a glance toward the high seas of demagogy.

"You know, Monsieur Callas, in my work as a judge I meet the French people when they come, as members of juries, to aid me in my difficult task. I am talking about the work I do every day in the courts of our beautiful provinces. And I can assure you that there is a true pertinence, a deep understanding and moral sense in our fellow citizens. I know that one must not lie to them or conceal from them a truth they have a right to know. But here, things are simple: I can't talk about an ongoing investigation."

The journalist, after a broad smile of assent, tried to restart the discussion. Apparently the judge would not discuss this rumor about baby skeletons that had been circulating in editorial offices and on the Internet since the day before. But what about the story of the Second World War lieutenant? Callas let himself go a bit:

"I understand, judge, that you can't tell us everything, and that is entirely to your credit. But allow me to speculate in your place. Let's imagine that someday we find the body of this Jean-François Lafitte, of whom Gemoni is supposed to be, if we believe the rumors, a sort of . . . reincarnation. Let's grant that he has been found and identified, following only Gemoni's directions, and even though no one knows where he is buried. On that hypothesis, it would be difficult to doubt this reincarnation, and we would find ourselves confronted by an extraordinary situation, to say the least. If that were the case, we would have to conclude that Manuel Gemoni in fact killed Tobias Darbier, alias Klaus Krinkel, in legitimate self-defense, so to speak. How could that be translated into juridical terms?"

Judioni gave a great laugh that was as false as it was out of proportion:

"A fantastic idea, I agree. But if ifs and ands were pots and pans, Monsieur Callas, there'd be no trade for tinkers. No, let's be serious. I'm not going to evade your question, don't worry, but I have to inform you regarding certain facts that are apparently not yet in your possession."

Jacob Callas's eyes began to shine. A scoop? The Holy Grail for a hack forever doomed to deal with trivia.

"Whatever we French discover, or rather imagine, I'm here to tell you that the accused, Manuel Gemoni, will be retried in the Dominican Republic. It is on that condition alone that the Dominican authorities authorized the departure of an individual whom they consider to be the murderer of one of their fellow citizens. Unless he is given the maximum sentence of thirty years in prison or the case is dismissed on sufficient grounds, as soon as his trial here is over, he will be sent back to the site

of his crime. And over there, I doubt that the police will enter-
tain the kind of woolly hypotheses that Superintendent
Mallock, for whom I have the greatest esteem, is so good at
forming."

Callas was delighted. A scoop plus a personal attack, what
a dream! Above all, keep it going:

"It is also said that the superintendent's behavior has been
strange. He is supposed to have taken hallucinogens and participated in other hypnosis sessions. What do you think of that,
as a judge?"

"One must never anathematize anyone. I am concerned
with the facts and nothing else. Countless remarkable political
figures have been besmirched by malicious rumors. Let us be
very careful. But be assured that there will be no weakness on
my part. If a mistake has been made, at whatever level of the
police hierarchy, I shall be merciless. We cannot tolerate the
slightest deviant conduct that would endanger justice in our
nation. Superintendent Amédée Mallock, to whom, I repeat,
our country owes so much, will probably someday have to
explain certain excesses that are, rightly or wrongly, attributed
to him. And I have no doubt that he will do so, and, I hope, as
soon as possible. In the meantime, he continues to enjoy my
complete confidence."

"So why don't you replace him?"

"I am only a simple judge, Monsieur Callas."

"Well then, what advice would you give him?" the journalist persisted, praying for the comment that would create a
polemic.

"Perhaps to show more humility. He is a public servant, and
as such he has to be irreproachable. He should get into line
and not open himself up, as he usually seems to do, to so many
rumors because of behavior that is more than controversial. A
friend told me in detail about the hypnosis sessions, and it's
quite appalling."

When Mallock finally decided to turn off the TV, he had lost any calm he might have gained. He was used to being attacked by jerks. But that didn't mean he liked it, or found it amusing.

In his view, there were more serious things than having to endure a few snubs on television: it was what they implied more generally. Even all tarted up, the true and the just interested no one. Idiots, hypocrites, windbags, lobbies, and the corrupt gathered together in the great liars' fair. There they exchanged rumors and gossip, personal promotion and propaganda, without having to fear anyone.

"What good does it do to curse imposters?" Amédée whispered to Mallock to try to calm him down.

There was at least one positive point in the interview with the judge. He now knew where the newspapers were getting their information. It was Maître Pierre Parquet who had confided in his friend Judge Judioni.

"Damn it!" he cried out loud as he picked up his telephone.

After all, he'd warned Jack. It's dangerous to annoy a hibernating bear.

36

Thursday, December 19, Fort Mallock

Outside, between two waves of intense cold, it had begun to snow again, timidly. The little sparse flakes fell in silence, one by one, like paratroopers dropping behind enemy lines. Mallock adjusted the collar of his overcoat. The asphalt was covered with a thick layer of ice and people were walking with their feet spread wide apart like penguins on an ice floe. The superintendent did not regret having chosen to add crepe soles to his equipment.

To forget the judge's wounding remarks, Mallock forced himself to keep his mind busy. First of all, he had to assess the whole situation regarding Manuel Gemoni. And start by going back to the very beginning of the investigation. Hadn't he left something by the wayside? A lead, a comment, an expression on Manu's face? He concentrated, and the snowflakes stopped falling, the sound of cars disappeared, and the capital evaporated. When the outside world reappeared, he was about to cross the Seine.

Two things had come back to him.

What Manu had said at the end of their first conversation: "He seemed to recognize me when I attacked him." Mallock hadn't remembered this phrase because at the time he couldn't explain it. He'd put it in the big pile of "nonsense." That was no longer the case. He could either choose to adopt, once and for all, the hypothesis of reincarnation, and find in this recognition a kind of confirmation on the part of Krinkel himself upon seeing his victim again, sixty years later, or he

could decide to remain in the rational, and then he could justify this remark by pointing to the obvious physical resemblance between Manuel and the late Jean-François Lafitte.
Mallock sighed. How could they have done such a thing to
him? A case in which all the clues led systematically to opposite conclusions.

His thoughts were interrupted by an urgent appeal from his
eyes, which were clamoring for his attention. *Come see,
Mallock.*

In front of him was the frozen Seine, with a barge caught
right in the middle. A little farther on, at the foot of Notre-
Dame, there was a tour boat, partly crushed by the pressure of
the ice and without a single windowpane intact. When the ice
thawed, it would sink immediately. Great, one fewer!

After an amused glance, Amédée continued on his way and
the course of his thoughts: the second thing he'd forgotten,
Manu's blood test. The one he'd requested at the outset, the
day when Julie came to see him. Since then, no one had spoken to him about it again. At the time, the hypothesis that
Manuel might have been drugged had seemed to him one of
the possibilities that shouldn't be neglected. The techniques of
hypnosis, combined with substances that made it possible to
compel someone to commit acts of violence without his assent,
were not an invention of spy movies. An organization or an
interest group could very well have carried out Tobias's murder by remote control. This was all the more credible now that
they knew Krinkel's criminal past. But then why would they
have chosen Manuel Gemoni for the job? That remained to be
elucidated. Mallock resolved to inform himself regarding the
results of this blood test as soon as he arrived at the Fort.

Then he caught himself grumbling, all by himself, out loud,
as he walked alongside Notre-Dame. The drug hypothesis now
seemed to him a little more plausible with each step he took.
So simple and so obvious that he began to worry. What if his

orders hadn't been followed? What if the Dominican Republic had kept the samples? What if they'd been lost somewhere between the Caribbean and 36 Quai des Orfèvres? What if they were out of date and couldn't be analyzed? What if the quantity was insufficient? And what if they hadn't been kept refrigerated . . . Damn, there's going to be hell to pay, the bear growled.

He had hardly arrived at the Fort before he ran into Julie.

"And the blood tests? Where are we with those?"

Julie opened her big doe eyes wide.

"What blood tests?"

Here, Mallock could have fired. The prey was trapped, looking right at him, in his crosshairs. The hunter's index finger was in perfect position on the trigger. All he had to do was pull: bang! Shoot a big one right between the eyes. But it was a little too easy, and frankly, little Julie didn't deserve such a fate.

So the bear in crepe soles lowered his weapon and explained patiently:

"Remember. When you came to see me about Manu the first time, I told you to ask for a blood . . . "

"Oh, yes! Of course."

Mallock's blood temperature fell below boiling.

"Don't tell me you didn't ask for the analyses?"

The rifle was up again, cocked, and Mallock felt ready to shoot once more.

"Of course I did. I didn't go to check the results, is all. But the Dominican authorities did send them to us in response to my request. In fact, we must have received the blood samples on the day you left to go over there. Since I didn't know what you wanted to do, I waited until you got back. And then, with all this hypnosis business I didn't think about it."

"Neither did I," Mallock acknowledged in fit of magnanimity. "After all, the main thing is to have the samples. We need a complete toxicological analysis. I want to be sure that Manu was not simply drugged."

"I'll go down to ask them to do what's necessary, Boss. It'll go quicker if I talk to them in person."

"Fine, I'll be in my office."

Then he hesitated for a few seconds. Should he tell her?

"Julie, I'm going to call Jean-Pierre Delmont, the ambassador who dealt with your brother. I'm going to try to confirm this business about a second trial. I suppose you know about that?"

Julie's eyes filled with tears as she nodded.

"Take it easy. I swear I haven't had my last word. O.K.?"

As a response, Mallock received a sad little sniff. He was satisfied with that, and went on:

"By the way, call Bob, would you? I want him to come see me in my office."

Mallock had some difficulty in reaching Santo Domingo. In the end, the ambassador called him back.

Delmont sounded embarrassed.

"Really sorry, Superintendent! That is unfortunately correct. Manuel will not escape a second trial. The Dominican authorities were inflexible. That was the sole condition on which they were willing to allow him to leave the island. That solution was ideal for them. They were afraid of being responsible for his death and all the tourist problems that would accompany it, but they also weren't prepared to let their territorial *cojones* be cut off. We'll let you have him, you take care of him, put him on trial, and afterward, back to square one."

Mallock growled an oath.

"I wasn't involved in this," the ambassador tried to explain. "It was between the president's office and the Quai d'Orsay. When we met, I can swear to you that I didn't know about it. If it's any consolation to you, I even threatened to resign.

Obviously I thought I was far more important than I am. My attempt at extortion amused them and they didn't fail to tell me that. I was pretty annoyed, in fact."

Even if he didn't have the heart for it, Mallock couldn't help retorting:

"You see, you're concerned about your *cojones* too."

"You're not wrong about that, Mallock . . . Touché! I picked up the little fragments of my pride and brought out the heavy artillery. You know, Superintendent, one doesn't serve in a position like mine for long without having an opportunity to build up one's own collection of exotic documents and anecdotes, if you see what I mean."

"I have a vague idea," Mallock smiled into the telephone.

"It's thanks to that that I was able to negotiate those two exceptions."

"Namely? I'd like to hear a confirmation from you on this point."

"Well, if he is given the maximum sentence, our thirty years without possibility of parole, or if the case is dismissed on sufficient grounds, they have agreed not to exercise the right to return him to the Dominican Republic. And that is assured; they've signed and can't go back on it."

"Maybe, but it isn't going to be easy. According to his lawyer, in this case he's risking a sentence of five to eleven years. And then we're—"

"It's up to you to get the 'current state of affairs' changed. It's in your hands. It would be better for him never to set foot on the island again."

"What do you mean?"

"Don't forget that I tried to warn you about the dangers on the island."

"What do you mean?" Mallock repeated. "Are you alluding to the *brutos*?"

"Whether Manuel spends one year or ten in prison, returning to the island would be equivalent to a death sentence for him."

Mallock knew that but wanted to hear it said to him one more time. Like a door that is slammed or a bridge that you blow up behind you. For Amédée there was henceforth only one thing to do: seek an acquittal.

He had hardly hung up before Daranne appeared in his office. He was wearing his bad-day face. And there was a scratch on his temple.

"Do you have a problem with my report on the Gemonis, Boss?"

"No, not at all, Bob. But it looks like there's a problem with your face."

Daranne put his hand alongside his eye.

"This? It's nothing. I slipped on that damned ice. In fact, I fell down three times, just getting from my car to the Fort."

Then Mallock made two decisions. First, not to even smile, because his collaborator wasn't in the mood. Second, to offer him a cup of coffee.

As he turned on the percolator, the telephone rang. Mallock signaled to Daranne to answer it, indicating by his gesture that he wasn't there for anyone.

"Bob Daranne here. What is it?"

Then a minute's silence, followed by:

"Sorry, this isn't Monsieur Dublin's office. What did you say?"

" . . . "

"Captain Daranne, and you are?"

Bob seemed surprised.

"It's somebody who wants to talk to the chief. I told him that this wasn't Dublin's number. He said he was Judge Judioni. I don't know; do you want to take it?"

"Yes, let me do it."

The rest of the conversation took place before the eyes of a completely astonished Daranne.

"So, Judioni, you want to talk to my boss?"

" . . . "

"A real bastard? Maybe, but in legitimate self-defense. I warned you not to pull my string too much. On TV, you—"

" . . . "

"I can hardly wait for your counterattack. But watch out. There will be reprisals. I've still got some aces up my sleeve . . . "

" . . . "

"Yes, of course. I love you too, pal," Mallock finally said before hanging up on him.

He looked up and glanced at Daranne, smiling:

"Don't worry. It's just a little clarification. The judge didn't appreciate me mentioning a couple of things about him to a journalist friend of mine."

"Your friend Margot Murât, Boss?"

"Drop it. How's it going?"

Daranne hesitated a few seconds and then gave up. After all, he trusted his boss.

"Oof! It could be better."

He ran his thumb over his red and white mustache.

"It's over with my wife. I don't know what she wants anymore, but in any case it's not me. Too old, too stupid, too everything, too nothing. She's like my sons, they're disappointed by what I've become. With my stupidities, I've managed to get them all against me. Great job, huh? Except maybe for the youngest, who still has a minimum of respect for me, the rest of the family avoids me."

It was sad, even if Daranne had brought it on himself. Authoritarian and not very affectionate with his sons, he'd made their childhoods an ordeal of screams and slaps. As for his wife, he'd treated her the way any macho does. Without malice, he'd simply seen her as a sort of maid with a lifelong contract, ensured employment with a whore option for Saturday nights, plus the quick little blow job on triumphant mornings. Given all that, it was hard to believe that he loved them, and yet that was just the way he was . . .

"I'm leaving this evening to repair a wall that has collapsed in Luc. I'll be back on Tuesday for Christmas. My sons are doing me the honor of coming to dinner at home."

Mallock was uncomfortable. Daranne didn't usually reveal his moods. Should he pretend he hadn't heard anything or encourage him to spill his guts? Mallock chose the latter option.

"You aren't telling me everything and that bothers me. That's why I called you in. You worry me, old man."

"I hope you're not afraid that I might do it again, Boss?"

Daranne was alluding to his attempt to commit suicide the first time his wife left him.

"No, not really. But a little. I've warned you that if you tried that again, I'd shoot you. But my impression is that professionally, things aren't going well. I sense that you're less involved, less interested in the investigations."

Daranne scratched his head.

"You're right, I'm not with it. In everything, in fact. The tiniest gesture, the words I say, always off the mark. I don't know quite how to put it. If I say black, that's because it's white. I go to the right when I should have gone left. I even laugh wrong, not when you're supposed to. Every time, I look like a jerk. That's what getting old means, sometimes. In fact, I think I'm broken and too old to be fixed. Too unhip to make it worth the trouble. Do you see what I mean? And then, don't tell anyone but at the slightest little thing I start crying like a girl. It's hard to realize that you're worthless both professionally and emotionally. It's a helluva failure. There, see, just talking to you about it is setting me off again, I feel like I'm going to start bawling."

Daranne grabbed a big Kleenex and blew his nose so violently that he let a series of farts out of his other end. Mallock looked at him and felt like weeping and laughing at the same time. It was true that Bob was really not with it.

Amédée took a deep breath:

"I know you don't much like people telling you this, but somebody has to do it. You're depressed again, Bob. And you know what you have to do. A little visit to the psychiatrist you saw the other time, a few 'magic pills,' and you'll be good as new. So don't give me any shit about your macho notions. You saw that treatment helped you the last time, right?"

"Hmmph, maybe. But I don't know if I want someone to help me. If I'm no longer capable of handling it myself, then—"

"Then what? Are you going to mess around with your piece again, as they do in those stupid American films where the cop finds nothing more virile to do than sob and stick the barrel of a gun in his mouth?"

"I didn't say that, Boss, but . . . Anyway, the shrink I saw the last time has retired, so . . . And then, it's true that I feel out of it, completely out of it. For example, I don't understand anything about this business with Julie's brother."

"Don't worry about that," Mallock shouted at him, "I don't understand it either. I'm lost. Mallock has been knocked out. So? Am I going to shoot myself? Hell, no! I'm just going to continue . . . "

Daranne was a little thrown off balance by his boss's outburst. He sensed that Amédée was sincere.

"Then why haven't you gone about it . . . normally?"

"What do you mean?"

"I don't know. The way you conduct a normal investigation. We arrest a suspect, we take his prints, we put him under the tanning light, we suck his blood. We search his house and question his neighbors. Little by little, we ferret out everybody. It's always a family member or a neighbor, isn't it? Well . . . You haven't even made a neighborhood investigation, here in Paris."

"Because we do that around the scene of the crime, silly. And in this case the scene of the crime was an island. Not here! I got involved after Tobias's murder, not at the time Manuel disappeared."

Bob took on his beaten dog look again. Mallock felt bad. He didn't know quite what to do with either the man or the situation. He too had only one desire: to leave for Normandy, to shut himself up in his house and hibernate. His chronic fatigue and depression, along with the confounded tangle from which he'd been struggling to extricate himself since the beginning of this investigation, had consumed all his energy. He would need strength to straighten out the twisted path that lay before Daranne.

Amédée grew frightened. If he didn't have enough determination to help his friend, if he didn't do anything, the dope might shoot himself. He abruptly made up his mind. Picked up the phone and dialed the number of his own shrink.

"Hi, it's Mallock. I know that I'm not supposed to do this, but listen . . . "

A quarter of an hour later, Daranne, who had spoken to the psychiatrist, hung up.

"I'm supposed to see him on the 27th at 10 A.M. Unbelievable, isn't it? I will have seen my sons the day before. My feelings should still be fresh."

"I'd have preferred for him to see you sooner."

"He couldn't. He seems like an unusually nice guy, especially for a shrink."

"He is," Mallock interrupted. "Now get out of here."

37.
Friday, December 20

He woke up at noon.

The answering machine was blinking, his inbox was overflowing, and the sun was shining. There are mornings like that when it isn't even morning anymore. Mallock grimaced. His back and his head still hurt. Outside, the day had begun. The world obviously had no problem getting along without him. That was a disagreeable feeling, even at his age. Why in the name of God can't we remain, once and for all, the center of the world? As when we were cooing with the nipple in our mouth? Instead of having to keep going on and on, farther and farther . . . as far as the brink, as far as the abyss? Until death follows!

The preceding evening, Mallock had drunk more than usual. And he usually drank quite a lot. But there was Bob's sorrow. His own concern. Judioni's voice. And his words: "a real bastard." He didn't like that. And he didn't like playing the informer, either. Two or three years earlier, he would never have made the phone call in question.

Stool pigeon, a little voice deep inside him whispered.

That would hurt for a few days yet, and then it would go away. But it made him doubt. Doubt himself and what he had become. Could it be that he had turned into a "real bastard" without even realizing it? He needed two glasses of whiskey to drown that incipient panic attack. To shut up that big wave of fear. He caressed his bottle of single malt affectionately. In moments like these, only alcohol could perform that miracle.

And it did it without asking anything, without moralizing, and without making its patient wait in the antechamber of guilt.

Wasn't alcoholism great?

No, but neither was sorrow!

Mallock regularly found himself caught between the two and called upon to choose. He gave in to sobriety only when forced to.

One does not choose despair lightly.

Already 1 P.M. Mallock put on his outfit for very cold days and went out to visit the bookstore run by his friend Léonid Scheinberg.

While he was in Nazi prison camps, the young man had promised to convert when he got out. The day of his baptism, in July 1949, he'd taken advantage of the event to change his name. This homosexual Jew who was also a freethinking ero-tomaniac made a very strange Catholic. Not the recruit of the century, the old priest at Saint-Placide who carried out the renaming must have said to himself. On that day Léon Galène, alias Léonid, who had had time to triple his weight since he'd arrived at the Gare de l'Est, had promised himself to do a ton of things, such as not speak for a year, see an aurora borealis, never lie again, either to himself or to others, eat ortolan, laugh underwater, open a bookstore, and do everything he could to recover the lightheartedness he'd had when he was three years old.

And the most incredible thing was that he had kept all his promises.

The little bells hanging from the ceiling tinkled. The shop was empty. At the very back, among the piles of books, stood Monsieur Léon. He was still very handsome, with his blue eyes, his big Ashkenazi nose, his full lips, and his silvery hair. He was short and always wore plain gray suits, blue silk ties, and two-tone shoes, flat black and patent leather. A kind of elegant uniform or a retro look, as we would now say.

"Greetings, wizard. So, you've been up to your old tricks!"

Surprised, Mallock wondered what his old friend was alluding to.

"What do you mean by that?"

"Don't play the innocent and give me a little time."

"But I didn't say anything!"

"What about the photo you sent me, was that just an accident?"

Mallock almost asked what he was talking about but then changed his mind. They'd go into that later. Especially since he was hungry. The bear hadn't eaten much since the night before. Bear irritated, bear no eat, so bear starving.

"It's almost two o'clock. I'm afraid the restaurant won't take us anymore."

"Go ahead, I'll join you. Were you planning to go to the Marseillais?"

"Well, yeah, unless you've got a better idea."

"Frankly, I don't care. You will understand why when I bring you the result of my research."

"Is it positive?" Mallock asked with dread.

Léon hesitated.

"Let's say that it's the chef's surprise. It's even the surprise of all surprises."

Mallock stifled his curiosity and went out into the street, heading for the Paris-Marseille restaurant.

When he got there, the owner laughed and shrieked:

"Oh my God, I can't believe it. Mooosieur Superintendent!"

"The comedy of repetition is your thing, César. You're not going to serve up the same refrain every time I come here, are you?"

"Especially since I have no excuse, I was expecting you."

"How's that, you were expecting me?"

"Well, yes! Your harem is already there. I seated them at the back. You're going bad, Superintendent, you're making them wait for you like a real macho from back home."

"What harem are you talking about?"

"Your girls, the two lookers from last time . . . Do you have more than one harem?"

From the back of the room, Kiko and Julie were smiling at Mallock.

"Great minds think alike, girls. Did you come back to try to seduce big César?"

They both got up to embrace their superintendent.

"How about you, you don't come here just for the cuisine, do you?" Julie asked mischievously.

César backed away, raising his arms.

"Oh, damn, a firing squad, a trio of cops. I'm getting out of here before you do something you shouldn't."

Laughing, Mallock took a chair and sat down at the table next to them.

"Am I bothering you? Because I can go . . . "

"Of course not. On the contrary, Kiko and I were just talking about going to see you to find out where we are. And then I've got some hot new information."

With this weather, anything hot was welcome.

"Go ahead, Julie, out with it."

"Jo tried to reach you this morning. I was the one who took the call. She confirmed that the hair found on the site, next to the well and the chain, the hair that is supposed to be Krinkel's, if we believe Manu's account, does in fact correspond to the samples brought back from the Dominican Republic."

"What samples?"

Mallock was at a loss.

"The ones you asked Daranne to get behind my back, Superintendent. The ones taken from Darbier's corpse."

"It's not good to be bitter, Captain," Mallock smiled, happy with the news.

There was no longer any doubt, Klaus Krinkel and Tobias Darbier were one and the same person.

"Finally, something concrete, expected, and logical. I was beginning to lose the habit. And what about Manu's blood tests?"

"The Judicial Identity guys handled that. But there, too, I had the results this morning through Jo. Negative. There was nothing in Manu's blood, no alcohol, no drugs."

Mallock gave a little growl like a bear going back into hibernation. He would have liked to find a nice cocktail of drugs. Well! As with all the information in this case, he'd have to deal it.

"Nothing else?"

"Yes, but I don't know if Kiko needs to hear it."

Kiko gave her a dark look.

"I have more right to know everything about this case than the two of you put together. It's the future of my husband and my family that is at stake. Not yours! What's the problem? Are you afraid I'm going to transmit information to Manu? I've sworn to you that I will never say anything. I want to know the truth, not fabricate it."

Julie heaved a deep sigh before turning to Mallock and saying:

"The little bones we found are in fact human. They are apparently those of two children aged six and fourteen months. We even have their names. They correspond to statements filed a few days afterward. One at the office of the village's mayor, the other in a gendarmerie a little farther away."

Julie paused before declaring, as if regretfully:

"There were, in fact, traces of charring and marks made by teeth on those bones. Human incisors and canines, but especially molars."

It took Kiko several seconds to grasp what Julie was saying. At the instant she understood, her hand flew to her mouth to try to keep a cry from coming out. Silence fell around them. Each was fighting with his demons and trying to control them. Rage and anger for Mallock, despair and incredulity for Kiko, a desire to weep for Julie.

Léon arrived during this moment of silence. He brought in on his shoulders a few snowflakes from outside that mixed with the two little troops of dandruff that had already been camping out on his old overcoat for a few days. He didn't seem surprised by the presence of the two young women, whom he greeted with a brief "Mesdemoiselles."

Julie wasn't satisfied with that.

"Don't you recognize me, Léon?"

"Oh, excuse me, Julie! It's that I've made such discoveries that they've completely discombobulated me. And then you're getting prettier and prettier. I don't know whether it's you or a woman who is still more beautiful . . . You're stunning, dear Julie."

"You old pervert," Amédée interrupted. "Cut the crap and spill it."

Léon took a deep breath full of regrets.

"As soon as I came back here, two days ago, I investigated. I'll spare you the details, it was rather difficult. Anyway, I obtained more information about this SS *Oberleutnant* from two friends who are historians. Digging around and putting serious pressure on all my contacts, I found one who ended up telling me the whole story. I warn you, it's crazy. No one knows whether it's true or false. But there is concordant testimony. It's huge, but I can't go on without . . . "

An impatient look from Mallock.

"Okay, okay, I'll go on. At the beginning, it's supposed to have been Himmler's idea. The other madman expressed the desire to gather together the elite of the elite of the *Schutzstaffel*, as if the SS itself were not enough for him. He already had a name for his collection of crazies, the SSS! The first S symbolized 'supra.' It might have ended there, because at first Hitler didn't think it would be useful, but that other sicko, Joseph Goebbels, adopted the idea and put his own twist on it. And then, bingo, Hitler went for it. The idea put forth by the Reich's propaganda minister was to spread genuine panic among the enemy troops and civilians by means of a rumor, but a rumor that could be manipulated because it was well-founded and especially because it was unverifiable. Before German troops arrived in an area, terrifying stories invaded the region. To feed these horrors, they are supposed to have decided to train specialized units in *Gesamtterror*: absolute terror. Six battalions of six men each, with six madmen as their leaders. The Devil's 666. It was still this fascination with two-bit mythology and stupid Prussian legends. You can be sure that these battalions would have had the right and the duty to behave in the most ignoble way. Rape, disemboweling, decapitation, torture, everything was to be done without restraint and with the greatest perversity. There was only one imperative: strike people's minds. They were also ordered to let one or two witnesses escape each orgy of violence. On the other hand, they were to leave behind as little proof as possible, and they were not to let themselves be taken alive under any circumstances. Curiously, it's the last point that helped discredit this story. The notion that they committed suicide and erased proof made it a little too easy to justify the absence of tangible evidence, even though now, knowing what we know, it explains why we weren't aware of it. Am I making myself understood?"

"The last part is a little confused. But that's all right, go on."

Mallock, like Julie and Kiko, had only one desire: to hear the rest. But his mind took off in a spiral: KKK, SSS, 666 . . .

The three scars on Darbier's skull. He began to think about DNA's double helix. Couldn't the myth of the superior race be expressed by a triple helix? A crazy idea based on genetic mutation by selection. Mallock had to force himself to return to Earth and listen to Léon:

"The rumor had to remain, if not unfounded, at least unproven. And it worked, in part. That's what I wanted to say, in fact—"

"What about Krinkel?" Julie asked, thinking mainly about her brother.

"Klaus Krinkel, KKK. Well, as you now know, he really existed. His itinerary passes through St. Petersburg. But he disappeared in 1944, killed during the landing in Normandy. He's supposed to have led the first and only battalion that Goebbels managed to assemble. It can be assumed that it consisted of all the members initially foreseen for the six distinct commandos, the thirty-six men whom Lieutenant Lafitte and his unit ran into. Another troubling aspect of Manuel's story is this business of fighting Krinkel with a pitchfork. It fits amazingly well with what we now know. All the documents, the rare photos, and the descriptions given by various persons agree on one point: the leader of the SSS was a very handsome man who had nothing in common with Tobias Darbier."

"So? They're nonetheless the same individual. We have his fingerprints and his DNA."

"I didn't say we didn't, Amédée. This is another one of destiny's dirty tricks. By an irony of fate, it was by disfiguring him that Jean-François Lafitte saved his life, in a way. The sadistic nature of his crimes had placed him in the first rank of those to be put on trial after the war. He should never have been able to escape. The few testimonies to the atrocities he committed, whether in Poland on the Russian front, make us pensive. And here legend rejoins history. Everything I found out about this fine gentleman, even his nickname, 'the Ogre,' has to be taken literally. You won't believe it, but there are abominable accusations against him and some of his lieutenants. Get this: even cannibalism. Horrifying stories of babies who disappeared. Keep in mind that I'm not saying they're true, and I think pain can lead astray people who . . . "

But Léon stopped. Mallock's and Julie's looks had been unequivocal.

"Why are you looking at me like that? Have you found something? How did you . . . "

"We found bones around the well. And unfortunately, Léon, they leave little doubt regarding this . . . legend that is no legend. Julie has just told me that the analyses confirm our worst fears. The size and the development of the little skeletons. And multiple tooth marks on the bones."

Léon's cell phone began to vibrate. He flipped it open, holding it at arm's length to locate the green icon in the form of a telephone.

He then pressed it against his ear.

"Yes, it's Scheinberg. I was waiting for your call. Yes, the inscription. Well?"

Mallock noticed that Léon had for once resumed his birth name. Then there were two minutes of silence. The bookseller murmured a series of exclamations. During this time, Mallock was boiling with impatience. He suspected that the call was connected with the business of the cross, but he didn't see how a simple object could put his friend in such a state.

"Incredible!" Léon cried, closing his phone.

"Did you find out to whom the initials correspond?"

"It's not 'to whom' but 'to what.' I'd turned those notorious initials, 'MPF,' every which way. I went through all the possible first names, then the composite names, like Marc-Paul. I moved from French to English, then to German. Finally, it was my two historian friends who freed me from that sterile effort. One of them looked at me as if I were the dumbest of the dumb. The letters mean 'died for France': '*Mort pour la France,*' MPF. At first, I was doubtful, but I ended up accepting the obvious."

Mallock was not really surprised, just vexed that he had not figured out the puzzle. Bravo, Wizard!

"But what was it doing at the bottom of an empty well in the middle of nowhere?"

"That, my dear, is what I've been trying to find out for the last two days. And I can tell you that I've annoyed a lot of people. All my contacts and the best experts have been exploited. Including the ones to whom you referred me. I labored a bit, but finally got lucky. An anonymous phone call, if you can imagine that. A man's voice, an old man, who asked me if I wanted to hear the story of that cross. He said he'd learned about our investigation through one of your contacts, Julie. I told him I refused to speak with people who didn't give their names. He hesitated, then asked me to forget his name immediately. So I promised, swore, crossed my heart and hoped to die. What the guy told me is so strange that I probably would have hesitated to believe it if I hadn't already had clues that led me in the same direction. If you said that this goes far beyond anything you could have imagined, you wouldn't be far off. We came to an understanding and he agreed to send a copy of all his documents to a third party whom we both know, a great specialist in this dark period, who was asked to analyze them and let me know his conclusions."

And there Léon stopped. As if he had said everything.

"Go on," Mallock said, encouraging him. "When will you have these conclusions?"

"I have them, Superintendent. That was the phone call I just received."

"So? What was the result?"

Mallock would have gladly strangled him to obtain more quickly the words that Léon must have stored up in his big bald head long enough to make the tension mount. For once it was the bookseller who had exclusive possession of the information, and he wanted to take advantage of it. All's fair in love and war. But he took pity on Julie and Kiko, whose looks were imploring him to tell them what he'd found.

"Well, I think I can finally tell you exactly where Jean-François Lafitte's body is. It all begins with a decision made by a famous general!"

38.
Tuesday, December 24, Early in the Morning

The fourth day of the snowstorm in Paris. And it wasn't over. Christmas would be whiter than it had ever been in the memory of Parisians. Mallock had difficulty opening the door of his building, which was blocked by several feet of white powder. Once outside, he walked as far as the rue de Rivoli, then headed for Châtelet.

It was still very beautiful. A new Paris, as if just revealed. A mad Paris, without the dirtying flow of automobiles. Without the carbon-laden air of urban vehicles. An unprecedented capital covered by several feet of immaculate snow. Rounding off the angles, draping the façades, it was nature that was taking back, in the form of snowflakes, its place within the city, a village of snow with heavy stone buildings. It was the sound of the wind, too, and that of silence, a voiceless phantom taking its revenge on the usual noise of the city. It was a few hundred Parisians skating on a snowy, frozen-over Seine. It was the beige, dirty Tour Saint-Jacques and the crunching sound of Mallock's footsteps as he trudged over these unprecedented mounds of snow. It was, impatient and amazed, his life that was leading him, in the cottony cold of this baptismal day, toward a revelation that might be going to change everything.

No more cars, no more buses, only the Metro was running, more or less, to irrigate the capital. So let's take the Metro. Mallock wasn't really a regular, but you have to make the best of things. And then it was a direct shot on line No. 1. A dozen stations where he would breathe in the smell of the plodding, feverishly impatient crowd. By chance, the superintendent chose a car that was full of women reading. All around him, their eyes were flicking back and forth, following the lines of ink in novels about other things and other places, following the thread of words to discover their meaning. The meaning of all this. So long as someone reads, there will be hope. Mallock was convinced of that, even if he wasn't quite sure why.

Not all the exits from the stations had been cleared. About one out of three. The others, buried in snow, had to await the transit authority's teams, which were, of course, overloaded. After the Concorde station, he had to continue on as far as Charles de Gaulle-Étoile before he could get out.

Outside was the Champs-Élysées under the snow.

The landscape was incredible.

The city, enlarged by its milky epidermis, resembled a lost metropolis, an Atlantis extending for miles. Toward the east, the whiteness of the snow set off the yellows and browns of the bas-reliefs on the Arc de Triomphe, a monumental edifice sculpted by a huge giant in the ivory of a titanic tusk. To the west, the gaze lost itself in the white stretching as far as the rolling plateaus of the Tuilieries in the distance.

Just as he emerged, the storm accorded the sun a few seconds to illuminate the scene and dazzle forever those who were lucky enough to be there. Mallock, fascinated by what he saw, had not immediately noticed Bob, who had probably just gotten out of the same train in the Metro.

"Damn, it's really coming down, Boss!"

Daranne had always had the rare ability to make any trace of poetry evaporate.

"You said it, pal!" Mallock replied in the same vein.

"So, is it the big day?"

Bob wore a magnificent child's smile. Mallock was delighted. It had been so long since he'd seen that kind of expression on Bob's face. He'd been right to choose him for the opening of the tomb.

"Who told you it was the big day?"

"You did, Boss. I don't even know what it's about. I thought I understood that all the others wanted to come, but that's all. I am very grateful to you for having taken me with you, but I can't be too late, I've got my special meal to prepare for lunch. I'm in a terrible rush. Did I tell you my kids were coming?"

Mallock didn't have time to answer, because in a moment the sky clouded over and a snow squall swept over the square.

"It's going to start snowing again, Bob. Let's hurry."

Daranne followed him as they headed for the Arc de Triomphe. The path that had been cleared to allow access to the monument was particularly slippery. Mallock took advantage of their slow progress to bring his collaborator up-to-date.

Three days earlier, Léon had delivered his revelation and they'd all been stunned.

At the bottom of the well, there had been only three identical sculpted crosses with the inscription MPF. The order came directly from General de Gaulle. The great man had made one of his democratic unilateral decisions. In his view, for this war, they needed a very special unknown soldier. They had to choose a body and entomb it next to the bier from the First World War. Considering the comments the Allies would not have failed to make and the reactions to be expected from the veterans of the Great War, he had decided to proceed secretly. "We shall inform the French people when the time comes," he had declared, how long that would be depending on his own will. De Gaulle was far too intelligent not to have already seen the limits of democracy and universal suffrage. The successive presidents of the Republic had been kept informed of the existence of this second unknown soldier, but none of them thought it useful to reveal a secret that had become awkward.

"But why so many precautions?" Mallock had asked. "After all, it was an honor; as in the First World War, everyone would have agreed."

Léon grimaced.

"That has nothing to do with it. You don't realize it, but the First World War was a still greater trauma. Ten million dead! And don't imagine that the burial of the unknown soldier at the Arc de Triomphe took place without controversy at the time. The whole affair was a terrible mess. Seventy million men had been in uniform. A million and half French people had died and three hundred and fifty thousand had disappeared. In fact, these 'absences' turned out to be an even bigger trauma for the families than the death of the victims. At the time, people were still very religious and considered these disappearances as a condemnation to nothingness beyond death. And then over several generations, millions of people had been wiped off the face of the earth, ranging from the sons of Edward Kipling to Louis Pergaud, by way of the aviator Roland Garros and writers like Péguy and Apollinaire. So something had to be done. According to my documents, the first person to have had the idea was the head of the memorial association Souvenir Français in Rennes, Francis Simon. The deputy from Chartres, Maurice something-or-other, took up the idea shortly afterward, adding the notion of the ordinary soldier. They had to take not an officer, but someone who would symbolize the peasant torn away from his field to defend his country. I'll spare you the details, but one year after the armistice was signed, the Chamber of Deputies adopted a proposal to bury a soldier 'disinherited by death.'"

"And then?"

Mallock was getting impatient.

"Then things went wrong. As so often happens in France. Everybody had to get his word in. The government wanted to take advantage of the second anniversary of the armistice to celebrate the fiftieth anniversary of the Third Republic and transfer Gambetta's heart to the Pantheon. But then the royalists associated with Action Française and the Camelots du roi attacked the 'whore'—that's what they called the Republic—and opposed the burial of the unknown soldier in the Pantheon. For its part, perfidious Albion was preparing to beat us to the punch. The British parliament had rapidly passed a law and arrangements had been made to bury their unknown soldier in Westminster Abbey in a few days. To top everything, it was learned that somebody named Binet-Valmer and his friend Boicy were getting ready to go dig up their own unknown solider and throw him on Gambetta's catafalque. Finally, all these people got more or less back in line. And on November 8, by some miracle, an agreement was finally made—except for the socialists, who thought that the unknown soldier was now a right-wing concept to which they would never submit! On November 11, after following Gambetta's heart to the Pantheon, the body of the unknown soldier, carried on a gun carriage, was placed under the Arc de Triomphe. But it was not buried until the end of January the following year."

"And the choice? How did they make the choice?"

As always, Léon had all the answers.

"Eight groups of soldiers who were unidentified but wore French uniforms were exhumed in each of the areas most affected by the war: Flanders, Artois, Somme, Chemin des Dames, Champagne, Verdun, and Lorraine. Then the eight coffins were transferred to a casemate in the citadel of Verdun. After they were switched around several times so that no one would know where they came from, the coffins were placed in a chapel of rest on November 10. André Maginot, known as the Sergeant, had chosen a man named Auguste Thin, who had also been a volunteer, the son of a soldier who had disappeared during the war and a war orphan. It was Thin who, by placing a bouquet of flowers on the coffin, designated for posterity the man who was to become the unknown soldier."

After explaining all this, Léon returned to his main revelation: the existence of a second soldier symbolizing the Second World War. The officer assigned in 1945 to find the body of this soldier had taken the initiative of limiting his choices to three places and three bodies. The swallows' spring was one of them. So they now had one chance in three of finding the long-sought body of Jean-François Lafitte. Even if, for Mallock, the probabilities were far more important. He remembered his dream in the amber chamber. A French flag snapping in the wind, and below it, a blue, white, and red flame: no matter how hard he tried to doubt his visions, they were becoming more and more troubling.

During the following three days, Amédée had not been idle; he'd been working all his connections. He had also drawn on the fortunate existence of a precedent, that of a soldier named Blessy, who had been disinterred in the Arlington National Cemetery in Virginia. But in the end, it was above all the friendship shown him by the president of the Republic after the poison case that had allowed him to obtain the authorization to have analyses done on the body enclosed in the crypt hidden under the Arc de Triomphe.

In particular, it had been decided to leave this soldier in his place if nothing made it possible to identify him, which most of the "initiates" involved in the project thought the most likely outcome. In the contrary case, if it was indeed the body of Lieutenant Lafitte, it would be buried wherever his descendants chose. In that event, two options would present themselves: either closing up the crypt, leaving the soldier from the First World War alone in his tomb, or, continuing and respecting General de Gaulle's initiative, proceeding to choose the body of an unknown soldier buried during the Second World

War. He would then join, with great pomp, and this time, before the eyes of the general public, his compatriot from the Great War. This second option was preferred by the president, but his advisors had instantly recommended that the French people make the final decision, probably by means of a referendum. "Sometimes it is good to let them have the illusion, if not that they control anything, at least that from time to time they serve some purpose," grumbled Mallock, whose opinion had not been asked.

Mallock and Bob finally stood beneath the imposing monument. Like everyone else, they couldn't help looking up. A kind of reflex or mystical salute to the majesty of the place. On the ground, the mass of swirling snow was making the flame vacillate as much as the superintendent's certainties. Who would have thought that a journey to the Dominican Republic, a witch, a giant jungle vine, and a simple sentence—"I killed him because he killed me"—could have led him here? To this place dedicated to so many young men who had been slaughtered? What a journey!

As he entered the west pillar, Mallock tapped his shoes and tried to brush the snow off his clothes. Present inside the Arc de Triomphe were, in addition to the two cops, a representative of the president's office, Judioni, the representative of the Ministry of Justice, accompanied by a bailiff, the head curators responsible for historical monuments and for the Arc de Triomphe, Mordome, and two assistants carrying metal cases.

After a whole series of handshakes, even between the two great friends (Mallock, two hundred and twenty pounds, black T-shirt and black jacket on the one side, and Judioni, one hundred and forty-five pounds, pink shirt, and red tie, on the other) the little group headed for the first door, on which was inscribed "Warning: Danger" with a silver lightning bolt over it. Then they had to pass through two other access rooms that were closed by a series of locks and bars.

In the middle of the last room, a strong light shone from a trap door on the floor, splashing on the ceiling. Obviously, nothing had been set up for visitors. They had to use an iron ladder to descend into the final crypt, the most secret in France. The sight was astonishing. Mallock thought of the Blake and Mortimer comic books he'd devoured as a child.

Cut into the stone, the cenotaph was lit by two Balcar lamps. The soldier's coffin stood in the center, enigmatic as the untouched sepulcher of some priest of ancient Egypt. The two assistants, helped by Mordome and the curator of the Arc de Triomphe, started unscrewing the lid. Rust had infiltrated the fibers of the wood. Unpleasant creaks, like chalk screeching on a blackboard. The participants grimaced. Despite its modest size, the room had a sort of personal echo, a resonance that some people would call lugubrious. But how could it have been otherwise?

Mallock and Bob were obliged to come help the four men lift the lid and place it against one of the walls. As they turned it around, they noted with astonishment the reason it was so heavy. It was lined with lead, a sort of ship's ballast in reverse. Almost seven hundred pounds of metal to seal the secret of this identity.

Once the lid had been set upright at the back of the room, in the shadows, they all approached the catafalque to see what was in it. What were they hoping for? An empty bier? An Egyptian mummy covered in gold? A perfectly preserved man in a uniform, smiling from beyond death?

At the two corners, video cameras on tripods were recording the whole scene. The heads bending over the inside all saw at the same time the poverty of the contents of the treasury: bits of stone and bone in ochre and ivory tones!

"You can proceed," Judioni declared, after having glanced at the two other officials to see if they agreed.

Then Mordome turned, as if Judioni's remark was of no importance to him, and said to Mallock in a loud voice:

"Mr. Superintendent, I am at your disposal."

Amused, Mallock played along.

"Mr. Professor, I shall let you operate."

Mordome, concealing a smile, opened the big leather instrument case he'd brought with him. It rolled open on the long trestle table alongside the coffin. The metallic sound of the instruments banging against each other resounded in the crypt: Granat calipers, anthropometric compasses, mallets, a Rowe clamp, a gouge, a periosteal elevator, a bone forceps, a stripper, Sims scissors, tongue clips, Halstead hemostats . . .

Mordome and his assistant began selecting from the earthy mass what most resembled bones, as well as various dried pieces of tissue or perhaps skin. Then they lined them up as if on parade in an order that meant nothing to anyone but themselves. In a separate plastic bag, they isolated what seemed to be hairs.

In the silence of the crypt, the calm, serious voice of the medical examiner resounded like a prayer:

"We can note the presence of numerous very large stones that have nothing to do with the corpse. They may have been put there to make up for the weight of the cadaver, which was probably incomplete, or perhaps out of negligence. To return to the skeleton, the cranium is intact, although fissured in several places, the main bones of lower limbs are also present and in relatively good condition, as well as a few vertebrae. Correction, or rather a clarification: the right tibia has been fractured."

Mordome was silent for a few seconds, long enough to examine the two parts of the bone under a magnifying glass. When he resumed, he had his answer.

"The fracture occurred *ante mortem*."

Then he went on in silence. With the help of his assistants, he continued his macabre inventory for twenty minutes. One of the assistants crushed a piece of bone with a mortar, put the resulting powder in a transparent liquid, and inserted the test tube into a small centrifuge they had brought with them in one of the large metal cases. A few minutes later, a minuscule print-out emerged with a sound like that made by an adding machine. Mordome read the result before carefully attaching the printed paper to the test tube.

It was at that moment that the imprudent Judioni thought he could intervene:

"Will you be finished soon, Doctor?"

To which Mordome replied without even deigning to turn around:

"I'll be finished when I'm finished. Don't worry, Judge, you'll know. That will be the moment when I turn around and say to you, 'I'm finished.' Until then, I'd like everyone to be silent. One last thing, it's 'Professor,' not 'Doctor.'"

Without waiting for a reaction, Mordome started removing and vacuuming up everything that remained at the bottom of the coffin. The table, even though it was four yards long, was covered with bones and shapeless fragments. Then they conscientiously sifted the contents of the vacuum cleaner and sorted out the smallest pieces according to their size. The remaining contents of the sack, which were dark in color, must be earth. Mordome asked one of his assistants to analyze the latter, and then began to dictate again:

"The fact that we have discovered such a large quantity of earth and have found only part of the main bones, as well as the absence of most of the smallest bones, tends to prove that we are in fact confronted by a body, parts of which were removed, in a very rudimentary way, long after death. At least two years after death. We can also state, without the slightest doubt, that the body in question has spent time in the earth."

Mordome continued to work for another quarter of an hour, and then asked:

"Mallock, could you come have a look at this?"

He'd forgotten to use the title "Superintendent."

"I've found the body's atlas. The good news is that this vertebra is in fact deformed, perhaps as a result of a bullet, but the bad news is that no projectile remained in the neck, or in the axis, either."

Mallock grimaced. That would not be enough for him to claim that they had found incontestable proof. Lieutenant Lafitte had been hit by a bullet that had lodged between two vertebra in the neck, the atlas and the axis. This was an acknowledged fact registered in the army's medical documents. Had the bullet been found between the two vertebra, Mallock would have had his proof.

"You don't have anything more? What about the soil?"

Mordome turned to one of his assistants, who handed him two sheets of paper, whispering, "It's positive." The medical examiner rapidly compared the two soil compositions, the sample that had just been taken and the baseline sample.

"Here there is no doubt, it corresponds exactly to the one you had me analyze."

"What soil are you talking about?" Judioni demanded. He had no intention of being left out for too long.

"The soil taken from the bottom of the well," Mallock explained. "The soil in the catafalque is exactly the same. Thus one thing is certain. The body of this soldier comes from that site."

Judioni paled. That didn't suit him at all. He wanted only one thing: to have Mallock on the ropes and put an end to this preposterous affair.

"Let's assume that this tells us where the body came from; that still doesn't tell us that this corpse consisting of a pile of fragments is your notorious Jean-François Lafitte. You must understand that, given the very strange nature of your theory, we cannot be satisfied with this discovery alone."

Judioni was not wrong; a jury would find it insufficient. Mallock had already discussed this question with Antoine Ceccaldi. The prosecution could be counted on to argue that casting doubt on Manuel's guilt and backing up a theory as questionable and fantastic as reincarnation would require evidence more convincing than a single deformed vertebra and a soil analysis, even if the latter proved that the body did indeed come from the well, a site itself identified and located solely on the basis of information provided by Manuel Gemoni. What they needed now was an indisputable identification of the body.

If they could prove that this cadaver was in fact that of Lieutenant Lafitte, then how could Manuel have divined that it was in the well? In front of a jury, as strange as it might seem to everyone, there would be only one possibility: recognize that they were confronted by a case that resembled a phenomenon of reincarnation. And that, contrary to what Mallock thought, was a case that could be argued.

Ceccaldi had told him about precedents in India, England, and Germany, proven examples.

In Manu's case, even if the jurors refused to admit the existence of the phenomenon, they would be compelled to grant the accused the benefit of the doubt. If one added to that the benefit of the extenuating circumstances connected with the victim's identity, one could reasonably hope, if not for an acquittal, at least for a light sentence, and perhaps even, given Manuel's lack of prior offenses, a suspended sentence. But they weren't that far yet.

For the moment, nothing allowed them to connect this pile of bones and Lieutenant Jean-François Lafitte. Case closed. Everybody packs away his hopes and Julie's brother goes to prison. Making the most of his advantage and of Mallock's obvious dejection, Judioni said:

"Gentlemen, I believe it is time to close the coffin and leave in peace the remains of the person who is now officially the unknown soldier of the Second World War."

The president's representative added, as if to seal the coffin:

"I shall report this to the president. I believe that within a week he will give a speech on television to inform the French people of this soldier's existence and make his presence here official."

Mordome was resigned to the outcome and had begun, with the help of his assistant, to decant the various pieces of the puzzle into the now empty coffin. To set his mind at ease, he examined the largest pieces once again before carefully replacing them in the casket. He looked with special attention at an oblong, cracked object he had not succeeded in identifying, and which he picked up again and shook, as if trying to guess what was in it.

"What is that?" Mallock asked, clinging to this last hope. "It looks like a pouch."

"No, sorry, it's a piece of the intestine. The part closest to the stomach, the duodenum. It was its form that first surprised me, and then its weight. But that's all it is, unfortunately."

Then he concluded, for the benefit of all those present:

"I'm finished."

As in a nightmare, Mallock saw the little group, only too happy to have completed this delicate mission, head for the metal ladder, chattering like magpies. They all had broad smiles on their faces. Those assholes were already enjoying their Christmas dinners and opening their gifts. Mallock would gladly have shut them up inside the crypt to deprive them of their celebration.

They were all startled when Mallock shouted:

"Silence! Be quiet!"

Mordome looked at his friend with concern. Had he lost his head? Judioni was more direct:

"Superintendent, get a grip on yourself. One has to be able to accept failure."

But Mallock was calm. He stood there, listening intently.

"Don't you hear anything?"

"Nothing, apart from you and your shouts," the curator said, offended.

"Music," Mallock insisted. "Coming from the coffin, I think."

Surprised by such a statement, the whole group fell silent to listen.

"There's nothing at all," Judioni said. "You're off your head, Mallock."

Judioni must have thought he needn't use Mallock's title. But he was far from having seen everything yet. With a person like Mallock, you always have to be ready for anything. Mordome knew that, but he hardly expected what was about to happen in front of him.

Amédée stood there as if frozen in the silence. The omnipresence of amber throughout the investigation could be no coincidence. Amber still had things to reveal. Who had recruited those insects, those involuntary pilots? Why had they been sent to the future in their microscopic capsules of resin? What was their message? Caught in a drop of thought and blood, couldn't souls also be immobile travelers? In the well, there were thousands of swallows, in the amber vial there was ayahuasca, in the earth there was a cross, in Manu's mind, another man, and in . . .

Mallock rushed back to the coffin and began rummaging around with his big hands among the various bones. The officials, stunned, watched him with the expression you assume when you think somebody has lost his mind. A mixture of reprobation and sympathy.

Sympathy for the Superintendent: that sounded like the title of a thriller.

Suddenly, Mallock stopped and raised his right arm in the air, with a smile of victory on his face. He'd found the pouch-like object that had intrigued Mordome for a moment.

He carefully placed the object on the table, observed it very closely, stood up, grabbed a mallet and, with a sudden blow, shattered the bit of intestine.

The assembly was stupefied.

Mallock, without paying attention to anyone, was now blowing on his discovery and dusting it off with a brush. When he finally turned around and faced the little group, music filled the crypt. A magical moment: the notes began to ricochet off the stone, like the pearls from a necklace falling on the pavement.

Mallock was holding in his hands, between his thumb and his index finger, the ultimate proof that Manuel Gemoni's fantastic ideas were nothing of the sort: a pendant in the form of a heart, opened to show two yellowed portraits, was playing Erik Satie's third *Gnossienne*.

39.
Tuesday Afternoon, December 24

It seemed that now they'd seen everything. Mallock was organizing a Christmas Eve party. All his friends in a flurry of preparation. In a paradigm shift, Amédée was becoming civilized. It was a little late to send out invitations, but he had nonetheless managed to get enough people together to make a good-sized group.

Claudius, of course, GG and Machi, Kiko and Julie, who hadn't been able to stop smiling ever since the discovery of the locket, Jules, who was always where Julie was, Mordome and his partner, who had cancelled their own party to celebrate "that" with the superintendent. Michel had come in from Rambouillet. Ken had not been able to get away from his in-laws. Beatty was in Dordogne with her new boyfriend. JF was also in the provinces, near La Rochelle. As for Léon, Mallock had gotten the impression that a certain new acquaintance made during his research on the cross had to be explored. Whether male or female was not mentioned and or important. Amédée sincerely hoped that this would be for Léon the companion he'd been so long awaiting. He had also called Bob to invite him to the meal. But Bob had reminded him that this was the big day. He had succeeded in convincing and assembling his whole flock, and he was as happy as a boy with his first bike. In all, there were nine guests, and that was perfect for a big Christmas dinner at the home of the superintendent.

At noon, as soon as he returned from his office, Mallock had rushed to the phone to order half a suckling pig from his butcher. That little morsel was for his female guests. For the men, the real men, he'd gone to his poultry man at the Raspail market:

"Can you get me five grouse for this evening? Don't say no!"

There was no machismo in the choice of dishes. It's in the genes. Only a man, a real man with whiskers, is properly equipped to eat grouse. Women hate it, that's just how it is. Mallock just wanted all his friends to be happy.

When he got home around 3 P.M., Mallock noted with relief that everything had been delivered. He immediately prepared a marinade, cleaned the five grouse, and laid them raw in the marinade. He added a few cloves of garlic, laurel, and thyme to the half suckling pig and put it in the oven at 250°. For the last half-hour of cooking, he made a mixture of honey, sake, and soy sauce to baste the skin before setting the oven on grill. Then he had only to take out of the freezer the fresh chestnuts that Julie's mother had sent him, lovingly "shelled in Corsica." It was written on each package with the date of processing.

In ten minutes, everything was ready. It is a curious legend that cooking is a long-term operation. After having put foil over the game, Mallock went down to his cellar to choose a bottle of Côte-Rôtie, with a Pommard representing the Burgundies and a Pomerol the Bordeaux, wines that would have the power to stand up to the grouse. For the suckling pig, two bottles of Saint-Julien would do. An '81, a forgettable year in every respect, and an '82, a glorious year for Bordeaux wines. All he needed then was a green, a salad of fresh spinach, with a little shredded arugula and lots of herbs. His produce man had promised him delivery by 7 P.M. at the latest: "It's Christmas Eve and my wife is attached to traditions, so I close around six. I'll drop off what you need on my way home, Superintendent."

Why should there be only disadvantages to being a well-known cop?

To finish his preparations, Mallock put three bottles of Sail-les-Bains mineral water in the door of his refrigerator.

He thought the design was brilliant.

At five, he called the Ministry of Justice. For once, they had moved rapidly. Aware of the impact that the results of the investigation might have, they had decided to continue the trial behind closed doors. That would be announced on Thursday. Manuel's family and his lawyer had already given their consent. In a public trial, a possible acquittal on grounds of reincarnation would produce, if not necessarily a bad impression, at least a hell of a mess. So everyone had rapidly agreed to keep a low profile. No one had any interest in generating all this publicity that could only cause problems. Mallock agreed, even if no one had asked his opinion. In fact, this decision, made with such celerity, had put him in a very good mood. There seemed to be an excellent chance of gaining a dismissal. With any luck, one could even hope to see Manuel released in time for New Year's Eve. Kiko and Julie were going to be wild with joy.

He hung up and rubbed his hands. The investigation looked like it was going to end with an apotheosis. Nobody knew exactly how it would turn out, but it didn't really matter, after all. He would have won, and that was good. It was still the same feeling of accomplishment and relief. As if, for a few seconds, all the injustices in the world, ever since the beginning of time, had been waved away by a magic wand. It wouldn't last long, but it was still that much in hand.

At 8 P.M., his friends all arrived at practically the same time. Amédée had just basted the grouse to thicken the gravy. They immediately sat down to table. Mallock was against aperitifs. Why drink alcohol and eat junk food, when good wines and delicious dishes were in the offing?

Happy to see each other, and to see their Amédée so happy

and relaxed, they did justice to the meal. As they ate dessert—Mallock had just served them a rum soufflé with vanilla ice cream—Jules brought up the already famous "scene of the heart-shaped music box."

He addressed Mordome first:

"Tell us, since you were there. How did that happen? We'd like to know the details."

Mordome indicated that he first had to swallow an enormous mouthful of soufflé he had just put in his mouth. Then he said:

"To tell the truth, I didn't see it coming. I think everyone believed our Amédée had gone off the deep end. He looked like a man possessed. When he turned around with the golden music box . . . "

Mordome fell silent for a few seconds. He was moved:

"In any case, I can tell you that it's a moment I'll never forget. It was magic!"

"You don't know how right you are, Barnabé. Everyone was taken in!"

"What do you mean, taken in?"

"You didn't understand how I went about it?"

"What did you do?"

Mordome didn't understand what Mallock was implying.

Amédée seemed to hesitate. Then he said:

"Just between us, I'm going to admit something to you. I didn't really know what to do to save Manuel, so since I was certain of his innocence, I did the only thing that could get him out of this fix. Can't you guess what it was?"

Jules and Mordome on the one hand, and Kiko and Julie on the other, looked at each other uneasily and doubtfully.

Julie broke the silence:

"Nothing illegal, Boss, I hope?"

Mallock hesitated again. Suddenly he seemed less sure of himself.

"To be straightforward, it's not really straightforward. But at my age, we can sometimes allow ourselves to manipulate the law a little, can't we?"

His whole audience paled. Hearing Mallock say such things was something new.

"What did you do, Boss?" asked Jules, who was no longer smiling.

Mallock looked like a mischievous child as he dropped his bomb in the middle of his audience:

"Since I couldn't count on this cadaver to authenticate the lieutenant, I simply had a clockmaker friend of mine construct a heart-shaped music box. No one knows about it, if it still exists. It was safer to bring it with me into the crypt than to stake everything on chance. Like a magician, I distracted people's attention, and while I had my back to them, I rubbed the locket in the dirt, turned on the music box, and voilà! The case was in the bag."

A leaden silence fell over the room. No one dared speak. Mallock continued to smile.

"Well? What's your problem? Did I say something stupid or what?"

Julie spoke first:

"Surely you didn't really do something like that?"

"Why not? You're not going to tell me that you're sorry I did it? Manu is going to get out of jail. That's what counts, isn't it?"

Kiko came to his defense:

"It's all right with me. As you said, so far as you're concerned, the end justifies the means."

The room fell silent again.

Mallock, suddenly uneasy, seemed to wake up:

"You're not going to turn me in over this, are you?"

His friends unanimously reassured him. Of course, they would keep this to themselves. They didn't approve of it, but they had no choice.

That was when Mallock said, in a severe tone:

"And the law? What are you going to do about the law? Aren't you ashamed?"

Looking at the stunned faces of the people around him, Mallock broke into laughter, an enormous laughter that brought tears to his eyes.

"My God, did you believe me? I was joking. Good Lord, you're gullible. The little gold music box was really in the tomb where I found it. I'm a police superintendent, not a faker, kids."

"You scared the hell out of me!"

Mordome, like all the others, was relieved.

Mallock explained:

"Sorry, with all this tension I wanted to let off a little steam. The discovery of this heart-shaped gold music box was a moment of pure magic. It was like a miracle! No matter how much I hoped for it, I couldn't really believe it. Finding the bullet in the vertebra, yes. But finding this object, never in a million years. When I saw it in the dirt, shining and immaculate, tears came to my eyes. That's why I didn't turn around right away, if you want to know the truth. A hell of a sensation after so much uncertainty, investigations, and mystery. I could have wept. In fact, I did weep!"

Finding this golden object embedded in the lieutenant's petrified flesh must in fact have been extraordinary.

"I sincerely believe that except for Carter, when he was the first to stick his head into Tutankhamen's tomb," Amédée went on, "there are very few people who have had the good luck to experience such an emotion."

"Was that any reason to scare us half to death?"

GG had been afraid for his friend. That kind of manipulation could have had terrible consequences for Mallock's career, and then some.

"The idea of the hoax came to me as I was making the soufflé," Amédée admitted. "But I didn't think you would be so easily deceived. Besides, I'm not sure how I should take that."

"In any case, the discovery of a golden heart that makes music in a bit of fossilized intestine is pure 'Dédé-the-Wizard,'" Julie said.

"There's nothing magical about it, you know. I didn't have a vision, I really heard the music, and I even know why. It's the lieutenant's ghost that gave me a sign, helped by our favorite professor."

Mallock turned toward Mordome.

"When you picked up that piece of intestine the first time, you put it down on top, next to the lamp. Then you picked it up again and even shook it. The heat of your palm and of the lamp, plus the movement, must have been what started the music. What remained of the oiled parts came back to life, so to speak. As is often the case in such moments, the slightest details then came back to me. Remember, at the end of the third interrogation, it was Jean-François Lafitte himself who told us, in Manu's voice, 'I had no other choice, so I swallowed it . . . ' After that, it was easy. The little pouch was the only thing in the coffin that could contain something; the rest was bones or soil. You even told me that it was probably a piece of the intestine, and you added that it had seemed to you 'heavy.' So I grabbed the mallet like a madman."

"Another great story to put down to Mallock the Wizard's credit," Jules concluded in his turn.

"Not entirely," Amédée insisted. "Since you're behaving so well, I'm going to explain where my . . . inspiration came from. At least I believe it did. And you can be sure that this is no joke, I promise you, on my honor. It's a marvelous story."

Julie glanced at her Jules: they loved it when Mallock started recounting his memories.

"One of the various things I did to cope with my herniated

disks was a course of physical therapy. Stretching and exercises for the abdominal and dorsal muscles. I did that in the swimming pool near my apartment. And it was there, four or five years ago, that an old historian who was splashing around in the water with me told me a very wonderful story that was one hundred percent true. To respect his request for discretion—I think he intended to make a book out of it—I'll limit myself to the essential points. The young son of one of our emperors— the choice is limited—had been sent to be brought up in the home of a . . . let's say Austrian, princess. The problem was that the tutor who'd been sent with the little prince fell in love with the aforesaid princess. I know, I know, this seems silly, but the worst thing is that it's all perfectly true. The princess's family asked the Emperor of the French to bring his kid home, along with his tutor. You follow me?"

"Absolutely, Boss," Julie replied, taking advantage of this pause to serve herself a little more soufflé.

"When he was about to leave, the little prince, who despite his young age had also fallen in love with the princess, went to find her to say farewell. Like the adorable child he was, he gave her the most beautiful thing he could think of: an apple!"

"An apple? And that's what put you on track for . . . "

"Patience! patience! During the following decades, no one dared throw away or sell the famous apple, which had become Historical with a capital 'H,' and it has still remained in the princess's family. Over time, more than two centuries, it slowly petrified. In the late 1960s, children were playing in the room where the relic was displayed, resting on a cushion and covered with a glass cloche. A particularly clumsy kick of the ball changed history! And the apple, as it fell, broke into countless pieces."

Silence in Mallock's living room.

"Tell us the rest, the rest," Julie and the others began to cry.

"Well, guess what happened?" Amédée challenged them.

"The kids were severely scolded," Jules ventured.

"They spent a fortune trying to put the apple back together?" Claude suggested.

"The remains were put in an urn, and that gave you the idea that . . . "

"There was a big worm inside it?"

"No, a butterfly, and it flew away!" Kiko cried.

"Bravo, that's very nice, Kiko, but no, nothing like any of that. The old lady, the princess's great-great-granddaughter, bent over the pile of fragments on the floor. And the children heard her weep. Big sobs that she couldn't stop."

"I understand her, the poor woman, the damn kids," Claude grumbled.

"They weren't so bad," Amédée went on. "The boy responsible for the disaster approached her. He was very upset. He loved his grandmother very much and was aware that he had made the mistake of his life: 'I'm sorry, Granny,' he said, 'but please stop crying, we're going to glue it all back together. You won't see anything,' he promised her. Then the grandmother turned around, with a big smile on her lips. 'I'm not crying out of sadness, my darling. I'm overwhelmed by emotion. Look!' And the old lady held out to the child a gold ring adorned with three stones that shone in the autumn sun, the little prince's gift to the pretty princess, a gift he'd had the idea of concealing in the apple. By the time she ate it, he would be gone. Then she would discover the little marvel so cleverly hidden at the apple's center. That way she would never forget him, he thought. But by deciding to keep the apple as a souvenir, the young woman never discovered the little prince's lovely gesture."

A loud murmur from the audience.

"There you have it, kids, that probably influenced me unconsciously and encouraged me to break the petrified piece in my turn. So . . . "

" . . . We must always listen to stories told by a very old man, even if he's our superintendent," Julie said, laughing.

"That's the most marvelous ending imaginable," GG decided.

But another person still had something to say.

"Nah . . . I prefer the Mallock-the-Magician version with the false golden heart," Kiko mumbled, sulking.

The group greeted her point with a big collective laugh.

Of course, the rest of the meal was devoted to the subject of reincarnation. Those who believed in it before the case had it easiest. But those who had expressed doubts the day before continued to do so. As if Manuel's adventure hadn't changed their convictions at all. Belief had nothing to do with reality or truth, on the contrary. Mallock, who was still very pleased by his joke and the success of his story, decided he didn't give a damn. Whether it was reincarnation or something else, it would probably get Manu out of prison; everybody was happy about that, and that was the main thing.

Like an echo of the magic heart, the bells of the Saint-Merri church sounded the twelve strokes of midnight. It was December 25, Christmas Day, and for once, with the snow falling and smiles on everyone's face, it really felt like it.

Champagne.

Kisses.

The dinner went on until three in the morning.

When the guests had left, Mallock decided to do the dishes. He didn't want to leave a mess like that for poor Anita to clean up. Just as he finished and was heading for his bedroom, the telephone rang. A smile on his lips, he went to answer it. At that hour, it was certainly one of his guests who had forgotten something. He hadn't had time to make a tour of the apartment.

"Who's the scatterbrain?" he asked when he picked up the receiver. He listened for two minutes and his smile froze.

"I'm coming."

That was all he said. He walked over to the bar and poured himself a big glass of whiskey.

When he sat down on the couch, he couldn't help sobbing.

Bob Daranne had just committed suicide.

A bullet in the mouth.

Without taking the trouble to consult their father, or even to inform him, none of his children had come. So Bob had remained all alone in front of the big table full of food. Then he'd decided that enough was enough. He'd taken a gun and swallowed, as his only meal that night, a 7.65 mm bullet. He'd promised Mallock never to commit suicide with his service weapon, and he'd kept his word. He'd used one of the guns in his collection, a Browning M1910, the same model that had launched the First World War when it was wielded by Gavrilo Princip, the assassin of Archduke Franz-Ferdinand of Austria in Sarajevo in 1914 and that had allowed Paul Gorguloff to kill the president of the French Republic, Paul Doumer, in 1932. The caliber of this pistol was modest, and the emergency medics had been able to restart Bob's heart three times. They were able to stabilize him before taking him to Cochin hospital. There, a whole team had done everything they could to save his life.

In vain.

Mallock's tears were still flowing when he put on his overcoat to go to his friend's house. His sons were going to arrive there and they would need him.

He'd loved this guy with a crew cut, and he'd go on loving him for a long time still.

Too often, life answers questions we haven't asked. It tricks us, traps us, catches up with us. Very often we fall. But we get up again, as we did when we were children. I give up! Not hurt, not even dead. In the garden, as kids, we always began again. Beep beep! Even blown up, crushed under an army of anvils, we began the following episode, like the Road Runner, as good as new . . . When we've grown up, we still play with the same ideas of immortality.

And then life humbles us.

Devastated, Amédée went out of his apartment and then turned around to double-lock the door.

41.
Thursday, January 2, Early Morning

That morning, Mallock opened his eyes with a grimace. Outside, the sun was already shining brightly in a clear blue sky. The impressive rise in the temperature that had accompanied the new year had begun attacking the mounds of snow and ice. The thermometer had gone from fifteen to fifty degrees. In his bedroom, on the chair at the foot of his bed, Mallock saw his red *fourragère*, a decoration he put over his left shoulder after having donned his uniform for important ceremonies.

At 11 o'clock, he was going to the Père-Lachaise cemetery for Captain Daranne's burial.

Bob's. "His" Bob's.

The telephone rang.

"No bad news today, I've had all I can take," he grumbled before he picked up.

"The case was not dismissed," Antoine Ceccaldi's lugubrious voice announced.

Brought up for immediate trial, Manuel had just been given a so-called symbolic sentence that was not insignificant: three years in prison. With remissions, Julie's brother would be out twelve to fourteen months later.

To be sure, the sentence was more than magnanimous for a murderer, but there was the notorious "tourist" clause. In conformity with the agreements made with the Dominican authorities, this sentence was going to give Manuel a right to a return ticket and free residence on the island, once his sentence had been served in France. The Dominican government wouldn't do him any favors and would make sure all its own prerogatives were respected, its sacrosanct national sovereignty. Over there he would probably get fifteen to twenty years. And then there were Darbier's *brutos*.

In fact, they had to start all over.

As he put on that damned uniform that seemed to shrink a size every year, Mallock started sighing and swearing.

An hour later, his anger had given way to sorrow.

Mallock was facing a varnished coffin covered with a French flag. To his right, four young carrot-tops, hanging their heads, looked overwhelmed with grief. Perhaps they were, in fact. People don't all react the same way, and he didn't know enough to judge. With a lump in his throat, he thought that Bob had finally managed to do it, if only in a cemetery and around a muddy grave: he had gathered his whole family around him.

The melting snow had produced countless streams that were running through Paris with a great sound of rushing water. Beige torrents, thousands of gallons of café-au-lait attacking alleys and gutters. And also funeral vaults.

The Daranne family's vault was already three-quarters full of water. Mallock wondered how the morticians were going to manage. He could hardly imagine them lowering the casket into the brownish liquid, with bubbles gurgling out of it as the air inside the coffin escaped. Bob had experienced too many humiliating or ridiculous situations during his life, and it was out of the question for his death to be still another one.

"It's all right," the undertaker replied. "We'll pump out most of the water, and then wait until the grave is perfectly dry. We'll probably put the earth back in the day after tomorrow. Don't worry about it, we do this all the time."

Then he added:

"In any case, we can't do anything else. The coffin won't sink, it'll float. So you can imagine."

Mallock had to repress a desire to laugh. Daranne had no peer when it came to always finding himself in grotesque situations. Mallock saw him again: tied to a lamppost, naked and in the middle of the winter, by a gang of hoodlums, jailed by the gendarmerie for soliciting because he was wearing stockings and a bra, emerging covered with garbage from a bin that had picked him up and dumped him in a waste disposal center, or still stinking of fish the day the Prefect made a surprise visit to police headquarters. There was also the evening when he'd begun to tell a young recruit the most horrible stories about the former head of the Paris police; she'd turned out to be the latter's daughter. Not to mention the numberless times his wife came to headquarters to read him the riot act and drag him off, humiliating him in front of his comrades. Bob had spent his life playing the hard-boiled cop and being rebuffed by everyone. The truth about him, apart from his uprightness and loyalty, was that though his brain was not very big, his heart was huge, and so was his awkwardness.

"Bob, I'm going to miss you," Mallock murmured, with tears in his eyes and a painful laugh caught in his throat.

When the ceremony was over, Mallock, Julie, Jules, Ken, and Jo went to a café. They picked the closest one. They weren't ready to separate yet, or to speak either. It would be for the boss, his closest friend, to decide when the silence could be broken. Mallock knew that. He'd already assumed that responsibility when they were mourning earlier deaths, and particularly the most painful of them all, that of his Thomas. In the latter case, he had still not given the signal, and six years later silence continued to reign, it being forbidden to mention the subject in front of him. Three weeks before, he had surprised himself by breaking the silence he'd imposed on others by uttering Thomas's name while he was talking with Ken. Was that perhaps a sign?

"Some ten days ago, Bob took me to task," he began. "He talked about a normal investigation, in which we arrest suspects, take fingerprints, canvass the neighborhood, the whole shooting match. What he said exactly was: 'Little by little, we ferret out everybody.'"

The four young captains smiled the same melancholy smile. Mallock continued:

"To him, the way the Gemoni case has developed didn't seem normal. Well, he may not have been wrong. Especially since we now find ourselves, as you know, with a sentence that raises a problem."

Julie was looking sullen, the way she looked when she was trying to keep from crying.

"So in his honor and in order to set my own mind at ease, I said to myself that we should try to forget the investigation the way I've conducted it, which has probably been too personal."

A general silence.

"I'd like us to give ourselves twenty-four hours to see if we haven't overlooked a quite different lead. We have to focus on the slightest bit of evidence that hasn't been used, or that doesn't fit with the version we've adopted. So far as I'm concerned, I have trouble imagining another explanation for all this, but Bob's words continued to haunt me, even before he died. And then, we don't have many other choices. Manuel is in great danger. I think you've understood that very well. If we reason in a very common-sense way, there may still be something to dig up. Consider the episode of the little music box. It was as if the lieutenant's spirit had made it start playing again. But it was probably more prosaic than that; it was the combined action of warmth and movement. Two tortuous stories for a single phenomenon. Isn't there another explanation of what happened? A different reality that is far more rational and that no one has yet glimpsed? An interpretation of the facts that might convince the most refractory critics and allow Manu to be freed?"

Mallock's harangue met with a total lack of reaction on the part of the group. Only the respect they owed Daranne's memory prevented them from protesting. Even Julie showed not the slightest enthusiasm.

Ken preferred to conclude:

"We'll bring you everything we find tomorrow night. But there isn't . . . "

"Above all, no 'buts.' Rack your brains. Think 'differently.' Erase from your memory everything you now know."

"That's easy to say," Julie grumbled.

"We have to wipe away all the stupidities and hypotheses we've been working with since the beginning of the investigation."

"And just how do we do that?"

Julie was too upset to have the slightest positive thought. Their stupid old Bob was dead and her brother was in great danger again.

Mallock decided to theorize a little to reassure his troops.

"I'm asking you to carry out an act of . . . descotomization."

His four lieutenants gave him quizzical looks.

"It comes from *scotoma*. In ophthalmology, it's a part of the visual field that has gone dark, blind in a way, as a result of damage to the retina. In psychology, scotomization is the psychic act that consists of erasing, in a selective way, an event that is often painful or even intolerable for the person who has suffered it. It's a denial of reality, an auto-therapeutic act that consists of removing this traumatic memory from one's consciousness. Today, despite what we've discovered, you've got to persuade yourselves that there's another solution, something that has escaped our visual field. Imagine an inkspot that concealed part of the story . . . "

"O.K., we're all going to work together and the devil be damned if we don't find something."

Jo had just positioned herself within the group for the first time.

"There's a fourteenth-century Franciscan monk," she went on, "who formulated a principle known as 'Occam's Razor.' It consists of always choosing the simplest, shortest, most obvious solution. And in Manuel's case, without accusing anyone, it can't be said that we made things simple!"

"Jo's right, we have to look for something obvious, far removed from all my divagations."

This last sentence sounded odd to the team. In fact, no one believed it, really. The story had been worked over far too much for them to be able to hope they could still dig up something.

42.
Friday, January 3, 7 P.M.

Friday evening, Amédée could only note how few clues and new leads his lieutenants had come up with. Captain Ken Kô Kuroda, the nice-guy KKK, had made two piles.

On the right he'd put the pieces of evidence corroborating the thesis they'd already adopted. They were too numerous for Mallock to be able to consider them all. Among the new ones, the only ones he had asked for, were those brought in chiefly by Jo. The two DNA samples had been analyzed and checked. Jean-François's lock of hair, which Mallock had borrowed from his fiancée, did in fact correspond to that of the hair found in the well and that taken from the coffin. In the same way, the DNA of KKK the ogre, also found near the same well on the scalp the lieutenant had torn off, had proven to be identical with that taken from Darbier's corpse.

On the left, in a much smaller pile, was the evidence that was deemed to be new and did not fit into the logic of the first explanation. There wasn't much, in fact. Nothing decisive or really useful.

However, Jules had ended up taking the matter seriously and had even undertaken, with Julie's help, the neighborhood investigation that Bob had called for. The result was forty-eight files, beginning with a photo of each of the persons visited over the past two days. Mallock looked through them without seeing anything strange. On top of the pile, Ken had put a red "X" on one salmon-colored file. Mallock opened it without enthusiasm.

It was over, and down deep he knew it.

All that was lacking was his agreement, an admission that he couldn't do any more, to close the case and move on to other things. That decision was much too painful for him not to try desperately to gain time. He opened the folder without succeeding in repressing a deep sigh.

In the course of a fingerprint comparison that Jules had instituted to see if a point of intersection could be found among all the prints that had been taken during the investigation, an ambiguous outcome had appeared. Although only partial, two prints seemed to belong to the same individual. One of the prints came from the cross found underground, the other from the videocassette that had started everything.

It was impossible: with sixty years separating them, only contamination could explain the phenomenon. The cross and the cassette had been moved around a little too much. Someone could have touched the two pieces of evidence, forgetting to wear gloves. But who? If it were a member of the police forces, his prints would have been identified. Without mentioning that the evidence had rapidly been sealed up in protective plastic bags. They had to find someone who could have had access to the two objects before everyone else and who did not think about protecting himself. That was implausible. Once again, the investigation of the swallows' well was challenging the superintendent and driving him into a corner.

After he got home with the principal files of the counter-investigation, Mallock fell asleep and dreamed about this fingerprint. When he awoke with a start around 2 A.M., he had only one image in his head, a strange image, just a screaming color: violet, a vibrant mauve, almost fluorescent. A color and the certainty that he had to call someone, the lieutenant's fiancée.

Calling a lady of that age at such an hour required him to offer her abundant excuses.

And that's what Mallock did.

"How can I ask you to pardon a call at such an hour of the night? I'm ashamed to call you so late, Madame, but I have to ask you a question. You're the only person in the world who can answer it. I hope I haven't frightened you?"

"Don't worry, Superintendent. You know, at my age people sleep only by fits and starts. I was awake and was getting ready to make myself some herbal tea. What can I do for you?"

Mallock stammered. Put up against the wall like that, he felt a little idiotic. Especially since his question was anything but orthodox.

"Regarding Lieutenant Jean-François Lafitte, if I ask you what the color violet means to you, or reminds you of, can you think of anything?"

Marie Dutin didn't really seem surprised by the question. When you're over eighty, you've already heard everything.

"The color of the ribbon on his Croix de Guerre," she replied without hesitation.

"But the ribbon has green and orange stripes, if I remember correctly?"

"Usually. However, because at that time the Croix de Guerre were being made in great haste, they sometimes ran out of striped ribbon, and they used pieces of violet-colored regulation ribbon so they could still have the necessary length for the decoration. My Jean-François's ribbon was practically mauve, with only a small part striped red and green. He wouldn't have been happy about that. It wasn't a color he particularly liked."

Mallock waited a moment before speaking again. He wanted to leave her time to think. Urged on by her interlocutor's silence, the old lady seemed to hesitate before continuing:

"There's something else, but I don't think it's related."

Mallock sat straight up. Without knowing exactly what it was, he knew that what she was about to say was what he'd been waiting for.

"Please tell me anyway. What are you thinking of?"

"You're going to think I'm foolish. But the color violet always makes me think of Gavroche, the young soldier my Jean-François took with him."

"Why?"

"Well, he often wore mauve pullovers and shirts."

"Is that all?"

Mallock was surprised. No vision, no sudden illumination.

"Poor Gavroche, he had such beautiful eyes. I'd never seen eyes like that, and I haven't since then, either. They were hypnotic. That's why he wore violet, to go with the color of his eyes."

There it was.

Mallock warmly thanked the old lady and asked her again to pardon him. He hung up slowly. His heart was pounding and an involuntary smile lit up his face. Who could have touched both a cross buried under yards of earth in 1945 and a videocassette sixty years later?

Bob had been right.

It was 3 A.M. when he got to Léon's place.

"Could you find me the name of the man whom General de Gaulle asked to choose the unknown soldier?"

Léon, wearing silk pajamas and a dressing gown in the same material, looked at his friend as if he'd lost his mind.

"Do you know what time it is?"

Mallock looked at him imploringly.

"You know me. You're fully aware that I wouldn't bother you if it weren't important."

Grousing, and looking like Sacha Guitry in his dazzling outfit, Léon signaled to him to follow. As he headed for the living room, he began to give a grateful Mallock the reply he sought:

"It was a lieutenant, one of the general's aides-de-camp, who was assigned to look for an unidentified body."

Mallock wanted more.

"His name? Do you have his name?"

The old bookseller sank into the deepest of his armchairs.

"Why do you need to know that? I remind you that it's top secret and that the person who told me would deny everything if you tried to use this information for an appeal or something like that."

Automatically, as he always did when he came to get information or have a chat with his friend, Mallock had begun making coffee.

"Yeah, I suppose he would, but that doesn't matter. I just want to know the man's name. I need it to close the case."

The boiling water had begun to sputter as it passed through the filter. The smell of the coffee blended pleasantly with the fragrance of the piles of books and newspapers.

"Well?" Mallock insisted.

"No, damn it, Amédée, I can't tell you. I'm sorry, but I gave my word. And don't tell me you really need it, I won't believe you."

Mallock just began to fill two cups. One black and without sugar for Léon, the other with sugar and a bit of milk for himself. Then, with a big smile on his lips, he handed the old bookseller his cup. He held it just a few inches from Léon's outstretched hand, looked him in the eyes, and said:

"What would you say if I told you his name is Gaston Wrochet?"

Léon took his cup and pointlessly stirred it with the little spoon that was in it.

He looked up at Mallock.

"I'd say you're a goddamn wizard. That's what I'd say."

Mallock burst into laughter. And like a magician, he pulled out a photo.

"This is the guy, isn't it?"

Léon gave up and Mallock took advantage of his surrender to ask a last favor.

"Come on, one more effort, old man, be nice to your favorite superintendent. Give me the file you put together. I promise not to open it."

"I already told you that my informant gave it to a third party."

"Knowing you, there's no chance you didn't manage to get the documents back. You like old papers too much for that, Léon."

Without even trying to resist, and without asking the reason for such a request, Léon rose from his chair. Majestic in his Super-Guitry costume, he moved toward the back of the shop.

"You stay here, Superintendent. I'm going to get the file I don't have. So I can not give it to you."

A few minutes later, still stirring his coffee, Léon Galène was watching Mallock go through the papers. Among the official correspondence with the president's office, there were reports written in English. More surprisingly, he found, in a tracing-paper sleeve tattered by time, a piece of paper that had been rolled several times and was still wrinkled. Along with a small copper tube. Amédée looked up. His friend, who was one step ahead of him, was already handing him a magnifying glass.

"Thanks. Do you have any idea what this is?"

"Yes, it's a band for a carrier pigeon. Decipher the inscription."

Mallock bent down and read "Lord de Gaulle." The name of the pigeon that Lafitte's unit had taken with it. And also the explanation for what Manu had said at the beginning of the investigation: "It's done, de Gaulle is flying off . . . It's terribly cold, I'm falling in the wind."

Then Amédée decided to put a little fingerprint powder on the note, on which was written: "Saint-Jean mission compromised." Léon still had a little fingerprinting set from the early twentieth century that Mallock had once given him "to take care of." Mallock bent over the paper for a few minutes, and then said simply: "Bingo." It matched the print taken from the cross and the one found on the cassette.

"It looks to me as though you've hit the jackpot again. And so we're going to have to congratulate you again on your perspicacity! Don't you get tired of always being right?"

Closing the fingerprint powder box and handing it back to Léon, Mallock explained:

"I'm not the one. Daranne. It was Bob Daranne who was right. Nothing is as good as the traditional, tried and true methods, and he was the one who stuck to them, the old devil."

All down the line, Amédée thought. "It's always a family member or a neighbor," Bob had reminded him. Even the use he'd just made of dactyloscopy to catch the perpetrator was entirely traditional.

Suddenly Mallock realized that he'd just received, from beyond the tomb, the very last lesson of the man who'd trained him when he was just starting out. If he'd proceeded seriously and systematically, he would have gone to question Manu's nice neighbor who had recorded for him the documentary entitled "Tobacco and Cigars in the Dominican Republic, a Mirage or a New El Dorado?" In fact, mentally, he also blamed Julie. It was she who had been responsible for the investigation into her brother's disappearance. Far too worried about Manu, she'd bungled the job.

He looked at his watch. In an hour and a half, he could arrest the man. The perpetrator, the only one, the true one, Gaston Wrochet, a.k.a. Gavroche. A young man who must now be over eighty years old. To be sure, there were still plenty of holes in the new version Mallock was constructing, but he hoped the old man wouldn't refuse to provide the missing pieces of the puzzle.

To get another trial, they'd need new, conclusive evidence.

Impatient to go pick up his perp, Mallock went out in front of the bookshop to wait for backup. Julie, of course, Jules, and a couple of uniforms to make the arrest. He tapped his shoes on the frozen ground. That night, the temperature had fallen again, freezing the last little rivers of melted snow in the gutters. With his head ducked between his shoulders, Mallock seemed to be expecting blows. Those of a fate that could still play nasty tricks on him. It had been doing that ever since the beginning of this case. Unless . . .

Mallock shivered. Yes indeed! Unless . . .

43.
Saturday, January 4

T he church of the Madeleine had changed religion. Rising at the end of the rue Royale, draped in its layers of snow, it resembled a giant Berber tent. Mallock, Julie, Jules, and half a dozen uniforms had parked as best they could on what remained of a little recess at the corner of the boulevard Malesherbes and the Place de la Madeleine. Kiko, wearing a red ski jacket, was waiting for them in front of the building.

"He's on the floor right above us."

"Don't you live on the top floor?"

"Yes, but Monsieur Wrochet lives in the attic. He rents an apartment made by combining several maids' rooms."

"Do we have to go up on foot?" Amédée asked uneasily.

"No, there's an elevator that goes all the way up. In his condition, he'd never be able to climb that many stairs."

"Does he have trouble walking?"

"He's had several heart attacks, I think. He spends almost all his time in a wheelchair, and has everything delivered. On several occasions, Manuel and I have offered to go shopping for him."

When they arrived in front of the main door to the suspect's apartment, Mallock rang the bell. Then he knocked, before finally making up his mind to shout:

"Police! We have a warrant for your arrest. Open up, Monsieur Wrochet!"

Then, since he didn't feel like waiting, Amédée broke down

the door. He did it himself because he was big enough. But also because he really wanted to. Smashing in a door is a great tension-reliever, especially when you're in the state he was in.

Generally speaking, old people are found peacefully lying dead in their beds or next to the front door, having collapsed there in a last effort to get help, or perhaps out of politeness, to let their neighbors know that they're dead. Here, as in this whole case, things were very different.

Old Gavroche's apartment was jammed with stuff. There were piles of books everywhere. Maps, photos, and war souvenirs in what seemed to be the entry hall and the living room. After the kitchen, which was equipped with two freezers and loaded with canned goods, the third room was in relatively good order. In the center stood a big desk, very medical-looking, and a couch. It was certainly there that Wrochet had treated Manu's headaches. The bathroom, which was next to the office, was all set up so an invalid could manage on his own. There remained only one door, all the way at the back of the apartment, probably that of the bedroom. Mallock hesitated to draw his gun.

He preferred to repeat his warning:

"Police, we have a warrant for your arrest. Open up, Monsieur Wrochet!"

Then, after a minute of silence, he shouted:

"Please, Gavroche!"

Then he tried to turn the doorknob. Everything was locked tight.

In the meantime, one of the police's locksmiths had arrived.

"Go ahead, open that for me," Amédée said, beginning to lose his temper.

At Gavroche's age, it made no sense to barricade himself that way. And it also didn't correspond to the image he had formed of Lieutenant Lafitte's friend.

After a few grunts, the locksmith turned to Mallock.

"It's odd, Superintendent, it isn't locked. Something else is blocking the door."

Amédée sighed, stepped back, and then slammed his body into the door. The door literally exploded and Mallock fell into Gaston Wrochet's bedroom. Or rather, into an enormous pile of snow.

Under the roof, the room, which was located right at the corner of the boulevard Malesherbes and the Place de la Madeleine, was triangular in shape. The big fanlight on the right side being broken, the wind blew through the room, filling it with ice, snowflakes, and dead pigeons. A room frozen solid, with a bed in the middle, covered with sheets of snow, with just an arm with twisted fingers emerging from this shroud of ephemeral marble. It wasn't Rousseau's fault, or that of Voltaire: Gavroche's hand blamed the winter air.

"Suicide?" Jules asked Mallock.

"Or an accident," he replied.

"It's incredible," added Julie, who had just joined them in the room.

Mallock went up to the bedside table and tried to wipe off the snow with his hand.

"In any case, this didn't happen yesterday. There are several layers of snow, with ice underneath."

Then, just to be sure, and because someone had to do it, he decided to clear the snow off the place where poor Gaston's head had to be. It took him more than ten minutes to scrape off the layer of snow and ice. He ended up asking someone to bring him a little hot water. As he carefully poured it, he saw gradually appearing the face of Gaston Wrochet, Lieutenant Jean-François Lafitte's Gavroche. It was a handsome face, lined with wrinkles and old sorrows, and with two unbelievably luminous eyes with violet-colored irises, gleaming under an inch of transparent ice.

Gavroche was no more, and with him had disappeared

Mallock's witness and perhaps his story. Julie, whom Mallock had briefed as he was going from Léon's place to the apartment, looked at him apprehensively.

"Now we just have to find a file or a letter," Amédée replied to her mute question. "Otherwise we're in trouble."

"But we still have enough evidence. With the testimony from . . . "

"Don't waste your time. I'm not the one you have to convince. A file, a letter, a photo . . . anything is good. But with this mess!"

Julie understood the message, and started searching, full of hope.

After two hours, the three of them looked over what they'd found. Nothing, or almost nothing, that was interesting. Of course, there were his papers, a few photos, notably two showing him with the General de Gaulle, but no confession, no diary, not a single letter. More out of habit than anything else, Mallock had then gone back to examine the cadaver, which they had begun to free from its coating of ice.

The violet eyes, wide open, seemed to be trying to pierce the ceiling. *What a look*, Mallock said to himself again before leaning over the body. A rapid examination suggested heart failure. To judge by his grimace and his right hand clasped tight on his torso like a bird of prey's claw. As for the date of death, it would not be easy to determine. It wasn't recent. Two or three weeks? The body had been mummified by the cold. The bones of the face protruded, and the lips, as they froze, had bared the teeth. Gavroche seemed to be mocking the mystery he'd left behind him.

Jules and Julie came in. Julie couldn't help insulting the corpse:

"This old bastard left us nothing. What did he do to Manu? Damned old jerk!"

Mallock preferred not to respond. He understood the

young woman's frustration. He continued to look at Gavroche's hand, clenched as if it were going to open up and reveal a truth. Then he looked at the left hand, which they had seen first, sticking out of the bed. Once again, he felt certain there was something to be understood here, a sign to be decoded.

He went back to the living room and started searching again. Behind an old hi-fi, he found several audiocassettes piled up. He took one of them at random and slipped it into the player. In the large room, the quavering voice of an old man started telling a story, the story of his life.

"How did you know?" Jules asked.

"His fingers. Go have a look. They're deformed by arthritis. He couldn't write anymore. So I thought that maybe . . . "

Forgetting the hierarchy, Julie planted a big kiss on her superintendent's badly shaved cheek.

44

Mallock went back to Wrochet's apartment the following day to classify and listen to everything. The development of events had quickly seemed to him to have its own logic, strange but obvious, almost simple.

Gaston Wrochet told a story of friendship and bravery. In his quavering voice, he brought Lieutenant Jean-François Lafitte back to life: "We formed an incredible pair, he with his big dark eyes and I with my sorceror's eyes."

Far from being the serious, monolithic person Mallock had conceived, Jean-François seemed to be full of good humor and imagination. He played the piano, drew marvelously well, and, even though he was rather short, he attracted like a lighthouse all the young people he met. Girls too. An engineer, he had entered the army in Saumur and was quickly promoted to lieutenant after a lightning-fast training of three months. It was during this period that Gaston had come to know him, in "the great stroke of good and bad luck in my life." His lieutenant had taken him under his wing, perhaps because Gavroche was by far the most at sea in the division, or perhaps because he was a war orphan and alone in life. For someone like Jean-François Lafitte, who was surrounded by love, that had seemed a very cruel fate. Much more than it did to Gavroche who, to judge by what he said in his confessions, didn't really suffer from it: "You know, I'd always been alone, so . . . The lieutenant was always there for everyone. And he didn't make much of it. He took it all . . . how to put it . . . lightly. We were all very worried about him when he was wounded. A bullet had been lodged in his neck. He was in danger of being paralyzed but that didn't seem to bother him. He simply put on what he called his bandage: a white silk scarf. How could anyone forget such a man?"

The first cassette ended there.

In fact, they were not all full, and none of them had been recorded on both sides. Gaston must have found that too complicated. The better to keep them straight, he had labeled each of the cases in a lovely old-fashioned hand. On the first one, he had written: "My first encounter with Lieutenant LAFITTE."

On the second cassette, labeled "March, 1940/March, 1944," the old man told all his anecdotes from the military period. Particularly, the three months of training before they parachuted onto French soil. His name change, as well. "It was my lieutenant who shortened Gaston Wrochet to Gavroche. It seems obvious when I think back on it, but he was the one kind enough to think of giving me that name. I was the youngest of the group and I had an accent so thick you could cut it with a knife. From that moment on, everyone called me Gavroche, even the British."

The third cassette, "LA MISSION," began with an account of the night in May, 1944. "He did everything he could to prevent me from going along. He never stopped telling me that I was much too young to die. Because as he saw it, this was a suicide mission." The old man described in detail all the tricks he'd used to get into the plane. And then he had to jump: "In complete darkness, at an altitude of a thousand yards, when you feel your parachute catch fire you know you're finished and you say your last prayers." But Gavroche had been lucky. Even under those circumstances, his parachute had slowed his fall sufficiently so that he survived a rough landing in a tree. He had remained there for six hours, caught between two branches, wondering who was going to find him first, a

Frenchman or a Boche? By chance, he was the one to whom Lord de Gaulle had been entrusted, and the pigeon and he had kept each other a little warmer as they waited to be found. On the cassette, he talked about his long dialogues with the bird. Of course, he did all the talking, and it was funny and moving. Fortunately, he had been discovered by a group of resistance fighters. As early as the following day, he'd heard about two sabotage operations that had just been successfully carried out, and he'd recognized his lieutenant's style. Alone, and despite his new friends' advice, Gavroche had decided to try to rejoin his unit. He'd headed for the third regroupment site, Biellanie 3, where he thought he might find his squad.

From that point on, it was in a voice broken with sobs that he described what happened that night. He'd probably tried to tell the story several times before, but the emotion had been too strong. His voice was hoarse and trembling. Hidden in a tree, Wrochet the simple soldier had witnessed all the acts of violence perpetrated by Krinkel's unit, as overwhelmed by the sufferings of his friends as he was terrified by the idea of being scented by one of the dogs. Particularly because of his pigeon. So he'd decided to let it go, after having written the message informing the Allies of the failure of their last attack: "Saint-Jean mission compromised."

Lord de Gaulle had flown off, passing over the clearing and the well where Lieutenant Jean-François Lafitte was being tortured. Gavroche was sure that he must have seen and recognized the pigeon.

Without omitting the slightest detail, Gavroche then described all the atrocities committed by the SS *Gesamtterror* unit. Everyone had to know what had happened in that clearing. For him, it was a revelation, the bloody, howling nature of barbarism, its terrifying cry, its infinite character. An unsuspected potential of humanity. A capacity hidden from ordinary mortals. Plucking the eyes out of a living person as one might swallow an egg, listening to his death agony as one might delight in symphony, disemboweling one's fellow man until his last cry as one might a fish. He'd never gotten over it. What he'd seen, but also his inability to do anything about it. "I asked myself whether I shouldn't hang myself from a branch and have done with life. A bit of parachute cord, a final jump, and bingo! No more Gavroche. Three days went by before I could make up my mind to climb out of the tree and walk the earth once again, on a planet the Nazis had soiled forever; I felt a terrible shame."

On another cassette, he recounted his return. On the case he had written "MPF 45/46." By a fortunate concatenation of circumstances, Gaston Wrochet had become one of General de Gaulle's aides-de-camp when he returned to France. And when the general had asked one of his close associates to volunteer to find and choose the person who was to become the Second World War's unknown soldier, Gaston had not hesitated. With the greatest secrecy, he had gone with two other veterans to dig up their lieutenant at the bottom of the well, leaving there the regulation cross that Gavroche had decorated with bronze leaves at its extremities. Then, to be sure that his lieutenant would be the soldier chosen and honored, he had separated his remains into three parts, supplementing them with stones to provide the necessary weight. Whichever coffin was chosen by lot, his friend would be the one elected.

At the time, that had seemed to him important. More than that: vital!

Initially, he'd thought that he was doing that for his lieutenant, and then he'd understood that it was a desperate attempt to redeem himself. He was angry at himself for not having come down from his tree and gotten himself killed in turn by making a gallant but doomed effort to come to his friends' aid. He forgot that his friends were already dead and his lieutenant dying.

Guilt is not an exact science.

But his extravagant plan had worked, and Gavroche had felt the presence of his lieutenant under the Arc de Triomphe as a kind of consolation. For what, he didn't exactly know: his death, his torture, his disappearance, his absence? A little of all of that, probably.

When he had returned to civilian life, he had opened an office of neuropsychiatry specializing in hypnosis. The intensity of his gaze, even if some people claimed it was of no importance, gave him a certain aura and credibility. In fact, his hypnotic abilities proved to be superior to those of his colleagues. Despite this advantage, which quickly became known and renowned, he continued to study other healing techniques and to practice his art in various countries. For him, the important point was to do something, to give people hope again, and especially to alleviate bodily suffering. This last point was an obsession for him, and although everyone admired him for that, he knew exactly where this vocation really came from, from what he sometimes called his "original sin." On the fifth cassette, Gaston Wrochet expanded on his methods and experiments, his art and the medications he used in connection with it. One felt that he still needed to transmit things, as if he were afraid of carrying off with him some detail that would have made it possible for someone to escape suffering.

The sixth cassette recounted his life as a healer and professor, and it was only starting with the seventh cassette that he finally came to his meeting with Manuel Gemoni and lifted a corner of the veil. "I am not about to forget my encounter with Manuel. From that day forward, I lost my peace of mind and the health of my body." Then came the sound of him blowing his nose noisily, but without ceasing to talk. "He appeared before me, like the statue of the Commander before Don Juan.

It happened in the Palais des Congrès a little more than three years ago. That man was the spitting image of my lieutenant, his twin, his clone . . . his reincarnation. My heart had always been my weak point and I had already had a minor heart attack, but this was much more serious. It made no impression on him. He continued on his way without even seeing me. But I felt ill and thought that if I sat down for a few minutes everything would be all right." For the same reason, before he was shot down, Krinkel had thought he recognized Gemoni. He too had been convinced that it was Lieutenant Lafitte, whom he had tortured sixty years earlier. Everything was suddenly so obvious. "This second attack almost caused me to finally rejoin my lieutenant, if I also deserve to be in Paradise." The old man then explained in detail how much this attack had weakened him physically. Shortly afterward, he decided to take up residence in Paris so he would not have to move around too much. Then there was another coincidence. An apartment opened up in Gemoni's building. "The floor just above. All the way up, a lovely place in the attic. Exactly what I'd been looking for. And then, once the first shock was over, I realized I wanted to see him again. So I decided to move in. That just shows that fate isn't to blame for everything, we often give it a helping hand."

Just after that sentence, a telephone could be heard ringing and it was apparent that the old man was doing his best to answer it. Then he could be heard talking in the distance until the end of the cassette. He hadn't realized it, since the rest of his account was found at the beginning of the ninth cassette, the eighth containing only advice and recommendations for the benefit of his students.

On cassette No. 9, he described the first documentary on the Dominican Republic. Klaus Krinkel appeared twice in the film. "Then I really almost fell apart. I don't know how my heart survived it, but my head sustained a serious blow. My hatred for that man drove me crazy. That bastard wasn't dead!

It wasn't possible. It was unbearable. Suddenly I saw in Manuel the hand of fate. It was my god or my lieutenant who was showing me the way. I even told myself that I was being given a chance to redeem myself, to kill the bastard. As I should have done in '44, by jumping out of my tree to rip his throat out with my teeth. But I was now too old, and my heart condition made it impossible for me to do anything. So everything seemed to me simple, obvious, as if it had been written. An irony of history, another one: the day before that broadcast, my young, pretty Japanese neighbor, Gemoni's wife, had run into me and asked if I could do anything to treat her husband's terrible headaches. She'd read an article about the technique I used. She was the one, in fact, who asked me to hypnotize Manuel!"

That's why Manuel was so willing to undergo hypnosis, Mallock thought.

"Just imagine! Sending my lieutenant's perfect double to kill the man who had tortured and killed him. It was written. I had no chance of persuading Manuel to do it and didn't even try. For me, my eyes and my abilities as a hypnotizer were part of a plan, a great design, an incredible puzzle that had just appeared in front of me, for me and for my lieutenant. I was insane, no doubt, possessed by hatred, but I regret nothing, now that I know Manuel was able to return alive. As soon as I've finished these recordings, I will go turn myself in to the police." Then there was a weird, almost childlike laugh: "I believe the superintendent in charge of the case is going to have the surprise of his life when I tell him the whole story!"

Mallock smiled. He didn't hold it against Gavroche; he knew he'd won, though it had been very close. If he hadn't come to the right conclusions, thanks to Bob, he wouldn't be here now. To be sure, the body of a certain Gaston Wrochet would eventually have been found, frozen to death in his bedroom, but no one would have connected it with the Gemoni case. All his effects and the precious cassettes would have ended up in the garbage. And Manu would have ended up in prison.

The old man continued his confession: "In five short sessions of hypnosis, plus a few suitable medications, I managed to condition him perfectly, to program him, as it were. All that remained was to try it out. So I lent him the cassette on which I'd recorded the documentary. And there, I was in for a surprise. He reacted even more violently than I'd expected. I didn't even need to give him the clues I'd collected. I'd programmed one or two sessions afterward, but they did not prove necessary. I believe that the horrors I witnessed, and that I had described in detail to Manuel, convinced him to act. On that subject, let it be noted that the theory that holds that we cannot make someone do something under hypnosis that he would not normally do is false. Hypnosis is far more powerful than one can imagine. In addition to my own practice, I refer to the experiments conducted by Hippolyte Bernheim, which were known to Freud and took place in the Saint-Charles hospital in Nancy. In substance, the murder of an unfortunate door, which had been designated as a dangerous man to a patient under hypnosis. A murder carried out with the help of a letter-opener. As well as the false trial that followed and the manipulation of the confessions obtained by Bernheim by simple suggestion." The old man blew his nose again, then the sound of a vaporizer could be heard, probably to administer a medicine. "Where I have no excuse is that I put his life in danger. He could have been killed. But as I already said, I had gone mad. Now I'm going to be able to right all the wrongs I caused and put an end to this masquerade. Tomorrow morning, I will call the police and my little neighbor to explain everything. I'm aware of all the suffering I've caused Manuel's whole family and his friends, but I am still sorrier that I used him, in a cowardly way, as a weapon. I have no excuse other than my hatred for Krinkel." Thus ended Gavroche's confessions.

Looking at the last inscription on the cover of the ninth cassette, Amédée read: "END: December 4, 1 A.M." On that date, Manuel had just been imprisoned. Then Mallock remembered the storm that had ravaged the capital on the night of December 3. The one that had shattered his neighbor's window and crushed the beautiful Christmas tree put up by the caretaker.

It had thus been a month since Captain Wrochet, Gavroche, had died of a cardiac arrest caused by the cold, the day before he was planning to turn himself in to the police. Had he done so, he would have spared everyone a great deal of suffering and questions. Mallock thought, promising himself never to admit it, that in the end that would have been a shame . . .

It was 7 P.M.

While he was listening to the last cassette, Gavroche's apartment had been invaded by the night and the cold. The captain's frozen body had been carried away by the men from the morgue. Rising to leave the hypnotizer's apartment, Mallock glanced out the window in the hall. Outside it was really dark. Obscurity as a malady, a malediction. What if there were never any sun?

Sometimes, Superintendent Amédée Mallock doubted everything.

Even the dawn.

EPILOGUE

Two Weeks Later

No snowflakes in sight.

The autoroute is deserted.

Mallock is driving fast to a different place, still determined to find peace there. The day before, Margot took a plane to Iran. He wasn't able to admit that he was scared for her. That, and a little more. Now he's angry at himself. But it's too late. Stupid bear. He turns off the radio, swearing. He's forgotten his iPod. In front of him, the promise of snow; the sky is loaded with it. His heart, too. A big glass of whiskey would have fixed all that, but he has a long way to go, so he abstained. All he can do now is sigh. It does no good to wash his hands, change his clothes and his memories, sadness still burdens him, like a persistent odor.

He'd so much like to recover his earlier euphoria. The one he had when he was twenty. With those moments of joy like so many clear skies. Three days earlier, Manu's release provided him with one of those moments. When you smile, your body feels light, and you're convinced, deep in your heart, that you'll never die. And neither will the people you love.

Amédée still feels the sweetness of Kiko and Julie holding him in their arms and covering him with kisses. And then Manu's smile, his tears as he embraced his baby. Yes, that was definitely one of those moments. Why was he so incapable of retaining them, of saving them somewhere on his big hard disk and playing them back in his moments of sadness?

When he was a child, he always caught the five rings with the little wooden stick.

*

Snow begins to fall again, suicidally, on his windshield.

Mallock starts counting up his troops: Jules, Julie, and Ken, of course, and then the little new one, Jo, Marie-Joséphine Maêcka Demaya. And soon there will be the big, lanky guy of Kabyle origin, Habib Al Azred, who has already been nicknamed Wik, a diminutive of Wikipedia. Five collaborators, a reconstituted hand, Mallock in complete form.

It's dangerous on the shoulders of the autoroute: cars are beginning to stop to put on chains. Amédée slows down, imagining the denouement of Manu's story, with his smiles, his tears of joy, Julie's thanks. These are the big moments in a cop's life. Even for him. So why not take advantage of them? The hell with it!

He accelerates in the storm.

A genocide of snowflakes.

Nothing is ever perfect enough for Mallock. There's always a hair in the soup, a piece of eggshell in the omelet, a pit in the clafoutis. But in this case, for once he's right. After having hesitated, he decided to keep to himself one fact that is more than disturbing. A few sentences that throw a strange shadow, a soupçon of doubt, on the perfect ending of this whole perfect investigation!

He opens the glove box.

Inside it is a cassette identical to the ones found at Gaston Wrochet's apartment. On the cover there is no number, no title. It contains the old man's doubts about what really happened. Little details that don't fit, and especially the business about the music box. Gaston, who read the newspapers, is certain about it. On the cassette he states that he has never seen this jewel or even heard the music. "Neither Marie nor my lieutenant ever showed me such an object. I would have remembered that." But then how was Manu able to mention it and speak about it on several occasions if Gaston Wrochet was not aware of its existence? Further on, old Gavroche added: "I don't say that it didn't exist, I don't know about that, but not knowing about it, I never spoke about it." He ended with a hypothesis: "I suppose it's only the result of Manuel's imagination." But Mallock absolutely cannot accept that hypothesis, since even as the snow continues to slow cars, he has the little golden heart, snugly tucked away in his pocket.

Amédée thinks back to what Mister Blue said when it was raining: "There are more things in heaven and earth, Horatio, than are dreamt of in your philosophy." The adventurer was right, and especially Shakespeare. But there you have it, a professional police superintendent likes to put everything in its place and hates above all finding himself at the end of an enigma with a doubt or with a piece of the puzzle left over. So he's made up his mind that he'll throw the cassette in the sea once he gets there.

Interchange. Toll plaza. A series of little villages.

Mallock finally slows down. Before going on, he makes a little detour to visit someone, a stop in Ampélopsis.

Two inches of snow cover the lane. Right in front of him stands a cute little house with a blue roof. He rings the bell. Waits. The door opens prudently. Behind it an old lady squints her pretty eyes the better to see who her visitor is.

"Ah! Mr. Superintendent. How happy I am to see you again. Come in, come in quickly, I'm going to make you some tea."

Mallock wipes his feet on a cast-iron grill half buried in the earth.

"Thank you, Mademoiselle, I hope I'm not disturbing you?"

"Certainly not. And then I haven't yet had a chance to thank you. It's thanks to you that I finally know what happened to my Jean-François."

"I'm sorry, but I can't stay. I have to be in the Arcachon Basin before seven o'clock."

Marie Dutin looks at him with astonishment.

"Did you come just to say hello to me?"

She still has the same silvery hair, powdered skin, and shining eyes, little diamonds bordered in mascara.

"Not quite, I have something to return to you, and I wanted to do it in person."

Mallock thrusts his hand into his pocket and brings out the music box in the form of a heart, just protected with tissue paper. This is the most elegant way he's found to put the last piece of the puzzle in the right place and finally close the investigation.

The extra piece will soon be sleeping with the fishes, and everything will have been said.

The old woman looks at the object without being able to identify it. Then she suddenly understands and her eyes fill with tears.

"Sweet Jesus, it's not possible!"

Her fingers begin to tremble like slender twigs as she tries to take the jewel Mallock is holding out to her. A little embarrassed to be the cause of so much emotion, he helps Marie by putting the object in the middle of her open palm.

That is where it belongs. The music box seems to fit there naturally, like a cat curled up on its favorite cushion. The old lady's face is now twisted with emotion.

Her chin is shaking and she has difficulty speaking:

"I kept it only a few days, you know. And it was so long ago."

"It still works," Mallock told her. "I took the liberty of having it serviced."

The old woman holds the heart to her marveling face. Then with her other hand, awkwardly, she pushes on the latch. The two yellowed photos appear, as the music begins playing the notes of another life. Overwhelmed, the lieutenant's fiancée nonetheless manages to smile through her tears.

But her whole body is trembling.

Gently, Mallock takes her in his arms.

ABOUT THE AUTHOR

Jean-Denis Bruet-Ferreol, who writes under the pseudonym Mallock, was born in Neuilly-sur-Seine in 1951. He is not only an author, but also a painter, photographer, designer, inventor, artistic director, and composer. Since 2000, he has dedicated himself to digital painting and crime novels.

EUROPA EDITIONS BACKLIST
(alphabetical by author)

Fiction

Carmine Abate
Between Two Seas • 978-1-933372-40-2 • Territories: World
The Homecoming Party • 978-1-933372-83-9 • Territories: World

Milena Agus
From the Land of the Moon • 978-1-60945-001-4 • Ebook • Territories: World (excl. ANZ)

Salwa Al Neimi
The Proof of the Honey • 978-1-933372-68-6 • Ebook • Territories: World (excl UK)

Simonetta Agnello Hornby
The Nun • 978-1-60945-062-5 • Territories: World

Daniel Arsand
Lovers • 978-1-60945-071-7 • Ebook • Territories: World

Jenn Ashworth
A Kind of Intimacy • 978-1-933372-86-0 • Territories: US & Can

Beryl Bainbridge
The Girl in the Polka Dot Dress • 978-1-60945-056-4 • Ebook • Territories: US

Muriel Barbery
The Elegance of the Hedgehog • 978-1-933372-60-0 • Ebook • Territories: World (excl. UK & EU)
Gourmet Rhapsody • 978-1-933372-95-2 • Ebook • Territories: World (excl. UK & EU)

Stefano Benni
Margherita Dolce Vita • 978-1-933372-20-4 • Territories: World
Timeskipper • 978-1-933372-44-0 • Territories: World

Romano Bilenchi
The Chill • 978-1-933372-90-7 • Territories: World

Kazimierz Brandys
Rondo • 978-1-60945-004-5 • Territories: World

Alina Bronsky
Broken Glass Park • 978-1-933372-96-9 • Ebook • Territories: World
The Hottest Dishes of the Tartar Cuisine • 978-1-60945-006-9 • Ebook •
Territories: World

Jesse Browner
Everything Happens Today • 978-1-60945-051-9 • Ebook • Territories:
World (excl. UK & EU)

Francisco Coloane
Tierra del Fuego • 978-1-933372-63-1 • Ebook • Territories: World

Rebecca Connell
The Art of Losing • 978-1-933372-78-5 • Territories: US

Laurence Cossé
A Novel Bookstore • 978-1-933372-82-2 • Ebook • Territories: World
An Accident in August • 978-1-60945-049-6 • Territories: World (excl. UK)

Diego De Silva
I Hadn't Understood • 978-1-60945-065-6 • Territories: World

Shashi Deshpande
The Dark Holds No Terrors • 978-1-933372-67-9 • Territories: US

Steve Erickson
Zeroville • 978-1-933372-39-6 • Territories: US & Can
These Dreams of You • 978-1-60945-063-2 • Territories: US & Can

Elena Ferrante
The Days of Abandonment • 978-1-933372-00-6 • Ebook • Territories: World
Troubling Love • 978-1-933372-16-7 • Territories: World
The Lost Daughter • 978-1-933372-42-6 • Territories: World

Linda Ferri
Cecilia • 978-1-933372-87-7 • Territories: World

Damon Galgut
In a Strange Room • 978-1-60945-011-3 • Ebook • Territories: USA

Santiago Gamboa
Necropolis • 978-1-60945-073-1 • Ebook • Territories: World

Jane Gardam
Old Filth • 978-1-933372-13-6 • Ebook • Territories: US
The Queen of the Tambourine • 978-1-933372-36-5 • Ebook • Territories: US
The People on Privilege Hill • 978-1-933372-56-3 • Ebook • Territories: US
The Man in the Wooden Hat • 978-1-933372-89-1 • Ebook • Territories: US
God on the Rocks • 978-1-933372-76-1 • Ebook • Territories: US
Crusoe's Daughter • 978-1-60945-069-4 • Ebook • Territories: US

Anna Gavalda
French Leave • 978-1-60945-005-2 • Ebook • Territories: US & Can

Seth Greenland
The Angry Buddhist • 978-1-60945-068-7 • Ebook • Territories: World

Katharina Hacker
The Have-Nots • 978-1-933372-41-9 • Territories: World (excl. India)

Patrick Hamilton
Hangover Square • 978-1-933372-06-8 • Territories: US & Can

James Hamilton-Paterson
Cooking with Fernet Branca • 978-1-933372-01-3 • Territories: US
Amazing Disgrace • 978-1-933372-19-8 • Territories: US
Rancid Pansies • 978-1-933372-62-4 • Territories: USA

Alfred Hayes
The Girl on the Via Flaminia • 978-1-933372-24-2 • Ebook •
Territories: World

Jean-Claude Izzo
The Lost Sailors • 978-1-933372-35-8 • Territories: World
A Sun for the Dying • 978-1-933372-59-4 • Territories: World

Gail Jones
Sorry • 978-1-933372-55-6 • Territories: US & Can

Ioanna Karystiani
The Jasmine Isle • 978-1-933372-10-5 • Territories: World
Swell • 978-1-933372-98-3 • Territories: World

Peter Kocan
Fresh Fields • 978-1-933372-29-7 • Territories: US, EU & Can
The Treatment and the Cure • 978-1-933372-45-7 • Territories: US, EU & Can

Helmut Krausser
Eros • 978-1-933372-58-7 • Territories: World

Amara Lakhous
Clash of Civilizations Over an Elevator in Piazza Vittorio •
978-1-933372-61-7 • Ebook • Territories: World
Divorce Islamic Style • 978-1-60945-066-3 • Ebook • Territories: World

Lia Levi
The Jewish Husband • 978-1-933372-93-8 • Territories: World

Valerio Massimo Manfredi
The Ides of March • 978-1-933372-99-0 • Territories: US

Leïla Marouane
The Sexual Life of an Islamist in Paris • 978-1-933372-85-3 •
Territories: World

Lorenzo Mediano
The Frost on His Shoulders • 978-1-60945-072-4 • Ebook •
Territories: World

Sélim Nassib
I Loved You for Your Voice • 978-1-933372-07-5 • Territories: World
The Palestinian Lover • 978-1-933372-23-5 • Territories: World

Amélie Nothomb
Tokyo Fiancée • 978-1-933372-64-8 • Territories: US & Can
Hygiene and the Assassin • 978-1-933372-77-8 • Ebook • Territories: US & Can

Valeria Parrella
For Grace Received • 978-1-933372-94-5 • Territories: World

Alessandro Piperno
The Worst Intentions • 978-1-933372-33-4 • Territories: World
Persecution • 978-1-60945-074-8 • Ebook • Territories: World

Lorcan Roche
The Companion • 978-1-933372-84-6 • Territories: World

Boualem Sansal
The German Mujahid • 978-1-933372-92-1 • Ebook • Territories: US & Can

www.europaeditions.com

Eric-Emmanuel Schmitt
The Most Beautiful Book in the World • 978-1-933372-74-7 • Ebook •
Territories: World
The Woman with the Bouquet • 978-1-933372-81-5 • Ebook • Territories:
US & Can

Angelika Schrobsdorff
You Are Not Like Other Mothers • 978-1-60945-075-5 • Ebook •
Territories: World

Audrey Schulman
Three Weeks in December • 978-1-60945-064-9 • Ebook • Territories: US
& Can

James Scudamore
Heliopolis • 978-1-933372-73-0 • Ebook • Territories: US

Luis Sepúlveda
The Shadow of What We Were • 978-1-60945-002-1 • Ebook • Territories:
World

Paolo Sorrentino
Everybody's Right • 978-1-60945-052-6 • Ebook • Territories: US & Can

Domenico Starnone
First Execution • 978-1-933372-66-2 • Territories: World

Henry Sutton
Get Me out of Here • 978-1-60945-007-6 • Ebook • Territories: US & Can

Chad Taylor
Departure Lounge • 978-1-933372-09-9 • Territories: US, EU & Can

Roma Tearne
Mosquito • 978-1-933372-57-0 • Territories: US & Can
Bone China • 978-1-933372-75-4 • Territories: US

André Carl van der Merwe
Moffie • 978-1-60945-050-2 • Ebook • Territories: World
(excl. S. Africa)

Fay Weldon
Chalcot Crescent • 978-1-933372-79-2 • Territories: US

Anne Wiazemsky
My Berlin Child • 978-1-60945-003-8 • Territories: US & Can

Jonathan Yardley
Second Reading • 978-1-60945-008-3 • Ebook • Territories: US & Can

Edwin M. Yoder Jr.
Lions at Lamb House • 978-1-933372-34-1 • Territories: World

Michele Zackheim
Broken Colors • 978-1-933372-37-2 • Territories: World

Alice Zeniter
Take This Man • 978-1-60945-053-3 • Territories: World

Tonga Books

Ian Holding
Of Beasts and Beings • 978-1-60945-054-0 • Ebook • Territories: US & Can

Sara Levine
Treasure Island!!! • 978-0-14043-768-3 • Ebook • Territories: World

Alexander Maksik
You Deserve Nothing • 978-1-60945-048-9 • Ebook • Territories: US, Can & EU (excl. UK)

Thad Ziolkowski
Wichita • 978-1-60945-070-0 • Ebook • Territories: World

Crime/Noir

Massimo Carlotto
The Goodbye Kiss • 978-1-933372-05-1 • Ebook • Territories: World
Death's Dark Abyss • 978-1-933372-18-1 • Ebook • Territories: World
The Fugitive • 978-1-933372-25-9 • Ebook • Territories: World
Bandit Love • 978-1-933372-80-8 • Ebook • Territories: World
Poisonville • 978-1-933372-91-4 • Ebook • Territories: World

Giancarlo De Cataldo
The Father and the Foreigner • 978-1-933372-72-3 • Territories: World

Caryl Férey
Zulu • 978-1-933372-88-4 • Ebook • Territories: World (excl. UK & EU)
Utu • 978-1-60945-055-7 • Ebook • Territories: World (excl. UK & EU)

Alicia Giménez-Bartlett
Dog Day • 978-1-933372-14-3 • Territories: US & Can
Prime Time Suspect • 978-1-933372-31-0 • Territories: US & Can
Death Rites • 978-1-933372-54-9 • Territories: US & Can

Jean-Claude Izzo
Total Chaos • 978-1-933372-04-4 • Territories: US & Can
Chourmo • 978-1-933372-17-4 • Territories: US & Can
Solea • 978-1-933372-30-3 • Territories: US & Can

www.europaeditions.com

Matthew F. Jones
Boot Tracks • 978-1-933372-11-2 • Territories: US & Can

Gene Kerrigan
The Midnight Choir • 978-1-933372-26-6 • Territories: US & Can
Little Criminals • 978-1-933372-43-3 • Territories: US & Can

Carlo Lucarelli
Carte Blanche • 978-1-933372-15-0 • Territories: World
The Damned Season • 978-1-933372-27-3 • Territories: World
Via delle Oche • 978-1-933372-53-2 • Territories: World

Edna Mazya
Love Burns • 978-1-933372-08-2 • Territories: World (excl. ANZ)

Yishai Sarid
Limassol • 978-1-60945-000-7 • Ebook • Territories: World (excl. UK, AUS & India)

Joel Stone
The Jerusalem File • 978-1-933372-65-5 • Ebook • Territories: World

Benjamin Tammuz
Minotaur • 978-1-933372-02-0 • Ebook • Territories: World

Non-fiction

Alberto Angela
A Day in the Life of Ancient Rome • 978-1-933372-71-6 • Territories: World • History

Helmut Dubiel
Deep In the Brain: Living with Parkinson's Disease • 978-1-933372-70-9 •
Ebook • Territories: World • Medicine/Memoir

James Hamilton-Paterson
Seven-Tenths: The Sea and Its Thresholds • 978-1-933372-69-3 • Territories:
USA • Nature/Essays

Daniele Mastrogiacomo
Days of Fear • 978-1-933372-97-6 • Ebook • Territories: World • Current
affairs/Memoir/Afghanistan/Journalism

Valery Panyushkin
Twelve Who Don't Agree • 978-1-60945-010-6 • Ebook • Territories:
World • Current affairs/Memoir/Russia/Journalism

Christa Wolf
One Day a Year: 1960-2000 • 978-1-933372-22-8 • Territories: World •
Memoir/History/20th Century

Children's Illustrated Fiction

Altan
Here Comes Timpa • 978-1-933372-28-0 • Territories: World (excl. Italy)
Timpa Goes to the Sea • 978-1-933372-32-7 • Territories: World (excl. Italy)
Fairy Tale Timpa • 978-1-933372-38-9 • Territories: World (excl. Italy)

Wolf Erlbruch
The Big Question • 978-1-933372-03-7 • Territories: US & Can
The Miracle of the Bears • 978-1-933372-21-1 • Territories: US & Can
(with **Gioconda Belli**) *The Butterfly Workshop* • 978-1-933372-12-9 •
Territories: US & Can